Dead Run

Dead Run

David R. Crook

Cyprian Publishing

CYPRIAN
PUBLISHING

Dedication

I would like to dedicate this novel to
Ronald David Crook,
my best friend, my mentor, and my father.
He was the most giving person I have ever met.
May he find the peace he deserves.
November 17th, 1940 to October 23rd, 2008

I would also like to thank two people that worked as hard
as I did to bring this project to fruition. Kerry Blair – thank
you for your support. Christine Wolfe – thank you for being
the first to back this project.

1

Introduction

My name is Ryan Prince. I am writing my personal account of the events of August 18, 2006 - easily the worst day of my life. While breakfasting, I read an article that clearly stated I had passed away the previous night in a horrific car accident. Unlike Wheaties, not the best way to start your day.

Mr. Samuel Clemons, Mark Twain as he was more commonly known, had a similar experience, and I will give a similar response: "The rumors of my passing were strictly exaggeration."

My therapist suggested I write about that horrible day so he can better understand my point of view. There are many who have refused to believe the events of that day, treating my account as farcical, a tale to be shared around a comfortable bar. There are few verifiable facts - I understand the doubt I see in their eyes when I retell it. The most concrete evidence is that simple newspaper article from that day, merely a blurb in Section B-4. Sixty-five words that would forever change my life. Samantha, my girlfriend, was drawn into the drama more or less against her will; an unfortunate witness to some of the bloodier events. I can also count myself among a lucky few who are still ambulatory after being shot twice. These scars still remain - ever-present. These two souvenirs are the only physical evidence that persists from that day. Yes, I saved the paper and the scars are now part of me.

It was difficult attempting to understand the events in which I was involved, let alone trying to explain these same events to someone else. Needless to say, next time I will remember my digital camcorder, or at least a notebook, or maybe a digital tape recorder. Everything occurred without nearby witnesses or without anyone to verify the facts; the reader can decide what to believe. I will just relay the facts the best I can. I do not believe any amount of education or planning would have prepared me for what happened.

I woke as I did every other day – doing nothing different, at least nothing I am consciously aware of doing. I am certainly a rat-in-the-maze kind guy, with very little deviation in my daily routine.

Did I deserve what happened? I am not sure; I believe we are at times the worst judges of our own behavior. I did learn an important lesson: There are many instances that we have little or no control over in the affairs of our lives. The ability to think and react quickly is as important as anything else we learn.

I am still plagued by the memories of that day. While the severity and intensity of those memories have faded, they occasionally still visit me in the night. I can feel the bullets rip into my body, the pavement rough against my face as I lay there bleeding. I can see every evil visited upon me.

Now, as I write these words, I try to live out the rest of my days in quiet anonymity. Yet daily I am plagued by this one rather annoying question. Why? I am no one of any renown. I manage a customer service office. I am the infamous cog that retains the momentum of the corporate wheel. I am the embodiment of the nobody.

I am a not now, nor ever have been, a member of law enforcement. I have not attempted to steal secrets or condone espionage. I certainly am not a hoodlum or drug dealer. I remain the boring middle manager. Maybe for others, this indicates I lack ambition. However, I am content with my life. I go to work and then I go home.

So it astounds me that I was thrown into the middle of the events of August 18. It happened all without my permission and not all within my understanding.

There still stands those 24-hours where I was dead. While my brain still functioned and I still drew breath into my lungs, to everyone else I was dead.

It was like a queer, quantum physics experiment gone awry. I now know how the famous cat in Edwin Schrödinger's thought experiment felt. Did the hammer fall after being triggered by a decaying electron? Or was safety ensured, the poison yet unreleased? If only there was someone who could open the box and look inside. For those hours I existed both alive and dead - no collapsing wave function could bring about just one reality. Because truthfully, I was dead to all those people that read the paper. Yet my own reality told a different one.

I discovered a lot about my abilities and myself during that 24-hour period. Those abilities of self-protection and eluding capture continue to astound me, even today. My new-found abilities did not come without a cost. There is now a rift with Sam. Once you are pushed to your personal limits you can either fold, and allow the events to carry you tide-like, or you can fight back. I choose the latter, and in doing so I have done many things of which I am not proud. But I am here to spin the tale for those that care to read along. Having been to the preverbal edge and looked over into the precipice, I did not falter. I persevered. It was Winston Churchill who said, "Success is not final, failure not fatal; It is the courage to continue that counts."

Many nights since I have lain awake and wondered if my actions were justified. Was saving Ryan Prince worth all that happened? The answer still evades; at last count, it was 50-50.

It occurs to me there are actually people who may have had a rooting interest, those who are still pleased that I am among the living. Mussolini touted the ends justify the means, yet I still have to face the man in the mirror, the person from whom I can hide nothing.

Yes, I am alive. Yes, I have held a gun to a man's head. I suppose justification for my actions will be judged - whether by divine being or the Karmic universe I do not know.

I can only relate I did what was necessary - not extreme, nor unjustified. Although justified or not, all my actions have not left me feeling virtuous about my Karma. Killing a man because he has a gun to your head does not make you feel any better about it the next day. My conscious over the last few months since has cleared, yet there are still nights when the worst of that day revisits me while sleeping - invading my own quiet time, When I am most vulnerable and unable to pick up some other activity, until the train of my brain finds another track.

August 18 was not about strategic planning and long-term goals. With that in mind, I will be as true to the sequence of events as I can be. I am writing this not only as my homework assignment for my therapist but for myself. I have to cleanse myself of the whole affair. I am fairly certain our recent group sessions, where I chose to listen instead of participate, as well as our individual sessions, where the talk of feelings is enough to bring out my ire, led to his insistence upon this mini biography. Sometimes talking about how we feel degrades the feeling itself. It is so difficult to look a stranger in the face and try to explain what, at the very heart of it, is inexplicable. Feelings are neither good nor bad, they just are. In our human condition, we assign a particular value to them.

I am a better person for living through that day I died, and now I appreciate the present more than ever, every second of my life I live like there will not be one to follow.

2

August 18, 2006 | 7:30 a.m.

I awoke to the sound of the rather annoying alarm clock interrupting my entertainment of three supermodels. I hesitated; even the snooze button could not bring me back to the hot tub. It was as if my alarm had maliciously removed me from them. I clung onto those thoughts for a moment or two, relishing the images as they slowly dissolved, not to be recalled.

It was a cool early August morning, the dampness hung in the air like a promise of what soon would follow in eight weeks, the air was more akin to mid-October than that of early August. The grey clouds that hung low on the horizon were dark and cold, mocking as if to say remember me. We in western New York knew that snow would be upon us soon enough.

I exited the bedroom and went to the kitchen to the left of the living room, the table tucked into a small nook. I could see the paper lying on the table, coffee still warming in the pot, the aroma of recently brewed coffee cloying in the air. A most enjoyable aroma in the morning.

My girlfriend, Maria Samantha de Saint Claire, or Sam as

she prefers to be called, left early, her car no longer in front of the apartment. I smiled and wished her a good day. We had celebrated two months of successful cohabitation. Although we talked about the next step, we never discussed when. Last night after a lengthy conversation with my folks, I came to the conclusion that today was that day.

I have been planning for this since the move in. She was not aware that I had $3,800 squirreled away for a ring, the RING actually. I will admit that this amount is not equivalent to two months of my salary. Does no one else realize that it's the jewelers themselves that set that precedent? I am a hopeless romantic; however, the logical side of my being agrees that $3,800 is plenty to spend on a piece of jewelry. I am due to pick up the ring on my way home from work. The jeweler called me yesterday informing me it had been sized and it is ready for pick up.

I was filled with anticipation. Although we had discussed such outcomes, I was still apprehensive about actually going forward. My mind told me I was being foolish, my heart told me a different story. I was about to walk a path that I promised myself would never be followed. Although one's heart is not as large as one's brain, we seem to make decisions according to the smaller of the two organs. We men having the obvious handicap of an even smaller third organ; therefore, there are now three competing thinking centers.

I was hesitant, spending most of the last few years pushing people away. I had some close friends and dated only casually. My divorce was still very fresh in my mind and I was uncertain if I could allow someone into my space, the only place I could truly be myself. Over the last two years, most notably the last two months, Sam had found a way past the wall I erected. It may have had a front gate that I was not aware of because she strode right into my inner sanctum with me none the wiser. Sam was as patient as a saint, she allowed me to work through my own problems and my own emotional issues. I love her; she is my life and the reason I get out of bed. Like a persistent tide, she eroded away my outer defenses until there was but pristine beach, open to all.

I was grateful my parents loved her as well. We Princes are a tight-knit group and she was welcomed in our clan. They were cognizant of the changes Sam had made over the last few years. They commented on how she had changed me for the better, and that I appeared to be happy when I was with her. Leave it to Mom and Dad to find what really resides in your heart. They know about my plans tonight. But they promised me they will sound surprised when we call to share our news. The celebration with be completed with free-flowing cham-pagne and one sparkling ring.

I left the bedroom and the supermodels behind me. My thoughts turned to Sam and tonight. The smell of coffee steeping in the pot and her perfume lingering in the air added to my already jubilant mood. I started to practice lines in my head, making sure to sound both sincere and romantic. I wanted the moment to be perfect.

The digital block numbers on the clock read 7:30 a.m., re-minding me that work started at nine and I would need to leave in an hour. I leisurely sat down to enjoy some coffee and read the paper.

I went straight to the sports section, looking for some updates from training camp; it was due to end soon. I lived for the Buffalo Bills. I bled Blue and Red. Reading through the sports section looking for something that would give me some hope that season would be the one. However, an unproven quarterback, a running back with a surgically mended knee, and an offensive line that was suspect did not fill with me with much enthusiasm.

Tickets purchased for opening day stood on the dresser, prominently displayed. However, that would not be until mid-September. I was looking forward to the game. Sam may accompany me. The games are always exciting - 70,000-plus filling the stadium. You can feel the crowd noise in your bones. That many fans chanting in unison is louder than jet engines on take-off. The noise level in the stadium often topped 120 decibels. It rocks you to the core. I often wondered what it's like on the field. We fans don't just rock it for the games in September and October; we fill this stadium in December regardless of the weather conditions. The best part about the game was tailgating and socializing in the parking lot amongst a sea of Bills fans. Watching fellow fans at their grills or tossing footballs around, the air filled with the pungent order of grilled meats of various kinds. Also, more beer than you can see at a distributor's warehouse.

Buffalo is a drinking town with a sports problem. We western New Yorkers don't require much of an excuse to tip a few, although the sports gods have given us plenty of reasons; a missed field goal that went wide right in the 1991 Super Bowl loss to the New York Giants, thus losing the game 20-19, and the no-goal during the 1999 Stanley Cup finals against the Dallas Stars. Brent Hull scored a goal in the third overtime even though the replay clearly indicated that his skate was in the crease when he scored. The officials refused to review the goal. Then there was the Music City miracle playoff loss to the Tennessee Titans in 1995. Immediately after the Bills had taken the lead late in the game, the only hope Tennessee had was to score on the ensuing kickoff. They did just that. The Bills are the only team in NFL history to make it to four straight Super Bowls and lose every one.

I sipped my coffee and decided to move onto the comics section, as I believed it to be the best part of the paper. I was listing all the reasons why the Bills were going to make the playoffs and just generally kick some ass while enjoying my favorite comics: Dilbert, Rhymes with Orange, and my other favorites. Call me crazy but Garfield was my hero, Dilbert my role model. Scott Adams calendars and memo pads adorned my desk. Part of my fascination centered on the fact, that I, too, spent too many hours in the cubicle jungle, sometimes laughing at the idiocy of corporate America.

Comics finished, I was reading the City Region section of the paper, knowing that my lazy morning was about to come to an end. The clock was working against me now as I had wasted most of the morning. I was due a shower and to start my day. Sipping the last of my coffee I was quickly looking through the city and region section, reading the police blotter on page B4, which would forever change my quiet existence:

Ryan Prince, 38, of 50 West Spring Street in Amherst, was found dead after his car struck a tree on Two-Mile Creek Road in Tonawanda. Alcohol was believed to be a factor. Prince was traveling on Two-Mile Creek using excessive speed when he lost control of his vehicle and hit a tree. There subsequently was a fire and the car was incinerated. No one else was injured.

My first instinct was not to worry. I was laughing out loud. Wait until Sam finds out she had slept with a ghost last night. Moreover, my friend Ed at work was going to have a field day with this. Knowing I was up for some serious ribbing, I figured he had at least a week's worth of material. We had a practical jokester in the office named Jason, I was certain to be a target for a few attacks from him as well. I never once considered it anything other than a mistake, or maybe there actually is another Ryan Prince living in here Amherst; it could happen.

I showered and dressed; we were having a product rollout tonight, sponsored by Nokia, one of our handset vendors. They were releasing the next generation of web protocol cell phones. These new handsets were able to access the Internet via an extremely fast connection, had the ability to access a variety of e-mail applications, and the phones came complete with mobile Windows, including such programs as Word, Excel, and PowerPoint. Nokia knew how to throw a party. Their last roll out had shrimp and lobster on the buffet along with made-to-order thick T-bone steaks. My mouth was watering in anticipation. I was not required to wear a shirt and tie on such days; I donned a lightweight polo with the company logo. Adding a lightweight jacket, my ensemble was complete.

I did the usual check prior to exiting the apartment: cell-phone on hip - check, keys in pocket - check, wallet in back pocket - check, big wad o'cash in money belt –check; apparently I was ready to face my day.

I exited the apartment by the back door, walking through the kitchen in the process. The door locked clicked into position and as always I tried the knob, confirming the lock had indeed engaged. I did live in a city with the lowest crime rates in Western NY; however, one cannot be too safe.

The wind seemed to blow through my lightweight jacket as if I were wearing gauze. While shaking off the cold I activated the garage door opener. I should be at work in twenty minutes as the majority of the rush hour traffic would be off the roads by now. Walking to the garage, using my remote to unlock the doors, my head lowered against the wind, I considered whether or not to return to the apartment and get a heavier weight jacket. I did not hear the beep-beep confirming that the locks had indeed disengaged. But I was already into the garage rounding the corner. It took me a moment to confirm the information my eyes were processing. The garage was empty. My maroon and gray Subaru Outback was not there. It was not on the street. I ran to the curb to confirm. I walked half-way down the block, nervously checking both sides of the street. My eyes and brain had finally reached the proper conclusion. I just discovered the difference between low crime and no crime.

Sam's car was also not parked at the curb; she couldn't

have possibly driven two cars simultaneously. I was looking for the car the same way I look for my misplaced keys, well they're not in my jacket or the pocket of my pants. I did not leave the car here or there. I ran out of options and finally admitted to myself the car was gone.

I returned to the apartment, unlocking the door and closing the garage door. Which in retrospect seemed odd, the car was already stolen. The proverbial horse had left the barn.

The phone was in the kitchen and picking up the handset I attempted to connect with 911, hands shaking, but there was no dial tone - the line was dead. I repeated the process with my cell phone, getting similar results, the nice recorded message letting me know that this number had been permanently disconnected. A disconnected cell phone can still access 911 services. I worked for the local cell phone company and knew the procedure inside and out. Even those customers that are legitimately deceased don't have the phone disconnected this quickly. The only way this would happen is if the ESN or electronic serial number was removed from the MTSO, the main telephone switching office, or the switch as it is known, which required someone with access.

There are also a variety of products on the market designed to block signals between cell phones and towers. These little items are gaining hold in the businesses. Currently, they are very popular with theaters and restaurants. All the annoying calls ruining fine dinners and great movies can now be stopped with these simple devices. Technology bridging the gap that common courtesy could not.

I have been with CellNY for over six years, cell phone attached to my hip, 24/7, since the day I started. A feeling of isolation crashed upon me. I would not have felt any more disconnected if I was on a desert isle with Gilligan and the Skipper, with only coconuts and jungle vines to set up a communication network. I couldn't even tell you where the nearest payphone is located. I haven't used one in forever. Not only was I dead but also I couldn't inform anyone of my current misfortune.

For the next five minutes, I was on autopilot. I ran about the apartment without focus and seemingly without any strategy. I decided if my cell phone was off certainly my other accounts were also closed. I took off my shirt and removed the money belt that had comfortably resided above my undershirt, now tucked securely under my arm. This was most inconvenient if I needed quick access to the money. I wore it over my shirt and under my jacket. I recounted the money and placed two hundred in my pocket. I needed to find out what else had been closed due to that false report. It occurred to me this may not be as funny as I originally thought.

My thoughts rocketed to Sam. What if she saw the article? She must know I was alive and breathing when she exited the apartment this morning. My parents lived out of state so they would not be affected; they were not an immediate concern. There were no other family members in town. There may be some co-workers that would be concerned or at least confused when I arrived at work. I wondered if my boss had attempted to reach Sam, her number is very easily accessed as it is on my account. I hoped her cell was not disconnected as well.

I did not really have much of a plan. I realized I needed to get to work and find out who deactivated my cell phone. A stop at the bank would be a good idea as well, not that I am incapable of spending $3,800 in a day. However, my goal of purchasing the ring was still my top priority. Therefore, any monies spent would have to be replaced. It also occurred to me that I may be required to work an hour or two today. My presence at the rollout would be required. It also occurred to me that a conversation with my boss would be forthcoming. I wanted to have everything solved before lunch, or maybe dinner.

My car now missing from the garage and presumed stolen, the laughter had ceased. While exiting my apartment for the second time that morning some rather strange thoughts worked their way through my skull. A) sometime last night my car was stolen, B) someone was pulled out of my car last night; unless I was having issues shucking my mortal coil and moving on to the great beyond, it wasn't me, C) did some crack head steal my car then drive into a tree, thus dying in a fiery wreck so intense that all they found was a clump of scorched carcass, D) why have the police failed to report my death?

They would have traced the plates back to this address and at least stopped by.

There are no official records that Sam resides there, she receives mail there, but only being engaged - or soon to be engaged - there is no Mr. and Mrs. Prince. My head was reeling. This was so far out of my normal daily routine. Second-guessing police procedure was not one of my normal Thursday activities. These questions could all be answered shortly as grand theft auto necessitates police involvement. And I could direct these odd inquiries toward folks that could actually provide an answer. Instead of pondering these things myself, which at the moment is only causing more questions than answers?

My mind continuing to look for answers when none were forthcoming. Was there something that was missed? I could not recall hearing anything out of the ordinary. I guess short of fireworks, I am not sure what night noises might arouse me from my slumber. Why would they steal my car out of the garage but not Sam's car, which was parked at the curb? The garage door would have to be opened and closed without the remote that resides either in the car or in our kitchen. It seems like a lot of trouble to steal the car then drive it into a tree. My car was four years old - not exactly a car that would get you a lot of money on the black market if such a thing exists? Was there someone out there that just was pissed off, and the trouble was worth the payoff? Maybe this mystery person gave my car to a drunk knowing that it would at least be involved in some minor accident. After living in Amherst the last few years having my car stolen had not entered my mind.

My whole world had been violated. Someone had the raw audacity to steal my car out of the garage. This was personal. Some additional safety measures would be put in place after a new car took residence in the garage. Complete with a top of the line in-car security system.

With no wheels, I was left with two options: either a cab or the bus. Our house in Amherst was close to Main Street and only a bus and train trip into downtown. I could be there in an hour if I caught a bus and also save about $40 from a cab ride. I took my cell phone with me and formulated the nearest thing I had to a plan.

Walking to Main Street I became more confused and concerned. I no longer thought this situation to be humorous. Twenty minutes ago my life was rolling along just fine, plans for a celebration looming, now a huge monkey wrench had been thrown into the works. I still wanted to keep my schedule - there was a need to complete my day, a need to end this day on a positive note. I wanted to be engaged before the sun set and unless I fixed this soon, it was not going to happen.

A bank was located near the bus stop and according to the schedule affixed to the window, I had fifteen minutes before it was due. I do not take the bus frequently but was familiar enough to know that $100 would not be acceptable fare. Entering the bank, I changed $200 into smaller bills.

My mind was elsewhere as I boarded the bus. I am dead, my car was stolen and driven into a tree, and burned into charcoal. I tried my best to construct a list of potential suspects. I take very careful notes on all customer interactions. It is a rather large database of customers. Complete with red flags on those customers that have actually made what I considered a real threat. More than once I was met at my apartment by an irate customer, thinking they could confront me at my home. Again these are things for the authorities and not a customer service retention specialist.

There is that thought that is always nagging you, there in the back of your skull, almost a dull pain if ignored. I ignored the thought for as long as possible before it took on a life of its own refusing to be overlooked. This thought is born from many an unpleasant experience with the ex-wife. So many in fact, that it was a mutual decision to move on before we killed each other in a murder-suicide, obviously whichever of us reached the breaking point first, well, you know. However, I have not seen nor spoken with her since the last of our court dates. Granted, I cried poverty to the best of my ability and she claimed that I was a millionaire. Sometime later a decent compromise was met. There was a drunken phone call about two months after that, insisting I come over and talk. I refused for two reasons: one that it seemed like a horrible idea and, two, I was thusly occupied.

I was not paying attention to the automated announcements on the bus alerting all riders that the South Campus Station had been reached and please get your ass off the bus and try to remember not to leave anything behind. I had reached my transfer point for the train.

I have ridden the subway into downtown on many occasions. Today, my mind was running circles and my legs were weak; I stumbled off the bus and headed down the long, steep stairway to the inbound train on the platform. The morning commute was drawing to an end, there were only about 15 other passengers awaiting the train. I felt the crush of the crowd, I felt uncomfortable in the mass of humanity pushing against me as the train neared the platform. My thoughts centered on what was ahead. I would need to have my phone reactivated, then involve the police and straighten this out. I was no longer amused by the report in the paper. I was concerned that my co-workers had heard the news of my demise.

I was concerned someone had the gumption to break into my garage and steal my car.

The 15-minute trip was completed without incident. The LRT system in Buffalo is not as extensive as its bigger brother in New York City, but it is well used by my fellow suburbanites. The subway operates in just two directions: from the University of Buffalo South Campus to the hockey arena and back; 7.5 miles in one direction. I have been told that the light rail system in Buffalo boasts the highest ridership per capita in the state, carrying over 20,000 passengers daily. I knew it was busy with hockey games and summer festivals. Moreover, it was very popular with patrons of Chippewa Street. Also, I understood the local transit authority, the Niagara Frontier Transportation Authority, contracted with the Buffalo Board of Education to carry students via the rail and other routes as well.

There are seven above-ground rail stations. The first is the theater station as is aptly named. The station is in the middle of the theater district. There are six theaters located within walking distance. The largest is Shea's, which seats about 6,500 people and is the only theater large enough to handle Broadway productions. The second station is the Fountain Plaza station. Sam's office is located at this stop. It is a commercial area boasting three major bank headquarters. The buildings were sleek, covered in glass and metal, their exterior shining when drenched in sunshine. This stop also services Chippewa Street or party central. The third station is the Lafayette station. It accesses a free concert series that is held from the end of May until Labor Day. The bands set up in what is known as "The Square." Depending on the band that was scheduled to perform, crowds can sometimes reach as many as 30,000. The main library for Buffalo and Erie is also located here. The library is huge, one of the biggest I have seen in my life. The library also housed a rather large rare book collection including an original first edition Mark Twain and the original plates that Audubon had used for his first field guide. My office is located near the Lafayette station. This station also offers a convenient way to the federal, state, and local court buildings. City Hall is also visible from this station. It is an impressive building and was constructed in the 1930s Art Deco design. City Hall was constructed in Niagara Square and was the terminus for Court Street. The building is square in design with blue, orange, and black accents with a larger central tower dwarfing the side towers, which I have been told is true to the form. The fourth station is Church Street. As the name implies there is an Episcopal Church adjacent to the rail station. St Paul's Cathedral was the main Episcopal Church in the city of Buffalo and one of the first constructed. The next rail station is Seneca and it is located adjacent to the ballpark downtown. Buffalo boasts a Triple-A minor league affiliate to the Cleveland Indians. The price of admission was reasonable and the atmosphere was very family-oriented, complete with fireworks for every Friday home game. The Seneca station was also two short blocks from Pearl Street brewery - a true microbrewery and a fine restaurant. The next stop was the Erie Harbor Canal station that used to drop off Sabres fans right in front of the old War Memorial. The name of the station was changed a few years ago after a construction project discovered relics left over from the original Erie Canal construction. The Aud, former home of the Sabres, has been closed for some time now, the last station is located in front of the new arena where the Sabres now play their game.

I exited the train at Lafayette Station. My office complex is called the Rand building - my home away from home. The building was named for Joseph Rand, an area banker in the late 19th century who would eventually manage the very first Marine Midland Bank. Mr. Rand was the chairman and this was the second bank in Buffalo to boast over a million dollars in deposits. Marine Midland was of course purchased many years ago; HSBC still holds offices on the first floor of the building.

I arrived at my office in about forty minutes. Not wanting to cause a scene, I decided to use the back entrance instead of the front door. There were fellow workers here that thought that I was dead, my showing up without any warning, would only add to an already bizarre situation.

It was a cool August morning when I awoke; the fact downtown is close to Lake Erie and is always cooler than the rest of Buffalo made the persistent breeze quite chilly. If not for the light jacket, I would have been uncomfortable on my short walk.

Every employee of CellNY is issued an identification badge allowing access to both entrances. I walked around the building to what everyone referred to as the nicotine alley. As always, there were those people huddled against the wind puffing on their cigarettes and looking rather unpleasant. One would think that would be incentive enough to quit, but as an ex-smoker, I can tell you it's not.

Ours is not the only office in the building and I did not recognize the people who at the moment we're taking seven minutes off their lives. I used my badge and keyed my number. My first choice of personal identification number was refused which is my mother's birthday, November 11, and I quickly discovered that security firms have no sense of humor. I keyed my numbers, which also happen to be the same code as my ATM card. I like simple and waking up dead was starting to ruin my day. I was granted access and I went through the door.

This way leads to the back entrance of the office and I quickly walked down the hall connecting the stairwell to the call center. At this hour everyone would be very busy handling customer calls; I should not encounter many others. I passed file storage and equipment storage, pausing momentarily at the entrance of the roaming department. Everyone, again, occupied at their desks and my arrival so far unnoticed. I was here to see the manager of the roaming department, as Ed has unlimited access to the switch, the main computer.

Knocking on his door he waved me in without first checking to see who was standing in the threshold. I shut the door behind me. When he ended his conversation and returned the receiver to the cradle. He stopped and looked perplexed.

"Aren't you dead? If not, you're late for work."

"Any day you wake up and find out you're dead is a day where rules do not apply."

"That presupposes you followed the rules when counted amongst the living."

I shrugged my shoulders. "I guess I mostly followed the rules."

"Mostly." His glance at me from above his glasses doubting the validity of the latest statement.

Edouard de Bar was the manager of the roaming department. Just a word of warning, it was unsafe to use his full name. If one tried it often resulted in a stern look or maybe a poke in the nose. Ed was by and not the tallest person I have ever met, he did, however, wrestle in college for a Division I school. During my first week at CellNY, when I was answering the phones, he single-handedly disarmed an irate recent ex-employee. The gentlemen came to work high on cocaine and rather pissed off at his dismissal, he also was carrying a 9mm Glock he had bought on the streets. He was looking for the manager of the call center and he had a full clip. Needless to say, after a few minutes with Ed, the would-be assailant was begging for the police and even attempted a lawsuit over the injuries he sustained. The man is stout. Although occasionally I may pick at Ed, that is one beehive I will not investigate with a stick.

For the most part, Ed's department interacted with customers that were not part of our network and were having problems using their phones on our system. Holidays and summer were some of the busiest days for Ed's department. We would gather to tell our war stories and to search out a sympathetic ear. Ed and I were work friends - we ate lunch together, generally shared the same world views and deranged sense of humor. We just never socialized outside of work, excluding vendor and product rollouts. We always promised to make plans, at the last roll out Sam and his wife Christy hit it off and Ed even had his daughter Yolanda attend, yet for some reason, plans for socializing outside of work or work situations never came to fruition.

"It's been an odd sort of day," I said. shrugging my shoulders.

"Yeah, how's that?"

"Well, I wake up and find out I died last night in a car crash, found out someone stole my car and I have no phone service at all either the cell or the landline. Other than that I have no complaints."

"Well, to what do I owe the honor of your visit?"

"I need a favor. Two actually."

"Okay."

"I need to know who called in to turn off my phone and I need it reactivated."

Ed tapped away on his keyboard, placed his chin in his hand and stared glassy-eyed at the screen, and said "Umm interesting."

"What?"

"Your girlfriend called to perm deactivate your phone. She rattled off both of your passcodes. Sorry, we thought it was legit."

"What time?"

"6:15a.m."

"She was sleeping at 6:15 a.m., or at least I thought she was. Can we pull the recording? I need to know if it was a female voice or Sam's voice. It's important."

"I'll have someone in your office pull the call. I will let

them know that it's for you. But maybe she has gifts of which you are not aware."

"Funny joking with a dead man is it. For favor two, I need a working cell phone number. I want you to set me up with a non-billable number. I need caller ID and caller ID block. I need you to set it up in the MTSO so there is no paper trail."

"How long?"

"For 48 hours, until I can figure this out."

"What do you think is going on?"

"I don't know. It feels like an episode of the Twilight Zone. I am going to call the police. This is quickly turning into a thing."

"Like Karma seeking its long-sought-after revenge, or 'why me' thing?"

"Ahhhh, option two."

"There, finished." He wrote down the number after a few moments of frantic tapping on his keyboard. "If you need any help let me know." His voice sounded true and the concern reverberated caution.

"You haven't seen me and you don't know this number right?"

"How can I see you? I am not a psychic boy on TV or the kid from the movie. Like all others, I ignore the dead."

Slipping out the backdoor unnoticed, I reprogrammed the phone with the new number. The process is easy on most models - impossible to difficult on others. Motorola has some phones that require you to enter a fourteen-digit code and follow it with twelve zeroes. This, fortunately, was not one of those phones. With the process complete, I called the police.

I told them who I was, and my car was stolen sometime last night. I informed them that the article in the newspaper was mistaken, and at last check, I was still alive. They advised that an officer at the police station could take the report.

"I don't have a car. Can we take the report at my house?"

The officer accommodated me and I returned home the same way I had arrived, on public transportation. The trip was uneventful, as there were fewer passengers on the train or bus. The Gillig bus announced my stop at California and Main. I had just ended a conversation with a less than helpful customer service representative at my local bank. He must have read the article, or he specializes in being obstinate. He thought me dead and would not open access to my accounts, even after I verified an unusually large number of passwords. Mr. Obstinate also reminded me that his supervisor thought me dead as well. Even more important, the computer was informed of my untimely death. Once the computer knows a thing, well, that just cannot be undone. He further informed me I shouldn't have filed a false report about my own death. I was truly speechless. A second call seemed merited; however, the bank remained steadfast in its belief that I was dead. They cared not to believe they were speaking to me directly and I ended the conversation with my asking about his personal belief of psychics and channeling the dead. He cared not to hear my diatribe as the call was disconnected. Rudely. If he had been working for me, he would have been seeking other employment.

The air had grown colder, the sun still fighting to break through the thick cloud cover, and it was nearing 10 a.m.

Walking from the bus stop at Main and California, my apartment is located on West Spring Street, which is just a block off of Main. As I turned off of Reist, walking on the south side of the street, I could see the Amherst police cruiser parked in front of my house, just down the street on the north side. I did not hasten my stride. I was told Officer Nicholas Flamel would be taking the report and meeting me for a statement. He disappeared around the corner of the apartment either to knock on the back door or peek into the garage.

I was still half a block away. The police have my temporary cell number and I figured if Officer Flamel was growing impatient, I would be receiving a call. Too far away to shout at the officer, I continued my slow pace, thinking about the upcoming hassles with the insurance companies and the mountains of paperwork contingent upon filing a claim, and generally convincing the world that I was indeed alive. At least I thought myself to be alive. My thoughts returned to the task at hand. I really loved the car. It had more than served its purpose and had gotten me through three winters - the all-wheel-drive had saved me on more than one occasion. Further, last month I had updated the car with a new satellite radio sound system. Ryan Prince may have been a mild-mannered customer service manager pushing some 36 years old, but I had an extensive music collection. It consumed the entirety of an iPod shuffle – 128 gigs. There was more than a monetary loss because I was fairly certain that I had left the iPod in the glove box.

I saw Officer Flamel come around from the back of the house to the front door and wait there. I noticed there was a white van parked across the street from my place. It appeared to be from one of the local HVAC companies. I continued down the block. Four houses now separated me from my apartment. Looking back at the van, I saw the back windows were painted with the company logo. I wondered if that made driving the van difficult.

Two houses closer, I saw the van door slide silently open. No one stepped out, which immediately appeared strange, causing me to slow my progress and assess the situation. What I did see was a barrel of a horribly long rifle accompanied by three smoky eruptions. The rifle was pulled back into the van before the barrel ceased smoking. More surprising was the fact that almost no sound accompanied the explosive force. The bullets hit their mark as Officer Flamel lay on the front stoop of the apartment, unmoving.

I stopped dead in my tracks, no pun intended. The day had started off weird enough and now was heading for surreal at warp factor ten. I did not even think about checking to see if the officer was dead or merely wounded, as men with high-powered sniper rifles complete with silencers don't often miss. I cared not to check their work. I did not want to hang around, figuring that the gunman also may be looking for me as well. I was terrified of what would have happened if I met with the officer a few moments earlier.

Had I not taken my time walking the final few hundred feet I, too, would be riddled with bullet holes and no one the wiser. This was no longer a mistake, this was no longer a mis-understanding, this was for real. I was now convinced that my ex was involved or even an irate customer. I have been accused on occasion of missing the obvious, however, a sledgehammer upside my head would have been subtler. This was the second indication that reading about my own death was not a mistake and I might be knee-deep in something I cannot understand nor control. Call me a coward, but I fled into my neighbor's yard.

3 |

August 18 | 10 a.m.

The yard belonged to our neighbors across the street, Charles and Lorraine Alexander. Charlie was a retired postal worker and first-generation Polish immigrant to this country. He reminded me of my grandfather. Charlie learned English out of necessity but he could very easily slip into his native language as well. I have attended many a party at Charlie's and he would speak Polish to his older family members, most notably his older brother, who had emigrated with him.

Charlie was a hard worker and a spendthrift. He was bigger than life, boasting a huge barrel chest, and was a very verbose, Jack Daniels drinking, extremely humorous, fun-loving man. He felt, above all else, his success in this great country was to ensure his accumulated wealth would see his family through. He planned on taking care of his numerous grandchildren and bought two houses for his children. Charlie was old school before old school was old school. He did not believe in the philosophy that good fences make for good neighbors. He had moved into this house about a year ago and his first project involved removing the fence that separated his property from the people with which he shared a back yard.

At the moment I was thanking him for his foresight as I ran like hell through his yard and his neighbor's yard, and onto Main Street; for the most part, I felt that my activities had gone unnoticed by those gunmen in the van. The fact that I was running and not bleeding all over the sidewalk convinced me I was correct. It did not, however, ease my current state of paranoia.

Main Street is a major traffic corridor for western New York. It started south of downtown Buffalo and ran to the outskirts of Erie county, where it merged with State Route 5, and then traveled alongside State Route 20 all the way into eastern New York State. Back before interstate highways were common, even before Interstates 290 and 190 were renderings on an artist's board, back before the Thruway was built in the 60s, Main Street and Route 5 were major thoroughfares in the area and the state. There was not a better way to travel from east to west. Although the interstates had lessened the traffic flow, Main Street was always busy.

I was looking frantically for either a taxi or a bus. Continuing west on Main Street and running as fast as my casual dress shoes allowed, I covered six blocks in what was record time. I was approaching Dickey's Doughnuts near Park Club Lane. This was a major hang out for those that made driving their occupation. Today was no exception, as the lot was full of cabs, a few police cruisers, and a Metro bus. To my luck, a cab driver was exiting the store with a steaming cup of coffee and a couple of doughnuts.

"I need a ride to Niagara Falls Memorial," I blurted out,

trying to catch my breath, hands on knees. "My car just broke down and it's an emergency."

In truth at that very moment, Niagara Falls Memorial seemed to be the furthest point from Main and Park Club Lane. The hospital had made headlines just a few days ago closing a labor dispute that had lasted years. Further, it was the very first thing that had entered my very frantic mind. The compulsion to run far and fast was undeniable. I had just run down Main Street wearing clothes that for the most part are not recommended for such activities. The thought, get safe, then call Sam was the only other coherent thought I had, other than the smoking barrel and the silenced shots playing back as slowly as my brain could manage. Frame by frame, slow motion smoke followed by the almost inaudible thffft, I must have heard that noise a hundred times before reaching my destination.

"I don't have time for charity." He pushed me aside.

I removed a hundred-dollar bill from my pocket. "I will double the fare if I can be there in thirty-five minutes."

"Deal." He moved faster than a man his size should do safely.

I am not Ann Landers but feel that this advice has lifesaving potential: Do not ever give cab driver a reason to drive faster than what they, themselves, deem prudent. It's about 10 miles to where Interstates 290 and 190 merge and you take the 190 north to Niagara Falls, crossing Grand Island in the process. It took only nine minutes to arrive at the merger.

Jeff Gordon would have been proud of how this man handled his cab through heavy traffic. I was expecting him to start rubbing some of the cars or get under their bumper to loosen them up. I was uncertain if the cabbie was tailgating or drafting. He may or may not have worn a helmet connected to a communication device. He also only made right-hand turns which I believe would have disqualified him from NASCAR.

The driver slowed because the traffic was always heavy along this route, more so during the tourist season. I was convinced that if there had been no traffic, we would have hit the South Grand Island Bridge and just jumped the four-mile wide Island completely.

Grand Island, according to local lore, is the largest freshwater island in the country. At roughly 40 square miles, it briefly splits the mighty Niagara River in two, before they combine forces at the Falls, thus creating one of the most spectacular views in the world. Each bridge is almost 1,000 feet long and there are four bridges in total; two bridges handling southbound traffic, the other two handling northbound traffic. There are two sets of bridges on the south side of the island, the other on the north side. Many a motorist in western New York will avoid the bridges entirely, choosing instead to add more than twenty minutes on their travel time to Niagara Falls by using Niagara Falls Boulevard. I can see their point. Being a cautious driver, I am very careful about crossing these bridges. One, they are narrow and offer only two lanes for traffic. Second, there are five toll booths and two lanes, do the math. Do the words mad dash mean anything? Three, at their apex the bridges are more than one hundred feet tall, allowing even the tallest ships access to the river. Fourth, the first bridge was built in 1935 - the subsequent bridges in 1965 - which makes one want to check inspection records before crossing. Fifth, after any particularly nasty winter weather the downslope on the bridges sometimes makes your car brakes ineffective. On more than one occasion I have slid, not drove, down the bridge. A firsthand interesting experiment in friction and inclined surfaces, which would have made any physics professor proud.

The view from the top of the bridge is breathtaking, featuring the panoramic Niagara Gorge. The view was hard to admire, as the cabbie drove too fast. His other hobby seemed to be tailgating and at several points, I almost ripped the panic handle out of the roof above my window. I tried to concentrate on the view instead of our progress. Maybe the paper was prophetic; today I would indeed die in horrible fiery crash caused by reckless speed.

Grand Island does live up to its name. Not only is it the most efficient way to the Falls, but also boasts two state parks, many boat harbors, and some of the most impressive green spaces in the area. People first settled on the island to get away from city life and all the issues that came along with it. Soon thereafter, it became a popular destination and housing and real estate is still a growing business. The island residents are not isolated; all the trappings of city life have found their way to it; grocery stores, movie theaters, and even an amusement park called the island home. Residents were no longer forced to make the trip across the bridges to buy life essentials.

Grand Island was first settled by the Huron then the Seneca tribes; it's ironic that we steal their land; er I mean buy the land for nothing, from such noble people then name all of our streets after them. I often wonder though, if those tribes thought they were taking us for a ride. There is a Native American expression that states, "We do not inherit the land from our ancestors, we borrow it from our children." A few years ago, the Seneca Nation was almost successful in suing to get their native land back. Their efforts failed but there were a few hairy moments for the non-native residents of that land.

Grand Island also offers your first view of the falls. While on the bridges you're still two miles from the vista, where you can see the ever-present thick, white mist hanging hundreds of feet above the water.

The cabbie managed to get me across the island and into Niagara Falls without causing my untimely death, arriving at Pine and Tenth streets, Niagara Falls Memorial. We reached our destination and he had kept his promise as we arrived in a little under 35 minutes. I doubled his fare, the trip cost me about $130. But I felt safe. My first order of business was to call the Amherst police and report an officer down. I gave them the address and then disconnected. I was not sure if the cabbie was watching or not; but I walked into the hospital, going to the cafeteria and ultimately out the back door, following those with nicotine habits and trying to look like I belonged in the crowd. I had never stepped foot in the hospital, so I relied on signs and arrows to point me in the correct direction.

When my day started and I found out I was dead, I had myself a good chuckle. Realizing now this was serious, deadly serious, fits of paranoia started to eat at my psyche. Every corner held a gunman; every alley hid the man with the sniper rifle, and every person on the street was tailing me. Every white HVAC van was tracking me down to finish the task at hand. I crisscrossed the street, stopping often to enter small stores. I was trying to determine if I was being followed. I was attempting a circuitous route to the casino - trying to be hard to track, but looking more like a lunatic trying to avoid the evil men out to get me. I saw Agent Gibbs attempt a similar ploy on an NCIS episode. That was the level of logic currently taking residence in my muddled brain. If I saw it on cable TV, then it must be true. I might want to watch an episode of Scooby-Doo in order to increase my investigation skills.

I just crossed my ex-wife off the list.

I wanted to call Sam, but I wasn't going to do it here. I needed a place to lie low. There were two such destinations within walking distance: the Seneca Niagara Casino on the US side and Casino Niagara on the Canadian side. It's about ten blocks from the hospital to the American casino. Instead of walking on Pine, a main artery, I took Ferry all the way to Third, and then Third to Wendell, thus avoiding main streets. I was certain that no self-respecting gunman would have been caught dead in such a neighborhood. There were obvious signs of gang activity and the normal corner hustle. It seems that people may have gone back to the cottage industry; nothing like working from home. Must be great to avoid the daily commute.

I am not sure why I chose Niagara Falls as my hiding place. It seemed logical. I had no ties to this area, as all of my friends lived in Erie County in the Buffalo area. I thought this would be the last place someone would come looking for me. I just wanted to get into a crowd and blend in.

The Seneca Niagara Casino is the renovated version of the former Niagara Falls Convention Center. The Senecas choose not to demolish the building; although, the outside of the building resembles the convention center, inside underwent a major face-lift. The outdated pale and yellowing tile had been replaced with plush carpeting. In some areas, there was a second floor where none had existed previously. The casino carpeting was plush and comfortable - an upgrade from the utilitarian look of the convention center. Native American art could be seen in every corner. Although the whole gambling floor was immense, the huge convention center floor had been broken into smaller areas. The space included the main gambling floor, a buffet restaurant that served everything from prime rib to Cantonese, various stores selling the usual Native American art, a sit-down restaurant, and an events center that hosted live concerts and shows. A poker room had been added with the recent Texas Hold'Em craze. The blackjack area was in the middle of the immense gambling floor and there were also four different snack areas selling food and a wide variety of beverages. There were three bar areas where one could relax, have a drink, and play video slot machines that were incorporated into the bar surface.

My destination was not the gambling floor. I went to the souvenir shop, purchasing a polo shirt, cap, and a light jacket, all embossed with the casino logo. My urban tourist camouflage complete, I could blend into any crowd. Exiting the casino, I made a leisurely walk to the Falls, traveling south on

Third Street, then to Rainbow Boulevard. Trying my best to look like a tourist and not a target, I stopped at points along the way, oohing and awing at the appropriate moments. I even aided a young couple acting as their personal photographer with the Niagara River as the backdrop. The river ran fast with white, foaming fierce waves. Although the tremendous roar of the Falls was audible, the raging river was nearly as loud, as the water gains momentum, readying itself for the fall over the brink. It was easy to be impressed by such a sight.

Once every few years, some yahoo in a boat would pass the "safe" area buoys and the boat would become unstoppable. Park Service personnel and local rescue teams would have to gear up to save the fool. The cost and danger to the personnel involved were often charged to the idiot of the month.

Following the river downstream was Rainbow Boulevard, where both terminated at Rainbow Bridge. This is the only bridge allowing foot traffic into Canada for the nominal fee of fifty cents. Deciding to cross the bridge, I went through the normal customs check. Obviously the Federal government was not aware of my demise, as I was ushered through customs without any hassles. It is the first thing that went my way since I woke up dead.

Niagara Falls is one of the wonders of the world. However, when it is in your backyard, and you have witnessed its glory on more than 60 occasions, well, it turns out to be just a bunch of water. I often wonder if the Egyptians feel the same way as the pyramids are just large triangular piles of rocks.

In order to not take the falls for granted, I enjoy showing first-time visitors the splendor that is Niagara Falls. Witnessing the awe-inspiring view through another person's eyes makes the trip worthwhile. As much as watching those same people pay $3.50 for a 20-ounce soda. But I digress. This plan for focusing on the first-timers has worked and renewed me somewhat. But I would highly suggest a visit to Goat Island on the US side of the falls. One corner of the island is directly over the falls, the water a mere 36 inches away. The noise is like a freight train gone awry. The cool mist envelopes your face and paints every surface of your body. The incredible speed at which the water plummets is an awe-inspiring experience.

I know a fall of 160 feet does not allow a body to reach terminal velocity. But as I stand at that one spot, I want Isaac Newton at my side doing the calculations longhand to prove it. Watching gravity pull the water to the rocks below, it looks as if the water nears an incredible and terrible speed.

The walk across to Canada is half a mile and comes complete with a tremendous view of Horseshoe Falls, also known as the Canadian Falls. Horseshoe Falls comprises 90 percent of the total water flow and is 170 feet high and some 2,200 feet long, with water falling a rate of 100,000 cubic feet per second. To give you some perspective, the helium-filled blimps slowly cruising around sporting events are filled with 5,000 cubic feet of helium.

I have completed this walk on numerous occasions, yet only once have traversed the bridge at night. The falls and the foam are illuminated via ten spotlights of various colors. The sight gets burned directly into your brain, as it is difficult to dismiss: reds, greens, blues, yellows, all mixing to form seemingly every conceivable color combination. The roar of the falls behind those seeking spotlights, as foam travels hundreds of feet in the air colored by the light, makes the tracking of it easy. It was the first time the roar did not seem so loud, as if my eyes attempting to view this panoramic of color briefly interfered with the ability to hear the full spectrum. One wonders if Leonardo da Vinci controls the lighting as it appears to be very close to perfection.

The cool day made the ever-present mist pest-like and not enjoyable. I paused at the halfway point to enjoy the view and remember how it appeared at night. The fact Niagara Falls is considered a desirable honeymoon destination is not lost during my contemplative period, standing on a bridge between two countries. Maybe I could take Sam here for a weekend. We have yet to visit. After this was all over, I would like to spend a weekend, hopefully celebrating our upcoming nuptials. But there is much to be resolved first. I remember that many years ago my parents, young and optimistic, stood at this very spot taking in the view, hands grasped, looking forward to what life had to offer. If only I could take advantage of the same opportunity.

Watching the water, feeling the sub-bass noise echo through my bones as it fell crushing the rocks beneath, I try to add some perspective to my day. Not an easy thing to do. I woke up dead and saw a police officer gunned down at my front door. I am involved in this somehow, I just can't believe how. I wondered if the cop was shot because he knew I wasn't dead. Which of course leads to the even logical next step, why would someone want me dead?

My mind was still trying to reach a conclusion concerning

the internal argument that has been raging since I jumped in the cab. Only one person has since been removed from the list. I had been called names that would make sailors blush; however, those are idle threats. Some people are never pleased regardless of the lengths you go to service their needs. I have been divorced long enough now that hurt feelings are a mere memory, at times I am sure my ex would want me dead, that is why she was eliminated earlier. I, like plenty of others, have angered many people, occasionally on purpose, sometimes without malice. I am no one. The list inside my brain should be brief; paranoia has greatly expanded it. I have begun to believe the only logical choice is a cosmic misunderstanding.

There is no doubt that this is big, bigger than me, and I am out of my league. However, I am not sure if the police should be involved. One man has paid the ultimate price. I could not have another death on my conscious.

Then there's Sam. If that officer died because of me, how long until they figured out that she also knows I am still breathing? Are they going to pay her a "visit" at her job? Pull her from her comfortable small cubicle and gun her down on the street? They killed an officer – what's going to stop them from killing a customer service manager? They, them, who -are these not the words of a person suffering paranoia? Seeing conspiracy everywhere yet not being able to name those involved.

Since I am not in the habit of pissing off random people on the street, the answer had to be in my database. Out of all those names, there would be one that may be the cause of everything that happened today. Still seems far-fetched. I talked with irate customers, not mobsters or drug dealers. Although one can never truly comprehend what resides in someone's mind, I cannot see another avenue to pursue. My database is accessible via an Internet connection; I have neither a computer nor access to the necessary programs. Sam does on her computer, her laptop she brings to work every day has MyPC loaded on it and also a WIFI card. Maybe I will call her soon, but for now, I am left to ramble like a lunatic about those, they, whoever was involved. One person was dead. Two, if you count the fact that I also was "killed" sometime this morning.

Hoping that I was in need of extensive therapy for a case of twenty-four-hour paranoia, instead of being in the middle of a conspiracy to ruin my life, then Sam was not in danger. What if I were being watched? What if they, whoever "they" was, saw me slip in and out of work? Would I anger these mysterious foes by forcing their hand? Would they gun down Sam because she knows the truth? I was second-guessing my original plan for contacting her.

Sam, the sound of her name in my ears is music; her voice a symphony. I let the sound of her voice echo through my mind. I let my thoughts wander while standing on the dividing line of two countries.

As always, I think about the first time we met. I made her acquaintance in the worst possible of all situations, a blind date. The infamous "I have a friend who has a friend" arrangement. I agreed to complete the last of our three-couple ensemble for an evening of drinks, a movie, and dinner. I didn't mind the plans, as I was not required to hold a conversation while the story played out on the screen. I have not been on many blind dates in my time; however, most have been disasters. I approached this date as I had the others - no expectations at all. No expectations led to no disappointments.

At that time, I was happy.

Or at least thought I was. My status as a bachelor meant my time was used as I deemed fit. I was dating no one and had mistaken this for supposed freedom. I would find out quickly my life was very empty.

I was working late that evening and agreed to meet everyone in downtown Buffalo. My office is also downtown, if anything it was very convenient; moreover, a co-worker had directions to call me in one hour, if necessary, giving me an excuse to exit the evening without hurting any feelings.

The bar was located on Chippewa Street, party central in downtown Buffalo. The place where all the twenty-somethings hung out, yet in this dessert of youth stood a lone oasis. The bar was named the Library, it had music played though an immense sound system at a reasonable level, no dance floor, no scantily clad women serving shots of Jägermeister from a tray, and the most comfortable oversized leather chairs this side of the nearest furniture store. This place reeked of old people - you know, those of us in our thirties, those of us that are half dead. I entirely enjoyed the place and often would go there and sit in a corner and quietly read while enjoying some signal malt scotch or a microbrew on tap. The bar was also equipped with a smoking lounge - the decor the same big overstuffed chairs- the music intended strictly for ambiance, the perfect decompression chamber.

My friend Steve, the first link in the multi-linked friend's chain, waved me over to a table they were occupying. Steve and I became friends through a rather curious set of events. Steve's office was in the same building as mine. We would run into each other occasionally. Steve is not easy to miss - he stands at 6'2" and wears Armani suits. His ties cost more than my entire wardrobe. He carries himself with confidence and when he talks he demands attention. You can always find him in a crowded room. Steve was a gifted conversationalist and could talk with authority on a broad variety of subject matters. He also was a gifted storyteller and extremely easy to talk to, even if you were not the extrovert he was. It was not hard to determine why women were attracted to this man.

One night four years ago, we were both exiting the building and exchanged pleasantries. Steve had two tickets to the Buffalo Sabres game but could not find anyone to accompany him. When he extracted the tickets from his jacket and asked if I wanted to attend, it was the start of a friendship that continues strong today. We have been friends ever since and have attended many games together.

Steve is a lawyer and his office occupied the 7th floor of the Rand building; he was the first scrupulous personal injury attorney I have known. He did not advertise; yet, he was never short of potential customers. He often turned away frivolous lawsuits and charlatans. He believed in personal responsibility. Although we had drastically different careers, we shared a similar bent on life. That was the bond that kept two very different men linked.

For the last few years, I have spent many an evening with

Steve and his seemingly endless stream of beautiful women. Steve went through ladies the way most people go through undergarments. I often joked the only reason he carried a PDA was his cell phone memory was at capacity. I am still in awe he could juggle so many women and keep all their names straight. Often, I would play the part of wingman, entertaining his date's friend to clear the way for Steve. However, this did not last long, late nights in the middle of the week is far from my forte. His ability to juggle numerous women was only outpaced by his ability to party until 4 a.m. and be ready for work at 8 a.m. I was not surprised when I received the invite. He had pestered me to continue our nightly escapades. I declined, citing the normal excuses, but his persistence wore me down; moreover, it was Friday and not the middle of the week. I was not required to rise out of bed at 8 a.m. I was not keen on going on this blind date but Steve assured me Samantha would be worth the time. He was not forthcoming with many details, other than to say she was attractive, had a great personality, and was very intelligent. He would not tell me why they never dated. Other than not breathing or lack of intelligence, I was not sure what made a woman non-dating material in Steve's world. I sensed trouble.

I sat down and thanked Steve for the drink, as he had taken the liberty of ordering me a scotch. Quick introductions were made. Steve, as always, was accompanied by a very attractive female named Shannon - a beautiful brunette with hair so black I wondered if it was Clairol instead of God-given. She was taller than me and must have had many a Greek goddess in her lineage.

The other couple was Steve's sister- and brother-in-law, both great people who lived a few blocks away from me in Amherst, although we never had the occasion to meet. Both Sarah and Jonathan worked for Erie County, and their office was located in the Rath Building.

Arriving at the bar before my date, I had just finished work and required a few moments to process my day before jumping head-long into any conversations. I talk for a living, but when the life has been drained out of you through listening to customers wax poetically about their problems, this short period of downtime was a necessity. After a particularly stressful day, 15 minutes of silence was required. Customers these days are worse than they have ever been, no phone etiquette, screaming and jumping to conclusions, and the vulgarity has grown substantially worse even from our younger customers. And everything is a personal attack. Thank you daytime talk shows for your contribution to society. Thank you, Jerry Springer. These problems have only worsened over the last few years.

Enjoying my scotch and attempting to nod at all the right times I followed the conversation without appearing to be rude. I wondered if Steve had given these folks the heads up concerning my personal relaxation mode. Either way, no one seemed bothered or asked me why I was not taking a more active role in the conversation. Thinking one more drink should bring me back to human levels, I was scanning the bar, attempting to locate our waitress. I was the only person who had a view of the front bar and subsequent entrance. I elbowed Steve as a beautiful brunette walked into the bar. She was wearing a summer-weight dress with a light sweater. The dress was long, yet seemed lightweight, as if allowed, could float on its own. The pattern was colorful earth tones yet not obtrusive. Her long, black curly hair was showing auburn in the bar lighting. She had such grace - she did not walk but glided across the floor. She was not tall, yet not short either. I guessed about 5'6", and she had a face that I am sure Helen of Troy would be jealous of and a petite, yet athletic, frame. When Steve followed my line of sight he rose from his seat and rushed to greet her. I must have stood slack-jawed and wide-eyed as she approached the table. I was wondering if I had food in my teeth or my hair was out of place as Steve introduced us.

"This is Marie Samantha de Saint Clair."

"Sam to my friends." She extended her hand, delicate nails perfect, yet she had real strength in her hands. A strength that comes from solid work. Her perfume could have replaced Viagra. It spoke to those places deep inside. She told me later that she much preferred her middle name Samantha to the first name her parents had chosen for her.

"Sam its a pleasure." I did my gentleman's best to offer her a chair without tripping over my tongue. "Ryan, sorry."

"What an odd last name," she smiled coyly. I wanted to tell her that the position of smart-ass had already been filled and there were no expected vacancies but instead told her what my real last name was.

"My last name is Prince actually."

The group laughed at my expense, yet I was not trying to

joke. I was sincere. My cheeks heated and flushed, and I acted as if it was from the scotch.

After our introduction, the remainder of the evening went by far too quickly for my liking. We exited the bar and walked a few blocks to the movie theater on Main Street. Much to my surprise the ladies in attendance did not insist on a "date" movie but selected an action movie instead. I couldn't tell you what the movie's title was or which Hollywood stars were contracted to bring the writer's vision to life, or if I even enjoyed it. Sam, by my side throughout the movie whispering comments concerning the plot holes was very distracting. I had to restrain outright laughter on more than one occasion. The final credits played across the screen approximately four minutes after we sat down, by my best closest estimation.

The walk from the theater to the restaurant was again very quick. We walked along Main Street as the subway made its way south, Sam's arm wrapped in mine, her perfume lingering in the air. She would look at me with her perfect smile and beautiful blue eyes. It was heaven. We chatted easily during the brief walk. I was almost afraid to mention the chance of a next date, for fear of ruining the evening. I had never in my life felt as connected to one person after so few hours.

Dinner, like the movie, went off without a hitch and we exchanged phone numbers before the waitress had brought the check. We hit it off immediately, our rapport seemed to grow as the evening waned. I found myself wanting to know when I would see her again. I felt things. I had not actively dated in a while, instead enjoying the bachelor's life. I had known this woman for only a few hours and I would give up all of my supposed freedom to spend more time with her. She had a way that allowed me to open up. I felt like a child. This was not my first date with a very attractive female. Yet I was not in control of my tongue nor the part of my brain that did the thinking.

One thing we shared was similar occupations. She ran the customer service office at the Erie One Mortgage company as I did for CellNY. Customer service is not an easy job, contrary to popular opinion; it actually ranks in the top five most stressful jobs. That list is shared with air traffic controllers and postal workers. No joke. It was comforting to know that I could go home and not say a word for 25 minutes and not be pestered with questions as to my sullen mood. I was de-stressing and she understood that completely. I have broken off relationships because my girlfriend, wife, and/or friend did not fully understand this. Working customer service for an ultra-competitive cell phone business adds more stress to the equation. I spearheaded the retention department where every phone call started off the same way - "I want my phone off and I want it off now." I was constantly reminded at monthly company meetings that the only way to grow a business and customer base was through retention and sales. Once in a while, I required 30, not 15 minutes, and a tall glass of single malt scotch.

After my divorce, I promised never to marry again. I would cohabitate, I may actually get engaged but never marry. I never wanted to have someone that close again. I never wanted to have that emotional investment. I never wanted anyone to be within the inner sanctum. Once you love you're vulnerable; once someone knows you that well, they know how to push your buttons and where to stick the knife for maximum damage. I'd rather be alone than potentially put myself in that position again. I prefer stability to vulnerability, seclusion over companionship.

Sam changed every aspect of my so-called freedom. She opened my heart and owned my soul. What would I do without her in my world? Finding someone else that understood my whims, my mannerisms, and me is difficult. I have not calculated those odds but I am certain that Sam is a rarity.

We talked for over an hour the next day and made plans for the following weekend. After a few dates, both of us were comfortable enough with each other that future nights out were actually spent in, taking turns cooking dinner, enjoying wine, or a DVD. The relationship progressed slowly - there was no pressure or talk about what would happen next or what either of us expected. We just were, and let the relationship grow at a natural rate.

Sam was not one to talk about her past. I figured she had been hurt by some distant relationship, and if she wanted to share those experiences she was welcome to. I never pushed the issue. Sam was everything I could have asked for.

We had a connection, some non-verbal communication, a look or touch was all that was needed to convey 1,000 words. It's weird but after she left a room, I could almost sense her route, as if I was watching a boat skidding across the surface of a calm lake creating a wake in its path. Her very movements were recorded differently, as if by some special ability, or she held a certain importance over the rest of us. It was either that or her interaction just remained with me well past the normal half-life.

Sam understood me from the here and now and did not delve into my past trying to gain some understanding through wasted relationships. She did not want to see the luggage I carried or hid in the closet. She would listen as I relayed past relationships and past problems as intently as I would remember those special moments, the better times. I am not one who believes mystery spices up a relationship. I prefer to be open and honest. I did not push her. If she wanted to talk about her family or her past lovers, she was free to do so. Sam was not a person of mystery either; she chooses to share what she deemed important. I did not try to lead such a conversation.

She knew I was close to my parents and talked with them often. Family held a certain amount of importance and distance did little to cut those ties. She chose to keep the majority of her past to herself. We both knew and understood life is more than what happens to you. How you react and cope is just as important.

Three months ago Sam was spending many an evening at my apartment and jokingly stated she ought to move in. She did just that a month later. After a few weeks, it was evident and necessary to discuss our future together. This was our first foray into such a discussion and I remember spending all night on the sofa, Sam on my arm talking about marriage, our need to combine resources, and what sort of ceremony we sought. It was then I discovered Sam also had been married previously and she was not looking for some grandiose ceremony or the great expense of a large family wedding. She only needed a quiet civil ceremony attended by our closest friends. I was in total agreement.

After our discussion, I started to put money aside whenever I could. We combined our monetary resources and Sam purchased some furniture and put a feminine spin on my decorating choices. For once my furniture matched. Sam was impressed by my collection of towels that contained matching sets and that both the kitchen and bathroom had modern color schemes. I was impressed she never purchased a dust ruffle for the bed or made me sleep with ninety pillows. The colors she chose were earth tones and browns, blues, grays, and tans dominated the apartment. The decorating was neither masculine nor feminine but rather neutral in tone and color. The apartment was comfortable, having a lived-in quality. The furniture was inviting and the living room set was of a modern design - squarish and oversized. There was no room which was deemed out of bounds and for company only. We used every square foot of the apartment; within weeks the place was ours.

My thoughts came back to the natural spectacle I was watching. I did not know what to do next. I have no experience in dealing with such matters. Where does one go to obtain this experience? Although the "Dummies Guide To..." books have gained popularity, I doubt there is a "Dummies' Guide to Waking up Dead and Being Involved in a Conspiracy" version. I would wager such a book is more than likely a good read. Maybe there is a Cliff Notes book that I could browse through. If there were I would be on Amazon immediately.

I completed my journey to Canada. The casino, built and operated by a local Native American tribe, was just blocks from the falls. Passing easily through customs I headed west to the casino. I have come to believe allowing these casinos to function is a form of payback for the atrocities we brought to these noble people. An atrocity brought forth during the formative years of the greatest symbol of freedom – the United States. That could very well be the definition of irony.

At last count, five such casinos operated in and near New York State. There were two casinos in western New York, one in Niagara Falls USA and the other under construction in Buffalo, just 17 miles south.

Few places offered a better place to lay low; I guess a neighborhood bar where no one knows you is also a solid choice. I did not even notice at first that my cell phone was ringing in my pocket. There was only one person who has the number and I couldn't fathom why Ed would call. The number was blocked, thus not being displayed, but at worst I thought it would be a wrong number.

"Hello?"

"Hey, it's me." It sounded a lot like Ed. "Our discussion this morning set some things a rolling."

"Are you free to talk?" I asked, wanting more information.

"No, there are people close by, be careful."

"Can you tell me who...." The line went dead.

Ed ended the call. Every phone that had some customer interface could and would be monitored. He did not call me from his cell - I would have recognized the number. Only the calls on the floor were recorded, so I understood his need for caution. Although Ed never identified himself or myself, in my bones I knew it was him and my decision for action was justified. Either that or the 24-hour paranoia bug was contagious.

The phone calls are monitored but only voice is recorded; they could not and would not pull someone's dialed call report without a viable reason. Ed must have had company or thought someone may have been listening. I was not sure why he did not just call me on his cell. He must have thought the risk was merited. His call was intended as a warning. Someone else must have found out I am still alive, and Ed's strange call leads me to believe that it was not an ally.

I dialed Sam's work number hoping to get her soon. The phone rang once, twice, three times, and as I waited for voicemail debating whether or not to leave a message she picked up, sounding very winded.

"Mortgage services."

"Sam it's me. Please listen."

"What's up?"

"If anybody asks I am dead. Look sad if you can."

"I will try to look sad but it's a stretch," she joked. "What is this all about? If you're joking that is not really funny."

"Sam, there was an article in the paper stating I died in an accident last night. My car was not in the garage. I think I somehow got wrapped up in something and I don't know what. The phone was turned off at the house and my cell was turned off."

"Who deactivated the phone?"

"You did, or someone who had all my passwords and is well aware of our procedures."

"Jason and jokes, this sounds like him," she said, trying to make light of the situation.

"He could not have turned off both phones. I am very concerned. Can you try to access our accounts and drive by the apartment?"

"I'll do it over lunch. Can I call you back then?"

"No. I'll call you back in about two hours."

"Where are you?"

"Hiding."

"Where?'

"Around."

"Are you trying to be elusive?"

"No. I am trying my best not to get you involved."

"Aren't we in everything together?"

"Normally yes, but an officer was gunned down at our apartment today."

"What do you mean gunned down?" She asked, her voice holding a note of concern.

"Shot dead with a high powered rifle. That sort of gunned down. He was there to take my statement about my car."

"If you don't have a car, how do you know that? Where the hell are you?"

"Long story. I'll talk with you later." For the first time in the three years I have dated Sam, I hung up on her.

After disconnecting the call, I found myself wandering around the casino. Unlike the casino on the American side, this casino was built from the ground up. The hotel was completed a few years after the casino opened. It was ornate yet comfortable. While enjoying the décor and congratulating whoever designed the layout; I stood and admired a painting on a mirrored wall. The contrast between the reflective surface and dark motif of the painting drew my eyes immediately. There, just to the right of the painting, I saw a man showing more than just a general interest in my location. He was dressed like a tourist, complete with a digital camera strapped around his neck. His eyes locked on me while holding a phone conversation. I continued my wanderings, and he seemed to be shadowing my aimless jaunt. I sat down at a slot machine and put in $50 and pretended not to notice my new best friend.

I was playing video poker, not that it mattered, but the game involves rudimentary skill as well as a bunch of luck. A waitress approached, drink tray in hand. I was able to conduct my business and watch my friend weave his way around the casino, making a sort of wandering bee-line towards me. It reminded me of Billy from Family Circus fame. I tipped the waitress after grabbing a drink.

I enjoyed the beer even though I normally didn't drink at 11 a.m. but since I was dead I figured I deserved the splurge. I also felt it made me blend in better with the crowd. Gambling camouflage completed, my attention focused on the game. Four hands in I was up $20 bucks; maybe my luck was changing.

My paranoia circuits had been running full tilt all day. My shadow had almost closed the gap between us. He looked like the guy from the Apple commercials, mid-forties, couldn't peg him for the partying type, tan kakis and a shirt at least ten years out of date, and of course boat shoes. An artist could not have drawn it better. I finished my beer and decided to get another when my friend's pace picked up and he made sufficient eye contact.

I am not the best looking guy in the world, never claimed to be. However, many people have told me that I remind them of someone else, so I guess that I have the plainest looking face in the world. I guess that is why my career as an underwear model never came to fruition.

My new friend and shadow put a smile on his face and extend his hand. "Ryan, it's been a while."

A really long while as I cannot remember ever meeting this man. Although, in my business, it's not uncommon for me to interact with twenty to thirty customers a week. I would have remembered this guy; he belonged to the "older gadget guy" category in my database. People consumed with the insatiable need to buy the next greatest gadget are some of my favorite customers. They are extremely easy to please as they search the world for the next nearly useless bell or whistle, or other perfectly useless cell phone app. I felt myparanoia triple and the hair stand up on the back of my neck.

"Sorry you must have me mistaken for someone else, my name is Curt," I lied. Something about this man made my paranoia circuits start to jangle.

Gadget guy smiled tightly. "We went to high school together, remember?"

"No sorry, I did not go to high school in the area, I am here visiting."

I ignored him and went back to my game, drew three of a kind, which added another $15 to my account, then went double or nothing and was then up $50, doubling my previous investment. I motioned to the waitress and she remembered me, a cold bottle of Molson already in hand. I tipped her another $5 American.

I did my best to appear unconcerned and apathetic as the man looked rather confused. I then said, "I am up $50, you want this machine when I am finished?"

"No, no thanks."

"I didn't catch your name," I said, extending my hand. "Curt Russell, nice to meet you."

"I did not give you my name."

His, "I am friendly tourist" disguise melted from his face. His posture changed. The goofy smile of a few minutes ago was replaced with a cold stare and sneer. He looked as if he was holding back the world's best string of profanity. He really wanted to let it fly; however, his strong understanding of social convention prevented him from sharing his thoughts. I could be wrong, as he may have been suffering gas pains.

He wandered off. I knew that was not a coincidence. I was also not entirely sure that my bald-faced lies necessarily had the intended impact.

Sitting at the video poker machine, attempting to appear tourist-like with a calm vacation demeanor, I continued playing. Looking as if I wanted a waitress and taking a moment to survey my immediate area, I was looked for my new best friend. I turned to see him talking on his cell phone, too far away to hear him, but his gestures suggested he was not swapping recipes with a friend. He appeared to be looking for land-marks inside the casino. He was possibly relaying my position to whoever was at the end of the digital line.

I cashed out from the machine and began a nomadic wandering of the casino. I moved fast but not too fast as to attract attention, as if I had no concerns. I stood with other patrons at the elevator, participating in the mindless chatter concerning our current luck, and whether or not a lucky streak was on the way. One gentleman pointed out he had a map of all the "hot" machines on the floor. I find it humorous someone always has a scheme that will tip fortunes in their favor. Casinos exist because they produce enormous profits, those profits coming from the very patrons around me.

I rode the elevator to the next floor, found the stairwell, and climbed an additional two floors. The fourth floor possessed a buffet and coffee bar and east-facing floor-to-ceiling windows to take in the view. Although the tinted insulated glass made hearing the falls difficult, the spectacle was very pleasing to the eye as it is an entirely different view being able to see both falls simultaneously. After the two beers I consumed visiting the café on the first floor for coffee was a prudent alternative. Most of the booths were equipped with a slot machine or video poker.

With a tall steaming cup of Columbian coffee, I stuck a few dollars in the slot machine and continued my surveillance of the room. I choose a booth that offered me a reasonable view of the floor and the only entrance. The slot machine was located in the middle of the table, and I slid as far to the right as possible, making it difficult to determine if someone occupied the booth. Taking time to sip on my coffee between viewing the falls and surveying the floor, planning my next move was paramount. Time ticked away and what seemed like an hour was only ten minutes, my coffee half full and growing colder. My new friend either remained on the first floor or, I hoped, was focusing his efforts outside, giving up the search entirely. Exiting the Casino and catching another cab seemed to be my best option.

Niagara on the Lake, seven miles north, was a quaint village. As the name implies, it resides on Lake Ontario; further, it was a popular tourist destination. This being prime tourist season Niagara on the Lake would be very crowded. The streets would be filled to capacity with shoppers, participants in the seasonal theater festivities, and of course tourists. I could go get lost in that crowd. I considered buying a new shirt and trashing my jacket and polo. I normally do not consider clothing so disposable: however; I wanted to blend in to be hard to spot. Keep moving and keep them guessing. Whomever they were.

Guessing I just had an informal introduction to one of the players, I could not identify anyone else. I also had no idea how many of them were involved. Further, I have no idea what they wanted of me. Obviously, my flight to Niagara Falls had not gone unnoticed. I required a new hiding spot, a place to lay low until it was safe to show up in Buffalo and access that database. I doubted my abilities to have this fixed by dinner, or by tomorrow's breakfast for that matter.

The elevator reached the first floor and my new friend was nowhere in sight. I was relieved. There were a large number of stores in the casino and no tax was a big draw. I left the casino by way of the guest service wing; this leads to a huge ten-tiered parking ramp, the biggest in the area. It was a cool day, and the cold, damp concrete walls seemed like a refrigerator compared to the perfectly controlled atmosphere of the gambling floor. This level was crammed with cars but I was alone. I found the exit and headed down the stairs instead of the elevator. Thinking how bright I was and using my superior cunning to foil said bad guy's day. I increased my pace, taking two stairs at a time. Hoping beyond hope I would make it out of Niagara Falls in one piece. Hoping. Hoping. That brought a smile to my face and a short chuckle. My manager was always fond of saying, "you can place hope in one hand and spit in the other, see which one fills up first." I did not realize until too late that I ran him down exiting the stairwell. It felt like running into a wall. He was not the old flabby man I had thought. He was solid.

He had a jacket and a lump near his ribs that had not been there before. It was either a gun or a tumor, being super cunning I figured it was gun. Obviously I was not as talented at eluding capture as I thought. My new friend seemed very pleased. I wondered if the elevator would have worked to my advantage, walking out the front door instead of trying to be tricky.

"Shut up and do as I say," he commanded.

"Okay." I had my hands up and I was not sure why.

"Looking fairly chipper for a dead guy."

"Thanks. Feeling well too. Modern medicine is truly miraculous."

He chuckled evilly. "Well consider this little meeting fixing that problem," he pointed back toward the street. "Go. Now. I will kill you right now if you don't." I followed obediently. "Walk slowly, and don't talk with anyone," he instructed.

"I don't have a gun. Can I put my hands in my pockets? They are cold," I asked.

"Just don't make any sudden moves. Let's go."

"Yeah fine, where are we going?"

"We are going to play like tourists for a few moments. I am waiting for a call."

My cell phone was in my pocket and I was not ready to give that up. I rather wanted them to think that I was still flying blind, successful in eliminating all avenues of communication with the outside world, thus still dead. I was able to turn off the phone without arising suspicion. My brain was working overtime trying to figure out a way out of this mess.

My shadow continued to lead me around. We headed for the main area adjacent to Horseshoe Falls. Even though the day is early, all railing and viewing stations are full of tourists, witnessing the sight for the first time, experiencing crushing water, the omnipresent roar of 100,000 cubic feet of it pounding the rocks below into submission. The roar grows louder as we approached. Once at the falls, conversation becomes difficult, and raised voices of various languages can be heard. You do not need to speak the language to hear the excitement in their words or as it plays out across their faces. Joy needs no language. Laughter is understood by all, and the look of awe is universal.

Niagara Falls attracts about 16 million visitors a year, I

don't know how they calculate crowd estimates, but it seemed a good portion of those visitors were here today. The line for the Maid of the Mist and Cave of Winds was impressive, with Disney-ride sort of lines, and you could hear tourists chatting to pass the time until it's their turn to board. I have never been on the Maid of the Mist in my 60-plus visits.

The Maid of the Mist is a short, wet boat ride that takes onlookers to the base of the falls, within feet of the falling water and broken rocks. The sight is exhilarating and frightening. The boats are numbered and it is not uncommon for a boat to be decommissioned because it was damaged beyond repair. At last count, Maid of the Mist twelve had set to sea. I was content to look at the falls from the lower viewing stations or from Goat Island. It was not fear that kept me off those boats, as I can swim like a fish. But riding the Maid of the Mist was like flying in a plane with one wing – it could be exhilarating or could result in a less than enjoyable outcome that involved well thought out speeches and too many pretty white flowers.

4

August 18 | 12 p.m.

My new best friend was leaning on the railing and I was enjoying the sights. We were further along the walkway and the Falls were not directly in front of us, but rather off to our left. We were not sticking out, although I cannot say for certain how many others had more than cameras strapped to their person. Canada takes a dim view of illegal weapons. My new best friend was taking a great risk by simply carrying the gun.

The ground was slick with mist from the falls, and it seemed thicker today and the cooler summer air did little to dispel the cloud. The air was crisp as it is cleansed with the ever-present mist, hardly any odor hung in the air. Most rivers of this size and magnitude possessed the most unpleasant smells of decaying fish and weeds, but the mighty Niagara flowed too quickly for such odors to linger by the shore, the water scrubbing such particulate matter from the air.

It was only Noon; as the clock on the tower read directly behind me. I have been officially dead since about 1 a.m., 11 hours dead and rigor mortis had yet to set in. My supposed burned carcass torn from the charred remains of my car. That picture burned into my brain as if I had witnessed the accident, the grey-black corpse desiccated, the fat boiled off the bones, the carcass itself light enough for one to carry, yet two or more will handle the very fragile remains, the car stripped on all plastics and combustible material. I can imagine the smell of burned flesh and rubber suspended in the air, while steam pours off the cooling wreckage.

I break the cycle to refocus. It wasn't me who was pulled from the car, who it was I couldn't say. But here I stand leaning against a wet railing watching water fall and mist rise, wondering how long until this problem is fixed, the problem of me still breathing. Was the car a setup? Did they steal the car with the intent of having my body in it? Was it better to kill me off, then to just march up the steps and pull the trigger? Did they not want to involve Sam?

Again questions of the non-rhetorical type that had no answers. They have already started to rack up a body count. I am perplexed as to their actions. Why not just gun me down with a silencer-equipped pistol? Or a sniper rifle so far off you wouldn't even hear the bullet exiting the rifle?

Too many questions, yet the clock continues to tick, tick another second gone, tock and other minute passes, is there enough time to draw some conclusion? Or will I die without knowing the why? The clock has a real and palatable effect, as if every second matched a heartbeat, both winding down, nearing the end.

My new friend seems to have the situation under control, as he is packing and I am not. He knows something, he must have some idea why his superiors gave the order to follow and apprehend me. Yet, after the big song and dance with the car, why is there no bullet in my back? Do they need me for something? Is my life worth some value that I can bargain with later?

I do not know! The scream inside my head reverberated. I am trying to remain calm and cool on the outside, as I do not wish to appear rattled. Is there a way out now? A tightness started in my abdominal region; I shrugged it off to the effects of hot coffee chasing two beers. Truly, the stress of today, which is only hours old, is taking a physical toll.

In a pinch, I can throw my cell phone at him. Yet, I am sure this will do no good, as he has bullets and a pistol complete with a silencer. I am grossly outgunned. After witnessing that officer being shot in cold blood and now standing here next to my new friend, I am at a loss as to what circumstances have brought me here. Who can I ask? My friend is not talkative, or the officer that lay dead in my driveway, well he is not much of a conversationalist. I lean calmly against the railing losing myself in the majestic view; inside my racing heart is only outpaced by my brain that is suffering overload. A few hours ago I sat sipped coffee and had a good laugh about all of this, not now. I am certain that my new friend intends me harm and will go to whatever lengths to fix his problem.

The press of people around is both reassuring and annoying. This would not be the ideal place for him to stick a bullet in me. The tourists continued to vie for position at the railing, attempting to get that one photo that will impress their loved ones back home or maybe become this year's wallpaper on their personal computers.

They are unaware of the fragility of the human body and

how close they are to witnessing death. Occupied with the aperture of the camera and the focal point of the lens, they continue their activities in ignorance and oblivion. I want to run far and fast. Multiple parties are involved in all of this. My new friend is not the sole conspirator.

How far would I get before a high caliber rifle round found my back or my head? The silenced weapon would not be heard above the roar of the falls. No one would notice until the last embers of my life had burned out, and I lay dead. I would be nothing more than a statistic to most, a memory to many, and a loss to few. They would chalk it up to senseless violence - nothing more.

I stayed. I looked. My friend is on his cell phone keeping me within arms' length. His attention is not entirely focused on the call; he occasionally looks in my direction. I see him consciously find the butt of the gun hidden under his jacket; I wonder if he is calculating the time required to extract the gun and discharge a round. Regardless of how long it takes him to remove the weapon from its holster, he has plenty of time to fire, as I can only run so fast. I also noticed why he picked this area. Unlike the others, this is devoid of tourists, as we are about 100 feet removed from the best seats. There is no thick crowd of people to protect my getaway. I will wait for my chance. It may come or may never arrive. But to run now would be suicide. I watch as a few police officers walk about making their presence known. Even if I could run for help, I would be dead before the explanation of my visit was clear. As fast as I can run it is doubtful I would outrun a bullet.

I continue to be enamored with the tourists, studying

them as they moved like a single entity, as they jostled at the railing, their voices merging, sounding like an alien language. You could almost hear their collective heartbeat. I wondered how many of these visitors were here on their honeymoon. I wonder how many will think this the best vacation ever, spending countless hours relaying the beauty and majesty that is the Falls showing countless hours of video to unmoved relatives. The Falls has that power over first-time visitors, its view is for lack of a better term awe-inspiring.

My mind wandered like a drunken college student in a strange town. I put the train back on its track. I should be at work, trying to get through my day, trying my best to remain calm while being screamed at, trying my best to remain calm after having to reprioritize my day for the fourth time, trying to remain calm while filled with anticipation and nervous energy counting the minutes until the hands reached 5 p.m.

I can picture my drive to the jeweler on Main Street, only minutes from the house. It's a mom and pop store that promised today to stay open past their normal 6 p.m. closing time in case I am running behind schedule.

Then I try to picture Sam's reaction as the ring sparkles from its perch inside the box. My well thought out plans for today are quickly turning into a chaotic mess. My new friend continues his conversation. He records every twitch of my muscles - watching waiting - for my run. Trying my best to remain calm and appear unconcerned, I remain unmoving at the railing. The sight of the Falls and the thunderous roar is hypnotic and you can lose yourself in it.

The scenic Niagara Falls is proof that there is a higher presence - one above the concerns of man. I have never claimed to a disbeliever, I believe in God the omnipotent master of all he surveys, and God with his gentle influence. Maybe he enjoys our reaction to this splendid view. Certainly, there are more efficient ways to convey water from point A to point B. This spectacular view beckons to a higher being. One that wished us mere mortals, walking this blue sphere, could find purpose behind such a sight: something to entertain our senses.

Yet, I have not felt the need to pray to a higher power, to plead some way out by asking for mercy. Figuring I was in this by myself. Either I find a way out or cease breathing. I could not simply utter a few words and leave the rest in His hands. Life has taught me that determinism is the rule upon which the universe rotates. We are free to make our own choices and sink or swim on our own merits. God's role is simple: Infuse each of us with the necessary skills.

God does not hand down the same skills to each person. We have our specialties and certain attributes. The world would be boring and commonplace if everyone was born to be in customer service, or born with the skill to build a house. We are not always trained for what we face - this is called learning, it's called gaining experience. We all must grow as people, use our mistakes as course corrections, gaining experience as much with our success as with our failures.

As much as I wished Sam was here to offer her guidance and advice, to involve her in this mess would be the equivalent of signing her death notice. Either I would find a way out of this or I would not. It was that simple. There would be no reaching out, no calling for mercy at the eleventh hour, I was in too deep, and why or for what I have no idea. But I would swim to the best of my abilities or die trying. I decided that it was time to take some initiative.

"What did I do to deserve this?" I asked, probing and hoping for some answers.

"You know too much."

"I have been telling my girlfriend I know everything; I guess that's confirmed."

"What you know has gotten people killed, people much more important than you."

"What could I possibly know? I work for a cell phone company. Has our new roaming plans bought modern society to its knees?"

"There is a war going on you know."

"Really? I was wondering why all those soldiers were dying."

"You have something that could ruin it all, ruin everything for us."

I shook my head. "I think you are sadly mistaken. I know nothing that could be considered unsafe for anyone, not to mention national security." I turned to look at him. "What possible knowledge do I have locked somewhere in this brain? I am a manager at a cell phone company, I talk to pissed off customers. I save accounts. I train new people and monitor phone calls. I am not trying to play dumb, but before you fix the problem I would like to know why I am going to die."

"I was not told the extent of your knowledge in our operation, or how you obtained that knowledge. We've been watching you for some time. Keeping tabs."

"Is that a euphuism for tapping phones?'

"Take it to mean whatever you wish. Our contact was given the make and model of your car. He carried out his orders, as will I. But for whatever reason you were not in your car."

"I hadn't noticed."

"Just our luck some crack head stole your car last night; our contact was convinced he completed his job when he heard your car crash into the tree. He said the car was running away like you knew we were coming."

"Well, I am as surprised as you, trust me. When did you realize I was not quite as dead as you had hoped?"

"One of our men saw you exit the subway this morning. We have been tailing you since. You're very clever for a man who only works for a cell phone company.'

"I thought we had already established the fact that I am, after all, a genius."

He reached for his gun in the holster as if to remind me who was in control and who was screwed.

"Who do you work for?" He barked out. "We'll make this easy when you tell us who you work for."

"Okay, CellNY. Do you need a copy of my W-2?"

"You seem very calm for a man about to eat a bullet."

"My people are all over the place. They see me, they will keep me safe." I was trying for sarcasm but it only caused him to make a phone call.

"We need to move him now, he has backup."

I literally stifled a laugh. This man had no understanding of the subtle world of sarcasm. He grabbed my arm and insisted I follow. He turned back toward the ramp. He started speaking into the cuff of his jacket and it was then that I saw the beige, skin-colored cord reaching his ear. Was this man government issue or just well equipped? It's not like this was standard inventory at Radio Shack.

"Pull out to second position." He sounded determined. "No, I will handle him. No. I have papers."

This is all I heard from him, not knowing to whom he was speaking on the other end. I almost laughed out loud again but felt comfortable forcing his hand as if I had back up. How could anything sound more absurd? Who was I working for? Indeed. At the moment I could have said both Santa Claus and the Tooth Fairy because this day was turning into one of those "Once upon a time" kind of days. The only thing missing was a magic dragon and a white knight. The only person in distress at the moment was me. God willing it ends with happily ever after.

The walk from the Falls to the parking ramp is approximately four-tenths of a mile, uphill. My new friend had a firm hold on my upper arm and was glancing around wildly, threatening to use me as a shield if bullets started to fly. I am not sure if our walk set any world records, however, I was winded when we reached our destination and climbed two flights of stairs bringing us back to his car.

My new friend no longer reminded me of the guy from the Apple commercials. He was a man that demanded respect - a man who took great pride in the fact most people feared him. When he flexed his muscle he demanded action and results. He also apparently was in charge of this fairy tale, this nonsense. I also had no doubt sometime later today he was going to shoot me and end my life.

"We're driving across the river. Take this," he shoved a driver's license into my hand. It had my picture but not my name. "When they ask for ID give them that. Place that ID in your wallet now. I don't care what you do with your legit ID, you won't need it for much longer," It was his turn to stifle a laugh.

"Why can't we walk?"

"Why do you care?"

"Nice day for a walk is all." I was hoping we would walk across the bridge and custom agents may have noticed that earlier I passed through with another ID.

We completed our journey, backtracking from where we had been a few moments ago. Fred - I decided to call him Fred because shadow Mr. Killer seemed a little formal, and he obviously wasn't going to tell me his name - was busying himself talking into his cuff. I was wondering how this was supposed to make someone seem inconspicuous. It made them stand out as if talking into one's cuff had yet to make it big as a new fashion trend.

He was talking in short staccato sentences. Talking in code to whoever was listening, I felt like I was in the middle of a bad spy movie. Fred not only looked worried but also was paranoid like me, glancing around the corner, looking into stairwells, gun drawn. Just to have some fun I made a few gestures in the air that were absurd and meant nothing at all. Fred stopped abruptly, drawing his cuff back to his face and speaking hurriedly to his co-conspirators.

"We've been made in the garage. He signaled his shadow."
I was upset because he was my shadow - no one else. Ask Sam,
if anything I am loyal. I am a one-shadow man; society was in
need of a scrupulous man such as me.

I heard a car engine start, felt the low rumble of as it drew
closer. In a fit of paranoia, I had the intense feeling that whoever was behind the wheel intended to run me down. The car
stopped a few feet before it reached me and Fred's partner
exited the vehicle. Fred had me remove my jacket and he felt
me up like a teenage boy with his first girlfriend. He accosted
me as he searched for a wire or tracking device. The search
was extremely thorough, making me feel very vulnerable in
the cold garage. Fred searched while man number two held a
gun to my back. His search was so intensely centered on locating a wire, my cell phone remained in my hand and was
undiscovered. After his search, he returned my jacket, which I
promptly donned.

Fred found my cash and this development made him more
concerned than ever. I was thrown into the back seat rather
roughly but did not think that the time was right to lodge a
complaint. Fred and guy number two started chatting in the
front seat of the car.

"Someone fronted him over $2,000. He has been working
very quietly today." Fred said.

"Did you report this to headquarters?" Man number two
asked.

The fact this was a question and not order led me to believe that guy number two was an underling. This was a fol-

lower and not the leader of this merry band of brothers, confirming my belief that Fred was in charge.

"Not yet, when we cross. There's a safe place for such matters."

"How many did you see?"

"One, maybe two; he signaled one of his men. The man responded."

"Okay, I will cross in the other car. You take him. Did you find a tracking device?"

"No, nothing."

"Did you check his jacket?"

"He just bought the jacket at the casino over on the other side. He was trying to sneak out quietly. I found him in the garage. The same with his hat. He threw them out at the casino - maybe someone will want to check that out?"

"Sounds good, careful with this one, he is not what he seems. He must be higher in the organization than we thought."

"We'll waste him at the safe house and throw him in the gorge. It will take weeks before anyone finds him." Fred took a moment to make eye contact using the rearview mirror to emphasize his words. He wanted me to know he was in charge and was not above getting his hands dirty, and when the time came, he would pull the trigger. I sat motionless as a big chill made its rounds up and down my spine.

The transformation in Fred's demeanor was near magical. Although he wore the same clothes and had not changed anything about his appearance; his face, once friendly, was now built on a confident sneer. There was real anger in his eyes and his posture changed. While he had appeared doughy and goofy in the casino, he now looked every part the methodical killing machine.

Man number two jerked open my door and grabbed me from the back seat. He pushed me into the front seat and advised me to keep my hands in my lap. I was also warned not to signal my backup or make any hand movements. Stifling a laugh, I stated I would comply; it was difficult to take them seriously. Yet they wanted me dead and I still had no idea why.

It was the absurdity of the entire situation. I was waiting patiently for the man with his camera to jump out between cars yelling "fooled you." Oh, what a big laugh that would be.

We exited the garage and paid the attendant, turning right out of the parking lot. The custom booths were up ahead. While we waited I was advised that I was to remain silent until spoken to and only give my name, which was Joe Smith. Thank God with the same birth date, which was both reassuring and alarming. If they knew my birthday what other information did they have on hand? They must know about Sam, which only made my stomach tighten even more. Are there men camped outside Erie One Mortgage, guns concealed in holsters? Are they watching my parents? How long have they been following me? Are any others at risk? Do they know what Ed did for me this morning?

These thoughts occupied my already overloaded brain. It was clear I was about to be driven out to "headquarters," questioned extensively, and no matter my answers sometime after dark what was left of me would be dropped in the gorge.

The fall of nearly two hundred feet ought to hide the true cause of my death.

My mind was focused on others, those still close to me that had a chance. I was on the verge of asking what I could do to ensure their safety, and if need be, I would run through every piece of irrelevant information my brain held. That should buy me a chance, a slim chance, but a chance none the less.

The queue continued to progress slowly. Much of the congestion was commercial traffic today and with new security measures in place only slowed our egress. Most travelers were not used to the new scrutiny and were impatient with the congestion. Not so much with Fred. He was busy with his cuff talking about an ambush at the crossing and that he wanted two cars and three teams to meet him in the USA.

"This guy is good he may have crossed the border to force our hand. There will be someone waiting for him on the other side. Count on it." I thought I was the paranoid one. I was slowly shaking my head, wondering why.

As I admitted earlier I have a plain face. There must exist some wicked international spy, or treasonous man, or an ex-husband that had run off on Fred's sister: one who had really pissed off Fred and his compatriots, and could have passed as my twin. With all the trouble and communication on my behalf, I began to believe there was a force of twenty men ready to spend their lives freeing me from the evil Freds. The cars were continuing their slow progress through the booths and soon it would be our turn to speak with the customs agents.

For those of you that have not had the pleasure US customs agents have no sense of humor and enjoy ruining a traveler's life. I had friends who played the smart ass and not answering questions to their liking, found their cars searched and torn apart. I tend to take the short answers to short questions approach.

Fred was sweating next to me. He appeared not to enjoy my unique brand of humor. I know the look - I've witnessed it on various occasions plastered on Sam's face. Fred sat convincing himself I might make trouble for him. Talking into his cuff repeatedly, talking in his own language of those involved. Fred opened the glove box, removed handcuffs, and promptly placed them on my wrists. He also removed some new ID for himself. It appeared to be a gold badge of some derivation. I did not get a clear look. But his contained only letters; like FBI or NSA, or CIA. I know that I was not A O K.

There were ten cars ahead of us. I could see Fred's underling in the line next to us. They appeared to be chatting via their cuffs. I guess you could say that Fred had made an off the cuff comment. I had to stifle laughter - my arcane sense of humor often entertains me much more than others.

"Okay, Mr. Smart ass, we're doing this my way."

Maybe I should have called him Frank.

I had an idea that was both brilliant and ludicrous all at the same time.

"Do you want to live?" I said this plainly as if I were talking about muffins and cookies, "Do you want to live?" I demanded, my voice monotone and logical.

Fred stared at me perplexed, his mouth was open mid-sentence, his eyes as disbelieving as mine.

"If you want to live you will drop me off immediately after

crossing the bridge and you will return my money. I will be picked up and taken to safety. Our response is going to be far from pleasant and swift. But I will let you live. If you say no, there is a man on the top floor of the parking garage. He has the most absurd talent. He can shoot a half dollar dead-on-middle from over a mile away. His well-trained finger and eye have you fully in his crosshairs. Since your skull is considerably larger than the infamous half dollar, I don't think he'll miss. He is only a few hundred yards away. He probably can make this shot in his sleep."

I continued deadly serious."All he is waiting for is a simple nod of my head. Do you really think I would have crossed into Canada without a backup plan? Don't you think we have already considered all your moves and have at the ready the necessary countermeasures?"

Fred's brow was now covered in sweat as we inched closer to the booth. He had no answer.

"Maybe my lone travel was to bring you out, to see how many of you there are. So what's it going to be? A simple nod of my head and a high powered rifle round will find the back of your skull, and your heart will stop beating before you can think about killing me. I ask again do you want to live?"

That of course was a bald-faced lie. It was the equivalent to going all-in with a 2 of hearts and a 7 of diamonds in Texas Hold 'Em when your opponent is holding a straight and there is $3 million in the pot. I put the same - can you guess if I'm bluffing - look on my face utilized by some of the world's best poker players.

The only other occasion I have ever attempted such an absolutely ludicrous lie was at the poker table and we weren't even playing for money. But I surmised these fine people only spoke one language. They were immune to pleads for mercy, but clearly heard and understood threats of this nature. Even if they decided to change their plans since they were convinced I had 'back up," maybe there would be an opportunity to run, maybe it was a long shot of such proportions I doubt that Vegas would lie odds on it.

I attempted to wear an angriest yet sincere look, not blinking to show him I meant business and that he needed to bargain. I stared through him, not at him. We were at a stalemate - the cars had for the moment ceased their slow march to the toll booths and the USA. He had his foot firmly on the brake, his right hand reaching for his gun, yet twice he hesitated.

"My man has his 50-caliber Marine sniper rifle at the ready; he's my main back up. Why do you think I stayed so close to the casino? A 400-hundred-yard shot is child's play for this man; In Kuwait he shot a guardsman at 1,100 yards in the desert in high winds. He sees me sitting here and he knows you want to cause me some degree of harm. You are within the crosshairs. Can't you feel the hairs on your neck stand up? I would not want to be where you are sitting. There is no place to run. Traffic is not moving and it is now an ideal time to ..."

(I am sorry to admit at his point that I had more or less stolen most of the last few lines from a movie of some sort, I don't really remember which one or else I would give due credit)

Fred flew from the car staying low talking into his cuff. He had reached for his gun and also produced a bi-fold wallet and went out fast, charging the customs agent booth. Never a good idea. Never ever a good idea when brandishing a weapon. I was waiting for my moment. Although still cuffed I opened the door the second Fred ran from the car. I was about to bolt from the vehicle when the door was slammed shut, almost taking my hand with it. The other man from the garage was standing there, looking content and waving his pistol the way a parent wags a finger at a misbehaving child. As much as I remained unaffected by events I could feel my heart pumping at full speed, threatening to crack some ribs.

Whatever ID Fred had shown worked well and as planned. We were waved through without the usual level of necessary harassment, our car given priority. We were allowed access to an unmanned booth with Canadian border agents on both sides of the car, with rifles seemingly coordinating with their American cohorts on the other side of the bridge.

Fred talking into his cuff again and more code more staccato sentences; we were driving well beyond the posted speed limit on the bridge. He sat low in his seat and bobbed his head about trying to avoid the imaginary sniper. I almost wanted to tell him it was a bluff. But for a brief moment, I enjoyed his reaction.

The bridge is about a half-mile in length and we reached the other side in seconds. I have never been on the bridge with a person driving 90 miles per hour. It is a fine way to ensure a night in jail or at least a few hours of police "questioning." He neared the American border authorities within a few moments, again access was granted to an open booth and we sped through. I now counted some five cars in our entourage, we led the pack but it was of no coincidence that four other black sedans were in the queue.

We came to Rainbow Street South. Fred slowed, allowing another car to pass us. This other car belonged to the waiting State Police and Niagara Park Officers; obviously there to explain our need to leave Canada in such a hurry. We slowed, and one other car stopped to join the police convention. We and the second car continued at a high rate of speed then slowed as we left the city, which under normal circumstances, is barely a ten-minute drive; when not having to obey the silly traffic rules the trip is much faster. We never traveled on the same street for longer than one or two blocks, often changing directions to suddenly get onto the 190, only to exit at the next ramp and backtrack. I certainly did not have any idea where we were headed, but I wondered if we were going to Cleveland first just to confuse those that followed us, my infamous backups.

I could understand the need to drive around as most of the available parking spots are filled with tourists. I was able to watch the trip however, my familiarity with Niagara Falls was well short of Fred's. The only thing I could ascertain; we were no longer in downtown Niagara Falls - in fact, we were no longer in Niagara Falls at all. It may have been Wheatfield or even North Tonawanda for all I knew.

Whatever our location, we took the long way to get there.

Pulling into the parking lot we were joined by another five others and two black sedans. I was left in the car watching this display. It was amusing that someone would use this kind of manpower to track me down. Today is an exception to my normal rat-race mentality. I find comfort in the routine. Being dead seemed to spur my adventuresome side; however, a big part of me wished I were at work listening to customers and solving problems. I would give a week's salary to hear someone cuss me out right now. I had a feeling that there were others, others watching, others tracking, ready to rush in here without a moment's hesitation to save me from these evil men. Although, it was more than likely my mind suffered an episode. I am alone in a way I have never been alone before.

The men were far enough away that I could not hear their conversation even after straining to do so. They stood in a circle and all I saw was the occasional gesture. After much discussion, the group went their separate ways. Fred and I were the last to depart. I was taken out of the car, still in my handcuffs. Fred opened the trunk using a remote and beckoned me to lie down. Another trip began and I was not certain of our origin and more confused about our destination. Why I had to get in the trunk I could only surmise was to hide our route and destination from me. I could only ascertain that Fred was driving nearly in circles, as we turned more than he drove straight.

After what seemed to be hours we stopped. I blinked from the bright sun as Fred hauled me from the trunk. We were in an office complex of sorts. I was not familiar with our destination and of course we had parked in the back lot. The lot was mostly empty, which I found very curious as it could not have been any later than 1 p.m. and one would expect the lot to be at capacity.

"Anything you like to say? We have a man that enjoys questioning assholes like you."

"Can I have my money back?"

"What?" Fred looked very perplexed.

"Well, I don't want to die penniless, thus fulfilling my father's prophecy." I did not care about the money. It was just a comfort to hold, as if it were my last ties to a reality besides this one, a reality where I did not die today at 1 p.m.

He handed me the money belt. With cuffs in place, it was wedged in between my hands. He spoke into his cuff. "We're here."

My jacket now draped over my cuffed hands, Fred's large gun poking my ribs, and my money belt all made for a slow progress to a rather large office complex. I did not know if we were in Niagara Falls or not.

Usually, these buildings all congregate in the same area of Pine, Main, and Buffalo Avenues, where there are industrial and commercial areas. These are kept away from the tourist area for esthetic reasons. Again, I wasn't even certain if this was Niagara Falls. We could have been in Lewiston or we could have been in Burt. All I knew was this was the end of the line. There was a copse of maples and pine that lined the parking lot; their numbers suggested we were no longer in the downtown area or the adjacent city region. The pine fragrance carried on the light cool breeze, it would have been enjoyable under different circumstances.

The building yields no clues. The name of the business was not written in large block letters for all to see. Advertising must not be all that important to them. It was rectangular in shape, composed mainly of concrete and glass, nothing outstanding. It wasn't anything a 10-year-old couldn't design with a crayon and construction paper.

Fred directed me to the back door, as he really did not seem to be a front door kind of guy. He may have to sign in and out of this building. What was he going to write? Fred and Hostage (soon to be corpse) in at 1 p.m.

He had stopped his conversation with his cuff. His eyes darted all over the place looking for my backup. I wondered if he was suffering a spasm. Fred's paranoia seemed worse than mine.

"You're a dead man," he whispered in my ear with too much spittle for my taste. He tensed and I could feel him moving his gun down my spine as we walked.

We rounded the corner. Another fifty yards to the door, another fifty yards to make my peace, as I was certain this was it. My existence would cease very soon. I was not contemplative. I did not see my short life flash before my eyes replaying the highlights like ESPN. I slowed my walk thinking about Sam, Mom, and Dad. Wondering what the future would have held for Sam and me.

I was not going to beg for mercy from this man. I was not going to drop to my knees pleading to his sense of fairness. If this asshole was going to shoot an unarmed man in the back, he would be shooting a proud man. I spent what little time I had left taking in all I could.

The sun was high in the sky and seemed warmer here being removed, however many miles, from the Falls. There was something reassuring in the rustling of the high branches and dark green leaves, several squirrels darted through the area and surrounding stand of pines. Birds being birds circled high above, some diving suddenly, maybe chasing bugs, maybe chasing thermals.

Either way, nature has a way of reminding all that regardless of the stupidity of man, regardless of our concerns; it will continue on - never ceasing. It is as if the universe itself would not be recording my death as it was that unimportant.

Niagara Falls and the surrounding area was home to a species of red squirrels and a few hung in the trees, more dancing on the electrical lines without fear of falling. The grass was freshly mown and the smell of cut grass and a mixture of oil and gasoline hung in the air. The area around the building was strangely quiet, birds circling overhead silently.

It was if they understood this building and chose to avoid it at all cost. The door loomed large. It was the point of no return and on the other side would be pain and death. I would never again exit the building drawing breath into my lungs. I would be removed via a body bag at some ungodly hour in the morning and taken to the gorge and tossed into the water. By the time my body was found it would be torn to pieces from rock and water, conveniently covering my murderous death. I made my peace with this world.

I felt Fred getting a better grip on his weapon, again slowly sliding it down my back, torturing and playing with my thoughts during the last moments of my life. I detested the man. He had done nothing to answer my questions. I was going down without ever knowing what caused my death. I am not by nature a violent person. I have restrained my temper for the betterment of my career. The tightness in my stomach returned, full force. I felt a wave of anger, festering and growing, ready to make itself known. I quelled its rise, regaining control and continued my walk. However, I had hatred for this man as he played with my final thoughts. I cared not to let this man win. He would not hear a whisper from my mouth nor ascertain anything from my actions. Our progress had brought us almost to the transom, twenty feet remained between me and the looming door.

I could hear Fred conversing with whomever, but I did not turn to look at my adversary. He may have been on his cell or talking into his cuff. Either way, it mattered not. Pausing, I said goodbye to everyone, whispering, "I love you Sam. I miss you already...." My sentence was cut short by the thump, thump of a silenced pistol. I fell to the ground. I felt a sharp pain in my side as I hit the concrete hard and fast.

5

August 18 | 1 p.m.

I could see the blood on the ground, a great pool encircling me. My face was wet and sticky, accompanied by a spreading wet stain on my shirt. My nose was most certainly broken - I lifted my head from the ground and the blood was streaming from my nostrils. It was choking me as it ran down my throat.

I was dizzy, unable to break my fall, my face the only thing slowing my descent. I could taste the blood, metallic and salty, filling my mouth; saw it pooling on the ground. My jacket was coated with blood.

I was disoriented, having lost the fight with the concrete sidewalk. I haven't broken my nose since my lacrosse days in college. The pain I felt was the worst since stopping lacrosse balls with my various appendages. The adrenaline worked it magic, as I am sure that shock should have overtaken me by now.

The biggest shock of course was the fact that I was still breathing. I was not complaining - just confused, very confused.

Lying on the ground I wondered why he hadn't shot me again and also wondering how he missed me when he was quite literally shooting from point-blank range. Pulling myself to my feet proved difficult as handcuffs cut into my wrists and my head was spinning from the unfair fight with cured concrete.

I rolled over onto my side, and from that position, I was able to sit on the ground. I was trying to clear my head while conducting damage control. Broken nose, check, gunshot wound check, bullet may still be inside me, check. Hands scraped to hell but functional, check, legs working, check, arms functional, check. My arms and shoulder hurt like hell and my forearms felt like fire. The worst pain came from the bones grating against one another in my nose, like dental tools on raw nerves.

Once I was able to sit up my head stopped spinning and cleared. I was better equipped to survey my surroundings. Fred lay still mere feet from my location. I understood Fred was dead, not dead like me but dead, dead.

I did not check for a pulse because I was still cuffed it was evident Fred was missing most of his head. Someone else had shot Fred; that is why his shot was errant, his final spasm missed the target and I was grazed by the bullet.

Most of the red stain, now painting my body and clothes, was from Fred, not me, which I was grateful for, except my new polo was ruined. I could feel the wetness; the shirt clinging to my back. No amount of Oxyclean was going to remove that stain. There was nothing on the market that could clear that thought from my brain. I could with perfect vision imagine the gore clinging to my back. I could not see the back of my shirt but one does not require an over-active imagination to discern the mess. The thought of what was making the shirt wet and heavy combined with my spinning head and faulty balance was enough to make my stomach do somersaults.

Most of the coagulating blood was not mine. Fred looked worse than I did. I spat on what was left of his head. I would have kicked his lifeless body if I had the ability to stand. I hadn't a clue what to do next. My nose was bleeding profusely with no signs of slowing and I was still in handcuffs. My body ached and complained of every move.

While contemplating my current predicament it immediately deteriorated further upon hearing someone come crashing through the bushes.

"Hands up!"

I did not turn to look at what I thought was Fred two.

"Can't. I am cuffed." I was trying for meek and defenseless. At this point, it wasn't a stretch.

"Are you here to kill me, like him?"

"Do not turn around. At the moment I am a friend. But that might not last."

I followed his advice and forced myself into statue-like compliance. He asked me to step away from the body and again I complied, rolling away and pulling myself back into a seated posture. That insignificant maneuver brought waves of pain through most of my body. I could hear him going through Fred's clothes and pockets searching for what I had no clue.

Thinking that the preverbal out of the frying pan into was fire was going to be written on my legitimate headstone, the stranger approached me from behind and began searching my pockets and clothes and pants. It was a very close inspection and any closer and we might have been dating.

"How do you know this man?"

"I don't. Met him at the casino on the other side."

"What were you doing here?"

"Well, he had a gun and insisted I follow. A very compelling argument. I was trying to keep from dying twice on the same day."

"Are you trying my patience?" A stab again to the ribs to remind me who had the gun and who was defenseless.

"I have had a weird sort of day and hard to explain."

"Turn around."

I was able to turn around without collapsing on the ground. My khaki pants were soiled with coagulated blood, grass, and dirt. I must be quite a sight. This stranger slowly unlocked the cuffs and handed me a hankie to clean up my face.

"Rough day?"

"Shouldn't we be going someplace before someone sees Fred lying here with no face?"

"You know his name."

"Not really, it's all part of the weirdness."

"You're coming with me."

"Meeting new people that like to drive me around apparently is my new specialty and I haven't even taken that course on how to influence people and make new friends," I said, and my new friend stifled a chuckle and directed me to a car. "Does everyone drive a black sedan?"

"They were on special. Let's go." He had trouble suppressing a laugh.

He then proceeded to place a blindfold across my face, throwing my jacket in the trunk ahead of me. Like Fred, he insisted I ride in the trunk. For the second time this day I was asked to ride in the trunk; twice in one day is a new record as far I could tell. Guinness may have to be consulted.

"Are you hurt? It looks like you were grazed. I can get you some medical assistance shortly." He was talking to me through the opened trunk as if nothing had occurred and this was normal fare for all.

"Just bleeding and my head hurts, I smacked the pavement rather hard. Surprised I haven't died a second time."

"Dying twice on the same day has to be a record right? You may not be dead but your nose looks broken." He felt my side. "It's just a graze - no entry wound. Sorry about the trunk but I can't risk you being seen."

"One I hope not to repeat." I grimaced as pain coursed through my body as I laid in the dark trunk.

I was again driven in what felt like circles; in the dark, my internal clock could not track our progress. We seemed to keep to city streets, as the vehicle was not traveling fast, and I never heard anything higher than third gear, although I could be wrong.

We never traveled on dirt roads or even those in disrepair, so the drive was smooth. I could feel the vibrations from the car's engine and drive train, the trunk smelled fresh, no lingering oil smells or of recent grocery purchases. It had an unmistakable new car smell. My mind drifted and the hum and the slight rocking motion of the car could have put me to sleep if not for the fact that the cramping in my legs had started.

It was difficult to maneuver in the trunk and there was not enough clearance to get my legs underneath me to roll over and find a more comfortable position. The bleeding had slowed but not stopped completely. My only revenge for this incident would be the rather large cleaning bill to clear the sticky mess I currently was leaving throughout the trunk. It would no longer carry that new car smell.

Our destination had been reached and the cramps in my legs were thankful the trip did not last long. Slowing, I could feel the pitch of the car move forward like we were on a steep decline. It could have been a parking garage. The car came to a complete stop and the trunk popped open.

"Is this him?" A new voice asked. Great. Now there were two of them.

"I think so. He attracted a lot of attention. At least ten men were watching him and following his activities."

"What for?"

"I don't know but they wanted him dead and fast."

"How long until they figure out we have him?" The new man sounded concerned.

"They probably know now."

"Let's find out what he knows."

They helped me out of the trunk and I tried not to groan as everything hurt. I was led into a building while they discussed me. I wanted to remind these fine gentlemen I was blindfolded, not deaf. But I guess my opinion was not sought after, and keeping my mouth closed seemed prudent. We entered a building, the large steel door was in desperate need of lubrication; the squeal of the hinges as it opened was excruciating to the senses. A moment later a guard asked the men to swipe their cards and sign in. He also asked who I was. They told him my name was Joe Smith. I almost laughed. I was searched for a gun but I did not remember either man checking my wallet for my legitimate ID.

The doors and the turns were too numerous to count unless we had just entered either a maze or a catacomb. There may have also been an elevator ride but I could not tell if it was up or down. After that, a long walk down a corridor that may have been carpeted, as our footsteps were muted.

I heard one final door slam and voices too distant to be discernable as if in another connecting room. A chair scraped across a tiled floor and I was guided into the chair. Once the blindfold was removed my pockets were emptied – it was quite a collection in the middle of the steel table - my cell phone, some $125 in cash, another $3,400 in my money belt, and my winning tickets from the casino. I have to remember to turn those in later. After recovering my wits about me, I was, without a doubt, in the middle of an interrogation room.

Bright lights, a single steel table, and two chairs graced the room, with an obvious one-way mirror behind me. It was just a touch below 68 degrees - enough to make one feel uncomfortable. Tom Clancy could not have created a better scene.

The person who saved my life was sitting in the chair opposite me, looking very disappointed, along with two men wearing white coats and stethoscopes. I assumed they were doctors, seeing Halloween was months off.

They insisted that I strip naked and given an antiseptic bath. It was not enjoyable. The nasty smelling liquid was not only colder than the room temperature but burned all of the scrapes and gaping holes. It could have been battery acid. I was uncertain whether or not the cure was worse than the disease, thinking that I was about to pass out and lose consciousness. It was the stink of the fluid that kept me in the here and now. My wounds treated, my broken nose mended; however, without the aid of any anesthetic, if I were not already on the brink of going into shock their activities brought me there.

I was hosed with off with cold water and towel-dried, shivering in the room I felt very exposed. I was given a blanket and advised that some clothes would be arriving shortly. I am aware the FBI knows a lot about us law-abiding citizens and the FBI keeps dossiers on most people, but it's humiliating when they know your pant size.

An agent, thus unnamed, walked into the room with a gym bag, which looked very familiar, although, I am aware that gym bags aren't all that dissimilar. Opening the bag, it contained some clothes from my closet and a pair of sneakers.

I was confused. "I know I have had a rather eventful day, but when did you have time to go to Amherst and grab some of own my clothes?"

"We were aiding the police in their investigation. An officer was gunned down in your driveway today."

"Why would they call you in on what was a local concern?"

No one answered my question. I continued dressing as I still felt very exposed and vulnerable.

"Ok, ok, I am starting to understand. You have been following me today. Along with Fred and his people."

No one answered that question either.

As these men watched me dress, I did my best to pretend they were not in the room. But my new ensemble was completed when one of my new friends walked into the room carrying my jacket. I had incorrectly assumed it was left in the trunk. I informed them they could keep it.

After being deemed fit, they directed me to a chair. I took it relieved. A few minutes ago I was hoping Fred's brain had not in some way stained me, now fresh as fresh can be I was being prepared for what was to come. The shirt I had purchased at the casino was lying on the floor and the mess on the back of the shirt was grotesque. Slasher movies never bothered me. I have watched "Faces of Death" One and Two while eating a sandwich, however, the grime on the shirt was gore like I have not previously seen.

In a very funny way, it reminded me of couscous in thick red tomato sauce. I felt bad for this guy because obviously some of the mess had been transferred to his trunk. There was a significant detailing bill on the way. By the time we reached our final destination, the trunk was not daisy fresh. Agent Boyle quickly took over. I only knew his name from the tag on his chest.

"Why did you refer to that man as Fred?"

"It was easier giving him a name instead of calling him hey you."

"What did he want from you?"

"He said I knew too much and they had to fix a problem. Putting a bullet in my skull would fix that problem."

"What problem would that be?"

"Okay, well I said I have a weird day so here goes." I explained the best I could about the item in the newspaper, about my cell and home phone being disconnected. I detailed my flight to the Falls and my subsequent capture by Fred and his men, ending with the moment Agent Boyle stepped in and saved my hide.

"What led you to believe that this was some conspiracy and not some mistake?"

"Seeing the officer gunned down in my driveway for starters. I was convinced."

"What were you doing in Canada, Ryan?"

"Hiding."

"Why were you hiding?"

"I woke up to read an article stating that I was dead and my car was missing from the garage. I spent a few minutes with a colleague at work. He stated that Sam turned off my account a few minutes after the office opened. Sam is my girlfriend and she was home until about 7 a.m. That's what time she told me she was leaving. I awoke at 8 a.m. and found out I was dead."

"How do you know she did not turn off your phone? Maybe she was mad or upset about something."

"Sam wouldn't do that. I work for CellNY and that is my lifeline to the office. She knows how important my cell phone is."

"But she could have, yes?"

"Yes, she could have."

"What is it, ah Fred, wanted from you?"

"He said that killing me would fix a mistake, a problem. He wanted me dead."

"Why?"

"He said I knew too much."

"Knew too much about what?"

I sighed, exasperated. My injuries were aching and this line of questioning is just going in circles. "I actually do not know."

"Come on, that sounds a farfetched."

"I run the customer service office at CellNY. What could I possibly know that could get me killed? Maybe he works for Frontier Cellular. They are our competitors."

"How did you get to Niagara Falls without a car?"

"After watching the officer being gunned down in my driveway, I ran to Main Street and found a cab. I didn't know what was going on."

"That doesn't explain the casino in Canada."

"Well, I had the cabbie drop me off at Niagara Memorial. I then walked to the casino on Third Street. There I purchased some clothes: the jacket, the polo, and the hat. Once I was convinced I looked more like a tourist than a dead man, I walked over the border and played tourist in the other casino."

"That all seems like some fast thinking for a customer service manager."

"I am gifted I guess."

Now it was Agent Boyle's turn to be exasperated. He pounded the table for emphasis. "Who do you work for and what information are you keeping from me?"

"People keep asking me that question expecting different answers, but it's still nobody and nothing."

My new friend then took off his identification card and threw it across the table at me. He inclined his head for me to pick it up. It read "Robert Boyle, Federal Bureau of Investigation." It looked legit but I have never seen an FBI badge before. He seemed very disappointed in my answers and me thus far.

"That badge means we can make some things very difficult for you and Sam if we need to."

I slid the badge back to him. "Agent Boyle, I think they have me confused with someone else. I have no idea what I could have possibly done to piss anybody off."

"We know all about you Ryan. Don't ever forget that. We traced some calls from this cell phone but it is not the number you have listed with CellNY. And you'll have to explain the $3,400 in your money belt."

"For the cell phone, I went downtown, entered the back door of the CellNY building, and talked with a colleague. He works for the roaming department and has access to the MTSO. He turned on the cell with a non-billable number. No paper trail."

"For those of us that don't speak cellular as a second language please explain."

"MTSO is short for the main telephone switching office, it's the main computer that controls our area."

"You defiantly seem gifted at this."

I inclined my head in his direction. "Thank you."

Agent Boyle was not pleased. His patience was wearing on

his face like a bad suit. He got up and paced. He glared; he spoke to the mirror and in general, was displeased with me. Some other agents entered the room, each wearing that same concerned and confused look. Each was assessing my story with their own bullshit meters.

"Explain the cash."

"I hoped to buy a ring for Sam today on my way home from work. I have been saving this money for about three months. We share credit cards and I did not want her to find out how much I paid."

"Why grab that money and why the money belt?"

"I woke up dead, no phone or cell. It was logical to assume my accounts were also not available. Then I saw a man get gunned down in front of me. I wanted to find out what was going on. I needed money and it seemed prudent to have a little carry around cash."

"$3,800 is not exactly carrying around money unless you're Trump."

"The money was for an engagement ring. You can call the store to confirm. The ring was sized and they called me at work yesterday."

"We just might call them Ryan. Why did you purchase a new hat and a new jacket at the store?"

"As I said I did not want to stand out. I wanted to blend in.

"But they found you anyway?"

"Fred told me I was being watched all day. I don't know if they were aware that I ran to the falls, or if they saw me someplace else. But as gifted as you want to make me look, my plan was far from successful."

"We captured parts of his transmission." Over the speakers in the room came the conversation concerning my signaling his supposed companions in the plot. I was laughing uncontrollably by the end of the ninety-second tape.

"You think this is funny?"

Composing myself I nodded. "You bet I do. Fred was more paranoid than me. He kept talking to whomever in his wrist cuff stating I had backup and other people there to assist me. The very fact I made up a bullshit story to save my life and they believed it just confirms my belief the world has gone completely nuts."

"Did you have other people, is that why you went to the casino, to meet someone?"

"I am beginning to think that I am the only sane person in this room. I just explained to you what I did. When Fred was leading me out of the garage to one of his associates, I waved at a man walking to his car. He waved back. I was playing the man hoping that I might be able to get away still breathing."

"You think fast on your feet. They teach this in cellphone mangers school?"

"No, but they do in the school of desperation. I was trying my best not to die."

"You have no idea why these men wanted you dead?" A vein bulged in Agent Boyle's forehead and he again smashed his hand on the table for emphasis.

"No offense, but you can ask me that question 1,000 times and you'll get the same answer on number 1,001."

"Let me summarize. You have over $3,400 cash for an engagement ring you were going to buy today, you saw a man get gunned down, ran to Niagara Falls, bought clothes that would peg you for a tourist, reactivated your cell phone in a way that is nearly untraceable, and you waved at someone you did not know to play on the suspicions of a man you call Fred."

"I know. I've had a busy day."

"How exactly did you think about all those things? You put some field agents to shame with your abilities today."

"No offense, but it seems like common sense to me. Also, if you don't mind me stating my paranoia radar was dead on today. Further, I actually started the day with $3,800 - I spent some along the way."

"Why did you take a cab instead of the local bus or Greyhound?"

"The cab was much faster. I was not going to the corner and wait for a bus when I can jump in a cab. Especially after seeing a police officer gunned down in my driveway."

"Do you know where we are?"

"Not sure, but I could take a guess."

"Fine. Take that guess."

"The new Homeland Security building in downtown Buffalo."

"How would you know that?"

"Again, it's just a guess."

The agent picked up the cell phone and turned it on. He made note of the number and then handed it to another agent.

"Would you like something to eat?" Agent Boyle was almost pleasant.

"Yes, that would be nice."

My faith in the federal government had definitely dropped a few points. They were making me out to be James Bond. Everyone who has ever watched a spy movie would have done the exact same things I did. Although I held an advantage working for CellNY as I could pull the trick with the phone. I hoped Ed had not been drawn into this as well. They were playing me, playing with my ego, they wanted me to confess my involvement. I would be more than willing to discuss my involvement at length, as long as I found out what the hell was going on.

I could also picture Sam being forcibly removed from her office to be taken in for questioning, maybe in the room next to mine. She's being questioned about her future fiancé's super-agent abilities. Could it be when you are trained to read between the lines you no longer can see the text? According to these fine folks anyone who has the innate ability to not die is now a candidate at Quantico. I don't know if I would consider it. I have to see their dental plan first.

I was famished. The events of the day had gone by in dream-like super-fast forward, yet I did not yet think that it was 2 p.m. I had lived this long, but my abilities to make it through the day were diminishing as I now have two groups who will be following my activities. It was evident the FBI was following Fred and his group, while Fred followed me. It was like a bad game of follow the leader. I was thankful Agent Boyle was able to save my hide at the last moment. He could have come crashing out of the bushes sooner; I guess he needed to make a grand entrance.

One wanted me dead for real and the other wanted to know why the first wanted me dead for real. However, no one seemed concerned enough to keep me alive. Other than myself, Ryan Prince super-agent. I was perplexed. They did not care whether I lived or died, they were interested only in why these other fine people thought it best I did not continue breathing. They indeed have been following Fred, they know more about him than I do. But the sharing of information had been decidedly one-sided.

I know nothing about what I am supposed to know about, therefore they must know that I know nothing about the thing, which everyone is stating I know everything about. So they must know I do not know what Fred and his comrades think I know because if I did know what they thought I knew and knew what Fred thought I knew. Then that would be new and I would not still be here in an interrogation room but rather somewhere with bars and open toilets. The threats empty and simply there to ensure I have been open and forthcoming about what I was cognizant of and when. I started to wonder what their role is in this entire mess. What do they know about what Fred thinks I know? I felt like a puppy chasing his tail, going around in circles yet making zero progress. If I only knew what they thought I knew what Fred knew, but not exactly what I knew. Well, I think the picture is clear, having nothing to offer, I may be losing my mind trying to figure it out.

Were they responsible for the car being stolen and burned in Tonawanda? Or were they behind the deactivation of both my cell and home phones?

I am certain they have IT techs that can hack any system. I would think having the FBI involved would mean one had an ally in their preverbal corner. Now I am wondering where they fit in this ever more confusing puzzle. It was certainly clear I was on my own and there would be no assistance rendered.

After an unusually brief period, I was further surprised when a man entered the room with a short, limited menu and notepad waiting to take my order. I took a moment filling out my preferences.

Agent Boyle was busy pacing about. He left many times only to re-enter the room after a brief absence. The other agents at the moment must have been busying themselves with real work. The tightness in my stomach was replaced by severe hunger pains. I had last eaten around 7:30 a.m.

My order arrived, the speed at which it was delivered lead me to believe it was not takeout. The ham and Swiss sub arrived as ordered and was delicious. It must run the taxpayers of the USA a few dollars to have such an establishment inside a government building - with the national debt and $900 hammers no wonder we are in financial trouble.

As I munched absent-mindedly on my tasty sub it occurred to me there were probably 150 such places located throughout the US, each with its own deli. I may need to send in my resume. Were there any with gyms or coffee shops as well? Screw the dental plan, get me a fresh deli sandwich and a good cup of coffee, I may work for the minimum.

I am not handcuffed, there is no gun in the small of my back, but I am also no further along the path of understanding why this is happening to me. This may or may not be some nondescript building somewhere in Niagara Falls, but what is behind door number one, still persists to be a mystery, a mystery which requires an answer. In my "mind-your business-stay-out-of-trouble-world," it seems I have made some enemies rather quickly.

I made a list in my head which consisted of people, at the moment, who I may count as allies. The list was quite short: Sam and Ed. Three against a large governmental bureaucracy and a band of killers. The deck was stacked in the house's favor.

I was wondering if Vegas would lay a line. What odds would they give me? If I have some extra cash and was willing to lay a few bills on Ryan Prince Super-Agent, I could very well afford a much more extravagant ring at 20-1 odds.

Once I finished my lunch there was an immediate pending intestinal need that required attention and soon.

Knocking on the two-way mirror, I said, "I can either make a mess in here or do it in the bathroom. Your choice."

Two rather imposing large agents, Agent Mountain and Agent Rocksolid walked into the interrogation room. I have taken to naming all these new friends. It would be a lot simpler if they wore name badges.

I may have underestimated my significance, or the threat level may have gone from orange to red. That would be the only reason two men the size of old-growth trees would be required to escort me to the men's room to have a bowel movement.

Both men made my 6'0 medium frame look quite inadequate compared with the chiseled, muscle-bound frames and each was at least 6"4". Both carried sidearms - as if I stood a chance against one of them.

They joined me in the restroom, I am not sure if they enjoyed that experience. After I finished what was necessary, I washed and dried my hands for over a minute, very slowly and deliberately. Passive-aggressive was the only defense I had against the two sequoias.

Once my toilet was completed each man put his arm under each of mine and carried me like a garbage bag. I am not sure if my feet touched the floor during the one hundred foot walk. When we reached the interrogation room there were a few more agents awaiting my arrival. I was rather unceremoniously dumped into the chair. It may have hurt a little.

"One more question." Agent Boyle said, again leading the interrogation.

"Shoot." I was trying for sarcasm.

"How is it a cell phone call originating in Canada is only picked up by cell towers on the US side of the border?"

"May I have my phone please?"

"Why?"

"Because I'm going to show you how easy it is to accomplish that."

I picked up my phone and showed the agent the setting list for roaming options. The current indication reading HOME ONLY. They looked confused and muttered among themselves.

"Okay, being a super-agent with some heretofore unmentioned super-secret agency, your phone has three settings:

home only, only A or B, or any. When a phone like mine is set to "home only," the only signal accepted must come from your home carrier, thus CellNY. It will ignore a stronger signal from another company. Cell towers operate on a five-mile radius. I am not five miles away so I can make calls from across the border and they appear on our towers only. Back before everyone had free-roaming this was a must. I do it as to not lose any of my features like caller ID, call forwarding, that sort of thing. They did teach me that in manager's school." I smirked at the agents.

The next hour or so, (this was strictly conjectured as no clocks were present), I answered questions as agent after agent took turns soliciting answers. There was a folder that I could assume was my FBI dossier. My mother's name, where she grew up, my father's name, and his background as well, where my parents lived now, naming all my present relatives, with a few "mistakes" thrown in to trip me up, their inquiries went back two generations. What did I know about Sam, and her family, my work history, my credit report, and just about every girlfriend I had screwed or thought about screwing. They may have known how many titties I squeezed, or condoms purchased. It was fun.

The more I answered correctly the more they seemed to anger and the more they tried to trip me up. It turned into a vicious cycle, short of a family reunion with the ex's family I don't think I have angered that many people simultaneously.

The continued questioning went on for a while. How long cannot be precisely determined as there were no clocks in the place and my cell phone was sitting in one of the agent's pockets.

The agents then took turns yelling, screaming, and throwing chairs about trying their damned to "break" me. There was nothing to break. It's like I was asking a square to be a circle or a brick to be a doughnut, there was no information that could be shared that already hadn't passed my lips. I was not protecting my sources or being obstinate. I was in total ignorance about the whole situation. I am a nobody as I have said before and their act was amusing.

Very few people understand customer service and the issues we face every day. I had been in the business for over seventeen years and you learn, you have to learn, to become emotionally despondent to such outbursts. If you do not learn this very necessary skill you're doomed. It's as necessary as a bus driver learning to drive and a teacher learning to teach. It is part of your skillset. You work on it every day, and every call, until the day arrives when you can have someone scream the most frightening vulgar words directly at you and you barely blink. I have on more than one occasion had to stifle a yawn while a customer screamed in my ear.

I not only deal with such issues over the phone but face to face as well. I get screamed at, sworn at, cussed at, finger pointed at my chest, daily threats about losing my job, my mistaken paternity, my mother's moral standards, my father's moral standards, being called an idiot, stupid, moronic, worse, my lack of job experience, my lack of the proper educational experience, my inability to be able to follow a conversation, the fact that I may indeed be deaf, constant threats to report my incompetence to my bosses, daily threats about reporting my incompetence to any media outlet willing to listen, threats about reporting my clear ineptitude to the FCC and our board of directors. I have been reminded that I serve no purpose, I am ineffective, and further, any form of primate with the innate ability of button pushing would be a suitable replacement, constant threats to track me down and teach me the necessary lesson, and the mention of dark alleys and chance encounters.

These agents were amateurs and I sat in my chair not moving, not really listening as the vulgarity started. The threats started shortly thereafter, stories would be told to everyone that I was drug dealing no good Al-Qaeda sympathizer, with direct contacts to the mob and every perverted form of child pornography that existed. I may or may not have abused small children and kicked some puppies as well. Worst of all there are witnesses that will swear that I was running with scissors.

I sat quietly. I sat still. I looked at my fingers and ran those said fingers through my hair. I looked at my shoes and counted to 1,000 more than once and thought about Sam and her world-famous chicken lemon. I thought about how a Jack and cola tastes after a rough day, how Speybourne is really the best scotch even though they don't advertise. I went through the entire Bills schedule in my head figuring they finish .500, hoping they steal a few games. I wonder if the time was right to invest in technology stocks once again, I wondered why Scott Norwood had missed that field goal in Super Bowl 25, it was freakish but one of the agents looked like my Uncle Jim who lived in Florida, how I always wanted to collect watches and I wondered if it was a really expensive hobby, and I recalled vividly my many experiences with Sam both in and out of the bedroom. I, however, never reacted to a single thing they said or a single threat they uttered. As experience has taught me, this angered them even more, since they did not have any energy from which to feed. It's difficult to vehemently argue if one party refuses to play the game. It's like fanning a flame with water - eventually, it just burns out.

A few of the agents so vigorously went about their jobs that ties were loosened and sweat was present on top of many a brow, spreading stains under arms. I was Mr. Cool, Mr. Relaxed.

Agent Boyle waited in the wings, no longer taking an active role in the interrogation. His role was so simple he was going to be the good cop, keeping these bad men from harassing an innocent civilian. After my last inspection upon my badly manicured nails, a bad habit developed right after I quit smoking, I pulled my chair away from the table, crossed my legs, and announced:

"You guys are boring me to death, when is the good Agent Boyle going to take over the interrogation er.... I mean questioning?" I thought Agent Rocksolid was going to take a swing. That pleased me deeply. The sweat was practically pouring off his forehead in a very convincing imitation of Niagara Falls.

"Okay, Ryan," good cop Boyle says, "you're a fairly cool man all right."

"I get screamed at for a living. I hope you didn't expect your little show to affect me in any way. Well, you broke me all right, I am KGB (with my best Russian accent which consequently is not that good) my real name is Boris."

I was laughing out loud and so hard I had to stop to take a breath. My nose was throbbing and my side was still on fire. It was well worth the 30 seconds of discomfort.

Agent Rocksolid's face was growing redder than Mars in summer. I could see his muscles tightening under his much too taut white dress shirt.

"We seem to be at an impasse gentleman. Either let me go or trump up some charges. I will need a phone to call my attorney. Now. I will not answer any more questions without a suit in here immediately. My attorney's number is in my cell you may call him if you wish."

I invoked, a lessoned learned while watching an episode of Law and Order. Whoever stated that broadcast TV has no educational basis, was entirely and completely, incorrect.

6

August 18 | 4 p.m.

The standstill had to come to an end eventually. The courts have not looked fondly upon holding prisoners without access to representation, not even terrorists. They had nothing on me they could prove - just supposition that indeed I was the best-trained secret spy guy around.

They allowed me to collect my personal effects. I counted the money deliberately and for all to see. I know none had been taken, but I could not resist. There is a part of me that emerged immediately after the divorce, it turns out I can be a real prick when needed.

I made sure my cell was still functioning. Blindfold was replaced and again I was lead off into a maze one hundred turns this way one hundred and fifty that way, and an elevator ride to nowhere. I was dumped in the back of a van. The crazy pattern returning again, making turns to confuse me and not allow me to get my bearings.

It occurred to me that we might not have left the Falls. I assumed we were in downtown, but that was never confirmed. Tracking time while blindfolded is not easy; therefore, we may be leaving the Falls now and taking the long way into Buffalo.

I had no reason to suspect otherwise, but I was certain Buffalo was our destination regardless of our origin.

My presence was required back into the middle of the fray. It occurred to me that this was a game, a feint, they wanted me in Buffalo. I was the bait for a huge fish. Maybe even the FBI could not penetrate Fred's compatriots. They were luring these men out of the dark using their fly reels and a big juicy lure-me-tied to the end. I realized now more than ever, that to survive this day I would need Sam and I needed to get out of sight.

I was like the expendable crewmember in the red shirt on Star Trek- the likelihood I would still be alive after the first set of commercials was not very high. All my resources would be required if I wanted to see daylight again.

Sometimes bait can be dangerous, ask the victims of the anglerfish. This fish has adapted a peculiar hunting method. It possesses a long appendage, at the end of it he dangles this bit of flesh and it dances like a worm luring his dinner a little bit at a time. Bait becoming predator.

I was unceremoniously dumped on the curb at the intersection of Court and Pearl Streets, just four blocks from my office. I removed the blindfold. The trip took less than twenty minutes, by my best estimation. I believe that I was, indeed, in downtown Buffalo. The black non-descript van without a license plate pulled away from the curb as if the driver were late for an appointment.

Cell in hand as soon as they completed their turn, I called Ed. It was now approaching 4 p.m. in the afternoon. He must have left for the day and I was without my emergency home phone list. I should have learned a lesson from the Boy Scouts concerning preparedness. I tried his cell number, and, getting his voicemail I left a message.

Thank God I was able to reach Sam as she was leaving the office. She sounded terrified and very concerned. I could not convey to her on the phone the danger that now faced us. We required a face-to-face meeting.

I asked her to meet me downtown with laptop in hand. She agreed, her voice shaking. She was horrified. I was beyond fear with everything that had happened thus far, my fear circuits may have burned out.

Our offices are separated only by one subway stop which is approximately four-tenths of a mile. Sam's job was located at the Fountain Plaza station, which just so happens to border twenty-something central Chippewa Street; along with bars too numerous to count, there were three coffeehouses, each with Wi-Fi connectivity. The laptop we shared I used for fun and she used for work. It had an integrated wireless card and PC Anywhere that would allow me access to my company computer.

I had PC Anywhere installed on my home computer and the IT department did not fuss when I put it on the laptop as well. I realized too late the reason they did not mind. I was reachable on vacation and was now required to carry it with me whenever I left town. One trip to Florida was ruined as I wasted a day driving around attempting to locate anywhere with a Wi-Fi signal. I was attempting to retain a business account with over 250 phones. Sam was not pleased after watching me spend two hours on my cell trying to retain the account. Not only did they remain a customer we analyzed the account adding another 50 phones and cutting their phone bill by a third. It was, I can say, the work of a genius.

My day had not gone so well. I was justified in following my instincts. There had to be something that had caused all the trouble. The secret had to be in my database. The one thought that continually runs through my brain, if this was not a mistake, and if my ex was not involved, and indeed this is not mistaken identity, the only factor remaining that would explain everything, was the database.

I could not access the company records from the PC Anywhere but I could access my hard drive. I kept extensive records for every customer contact, both over the phone and face-to-face. Only a few fellow workers knew I had this information. When I received a call from a customer stating we talked on such a date, I would access this database. It contained their account number and cell phone number and home address if merited, and also included extensive notation concerning their issue and how it was resolved as well as the cancel date of their contract. I would personally direct these customers into our stores with incentives two months prior to the cancel date of their contracts. I recorded a seventy-five percent retention rate with those customers.

If I knew something I should not know it would be in there, someplace. I want to find it, I needed to find it, at this point I believed without a doubt that my life depended on it.

And so did Sam's.

The Mug Stop like the other coffee houses was dominated by the younger crowd, as this street was their Mecca.

Normally I am not a fan of coffeehouses and in general as gas is expensive enough, but when a twenty-ounce beverage costs about $4, that works out to about $25 a gallon. Too expensive for my taste.

The Mug Stop was an intimate bar in its previous incarnation. It cannot claim the largest square footage of more illustrious cousins along the strip. As you enter this quaint establishment the counter is off to your right and there is limited seating. The counter was retained from the last enterprise that occupied this space- it was solid cedar with a well-worn and well-polished surface. There were two rows of small square metal and glass tables.

The place was packed with downtown workers, some high school students, and some customers preparing themselves for a night of overindulgence. The collective conversations of coffee patrons added an almost unpleasant white noise to the background. Most of the tables were full but I was able to find a seat in the back after walking past the younger customers, each boasting more metal than a Japanese sports car.

The décor was simple earth tones, mostly varying shades of brown coffee tones, cafe latte colored walls, mocha toned carpeting, everything trimmed in espresso, the drapes covering the two front windows Café Leche.

Some new age music spewed forth from the sound system, the artist CD was prominently displayed on the counter. I made a point of ignoring it.

The waitress approached, chatting away to whoever was on the other end of her Bluetooth connection.

"What can I get for you?' She asked, snapping her gum for good measure.

"How about a glass of water, a large black coffee, and a large French vanilla with two creams." I may not frequent these places but I am wise to the ordering procedures.

"What flavor for the first coffee?"

"None."

"Pardon?"

"None."

"Okay, we have syrups that can be added later which would you like?"

"No, just black."

"Well do you need...."

"No, just black, the recipe simple, get those environmentally friendly cups you use, fill with streaming hot coffee that I won't be able to drink for at least twenty minutes, place lid on top, just black coffee."

"Okay, just black." She walked away but before she was out of earshot I heard, "Can you believe some old guy just ordered a black coffee OMG, who orders black coffee?"

Shaking my head in disbelief, that exchange was the main reason I bought my coffee at gas stations and Dunkin Donuts. Within a few minutes, I saw my waitress weaving through the crowd, tray held high, Bluetooth device firmly planted in her ear and conversing with yet another friend on her speed dial.

Sam was immediately behind her, her laptop case bouncing off her hip, looking very sharp in a purple dress shirt and black dress pants. Her curly hair was bouncing in rhythm with her step. She was the most beautiful thing I had seen all day. She also looked pissed.

Sam's weariness was plastered on her face and the stress caused lines that I normally did not see. I did my best to relay today's events in a manner that could be understood; however, as the story developed the more apprehensive she became. By the time I recalled my captivity at the Homeland Security building and the intense scrutiny I was under, she sat with crossed arms and with a disbelieving look on her face. I doubted she had the patience for me to explain. She was growing angrier by the moment, her foot tapping uncontrollably, which I knew was her tell, she was not just mad, but pissed.

"Well, you've had quite a day."

"It's been eventful," I was trying to keep the conversation on the light side as she was ready to explode. I loved her to death and she did me, but our relationship was not immune to arguments.

She had a temper. I lifted my shirt enough to show her the bandage now adhered to my side. I explained that the doctors also had reset my bloody broken nose. The FBI at least patched me up and pronounced was well enough to sit in a chair and get screamed at for an hour. She looked shocked.

"What the hell is that?"

"Shh... I told you what it was. I got shot. My friends at the FBI refer to this as a graze."

"That better be a gunshot wound because I am in no mood to listen to this story you've been feeding me. What the hell happened to your clothes?"

"After being shot, causing much bleeding all over my

clothes, the FBI deemed it necessary to give me some new threads prior to their interrogation. Did you try to get money out today as I asked?"

"Yes. There was a message that our accounts had a pending hold."

"Because the account holder was deceased. Right?"

"Well, they did not go that far."

"Did you stop by the house?"

"Yes. It was cordoned off with yellow tape. They said Officer Flamel was supposed to meet you. He was shot three times in the back with a high-powered rifle. They still think you're dead, even when I told them we were together last night."

I grabbed the laptop. I went to the Buffalo News website and showed her the blurb in the police blotter section.

"Well, two things in your bullshit story work out."

"Sam, I am not making this up. Someone out there wants to see me dead. I don't know why."

"Why did that FBI agent come to your defense? What could you know that could help them?"

"I came to the same conclusion. They know why Fred wanted me dead, but they were not willing to share it with me. I was accused of being too clever today. Everything was too convenient. They think I was working for Fred and his entourage. Moreover, they let me know they thought I was connected with them and were angered when I could not aid them in whatever endeavors in which they are involved."

"You know when you talk like that you sound like a pretentious prick."

"According to most, I am dead. I think I've earned the right to talk any way I want."

She looked at me, her jaw twitching slightly as she gritted her teeth. Sam took a deep breath, exhaling it with deliberation.

"I don't know if you need a kiss or a whack with a heavy iron implement."

"I could use a kiss. It's been a rough day."

She leaned across the narrow table. I was able to meet her halfway and we shared a none-too short but enjoyable kiss. Our eyes met and again there was that immediate understanding that we have shared for so long. I am sure most of the patrons wondered why the old couple was making out in the middle of the coffee shop.

"Okay, why is the laptop so important?"

"There must be someone I talked who recently who has a connection to this. I plan on finding out who that is."

"What happened to your jacket? The one I bought for you?"

"It's in the garbage. I bought this one at the casino, remember?"

"So, this guy you call Fred, your shadow, you did it to give him the slip?"

"Yes. Well not exactly for Fred. I bought it before we ran into each other."

"Are you high?"

"CellNY drug tests remember, and if not for my intense feelings of paranoia I was convinced I would be dead, again."

"Who was driving your car?"

"I don't know."

"Why are these mysterious people trying to kill a manager of a customer service office?"

"I don't know."

Sam still thought I was under the influence because the tone of her voice held a dubious note. "You withstood hours of questioning from the FBI only to be released."

"I threatened to lawyer up."

"Something is very wrong here. It doesn't make sense."

"Really, Sherlock?" I was exasperated and my tone became rather sarcastic. "It took you all this time to put that together?"

Her brow furrowed and she rubbed her eyes. "I'm sorry. Would you believe me if I came to you with this story?"

"No, but you see that man over there," I inclined my head towards the door. "The one that just walked in?"

"Yes."

"That's Agent Rocksolid. He really doesn't care for me much."

She shook her head. "Neither did I until a few minutes ago."

I smiled. At least some of her humor was still intact. "Love you too. They released me so that I would lead them back to my secret hideout. I am sure that we will not be alone for the remainder of the evening."

Sam gave me a tight smile. "This paranoia is contagious because I am beginning to believe it."

I waved at Agent Rocksolid and he glared back. His shirt was rumpled and had pit stains. I smiled. He must be quite uncomfortable, as I had caused the man much distress and great puddles of sweat. The memory of his cranial veins pulsating through his skin and the anger in his eyes pleased me deeply. I stifled a laugh.

Surveying the room, no one else currently present appeared to be paying us much attention. I know Fred would not be here, as he had a previous engagement with a coroner. His other partner was not here either, just the FBI Agent that more than likely loathed my very existence.

Although in a public place, I did not feel safe and I certainly did not feel comfortable. I wanted to get the hell out of the coffeehouse, however, accessing my database was a priority.

I was overcome by claustrophobia as the crush of the patron's chatter and Agent Rocksolid's constant glare caused my fear circuits to veer wildly. They were on the verge of overheating and imminent collapse. I am not normally prone to such irrational fears yet, the logical side of my brain had apparently taken the rest of the day off, allowing its silly cousin "Mr. Let's Fear Everything" to run the show. Most of the patrons were young kids - barely twenty-somethings. It was apparent most could barely tie their own shoes and dress in matching clothes, yet to me, each posed a specific yet unidentifiable threat, each one was the next sniper in the van, each one carrying a pistol in their backpacks, each one there to apprehend me and return me to the cold room.

As a precaution, I set my privacy option on the laptop so no other Wi-Fi users could access my system. I could surf in relative secrecy. I struggled to act normal, as if this were any other day, just another trip to our favorite coffeehouse to enjoy the new age music, maybe preparing for a night out.

There were those in the crowd that met my gaze, while others looked away immediately; my paranoid brain could not discern which was the act of the guilty; those who met my glance without fear or those that could not look me in the eye. In my adrenaline-soaked brain, I somehow argued with myself the pro and cons of each position. This internal back and forth occurred while I sat there composed, participating in an arcane conversation with Sam. It was all strange, it was surreal.

"What's your plan?"

I was pleased our conversation again turned to important matters other than the robustness of the coffee or the blandness of the creamer.

"Plan A, don't die."

"Smart. Well thought out."

"Plan B, find out why these fine people want me dead. There has got to be something in the customer database that can point us in the right direction. We need to find it before anyone else does. The first group of friendlies is probably still looking for me."

"Agent Boyle really shot this guy Fred?"

"Yeah, right before he was going to blow my head back to Buffalo." I could still feel the gun at the base of my neck. "Heard two pops and thought I was dead right there."

"One more question. Do you really have $3,400 dollars on you? I want to see it."

I opened my money belt, trying not to garner too much attention, which mostly is difficult, and in a room full of coffee patrons nearly impossible. Doing so made my gunshot wound ache. The pain was tolerable, for now.

Looking inside, Sam asked what the money was for.

"Well, it's kind of a secret."

"Tell me now or I walk."

"It was for you. I was going to buy a ring today."

"What kind of ring would cost you...." The tears started to well in her eyes. "You were going to buy me the ring. THE ring."

"Yes. I was until I woke up and found out I was dead."

A tear slid down her cheek and I gently wiped it off. "What's the next step?"

"Call my parents, order invitations, plan a wedding shower, and set a date."

She smiled at me and sighed. "What's your plan for the rest of today smart ass?"

"Download my database here. Then run like hell."

"To where?"

I motioned for Sam to sit next to me. Even in the crowded space, she was able to turn her chair one hundred and eighty degrees and join me on my side of the diminutive table. I double-clicked on the Word icon and began typing.

"My dad owns a cabin just outside of Watertown. It is not common knowledge that he owns it. It's also a good cover as you have relatives in Syracuse."

I was sure Agent Rocksolid had some device to eavesdrop on us. Sam was starting to buy into my paranoia as she did not directly respond to my written statement.

"Well, I was thinking about going to Syracuse. My aunt lives there," I stated loudly, hoping my ploy was working.

"That sounds nice," Sam said, playing along. "I've never been there. I know I need to get the hell out of Dodge."

Continuing to utilize writing, I outlined my plan. "I am going to borrow a company van. Your car might have a tracking device. You go get gas, drive back to work. I'll meet you there."

She smiled and took over the keyboard. "Can I see what there is to do in Syracuse?" she asked, and I nodded. She typed: "That won't work. You'll have to come back with me. The new office security policy won't allow you in the front door without me."

"Oh, there are so many things to do in Syracuse. It looks like we can be there by 7 p.m. tonight," she said, her voice gleeful.

"Yeah, sounds about right." She gave me back control of the computer and I began the task at hand.

The rest of our stretch at the Mug was spent in idle chitchat under the watchful eyes of Agent Rocksolid, who, on more than one occasion, was talking into his cuff, certainly reporting our actions back to whoever was listening. Again the expense to the taxpayers seemed rather extreme. But they were playing their line, more than likely surveying the coffeehouse as was I.

They may have been in possession of photos from which Agent Rocksolid could match faces in the crowd. Instead of the less effective paranoia radar upon which I was so dependent. Like a master angler playing the line across the water, mimicking movements, trying to draw your prey from its hiding place. Luring that prey into some false sense of security, until the bait is so enticing, it cannot be resisted.

Agent Rocksolid was the master angler playing rod and reel to land his real catch. I am not an anthropologist nor a historian, but I would place a bet small fish have been used to catch larger fish since man first dipped a pole in the water. And today I was that small fish.

Watching Agent Rocksolid glare in my general direction, his face was buried in his cuff. This no longer struck me as odd after the day's events. I was hoping Fred's friends also were near and listening. So Agent Rocksolid could record their names and apprehend the real criminals.

My supposed trip to Syracuse may buy us some time, a commodity in very limited supply. Repeatedly checking the download counter on the database file, it seemed to go backward, as if the clock was running against us. I have seen movies download on dial-up faster than this. While the download of the file crept, the clock on the wall seemed to be breaking speed records, the second hand sweeping like an Olympic timekeeper.

To say time was the essence was indeed the understatement of the week. After being dead all day I felt the cool gray hand of the reaper. Our lives depended on a smooth and fast departure. We needed to disappear into the night.

Now.

7

August 18 | 5 p.m.

The download complete, we walked back to First Erie One Mortgage Company. I was in a hyper state of awareness, feeling exposed as we quickly moved towards Sam's work. On more than one occasion the hair on the back of my neck stiffened and I glanced behind us, looking for Agent Rocksolid. To say I was relieved when we entered the stately stone building is another understatement for the day.

First Eire One Mortgage was a subsidiary of Erie One Bank; the first floor of the enormous bank was anachronistic compared with the computer room just down the hall from Sam's office.

The floor of the bank was polished marble; the rails marking different teller lines brass. It spoke of a different time, when Buffalo was as big as New York City and the Erie Canal brought goods and services from all over the state.

Ships harbored at the port and used Lake Erie as their blue highway. Downtown was crowded; jazz filled the streets as patrons danced. Ferries operated daily, carrying passengers between Fort Erie Canada and Buffalo; businesses lined the streets and commerce was heavy. Money flowed into Buffalo like the water over the mighty Niagara Falls.

No one could have predicted what was ahead. Buffalo's reign would not last a generation. It was during this period that First Buffalo Savings Bank was formed. Incorporated in 1890, the initial investors read like a Buffalo street and attraction guide. The first to sign the charter included Millard Fillmore (yes, the President); John Ellicott (the surveyor who gave downtown its distinctive look, and who has a street and a building named after him); and Asa Ransom (one of the largest landowners when Buffalo was first formed).

The bank continued to grow as did the area, by the time World War I commenced Buffalo Savings Bank was the largest bank in the country, boasting tens of millions in deposits. It was in 1920 that the signature gold dome was added to the building.

The enormous first floor held fifty teller stations and fourteen bank offices. It was gaudy and it was ornate, and it was a true metaphor for the area at the time. The walls reeked of success, the place emanated enormous wealth.

Sam's company bought this bank after it changed hands from Buffalo Savings Bank to Gold Dome (no joke). Gold Dome went under as Buffalo went under, fast and without warning.

The '70s were not kind to Buffalo or New York State for that matter. The Erie Canal that had built Buffalo into a giant dried up as fast as disposable income. The Saint Lawrence Seaway contributed the last straw. No more ships, no more canal, no more steel plants. No more people. What was the second busiest port in the east hardly saw a boat that was full. Tourism stopped.

There was no reason to come to Buffalo. There was no reason to do business in Buffalo. Without the resources to support them, it was not long before the people began what would become a great exodus from the region. The population of Erie County in 1920 was two million; it now stands under a million people some eighty-six years later.

What was once the commercial hub for the area now finds the sidewalks rolled up by 5 p.m. Most stores are vacant; the great Main Place Mall only fifty percent occupied with more tenants leaving every year. Without the ballpark, home to the Buffalo Bisons, Cleveland's triple-A affiliate, the HSBC arena home to the Buffalo Sabres, and party central, there would be nothing to bring people into downtown, as there is nothing to see.

Erie One Bank opened up this relic and restored it is original grandeur about ten years ago. A ten-floor office complex was built adjacent to the original bank, connecting old with new, past with future. Sam's office was located in the adjacent office complex.

Companies that built in Buffalo and stayed in Buffalo were rare. Everyone was hopeful that restoring this landmark to its rightful beauty might be the impetus to restore downtown as a major commercial hub, thereby slowing the exodus of the regions' best and brightest leaving in droves.

I looked down at the marble floor, which was buffed to a mirror shine. The brass polished until it glowed. The bank was restored to its former glory, including the gold roof that was actual gold leaf hammered into its intricate texture. The ghosts of Buffalo's forefathers haunted this place; the ghost of Buffalo's past lingered in the halls, reminding all who entered of the glory days never to be captured again. In a real way, Buffalo itself had died inside these walls, on the polished marble, and in the gleaming brass rails.

Sam and I passed by the security guard, who was more interested in his preseason football game than scanning for potential criminals. He waved us through without much scrutiny. The guard's monitor beeped when Sam swiped her card, the final acknowledgment we belonged.

The mortgage portion of the building was very impressive; it was of a modern design where glass, metal, and polished concrete dominated. The green trim matched the copper oxide which coated the exterior of the older building and doors. The glass walkway connecting new and old was the perfect transition; complete with period ornamentation and modern flair.

The ride from the lobby to Sam's office was in a glass elevator that looked over the back of the building and the magnificent St. Michael's Catholic Church, which stood on at least two city blocks. Again a reminder of Buffalo's glorious past.

The offices here seemed more stylish and less centered on function. Although the normal "cubicle jungle" theme was present, accommodating some 35 representatives, the lighting and spacing between the workstations was much more aesthetic, bright lights were replaced with recessed lighting, the cubicles themselves colored to match the décor, and the carpeting gave the space a much more intimate feeling than the call center over which I presided.

Sam's office of sorts was off the main floor; it consisted of two walls, each perpendicular to the floor and the to ceiling. The space offered more privacy than my middle-of-the-floor, babysit-the-call center-kids area that I was accustomed to working in.

I dropped my body into the guest chair as Sam sat at her desk, calmly answering a few newly-received emails and checking the departmental voicemail box. She also spent a moment clearing her inbox. I watched as she distributed correspondence that would need to be handled tomorrow, leaving sticky notes on some desk blotters with obvious direction to how she wished they were to be administered. I anxiously shifted in my seat, my wound aching. We needed to get going.

Sam, however, was not in a hurry, as if life presented no concerns. She continued her carefree ways, taking care of some housework items. I saw her empty garbage cans and disposing of the rubbish in a central location in the closet. Her movements were slow and deliberate and without worry.

I was trying to understand and track her activities. What was she doing? I was wondering when her plan would be brought to light. I have been running so long today, sometimes relying strictly on instinct, and I was growing impatient to hear what she had in mind.

Sam is intelligent and gifted. She climbed through the ranks of the Mortgage Service department faster than I had with CellNY. It's not as if I thought her plan would not be feasible, I was impatiently awaiting its manifestation. I heard my own internal clock winding down all day and I was no longer was a man who cared about the rat race; the daily regimented schedule, planning one moment to the next. I was living my life in sixty-second increments. I was not buying any green bananas. Long term planning had no place; I could throw away my Palm Pilot and not miss it at all. My planner and my calendar could be burned for kindling.

I am, under normal circumstances, a very patient person. I have on occasion been accused of being too patient, too accommodating to a customer's rants, too willing to turn the other cheek. Some have decided that this is cowardice in hiding. I don't necessarily avoid confrontation, however, more often than not, there are preferable ways to solve problems without screaming and placing blame. Even though, it is difficult being the bigger person, the one who is willing to give in, the first to concede for mutual benefit. That is a price most are not willing to pay. For some strange reason, in a world where personal responsibility has failed, to the land of lawsuits and parents blaming video games and music for their own failures: the mere act of apologizing for something that truly is not your fault is considered rendering yourself neutered.

The art of negotiation may be dead and I very well could be the last person that understands the give and take of this art form. All of this being said, after all my years of training, being the patient engine that could, I was about to blow a gasket. I could no longer watch Sam clean her office when men that wanted me dead were but blocks away. Sam was focused on garbage cans and voicemail, inboxes and emails. There could be a sniper right now across the street in the parking garage waiting for me to exit the building, but at least she would have a solid jump on tomorrow's agenda.

"Don't you pay someone to take out the garbage? What are you going to do next? Shampoo the carpets?"

"Is there something bothering you?"

My temper got the best of me and sarcasm took over. "No, not really. How about I grab a gallon of white and touch up the stairway?"

She looked at me like I had just sprouted three heads. "What's your problem?"

"Not much - I woke up dead, got shot and people want to kill me. No worries."

She stood up, adjusting her shirt and slacks, sauntering in my direction. She paused, taking a moment to share another kiss, and with her arms draped around my neck, her blue eyes met mine and she smiled. Inside, I was ready to explode. I was not in a 'take your own sweet time' mood; rather I was in a 'let's run away and avoid more bullets' mood, 'let's not get locked in any more trunks' mood, 'let's not get interrogated' mood, 'let's not break any more bones' kind of mood.

"My love. These people you have angered seem to know us fairly well, correct?"

"Yes, they seem to have obtained a copy of our planning calendars."

"Well, let's act like today is any other day, then we will disappear right under their noses."

"How do you propose we do that?"

"I have a plan."

"A plan? Do you plan on sharing your stratagem with the rest of us before or after the dirt starts falling on my coffin?"

"How about now? I have access to a car that's not mine and will be nearly untraceable because it belongs to the bank."

Doubt flooded through me and I shook my head. "I still think that my dad's cabin is our best bet."

She nodded. "I agree. Let me just take just a few more minutes to tidy up in here."

"I am not trying to be an asshole, but time is well, running out." The urge and need to leave before we both got killed coursed through my veins.

"The more it looks like any other day means we throw them off our tail. Hence using the bank vehicle. But we may need to spend some of that nest egg of yours."

"It's just money and it can be replaced. I'll just use a credit card for your ring. It's not like it's a surprise anymore."

She stiffened. "You know when everyone says it's the thought that counts and it seems like a load of bullshit?"

"Yes, sure."

"This is not bullshit. And the thought did count. Thank you." She was fighting tears. Sam is not one to allow herself to be seen as vulnerable in public. She was much more forthcoming with tears in private. Not that it matters, but we both fall on the same side of the fence on this issue.

"Have I told you in the last few minutes that I love you?"

She brushed away the tears from her eyes. "No, you have not." For a moment her composure was restored.

"Well, if I hadn't awakened as a dead man today, we'd be engaged right now."

She kissed me. "I know. Let's make it through today and we can do it tomorrow."

"I wanted to do it today. Life sometimes blindsides you. I certainly did not see this coming."

"Nostradamus didn't see this coming?" She asked, finally grabbing her bag. "Okay. Let's go."

Relief that we were finally moving flooded through me as we exited her office. While Sam recalled the elevator, I was taking in the view from the glass atrium. I witnessed downtown coming to life as the lights on each building blinked on one at a time. Sometimes a whole building would light up all at once, which was quite the display. It pleased me to know people would be flocking into downtown shortly for Thursday in the Square and they, too, would witness this event. They would witness this fight against the dark. It was strangely reassuring sharing this spectacle with total strangers and it allowed me to feel grounded if only for a fleeting moment.

In the elevator, Sam's hand intertwined with mine was as reassuring as my witnessing the same things as others. It was almost as if we pronounced for all to hear that we were alive and we will fight into the night until the dawn's gray light greets us.

Sam removed her hand from mine, extracting keys from her pocket. She slid a key into the slot under the floor buttons, the one that all of us rule-followers assumed was for firemen only. She looked at me and smirked, turning the key all the way to the right, past the off position, and a panel fell open, concealing another panel with additional controls. She pushed a few buttons and the elevator began it's controlled descent. I watched as the numbers counted down 7, 6, 5, 4 3, 2, 1, then, much to my surprise, it continued for a while, slowing and finally resting somewhere below the first floor.

"Wait here," she instructed.

I complied, as I was not sure where here was. The air was moist and cool and the sound was amplified many times over as her footfalls echoed off the dark walls. The low-light made the area a safe haven for deep black shadows. It was not a place one goes rushing into without a flashlight and GPS.

Sam ambled off, disappearing into the blackness after only a few feet. The sound of her footfalls echoing off the concrete walls was reassuring. Light illuminated the area as she located the light switch. She hurried back to me, the sound of her shoes preceding her arrival, echoing as if ten women each matched the cadence of her stride. Sam motioned for me to follow her. I complied.

With a good deal of illumination, it became clear this was a delivery area of some sort. There were individual bays off to my right and I counted seven. The tire tracks and slick black oil stains were too numerous to count; this was a very well used area. I would venture to guess it saw almost daily use.

Parked to the far left was a company van, emblazoned with the necessary amount of logos, so no one had to guess to whom it belonged. The garage delivery area was empty except for this sole vehicle. Along the wall, there was a black box bolted to the concrete block, complete with a rather stern and sturdy lock.

This, too, felled to Sam, her now seemingly unending supply of keys allowing her access to the black box. She then removed a remote starter and a set of keys. With the speedy beep beep of the remote, she opened the door and slid into the driver's side of the vehicle.

The passenger-side window slid down its tracks, and she motioned to me. "Are you coming or what?" She pointed to an imaginary watch on her wrist, which to be truthful at first I may have missed the intended humor in her actions.

"I guess we are leaving now. Okay then. Let's go."

I buckled in as Sam informed me the van was used generously. It was utilized to shuttle employees.

The bank took pride in its employee-first approach and shuttled employees that did not have cars, as not all of their branches were assessable by public transportation. I did recall hearing about Marla, an assistant in Sam's office, who broke her leg from knee to ankle and was in a cast that made driving impossible. A simple solution was reached. Sam's boss, Terry Franklin, picked her up every morning, often arriving at work early to ensure her perfect attendance record was not marred.

"How do you have access to this floor and the van?" I didn't remember her mentioning using the vehicle at all.

"Mad skills babe, mad skills. I drove the van back in November 2000 during the snowstorm. Nobody asked for the keys back."

November 19, 2000, was one of the worst snowstorms to hit Buffalo in recorded history. What made it the second-worst of all time was that nobody died. The worst of the worst was the Blizzard of '77, which buried Buffalo for over a week. Many people froze to death, their cars buried under feet of snow; the rescuers arriving sometime moments too late to save them.

The snowstorm of 2000 did not cripple the city for weeks; however, it was the ferocity of the storm that made it memorable. We in western New York expect snow in November, Thanksgiving turkeys are often accompanied by lake effect flakes. The weather reports for that day had called for a dusting, or under an inch of snow, however, by the early morning commute, the anticipated snowfall total increased to three to four inches. The storm was supposed to start around noon that Tuesday afternoon.

The snow started at noon as expected, however, none of the meteorologists anticipated a high front over the lake that had not yet frozen over. The snow started to fall in increasing amounts. We had five inches of snow during the noon hour alone and by two o'clock looking out my office window I could not see the building across the street some sixty feet away.

The call came to close schools at 2:30 p.m., much too late. The mayor then asked everyone to evacuate downtown. Everyone did exactly as ordered. However, the egress from downtown was far from systematic and was driven by panic as workers left frantically trying to reach their children. Traffic on most surface streets leaving Buffalo was bumper to bumper for miles. The elevated expressway, prone to whiteouts and zero visibility, was crammed with cars within minutes of the evacuation order.

Too much snow, too fast, and too many people leaving downtown made for a disaster. It took more than four days just to move the cars out of the way to make room for the plows.

People slept in schools and fire departments. People congregated wherever there was heat, light, and food. Children were stranded on school buses and were evacuated to retail stores, universities, and anywhere that could accommodate them. It was a chaotic mess. I spent two days in Buffalo, my car parked in the ramp with no hope of clearing the abandoned cars out of the way, trapped like all the others.

Some fifteen colleagues like me were stranded at work. After the first twenty hours, the vending machines in the cafeteria were emptied of all food. We raided the cafeteria stores and that held us over for another two meals. I decided to take action and before we all starved to death I walked Main Street looking for a pizza shop which may have remained open. I ambled for about ten blocks before finding a Chinese restaurant. I do believe the proprietor was as pleased to see me as I was him.

Using a company credit card I purchased as much food as they were willing to cook. General Tao's chicken, Moo-goo Gai Pan, egg drop soup, chicken and snow pea pods, and a variety of beef dishes later, the bags were filled to capacity and the bill well over $200. I figured cold Chinese was better than warm water. Mr. Chang offered to drive me back to the office; he managed to drop me very close to the door.

I clamored over a few four-foot snowdrifts, careful not to drop the large box of food. When I reached nicotine alley, now devoid of its usual smoky haze, I used my badge to gain access and called upstairs. Very thankful people came out to help with the bountiful booty I was able to locate. The food was delicious and as we all gathered in the cafeteria, we were thankful to be in a warm building; moreover, the cable TV was still operational.

Downtown looked like a scene of a post-apocalyptic sci-fi movie. There were no people; there were thousands of abandoned cars, some doors ajar, snow filling the passenger compartment. It was odd. I won't say that people flocked to downtown in droves, yet the day after the storm, an eerie silence is all that filled the streets. The sounding train bell as it ran down Main Street was strangely missing, the combined engine sounds of cars gone. There were no sirens bleating down the street, the Doppler effect bending the sound waves as they rushed passed, no murmur of people walking main street, their boots pounding the sidewalks packed with snow. All that found me was silence as intense as it was complete. If questioned I would have agreed that I was the only survivor of the storm.

It was peaceful.

There were no buses present, as public transportation was shut down until the cars could be moved, thus making room for snow removal equipment. The plows would be allowed access to roads removing the snow clearing the way for buses and trains. Ninety-nine percent of all businesses were shut down, including local, state, and federal governmental agencies.

I drew my attention back to the present as Sam opened the bay doors so we could make our escape. Light came from above as the bay opened to its full twenty feet; the incline very steep. Sam maneuvered the van from the subterranean bay like an expert. I wondered how many joy rides had been taken without the company's knowledge. It brought a new aspect to her legit follow the rules personality.

Sam pulled the van to the top of the incline signaling her turn. There were no cars approaching from either the east or the west. Ours was the only vehicle on the street. It was not uncommon for Buffalo to be closed down after 5 p.m. as everyone was home and the drinkers had not yet arrived; that party would start later. More importantly, there were no police cars, no FBI black sedans. We proceeded east on Huron until we reached Oak Street, turning south. Oak Street offers an easy entry onto the 190 South which connected with our ultimate goal: Interstate 90 or the great New York State Thruway, also known as the Governor Thomas E. Dewey Thruway.

The thruway authority named the toll road in 1964, after one of our governors. Before running for office Governor Dewey was in the district attorney's office and made a career out of locking up mobsters. It's ironic the thruway is named after Dewey; as the tolls were to be removed years ago but instead the cost increased. Highway robbery indeed.

We would be on the road for almost three hours before departing at exit thirty-six, then traveling north on Interstate 81. So we had some time to think and go over my contacts that I have accumulated over the last six years as manager of CellNY.

We had not yet reached the 190/90 interchange when I called my boss on his cell phone. Those interested in my activities were aware I was desperate for transportation, transportation that would not be recognized.

As the phone rang, Victor's voice mail picked up and I left the message that I was not dead after all and could I borrow a van. Further, I was heading to Erie for a few days as I needed to clear my head. A feign inside a feign. I did not know if those involved in ruining my perfect day were listening or not, but if it bought us some time I would consider it successful. I knew to request the van was a reach but my boss was very accommodating.

I had worked for Victor Hugo throughout my entire tenure at CellNY. He was fair and he was aware that my direct activities put some huge bonuses in his pocket. Vic was one of the youngest regional directors in the company. He was responsible for all of the markets in New York State; Buffalo, Rochester, Syracuse, and Albany.

Further, we were expanding into Boston. There was talk about consolidating the two offices, ours in Buffalo and the other in Fredrick Maryland into one huge call center that would then serve a six-state area - New York, Massachusetts, Pennsylvania, Maryland, West Virginia, and Virginia. This conglomeration would be managed from Vic's desk.

We had both proven our worth to CellNY. Some of my retention strategies were incorporated into other markets. CellNY was one of many subsidiaries of Cell Southwest. In total, we controlled forty large markets and millions of customers. The Chief Executive Officer of Cell Southwest, Blanche d'Evreux, was due to visit in a few weeks. We were hopeful we would merge completely with Cell South. Once merged and no longer a subsidiary there would be many financial incentives and also the added stability of a being a Fortune 500 company.

In the next month, there would be much to celebrate. Vic would manage the market and I would more or less be his second in command. Together we would be responsible for an extremely large market of current and potential customers. We would be seeking new customers as well. In some ways a promotion for both of us with appropriate remuneration to follow.

Our current situation brought me back to this reality of now. No buying green bananas, no thinking past the next hour. I felt limp like I had gained 50 pounds of fat today. Gravity somehow was affecting me differently than others. Without a thought, I drifted off as the adrenaline had worn off and I crashed hard.

I was soundly sleeping within a few moments. However, the buzzing of my cell phone put an end to my run-away train thoughts and my dreaming of walking Sam down the aisle.

"Hello?" I answered groggily.

"Ryan?"

"Yes. Ed?" Through my brain fog, it sounded like my co-worker.

"Yes," he said quietly. "There is company upstairs asking questions."

I instantly became alert. "FBI Company? Government company?"

"Yes, with locals thrown in for good measure." Ed sounded

scared. I have never seen or heard fear from this man before. It was unnerving.

"Why are you calling?"

"You're in trouble Ryan. They've been following you all day."

"Yeah. By both good guys and bad guys. I was shot. This dying thing kind of ruins your day."

"Get out of town."

"I am trying like its London during the plague."

"I heard them talking," he said, barely above a whisper. "They know about the van. Vic just called them. He thinks you are in trouble."

"I am in trouble. Knee-deep when I woke up and neck deep now and I am standing on my tippy toes. Have they told you what I supposedly know - this dark secret worth killing for?"

"They subpoenaed company records. They wanted to know about how roaming works and cell towers and such."

I shook my head. "They don't know squat; I gave them a crash course today in roaming settings. It fractured their skulls." I let out a bitter laugh. "They think I am a spy."

Despite his whispering, I heard the incredulity in Ed's voice. "Stop it. Why you?"

"Because I did my best not to get killed, and pulled it off," I explained as the line went dead.

Ed's warning had no effect, it did not answer any questions and only solidified my current dilemma. The FBI, rods in hand, using a fisherman knot, had me secured on the line, the lure was being played out. I was overtaken by physical and emotional exhaustion. Contemplation, as it did so many times today, returned. My head was heavy as I leaned against the window of the van. My eyelids felt like lead and closed, losing the battle once more. I was sound asleep within moments.

8

August 18 | 6 p.m.

Sam received a phone call, moments after Ed had disconnected our conversation. I was again roused from a deep sleep. I was privy only to her end. But I could tell she was being evasive answering questions with short answers, glancing sideways at me occasionally.

This is how the conversation ended. "No I haven't seen him since we left the coffeehouse, I'm still at the office. Tell the guard to call me when you enter the front door of the complex."

She looked terrified. She hung up her cell and replaced it in her purse. Without a word or further hesitation, she increased the cruise control to 75 miles per hour.

"The guy you call Fred."

"Yah, what about him?"

"He died. Shot to death."

"I know I was there."

"They are going to pin that on you if you don't cooperate. They have contacted the local news agencies. You're being listed as a person of interest."

"Well, I always wanted to be famous."

She shot a look that told me sarcasm was not working right now. We were passing cars at a greater rate. I looked up and saw exit 48A Pembroke and Route 77, we had barely left Erie county, I had only slept for minutes.

"Whatever you know has pissed off a lot of important folks," Sam said. I could see her hands gripping the steering wheel tightly.

"Who were you talking to," I asked, my voice rough with exhaustion.

"It was Agent Boyle from the FBI. They are no longer buying the innocent bystander story."

"It's not a story, for Christ's sake he was the one who shot Fred. Obviously they are trying to set me up and force my hand."

"Well, they are at Ed's house asking him about your visit today."

"I know Ed called right before they called you."

"You owe him big. It sounds like he doing his best to cover your tracks. They have a multi-agency force headed to your office right now. They want to take you into custody for your own protection."

"Time is running out," I stated in a flat voice. "Let's switch at the next rest area. There should be one coming soon." She looked tired. I understood where such weariness came from. I felt like sleeping for a week. The remainder of today would require both of us to be sharp and any fatigue would lead to mistakes.

I was concerned Boyle was outright lying. I was attempting to understand their motives. I could only surmise about the validity of any forensic evidence. I immediately regretted leaving my soiled clothes with the FBI. They were drenched in Fred's blood and gunshot residue. I wondered if Fred was left on the sidewalk for the local police. Witnesses may notice a few FBI cars parked in a business area, collecting evidence. How long until the FBI "finds" my gore-soaked clothes and hands them over? It would not take much to convince a jury that I was indeed Ryan Prince super-spy, and had managed to gun down evil Fred. I am certain the fact I was handcuffed may be omitted from the proceedings. Technically the only witness to the crime is the one currently doing his best to shift suspicion to me.

The reason for Agent Rocksolid's presence at the coffee-house was now clear: they have a witness that places me in Buffalo, with a fresh set of duds, hours after the horrific murder. Security footage from the office would clearly show me dressed in my normal company garb. Defense item 7: Niagara Falls Casino footage showing Ryan Prince disguised as a tourist. Complete with a new jacket and cap; both items now part of the mountain of evidence that will be utilized to convict me of crimes I did not commit.

While Sam drove silently, I imagine her mind was attempting to understand the enigma our lives have become. I started to wonder if a police officer was truly gunned down, or was it set up entirely for my entertainment. I unconsciously did what they wanted me to do, they have been playing me.

Could it be they were truly convinced I was part of a larger group, that I had co-conspirators?

Anyone who follows my activities for a week would

quickly come to two conclusions: one, if I am part of some grand conspiracy, then most meetings must be scheduled at my house, and two, Ryan Prince likes his regimented life and in fact, is a big bore. I don't have many close friends and my time, every 24-hour period is very easily accounted for.

My mind has reached a logical conclusion. I was caught up in a conspiracy. I was not only the bait but the scapegoat. Even if I lived to see tomorrow, I may spend my remaining fruitful days behind bars. I have yet to hear any explanation as to my involvement in all of this.

Mafia? As strange as it sounds there have always been rumors organized crime controlled much of Buffalo, including the local grocery business. Everyone who had an opinion, which numbers exactly the number who are born with appendices, talk as if it were common knowledge. I have never seen such things take place. Of course, I am not of that ethnic background and work a legitimate job, therefore I am not sure if our paths would cross.

What if I had a few of these fine men in my database? Maybe I connected two of them without realizing the connection had been completed. Often I do rate plan analysis by searching for common addresses, and often pitch our new group plans for these users. Could I have drawn a line between two points that did not want to be connected?

They could assume I had access to call records, which I do, and have discovered something no one wanted to be discovered?

At my feet sat the answer to our problems, I just required about five years to extensively search the files. I have the skills to run some fairly complicated queries; I lacked any background in data analytics. Maybe a place to start such a search will be a query to find a common address for various account numbers.

The big blue sign announcing the next service area was one mile away was illuminated by the last of the daylight. Purple and orange filled the sky ahead of us. Buffalo lay 35 miles to our west and was still under the control of the sun. The sunset was reminding us of the importance of the next few hours. There remained about six hours until the start of a new day. There were many miles on the thruway ahead of us. I couldn't help thinking a miracle was required to stay alive.

My personal beliefs could not make room for miracles. One solves problems through intellect and deduction, sometimes creativity and luck, concrete answers to real problems. It was of the greatest import I discover the truth. It was my only leverage at this point - a rather large fulcrum would be essential to move the balance back to my favor. Imagine the teeter-totter with three large children on one side one small child on the other, the small child hanging perilously in the air, unable to move the three bigger kids, unable to jump off for fear of injury, hanging on until the other children decided to move. Even the good guys were manipulating the scene to their advantage.

If I choose not to cooperate I would be tomorrow's news and I would not be located on B3, I would be on the front page in full-color bold headlines.

Sam signaled and exited the thruway. We followed the sign directing us to the parking lot for passenger cars. McDonald's and their golden arches were located at this rest area. At this hour, the parking lot was strangely empty, only ten other cars parked awaiting their occupants. After being told I was on the fast track for a lead story at eleven I would have been more comfortable had the place been full. There was no one waiting in line.

I realized the van, not belonging to us, had afforded an opportunity to escape Buffalo. However, I am realizing it could very well be a liability. Not many vans in the Rochester area are emblazoned with the ErieOne Mortgage logo. Hesitantly we walked to the building.

George, who prominently wore a badge announcing he was part of the management training program, took our order, and was very friendly as if trying to set an example for the others. We purchased the food without incident as my mug had yet to make it on the local news. Aiding our cause was the fact that the only TV was fifteen feet away and tuned to MTV, which at the moment was playing a video for some band I have never heard of, and after watching thirty seconds of the video, I was pleased with my ignorance.

We arrived and left without making a ripple, not turning a single head. The gas attendant was staring at Sam, but that had nothing to do with my status with the FBI. That occurs during most of our public appearances. She was smartly dressed and her ensembles worked magic, extenuating her curves in all of the right places.

The van was only down five gallons however, we may need to divert our itinerary without much notice, and having a few extra gallons could be the difference between success and failure.

Sam tucked her feet under herself, curling up on the passenger seat, seemingly very comfortable and content. She was asleep moments after our departure. I was jealous as my size does not make sleeping in this van comfortable.

"Is the van painted or is it a vinyl wrap?"

"I am not sure why that is important right now," she said groggily. I could understand that feeling.

"Well, if it's a vinyl wrap, it can be easily removed. Paint would offer an entirely different option."

"Oh, I see, take off the wrap and we are just a white van."

"Exactly"

I pulled through the gas station. On the right, there was an area for trucks. A safe place for a trucker to pull over and grab some sleep. Also, there was little lighting. I found a place with deep shadows. It was deep twilight; the moon had yet to dominate the sky. I got out to take a look.

Upon close inspection, the van was indeed encased in a vinyl wrap. I cursed myself for not having a jackknife at my disposal. But a search of the van yielded a more useful tool - a box cutter. I started at the rear of the van. Once the vinyl wrap was compromised, the removal process was easy. Within ten minutes, the van was back to its factory imposed conformity. We were now driving the most non-descript vehicle one could operate, a plain white van.

I apologized to Sam, as I was certain that customization was not cheap. I got back in the driver's seat and moved towards the Interstate. Although I could have used some sleep, my energy was renewed. We just might make it to Watertown after all. There was a huge pile of vinyl now occupying the cargo bay of the van. I could dispose of that at the cabin.

There on the floor between us, sat the laptop. Either my savior or my mortal enemy. Can it provide answers or just produce more questions, leaving me with nothing, no more knowledge, no understanding, I hope just not dead?

I roughly meet face-to-face with twenty customers a week. There are not a lot of repeats. Also, I speak with another forty a week over the phone. I figured that puts me about twelve per day. There were over 25,500 recorded customer contacts. Having the database in Access allowed me to do a quick search by each data field.

The most recent entries would be the place to begin. This whole affair must have been prompted by recent events or some recent contact. The last six weeks would be a focal point. I doubted that someone I met two years ago has any bearing on today's events.

Of course, I failed to have added a field that read, "Customer will one day ruin your perfect day" or simply "Criminal". Next time I will know better.

Having some plan of action brought about a sense of accomplishment to this crazy day. I felt productive; I was being proactive. This was my first strike back, my only chance to make it to August 19 still in one piece.

If I'm fortunate enough to make some connection, to find this link between my database and some customer, what then? Do I obtain a handgun and shoot the bastard in the head, dumping his body in the mighty Niagara? Or go to the police?

By the time I could explain everything I discovered: I will either be taken to the nearest looney bin or be collecting social security when released from prison. These decisions will be made when I reach that destination, at this point if I find anything at all I can use to my advantage I'll be thrilled. There was finally a starting point in the preverbal search for the needle in the haystack.

The road waned behind us, traffic was light - mostly truckers sharing the road tonight. I have made this trip so often it was almost second nature, blindfolded I can still complete the trip. My mind drifted off, wandering when confronted by some much activity. My thoughts returned to my parents and family.

The New York State Thruway was not the most exciting of trips. The road was mostly in a straight line from Buffalo to Syracuse. There were no majestic mountains or scenic overlooks. While I ensured the van was steady in my lane, that I followed none of the other cars too closely, my mind wandered off the beaten path. Glancing at the standard AM/FM radio, I wished I was driving my Subaru. My car was equipped with satellite radio and I carried a collection of compact disks from my favorite bands. Their entire collection fit in the CD wallet hanging from the driver side visor, numbering seventeen. I was thankful those CDs were copies - the originals were at the apartment. I would only have to recopy all of my favorites, the music was still stored on my desktop computer.

As I flipped through the stations, I was unable to find one to my liking. And when I was fortunate to find a song or two I liked, the signal would deteriorate, and the songs were lost to static. The Yankees were playing today and the game would be transmitted on the local Buffalo sports talk station. I knew I could hold the signal until we reached exit forty. I fiddled with the dial and found the game on WGRZ 550, and with the play by play as background noise, my mind continued its aimless ways.

I have shared most of my past with Sam, as I wanted her to know how my experiences shaped who I am now. To know my history is to know me, I am not a man of mystery and don't pretend to be, what you see is what you get.

I had an uneventful childhood. My parents were kind and my sisters pushed me around until hormones set in and I grew eight inches in one year. But there were no tragedies, no beatings, and no scars on my body, or being, or soul. I never felt afraid of my parents - respectful yes, but never fearful. It was not a perfect childhood, as I believe no such thing exists. But the fond memories far outweighed the darker ones.

We were a rather large family. I grew up with three sisters and without the camaraderie of a brother. My parents worked hard, my mother was a nurse before nurses earned what they were worth. My dad worked at the local flooring and textile factory from the time he was eighteen until he turned fifty-three. We were not rich, although we were comfortable, and certainly, we never went hungry. We did a lot of family activities, like going to the movies together, camping once a year, and spent the weekends together doing whatever we could to entertain ourselves. In hindsight, those were the most enjoyable times of my life.

There were the usual normal bouts of rebellion during my

teenage years. And the usual dose of sibling rivalry was present, along with vows to never again converse with my oldest sisters, until either the Grand Canyon filled to the brim, or Hell suffered an ice age. But that was in the past. Over our adult years we were closer than ever and the atrocities we visited on each other during those formative years forgotten.

We did not bring up the past unless it involved laughter, or to embarrass someone who had the courage to bring a date to a family event.

My mother, God bless her soul, taught us all that humor cures many ills, and sarcasm allows us to laugh instead of cry. She also taught us to laugh at the world so you can learn to laugh at yourself. As I have said before, the sarcasm gene runs rampant throughout our family, and I believe my mother carried the defective gene first.

When we were young my father was doing shift work. He did not always share our sense of humor. As with the rest of us, now he is different, as time had worked its magic. He is my best friend and confidant. I love the man.

These thoughts always started at the same place and sought the same destination. I often wondered what had happened during those same formative years with Sam. She spoke very little about her family or friends. All I know is her mother's name was Jean Saint Claire and Sam resembled her somewhat. There was some event in her younger years that made her tough and stubborn, sometimes very independent. When she spoke about her past, it was with a venom that would kill a rattlesnake. Her beautiful face would transform into this rigid mask, one she constructed to keep the world at bay.

There were moments when even I could not penetrate her defenses. She gave me room when it was required and I had often paid back the favor. I never probed, never asked, unless given the opportunity. All I could surmise was that some tragedy had befallen my love. She had mentioned her mother only twice to me in three years; her father never entered the conversation, not on a single occasion. She never uttered his name good or bad. She made no mention of birthdate or wedding anniversary, or any other date of significance as if she believed she sprang forth from an egg.

My parents both played such a vital role in who I am, and in my life, I could not conceive a fight or argument breaking that very special bond. I am not saying we do not have our differences on a variety of topics; however, there could be nothing regardless, of the topic that could, for more than a week, keep me from communicating with mom and dad. This is not some sort of shortcoming in my own makeup, this has nothing to do with my own independence or my need, this was interdependence. We all needed each other in our lives, we needed to feel part of a greater whole. It was this love that kept us grounded. My personal toolbox was without the needed implements to understand this day; it also lacked the tools to understand Sam from this perspective. I could not understand how she could cut her parents from her life unless one of those unforgivable issues had occurred. That list is not long but boils the acid in my stomach. I have often thought about it, thought maybe her father was "inappropriate with her" and her mother let it happen. My life without my folks and my sisters would be quite hollow and different.

Sam would sit and listen to me tell stories of growing up, of Saturday nights and Michigan Rummy, of family movie nights, and of countless family gatherings. She enjoyed hearing about my extended clan. My father had three brothers and a sister and my mother had three sisters. Our family, when gathered, was quite formidable. We all grew up in central Pennsylvania and lived in the same city.

The family would gather for funerals and weddings, graduations and baptisms, and when I was in college, we were one hundred and ten strong. What I considered mundane family matters would fascinate Sam for hours. She also knew we all kept in touch via the Internet, and while some of us had moved from the old homestead we were still close emotionally.

I could not tell you if Sam had any family I knew nothing of cousins, brothers, or sisters. She had chosen to lock up her past someplace deep inside. I believe this to be a necessary evil but have not verified that.

The only personal history she has ever shared covered the last few years of her life. Not that knowing what someone did when they were three is all that important, but Sam has erased the first eighteen years of her life.

Sam moved to western New York when she was nineteen years old. She spent her formative years in Southern California. I am not cognizant of why she chose Buffalo, but one night she admitted the distance was as necessary as chemo to a cancer patient.

After spending a few months at the youth hostel and learning the lay of the land, she answered an advertisement for a roommate. She was accepted and moved into her new apartment a week later.

Sam shared an apartment on the Elmwood strip with four other females. She did not enjoy the experience. Unlike her new friends, she did not frequent the local bars, she scraped and saved every last dime like she wouldn't earn another. Further, she was not wrapped up in the dating lives of her housemates. Her focus on the non-drinking, non-dating conversation caused much derision in her household. Her stay on Elmwood Ave was far from enjoyable.

She found a job working in customer service with the local bus company, and after just a few months, was offered a promotion. This allowed her to find a studio apartment of her own. It was tiny, barely two rooms, complete with the smallest galley kitchen ever seen. And it was missing the four other yapping females.

The quiet thrilled her, the silence a symphony. She was able to concentrate on what she deemed important. Plus, she hadn't heard anyone vomiting in a toilet or trash can in months.

After a year of calling western New York home, she was able to apply to the University of Buffalo and receive the same discounted rates of permanent residents. Not only was Sam accepted but was awarded a large scholarship. And despite what may have occurred during her younger days, her studies never faltered. She continued to work full time and handle a large course load, maintaining a 3.8-grade average. Sam majored in accounting and held a concentration in computer technology.

Her choice of majors spoke to the person she had become as an adult and may aid in understanding who she truly was. Her interest in accounting and information technology was simple, numbers are easy to fix, mistakes easily remedied, and, computers are logical, devoid of all emotion.

I have learned Sam prefers solitude to being sociable. She strays from large groups; and while she does not avoid contact with other people, she does avoid the emotional baggage that comes from forming acquaintances. Very much like myself. Sam was not one of those people who had twenty friends. She knew a lot of people. She just chose to keep them at arm's length.

She told me once "you cannot always fix what's wrong with life. But you can always find the mistake in the ledger, you can always reprogram a computer, there is just no reset button on life."

Sam graduated from college in three years and immediately entered the MBA program at the University of Buffalo. While she attended graduate school, she kept her customer service job and was given different promotions until she was the lead supervisor on the night shift.

She completed her MBA in record time; she then applied for her job with ErieOne Mortgage as a front line customer service representative. While it was a demotion in title over her last job, she received a large increase in her salary. She also knew she would be able to work her way through the ranks. Within the course of a year, she was running the place.

I do not know if Sam's ambition and drive was a coping mechanism for something she had lost, or to perhaps it was a way to clench her fist, pointing it west in victory and pronouncing for all to hear "I told you so."

Sam is a proud person, yet she does not wear it for others to see. Hers is a quiet pride. This is partially due to the fact she does not display her life for others to view. She is private, which only makes me feel very special to share her life.

When things began to turn to more serious, and our relationship grew, some of my cousins began to email Sam. She enjoyed her first taste of family; she waited for their emails and was prompt in her response.

My oldest sister, Claire, was close to Sam; she spoke to Claire more often than I did. I loved to see the delight on her face when she would reiterate, word-for-word, the conversation that had just taken place. To witness Sam interacting with the Prince extended clan was very satisfying. It was odd as well. I had grown up in this environment, thinking that every family, everywhere, was like ours. That love and respect and togetherness was the theme, there was no one cowering in the corner, or having to hide the scars of physical abuse. Watching Sam interact with my relatives was like watching a caveman witness fire for the first time.

For everything she has given me daily, the fact I am in her life at all, giving her the gift of family is only starting to pay back my debt. I know we are closer because of it. My joy is her pain. My family a reminder of what she had lost. She could be bitter about it, insisting I spend my energies solely on her. However, she understands that my family bond gives me strength, and had she confronted me about it, she would be the one to lose.

There are people in this world that are bitter for no reason. These are the people who never have had a good day; their world is out to spoil their fun. They complain about the heat in the summer and the cold in the winter. These are the people who give an honest answer to the world's greatest rhetorical question, "how are you today?" These people are thrilled to share their daily misadventures, maladies, family issues, and maybe everything that ever has gone wrong in their lives. They never share anything positive. They could win the lottery and spend months complaining about the taxes. I find it difficult to converse with these people, I find it impossible to have them in my presence. They are a disease. Their goal is simple: destroy any positivity, combat joy, and kill happiness. They do not, or cannot, bring joy into their own lives. Their survival depends on eliminating it completely.

This list of unhappy people, often as long as the one Saint Peter has at his disposal, are many of the people in my contact database. They are, by and far, my least favorites. If you could design a cell phone that could clean your house, they would complain the dishes still had spots.

There are people who are bitter but for a profound reason. These people often had experienced great pain and loss. They wear it on their sleeves. Thinking that God awakens every day to ruin their lives. You often think they would get better with some professional help. I am not sure if they could ever know happiness. The grim, the bad luck, the loss, is all they know in the world. They wear it like a badge. I often feel sorry for these people, as much as I cannot understand their point of view. I try to remain upbeat and positive. I don't tend to worry about things that I can't fix – I choose to concentrate on those I can. These people often view me as a fraud – how could someone possibly have such a positive outlook. They prefer to think of it as an act, instead of embracing it.

Then there are people who have every right to be bitter but are not. They turn tragedy and disarray into happiness and joy. These people, like Sam, take what the world gives them. And no matter the circumstances, they walk with chin held high. Sam is like this. I see her sometimes succumbing to that other world, her mask at the ready. But she fights it, fights it until she knows she is in charge. A great man once said life is not what happens to you, life is how you react. Sam is a lemonade maker. I just wish I knew what had happened to her. It may give me some insight. But it's none of my business until she decides to share. We often see these people after some tragedy has befallen them. Like the man who loses both of his arms on the battlefield, yet comes home and has nothing but a smile to offer the world, overcome with gratitude that he still breaths. I have met people that have overcome such tremendous handicaps.

I have such a customer. Her name is Rose Lion. She is 100 percent visually impaired. Her mother and father took turns beating her when she was only three years old. She cried too much. Their constant beatings, and a brain in its early developmental stage, caused complications in her adult years. The bones that were broken numerous times are far from fully functional. One arm ceased growing when she was twelve. It hangs uselessly from her body, like a dead branch on a tree. Her optic nerves were so damaged by the savagery of her parents, they no longer worked. She was totally blind in one eye. I had the pleasure of sitting with her for an hour, walking her through every feature on her phone, aiding her with her setup, and adding phone numbers. She calls me once in a while to chat. I do not rush her off the phone and truly enjoy conversing with her.

Last year she was hit by a van while she and her guide dog were walking through an intersection. The driver fourteen years old and drunk at 4 p.m., took away her ability to walk, fracturing, beyond repair, both of her legs. I remember reading the story in the City Region section and I was moved to tears. Despite this horrible incident, Rose was back at work after only missing one month. She operates an advocacy group for handicapped teenagers and college students. She started the business with her own money and has substantially grown her business with charitable donations.

Since her accident, the proceeds from a civil suit were immense. She no longer runs just a business; she expanded her group into an institution.

Rose enjoys talking with those employed in white-collar jobs about perseverance and overcoming life's little pitfalls. She once gave a speech to four different groups of sales personnel from various companies. The topic of the speech was staying positive in today's world. After her ninety-minute speech not only was there no dry eyes, she increased her employee pool by four.

Everyone should be required to spend some time with this

very special person. You can learn a lot. It speaks to the fable concerning the man with no shoes who meets a man with no feet. Rose has no legs and one eye yet can see possibilities and beauty where those of us with limited vision see difficulty.

My cell phone was ringing. The incoming call breaking me from my thoughts.

"Are you going to answer that or should I?" Sam asked, sleep still apparent in her voice.

"Yes, please," I said and she handed me the cell phone. I answered without even checking the number.

"Yes?"

"Mr. Prince."

"That's me."

"Where are you going Mr. Prince?"

A shot of adrenaline and paranoia coursed through my body. I became instantly awake. "Who is this please?"

"Nobody you want to know."

"How did you get this number?"

"We all have connections, Mr. Prince."

"My name is Ryan. Why did you call me?'

"You need me Ryan."

"Need you for what?"

"I have information. I know the secret. Read the papers, Ryan, it is in the papers. The national papers Ryan. I know why they are after you; I know what bit of knowledge you have locked away in that head of yours. I want to help you, Ryan."

Was there really someone who was interested in saving my

life? "Why do you want to help? No one has offered me any assistance. Why you?"

"There are forces at work that you don't understand. Forces that have broken with the government. Forces who have their own agenda."

"Enlighten me then." I wanted to understand; I hungered for more information.

"The time is not right. When the time comes, I will inform you to the fullest. Remember you have a friend. Someone looking out for your interests."

"What do you perceive as my interests?"

"You're a man that caught up in something and all you want is for this to be over so you can return to your life and your plans with your lovely fiancé."

"Just make sure I am still breathing tomorrow." The line went dead. Did I really just have a conversation with someone who was an ally? Upon whom I could depend on when the time came?

"Who was that?" Sam asked, rousing from her deep sleep.

"I am not sure. He said he was a friend." I looked at the phone as if it could dispel the mystery. The number on my call log read private. No help at all.

"Well, what did he want?" She asked, her tone of voice betraying her annoyance.

"I don't know really. He didn't give me a name. He said he had information and that I should look in the national papers. There would be a story giving me a clue to discover what I don't know. He also said we could count him as an ally. He's on our side."

"What in the hell is that supposed to mean?"

"Your guess is as good as mine. There's another service area up ahead. Let's stop and pick up some papers. He also seemed to know a lot about us. He called you my fiancé. I have told no one about this except for the FBI."

"Okay," she stretched the sleep from her bones "I need to stretch my legs and get some coffee. Maybe there is a link between a story and someone in your database."

"I hope it's that easy."

We stopped for gas at a service area just outside of Geneva. You know gas prices are high when rest stop gas station prices seem reasonable. We had only traveled about 50 miles and the tank was not empty; again, I would rather have full tank than have to worry about stopping to fill up when bullets are flying.

The attendant did not look twice at me. I could have been his favorite rock star; however, his face was stuck in a fantasy football magazine, scratchpad close at hand. He was too engrossed in trying to fill out his roster to pay much attention to us.

Still, paranoia was setting in again. Was there such a disorder as intermittent paranoia? The FBI felt it necessary to publically report I am the one who killed poor Fred, even though they are well aware that was not the case.

Is it the FBI field office in Buffalo stating that I had gone rogue, as my mysterious caller had warned? Or was it nothing more than a bluff, trying to convince Sam to help bring me in? And when it looks as if she might not be able to aid them in their endeavors, the threats begin. I am aware through firsthand experience they are not above making idle threats, as they had thrown a variety in my direction.

This very moment they could be sending my photo to all the normal outlets. The New York State Police, other FBI offices (I think there are four others), the local sheriff's office in Buffalo, and media outlets as well. The gas pump abruptly stopped and I pulled myself to the present. I paid the attendant in cash and he handed me my change without breaking his constant stare.

I started the van and drove it back to where the convenience store and restroom were located. Sam jumped out to use the bathroom. I went to pick up some papers and grab some coffee and sodas.

Sam was not awaiting my arrival so I went inside to meet her. I also had to pee. This rest stop was similar to all the others along the thruway. There were two fast-food restaurants, a yogurt stand, a coffee store, a convenience store, and of course, restrooms.

I quickly took care of my business and I exited the restrooms. Sam was nowhere in sight. I checked at the Dunkin Donuts. She wasn't there. It seemed as each restaurant competed for customers by smell as much as by habit. The aroma of freshly cooked hamburgers, fried foods, and coffee diffused in the air. It was neither pleasant nor enjoyable: It was an assault on the senses.

I could have called her on her cell phone but I had left mine in the van. Standing in the middle of the main room I could see the entrance, Dunkin Donuts, and the convenience store. I slowly rotated in a tight circle, trying to survey the entire building in each rotation, trying my best to locate her quickly. Suddenly I could not remember how long I had been standing there spinning like a slow-motion top attempting to locate my betrothed. The clock in my brain told me I had spent an exorbitant amount of time. I immediately turned on my heel and ran out of the building.

The van was missing. It was not parked where I had left it. I again stood there slacked jawed, disbelieving, trying my best to deny what my optic nerves were correctly recording. Not that August 18 would ever be known as a banner day in the life one Ryan Prince, but losing two cars in less than 24 hours was rather irritating. Having two cars stolen in less than 24 hours seems as if the universe very well may be out to get me.

Basically everything I had left was in that van, my cell phone, my money, and Sam's laptop. They had found us before I could make 70 miles. They found us and now they have Sam. I do not have the laptop, I don't have Sam. I have nothing. It was over.

9

August 18 | 6:30 p.m.

My legs were no longer capable of supporting my weight. I collapsed onto the sidewalk outside the rest stop wondering how I could be so stupid. I had left the keys in the van without a second thought. I was going inside to meet Sam and we would then leave. My extended stay allowed someone to steal the car. I am not sure if this criminal pledged allegiance to the FBI or the FED (Fred's evil dudes), either way, it mattered not.

As if mocking me, seventy-five yards away, just on the other side of the parking lot, was a State Police station. If the FBI had truly listed me as a person of interest, I would sign my own death warrant by soliciting their help. But if it was an idle threat I could be alright.

I stood up, finding the necessary strength, shaky legs and all, bent on turning myself in. I hoped my sacrifice would ultimately help Sam stay alive. Once I was back under guard I hoped they would free her.

One shaky step followed by another I somehow traversed to the half-way point. My head hung low hands stuffed in pockets. I had given up my fight. Was it my own stubbornness or something else? Could I have done something different like involve the authorities' sooner? Or maybe stay at the FBI instead of leaving?

So engrossed in my own self-pity and feeling defeated, I paid little attention to the traffic in and out of the parking lot. I was not paying close attention to the revving of car engines or the squeal of brakes. My head was focused more on the texture of the parking lot then the movement of traffic.

I was run over by an unwary motorist.

At that moment, I truly did not care. My death, hopefully like my incarceration, should guarantee Sam's freedom and safety.

I hit my head on the hood and slid to the ground, striking my nose on either the pavement or a protruding auto body part. My nose was a bloody mess within seconds. My head was spinning.

There was a movie running through my brain, my overactive brain, one that featured Sam tied to a chair, muscled men, and Agent Rocksolid taking turns beating her. She was bloodied. Her black hair thick with sweat and blood; her constant pleas ignored. This sequence became more gruesome every time it restarted. I could hear her plead our innocence. Those men chose not to hear. Granted, I know I have an imagination on overdrive. I began to consider if this room was looming, approaching us faster than we could run. Could I avoid the room? Would I be beaten until my face was fat with swelling, unrecognizable, blood from every orifice draining profusely? I would give myself up to ensure Sam's freedom.

10

August 18 | 7:30 p.m.

I could feel more than one set of hands lifting me off the pavement. The metallic taste returned, blood staining yet another shirt. This shirt was an FBI issue so I didn't care. I was trying my best to get to the State Police station.

"Are you okay?"

I waved my hand, not caring who was speaking. "I'm fine, I just need a towel. My nose is bleeding."

"Out of my way, get out of my way now!" My concussion-addled mind was playing tricks on me. It sounded like Sam trying to cut through the crowd.

"That's the chick that hit him." Said another bystander.

"Yeah, she hit this guy, he was just walking in the parking lot." Said someone else.

Sam managed to get through the crowd, helping me to my feet, handing me a stack of napkins she had located. The crowd began to disperse after she had made it very clear that she was with me, and I walked into the car. Since the situation changed from a potential lawsuit to a potentially horrible domestic situation, those in attendance ran fast.

My head was clear again, the bleeding began to quell. I felt well enough to stand. I also had some questions that needed some serious answers.

"What the fuck were you doing? You were walking around like you didn't care. Like you had given up. I honked the horn three times before I realized it was you. I hardly had time to stop then you literally walked into the car."

I looked at her, hands-on-hips, eyes flashing. I was happy to bear the brunt of her anger. "I got gas, drove back to the rest stop so I could use the bathroom and catch up with you. After using the bathroom, I could not find you, and when I left the van was gone. I assumed that one of our new friends had taken it."

For a moment, she was taken aback. "I am so sorry are you alright?"

"I will be but I need a new shirt. I could think of nothing but turning myself in the hopes they would let you go."

"Who's they?"

"They as in Fred's people."

"Oh that they. I wasn't taken by anyone. You overreacted, ah, a little."

Now I was angry. I thought she was gone. "Then where were you? I was looking all over the place," I said tersely. "New rule. Cell phones with us at all times. Rule two. No more splitting up." I was not in the mood for an argument and made sure my tone of voice conveyed that.

"Accepted. I left the ladies' room and purchased these papers," Sam said, holding the bag proudly in the air. "Then walked out the back door nearest the gas station, and much to my surprise, no van. I walked around the front just in time to see a state police officer ready to write a ticket. I was angry at you for parking in a no-parking zone. I moved the van to avoid a ticket. I then saw you walking across the parking lot, head hung low. I beeped the horned repeatedly and you didn't notice. I pulled in front of you to get your attention."

Well, you got it alright. I moved towards the van. "Let's get out of here before we start leaving impressions."

"Ryan, are you all right? You are not yourself today."

I nodded. "I'm fine now. I really thought that you were gone. For good. I couldn't get the picture of you out of my head. I could see them killing you."

"Where were you going?"

"I was turning myself in to save you."

Sam looked at me, not knowing if I was dealing my normal level of bullshit or deadly serious.

"You're right. No more separation from this point forward. We stick together. Right?"

"Right."

Sam purchased four papers from the newsstand inside the rest stop: The Washington Post, the New York Times, The Buffalo Evening News, and the Toronto Star.

She was quick to point out our mysterious ally did not specify which national paper, but it wouldn't hurt our search to get a different perspective. Also, Toronto was only two hours from Buffalo.

Although we did not purchase any green bananas, we did add to the basic plan conceived at the Mug Stop. One, don't die. Two, run like hell. Three, stop for some different clothes. Four, find some commonality between all the papers. Then, with any luck, our search would produce a name I could run through the database, thus gain the one bit of leverage to use against our adversaries.

Our research could turn up enough information so we could go to the FBI for protection, instead of wondering when they would list me on America's Most Wanted.

We were very fortunate the area's largest outlet center was a mere five miles from the rest stop, offering a huge selection of clothing. And hey, we could save a few bucks in the process. It also should be very busy on a Friday night, creating the requisite camouflage to cover our shopping.

We will choose a store, buying only the essentials, and then run for Sand Lake. To the cabin and a bit of solitude. A chance to hide and to catch our collective breaths and assess the situation. Deep, relaxing, cleansing breaths, in through the nose, out through the mouth. After our collective exhale, we would combine our resources and attempt to solve the puzzle. Well, actually solving is not as necessary as piecing together enough data to at least form a coherent picture.

My family are puzzle people. When we weren't playing Michigan Rummy, we were taking turns, gathered around a card table solving puzzles, piece by piece. Our favorites were two-sided puzzles and photo mosaic puzzles. Each offered their own challenges.

Now I just was lacking the box top, to get an overview of the puzzle. I also lacked the lucky table and three other enthusiasts.

Sam was piloting the car, uncertain of my abilities after banging my head on the hood. As we rounded a lengthy curve on Route 414, a sign announced the Finger Lakes Outlet was up ahead.

The enormous factory outlet mall was just a few miles from the exit. We could complete our shopping and hop right back onto the thruway without wasting much time.

The outlet had over one hundred stores and a parking lot the size of four football fields. You could buy everything from sneakers to Corning Ware, from bras to leather jackets, from speakers to cologne. We chose one of the many clothing outlets to purchase some jeans and tee shirts. We were not looking for fashionable attire; just some things to see us through. We found a parking space within the enormous lot. I couldn't form a reasonable estimate as to the number of cars, buses, and vans parked within its confines.

Our target was closest to our parking space and offered all we required. I was extremely self-conscious about the mess on my shirt. I tried my best to ignore the drying goo as it felt sticky against my skin. I wore a smile instead of a grimace as I held the door, allowing Sam access to the store.

I, of course, garnered much attention with my bloodied shirt. Sam told at least four different cover stories while we made our progress through the store.

The store was not that large and many young people ran about, stocking shelves and chatting amongst themselves at a rate that was hard to comprehend. I took no more than two minutes grabbing two pairs of jeans and two t-shirts, neither one white. We had no issues finding what we wanted and were able to purchase everything we needed in a short time. Unlike most others I had dated, Sam was not a believer in the all-day shopping trip. She added to our haul two t-shirts, a sweatshirt, and a pair of jeans to the order. One employee was so moved by Sam's story, he allowed me to wear the shirt before completing our transaction. He also gave me a bag for my bloodied shirt. I had no intention of leaving it behind. I did not intend to lay a trail of bread crumbs for anyone to follow.

As we were cashing out, the young female cashier kept glancing at me as if she were trying to figure out if we had met previously.

"You look familiar," she said, snapping her gum at a higher than socially acceptable level.

"I get that a lot," I said, smiling and looking as unconcerned as I could muster.

"Anything else?" she asked, handing me my change. "No, thanks, have a nice day." We leisurely walked out of the store.

My earlier thought about preparedness made another run through my brain. At this point, I had unconsciously created a list of things I would need the next time I woke up dead.

The food court was all of 100 feet from the clothing store. I entered the men's room. The harsh light revealed a face only loved by the one who bore it. Two dark eyes looked back at me through the silvered surface, the circles under each a deep purple. My nose was swollen, and the right side of my face was dominated by a bluish reddish scab that was inflamed.

Turning both faucets on high, waiting for the mixing water to reach a desirable temperature, I removed my shirt. It occurred to me another personal record was breached twice today. I had broken my nose to the extent that it caused me to expand my wardrobe. Twice I was locked in a trunk, and twice I almost died. I should be recording these feats for Guinness.

I was alone in the bathroom. Carefully I turned my attention back to the mirror, spending a moment or two washing my face, ensuring that no blood was left behind that would cause someone to take notice.

My plain face again may be an advantage after all, as it blends well with any crowd, I deemed myself able and ready to face the next challenge.

I spotted my mangled face once more. It was not hard to notice. I might be able to blend in with a group of trick or treaters, but its only August.

Sam was sitting at a booth with a tall glass of soda. We wasted no time returning to the van. The cashier seemingly remembering my face had me worried once again. It could have been simply a coincidence but I was not willing to take that chance. Exiting the parking lot as quickly as possible without seeming to be in a hurry, the trail back to the Thruway was very easy, as the route was well-marked.

We had only lost about thirty minutes and we were back on the Thruway quickly. Our trip, once sidetracked, was now back on schedule, the van heading east. Sam trusted me enough to drive, yet she was not curled up on the front seat. She was very attentive about the traffic and my handling of the van. She looked at me the same way I have seen fathers watch their teenage daughters when they were behind the wheel gaining experience.

The man on the phone left me feeling anxious, the hairs standing at attention on my arm and the back of my neck. It occurred to me a third party was following my activities. I did not know what school of thought my new friends attended, the "why can't we kill this guy" school, or the "let's hang him out as bait" school, or maybe he prescribed to the "let's follow him find out what he knows then kill him" school.

Although the last few hours had passed without serious incidents, the tightness had returned once again. The stress, the running, the fear of losing Sam. I was unsure if I possessed the required fortitude to make it through the day. I am not a coward. I have proven that today. I have faced my mortality head-on. Truly, who is equipped for a day like this one? For a Marine, this day is probably nothing more than another day that ends with a "y". But the training they receive is much more intense than customer management training. I may be developing an ulcer.

Also, it was very perplexing that someone would be lending me aid. It did not quite fit with what little facts I had today. Moreover, I was wondering if my mug had indeed been given to the media. The interaction with the cashier had heated up my paranoia radar once again. I was fed up with the "let's play games with this guy" philosophy, why not come clean. Just say X and Y are in your database under Mr. and Mrs. John Smith. They are in charge of the RWS, or the infamous Runs with Scissors, a discrete underground covert operation.

I was not in the mood for games. I wanted someone to sit down and explain the facts, explain why I am here in a van running for my life, wondering if everyone other than Sam was conspiring to ruin my day. It was difficult to discern who was what, who wanted what, and who thought I expendable. Who thought I was of value, and of course, why. Why! My stomach was in a vise grip, painful, searing. I screamed inside, a feral scream. It did little to alleviate my discomfort.

I enjoy solving a variety of puzzles, whether picture, logic, or mathematic. But I do not like to be toyed with. I failed to understand what they gained.

Fred's group clearly wanted me dead. So what's the harm in telling me this secret, this knowledge that I possess yet do not see its importance. One would think that my ignorance of this "knowledge" would be a loophole. Had I done something which indicated I was aware, consciously or intentionally, of making connections that place others in harm's way? If I do not know, what they think I know, today has been a complete waste of time.

The FBI had clearly tailed Fred and his party - they had recordings of partial transmissions. I did not lead them to Fred, Fred led them to me. If they were more forthcoming with information, I might be able to direct them. This person, my new friend, he, too, had an agenda. Can he be trusted? Does he truly know the secret? Or is he here to drag me out of hiding, to bring me into the light? Or maybe he has set a trap for the other two?

The more I try to understand the further I am from an epiphany. It is hard enough to discern the motives of my fiancé whom I have known for longer than three years, how I am to comprehend the motive of three separate groups of such people?

If I weren't driving, I may have smacked myself up against

the head. Duhhhhh, who says there are three? The FBI knows a lot about Fred but was unwilling to share any information - retrieve and extract but not share. What if they were not seperate groups after all? What if they were the rogue group the caller had warned me about? Maybe Fred was not operating within the confines of FBI jurisdiction. Would this Boyle guy shoot Fred because he got out of hand? Fred was about to put a bullet in me and that may not have jived with Boyle's plans. It seemed extremely unlikely, but right now any theory at this point was a sound theory. This mystery man, he may indeed be part of the bureaucracy of the FBI. He is either in charge or a paper pusher that has had the answer mistakenly delivered to his desk. This man is FBI.

There were many resources expended on my behalf today. Although the FBI does not have unlimited resources, I am certain there are resources available at moment's notice. I was thinking my complex puzzle had just been reduced from 1000 pieces to 10.

I prayed that my latest partner to this insane dance was indeed correct. That the secret was in the papers and in my database. That way I had a chance, an outside chance, but a chance nonetheless. Again, where to start the search.

I know of four customers in the database with strong political ties outside of Buffalo. One was a congressman; he had an account with us and an account with our sister company in Virginia. The other two were legislative aides for a congressman, and the other a State Assemblyman. There was one Buffalo Sabre and two members of the Buffalo Bills. I could not imagine why they would be tied up in this mess. The two legislative aides and the congressman both were squeaky-clean. The congressman was a Republican who garnered support from both parties and his constituents loved him.

I certainly did not have any fields in my database marked informants, hates children, or kicks dogs. I was certain the paper would not be highlighted in bright neon yellow with, "hey Ryan look here" - big arrow pointing the way.

My mind was racing to make sense of it all. Possibly, someone I had a ten-minute conversation with is the cause of the day's festivities. It did not seem plausible. It still was easier to believe they were out to get someone else and I was drawn into this nightmare. Unfortunately, there was no waking from this dream. I have left two men dead in my wake. Granted, one had it coming.

I was thinking of the novel the Butterfly Effect, where the death of one butterfly by time travelers has immense consequences when they return to the future.

I meet with one person that was in hiding or did not wish to be seen, could it be that they were supposed to be dead? Potentially someone in the Witness Protection Program? One customer contact out of the thousands I have recorded in my database might be the cause of two men's deaths. Could it be someone that I spoke to about a voice mail problem or erroneous charges on their monthly bill? Could I have somehow extracted a secret so powerful to cause deaths and threaten national security? It was absurd. It made no sense. Even if I had stumbled upon a person in the Witness Protection Program, and I somehow had blown their cover, wouldn't the US Marshalls just relocate said person with a new identity?

I was not out to reconnoiter the secretive lives of our customers. My sole goal was retaining customers and service their needs to the fullest of my ability. In the end, maintain the profitability of CellNY.

I was a problem solver by nature, and by solving problems, I created lifetime customers of CellNY. Even if by chance I met with someone who did not want to be found, someone hiding out, someone that had secrets and a boneyard of skeletons hidden in their closets, it was not my MO to ask a lot of unnecessary questions. Determine the problem, solve the problem, negotiate proper compensation. The anatomy of customer retention.

I was not handing out twenty-page questionnaires, delving into their daily rituals or habits. I never probed into their personal lives. Of course, there were customers that choose to share some of their lives with me, some of the oldest entries in my database, these customers shared a little of their lives because they had nothing to hide, nothing that would find two people dead and me on the run.

Instead, I was left with 25,000 entries and one of those customers had secrets, secrets so severe as to force my hand and cause the events of today to unfold. It all seemed so absurd and surreal. There are 25,000 customers and yet one held the key; one was the key log in the jam that had become my life over these hours. I could only hope the search would be fast and efficient.

Sam at my side, sleeping, is now a part of this. I was torn because I felt guilty for involving her in this mess. On the other hand, I required her assistance. I don't know how far I would have been able to run without her direct help. The van idea was a brilliant idea. Her ability to remain fairly calm during a few rough moments, admirable.

As always, a rock that I could depend on in such moments. However, if at the end of this she is hurt, or worse killed, I not sure I could live with that bit of knowledge. Regardless, I would blame myself for whatever happened.

I had little choice but to find the clue to unlock the mystery before we both ended up with bullet holes in our skulls.

The weather cooperated for our escape to the cabin: No rain, dry roads behind and ahead. The setting sun filled the sky behind me with such variations of color - deep purple, violet, blue, and orange, thrown in for good measure with a hint of yellow.

The sun no longer ruling supreme over Buffalo - just another sign that the day is fading. I couldn't shake the feeling that this is my last sunset, my last night with Sam. I hoped that I was as smart as the FBI alleged.

It would not take them long to realize our destination. The land and cabin were both in my father's name. I figured two to three hours' tops, and they would come a calling.

We had many papers and 25,000 names and no supercomputer to sift through the data, just myself and Sam. My coffee had grown cold but I drank it anyway. We were passing the Montezuma Wildlife Preserve and I glanced over to see some birds floating on the water, some nesting in trees, their day complete.

The world was oblivious to my plight. There were no trucks or cars accompanying me on the road. An eerie feeling crept into my bones and numbed my soul. Maybe I was actually dead, burned to a crisp, and I had just failed to pass over?

Could it be all of this was the last embers of a conscious mind not ready to shuck its existence? I held my feet fast to the bottom on the floorboard. I needed to feel grounded. I needed to proudly yell for all "E Cognito Sum," I think therefore I am.

I needed to remind myself I still walk upon the earth, breathing deeply of the surrounding air. I did not think it wise to share my thoughts with anyone, not even Sam. I sounded certifiably crazy; such thoughts have no place in my world.

Sam often accuses me of being too jovial, too easy to joke, to reach for sarcasm. I was taught to laugh at the world. I was taught to meet hardship with humor. I could not find the silver lining or laugh away the events of the last ten hours. This was deadly serious business in which I have unwillingly become involved. It is through my own will and determination that tomorrow the sun shall rise again with me as its witness.

Exit 40 loomed ahead, so far the trip has been without incident. We should be at the cabin within the next few hours. Except for Sam sleeping beside me, I was alone.

I felt the world had forgotten one Ryan Prince. Could it be my ticket was punched and I was only delaying the inevitable - running from fate? I was not sure. I am a pragmatist, not a philosopher. I believe in real problems with concrete answers. I planned on spending my last few hours remaining solving this puzzle, this enigma that my life had become.

When I make it through this day, I will then wrangle with the headier issue of fate and destiny. There will be time later to sit back and wonder how I could have changed my day for the better, time to search my soul for the better answers.

11

August 18 | 8 p.m.

We had stopped at a comfort rest area, not a full-service location, as we were nearing the end of our day on the thruway. We took a bathroom break and bought some more coffee from a vending machine. My legs were cramped from sitting in the van. I needed to clear my head and stretch my weary muscles.

The last leg of our journey would be the most difficult. The last three miles a daunting task during the day, a dangerous drive at night. It was prudent I remain focused and alert.

Advice interlude number two: coffee out of machines is never good. In fact, I had better two-day-old coffee during my bachelor days. However, sometimes our friend caffeine comes in convenient sizes. The cup was emptied before I reached the van. The machine produced mostly warm coffee, it was more than a few degrees short of hot.

No one recorded our passing; no one paid us any heed. Either those other patrons at the service area had been traveling all day, or my picture had not yet reached the local media. The FBI may simply have bluffed, hoping I would succumb and turn myself in.

Back behind the wheel, I accelerated down the ramp that merged with the highway. We would be passing exit 39 very soon. Our destination closing in quickly, I set the cruise at 78 miles per hour. Most of the traffic was off the road - I had not seen many troopers tonight.

I thought that my breaking this minor law would go unnoticed. I looked at Sam, again asleep, her breathing slow and steady, her small size allowing her to curl up in the passenger seat. She looked very content; I do not believe I have ever been that comfortable sleeping in a moving vehicle.

The road lurched ahead as the headlights illuminated a small fraction of it, the high beams not very efficient. It occurred to me that this was a metaphor defining what my life had become. I have been forced to witness my life in small segments, reacting only to what was immediately in front of me. There was no magic crystal ball to peer into the future. I was restricted, able to think only about the next few moments. There was no amount of illumination that would clarify the events that had thus transpired. There was not a means by which I could view the entirety of what I faced.

My thoughts were interrupted as Sam had awakened. She was digging behind the seat for leftovers from our first stop along the great New York State thruway. I was about to warn her about the potential of bacterial contamination, but it seemed rather unnecessary. I felt that a potential botulism infection was the least of our worries.

Sam sat in her seat in a contemplative mood, absent-mindedly staring out of the window, watching the blur of landscape speed by. At first, the urge to interrupt her contemplation seemed necessary, but, stopping myself, I realized that there would be time for such conversations later.

I deactivated the cruise control and coasted up the ramp to pay my toll. The tolls were supposed to be eliminated in the '90s but instead, they went up. This really wasn't a time to squabble over a few dollars. I paid the attendant and continued my trip. The interchange over to Route 81 was ahead and so was the cabin. North we go.

Sam was quiet - looking out the window - not focusing just recording our passing. "Ever think this is just a dream and it will end with the alarm in a few hours?" She asked in a hushed tone, almost too quiet to hear.

"The alarm took me away from supermodels. I don't think you dream about being shot and having the FBI strong-arm you."

"Let's call your Dad, let him know were taking a vacation and using the cabin."

"Not necessary. I have a key. Plus, he is in Maine on his annual fishing trip."

"How long until we are there?"

"An hour to hour and a half tops."

"Where are we going again?"

"The cabin is at Stone Mills Lake, just northeast of Watertown. The lake and surrounding area are beautiful."

"Aren't you afraid to attract too much attention?"

"Most of the cabins are for hunting and will be vacant until at least early October. I doubt that we will see anyone. Plus, the cabin is off the main road and is on posted property. We will be safe until they find out the cabin is listed in my Dad's name. We may have as much as two to three hours of uninterrupted fact-finding."

"Then what?"

"I really think we will find something. Maybe we can then take it to the local FBI out here."

"What if they already think you're part of this whole mess?" Sam's voice was full of concern and worry. "They won't care what you say or any obscure bit of evidence you have."

"The state police may be a viable option and they have offices all over the place. Let's find what we need to find first. Without knowing what caused everything today, we're quite literally dead in the water."

She opened her mouth to say something but the right words could not be extracted. She just shrugged her shoulders and continued her unfocused gaze out of the window.

The rest of our journey would be fairly straight forward. We would stay on Interstate 81 for 72 miles until we reached the outskirts of Watertown - at our current speed, we would be there in under an hour.

Watertown, also known as the Garland City, was settled in 1800 by New Englanders who were looking to establish an industrial complex in the northeast. Although not directly on Lake Ontario, it was in close proximity.

Watertown was not huge by any standard, only boasting a population of 26,000, which accounted for more than a fifth of Jefferson County's total population.

I have traveled to dad's cabin more times than I could possibly recall, yet I spent very little time in Watertown. I have heard the downtown section is very quaint. Watertown can also lay claim to the first Woolworths, which was located in the public square.

Sam seemed awake and alert as if her question was answered by the landscape passing at the relative velocity of 74 miles per hour.

"Is there any food?"

"Is there any food where?"

"At the cabin. Is there any food at the cabin?'

"Probably not, we never store any boxed food there or any dry goods."

"Is there a fridge in the cabin?"

"Yes sure, it's not really a rough it kind of place. It's quite comfortable."

"We are coming up to Watertown now. Let's find a store and grab a few things."

I debated the wisdom of going on a shopping trip right now. The urgent need to get to the cabin and dive into the database was urging me on. "Well, I don't know. How about I drop you off and come back?"

"Rule #1 no separation. No one except that cashier at the store even pretended to know us. I think we are safe. Five minutes in and out what could it possibly hurt?"

My internal struggle debated for only a moment. We did need to eat. "All right. As long as we are fast. It still bothers my paranoia radar." I said forming a small radar dish on top of my head.

"Regardless of what, I think you could plead insanity. As

soon as the judge has spent more than two days with you, he'll know it's not an act."

"Thanks." She is absolutely right. I am, as they say, one of a kind.

12 ▌

August 18 | 9 p.m.

We were fortunate there was a store that had all we needed in the Salmon River mall. Although I did not recognize the franchise, it was located conveniently off the Interstate. We would shop and then we would leave behind us the smallest of possible wakes. No trace we were even there.

The store was small compared with the goliaths we frequented in Buffalo. The selection was not as large, but the store did contain both a fresh bakery and deli. The subs we ordered were being wrapped as we approached the counter. We took four with us, again the length of our stay was yet to be determined. But we do not plan on staying much after our reserves were depleted.

On the way to the checkout, we passed the snack food aisle and although it was full of unhealthy food, it was also full of comfort food. Two different bags of chips were added to our order along, with two separate dips and some soups. We walked around the store, actually enjoying the brief interlude from all that troubled us.

My radar was pinging but I ignored it. Something told me repeatedly get out, again I choose to disregard it.

While Sam was poking fun at an older couple who were arguing over the importance of sodium content, I finally understood what I had heard, what my senses had detected. A police radio.

There was no proof that indeed our photos had been circulated, however, I now can recall hearing the scanner close by as we sauntered down the last two aisles.

I stopped, grabbing Sam's arm, and gave her the universal sign for immediate quiet. The officer apparently was directly opposite our location in the next aisle. I heard a deep voice speaking in hushed tones into the radio.

But I clearly heard two things: A) they may have been spotted entering a store in the plaza, B) get a unit over here to find their car before they leave.

I walked over to the Butcher counter, my back to the officer. I stated loud enough for all to hear, that we could use some chops and that I was impressed over the freshness of the meat. I am not sure if this worked or if the officer actually had us under surveillance.

Unlike the stores we frequent in Buffalo, this small establishment seemed to be lacking any significant security equipment. I returned to Sam's side. The officer was making his way to the front of the store.

We walked quietly through the seasonal aisle, and for the first time in my life, I stole something from a store. I grabbed two baseball caps. One was pink, embossed with a New York Yankees logo. I am at the heart of the matter a true blue Mets fan, but in a time of emergency well, you do what you can. I also took out a Salmon River tee shirt, intentionally one size too big, removing the tag.

The old couple had forgotten their cell phone, oblivious to its fall form purse or pocket, during what was a heated argument over nothing. I dialed 411 and asked for the number for Jefferson County Sheriff's office. I accepted the additional charge to be connected directly.

I informed the nice young woman who answered that I just witnessed the couple from Buffalo heading south toward Route 81. For realism and effect, I gave her my actual license plate. I knew it currently resided on a fire-roasted wreck, but I was certain she did not. I also gave her a description of the van prior to its hasty makeover. I thought including the ErieOne Mortgage signage important.

I quickly erased the call form the phone memory and patiently waited until the Sherriff had received the call. Also, sadly, it confirmed indeed our pictures had been released. The Sheriff exited the store with a great deal of haste.

I tried to fake a southern accent, calling Sam by the name Billy Sue and acting a little louder than I thought prudent. Fortunately, we were able to use the express lane and there was no one in line. I handed the couple's phone to the cashier explaining in a horrible southern accent that I located it in the snack aisle.

My plan worked. We were out of the store faster than anticipated. I had parked the van close by for a fast departure. We walked with haste but did not run to the van. Upon exiting the store, I could see two cruisers, sirens blazing, speeding south toward Route 81. We very calmly entered the van and drove off.

Call me crazy, call me paranoid, call me whatever, but I found the entrance ramp for Route 81 South and intentionally drove two miles in the wrong direction, before reversing my course and taking Route 63 Northeast back into Watertown proper. It appears I will be spending some time in downtown Watertown after all. With the first good luck we had all day, Route 63 intersected Route 12 just east of town and traffic was non-existent.

We were back on the track, after only diverting our trip for about ten minutes and a few miles.

Neither of us spoke during our short trip circumnavigating Watertown. It was true the FBI had not been bluffing. The police all over the state had our photos and a description, of us. I am either a person of interest or a full-blown suspect.

They knew Sam as well. She, too, understanding the expression chin-deep in shit. She is considerably shorter than me, so she caught up a lot faster. The imaginary clock in our heads that has been ticking all day, ticking like a countdown, now had sped up.

We may not have as much time as I thought. How long until they connect me with the cabin? Tick tick tick tick tick....

We had better find a solution fast. Or else.

13

August 18 | 9:30 p.m.

Route 12 is a double lane road - barely a road – and hardly merits the prefix "Route." However, we would only be on the road for about four more miles.

The closer we get to the cabin, the more the roads deteriorated, as we were traveling into more rural settings. Sam was shocked when I turned east onto Vaadi Road, as the term paved can only be loosely used to describe the maintenance level of the road. She turned to me and I saw a disconcerted look on her face which stated, 'I am glad you're driving.' Her look turned to shock when I turned north onto Sandy Pine road.

Sandy Pine Road is an unmarked private road that runs for almost three miles and would ultimately bring us to the cabin. The dirt road was not serviced via any local or state department of transportation. The ruts were deep and almost impassable during the wet season. The road was desert dry now, bouncing us around like a super ball, hard enough to cause my ass to lose its grip on the seat and scramble what was left of my functioning cranium.

Sam constantly watched the speedometer, thinking I was

driving much too fast for the condition of the roads. This was more than likely the first, true, dirt road Sam had seen in her life. In the three years we dated, to my recollection, we had never left the city or surrounding suburbs.

I thought that she may have been watching a tennis match in her head, as it bobbed back and forth like a pendulum, look at the road, glance at the speedometer, look at the road, astonished by the speedometer. You get the picture.

"Are we in another country?" Her voice held a note of alarm. "Doesn't anybody take care of this road?"

"No."

"Why not? I haven't seen this many ruts in my life and I thought the potholes in Buffalo were bad."

"This is a limited service road. With limited access, no one is responsible for the upkeep."

"Are there people here year-round?"

"Yes. There are and they drive some fairly rugged four-wheel-drive vee-hickles."

"You're not really funny all the time, you know that don't you?" Her voice held more than just a touch of scorn.

"Of course not," I retorted. "I am hysterical 24/7. Funny doesn't start to describe my antics."

"Your right, your antics have yet to be defined for sure. They lean more toward, um, what's the word?"

"Hysterical, comical, blithe, hilarious, silly, ludicrous, jocular."

She reached over and punched me in the leg. I was happy she didn't slap me upside the head. My cranium had taken enough of a beating today. "Mr. Theo Sarus, that's about enough."

"I can continue if you'd like."

"More of that, I'll shoot you myself."

Laughter filled the cabin of the van. It was well deserved and broke the tension which had been plaguing us since we left Buffalo about three hours ago. Sam again directed her attention from road to speedometer, wondering when the longest portion of the trip would end.

The hazard that lay ahead was a suicide curve. It was dangerous to drive this curve much above 15 miles per hour. It was hardly wide enough to accommodate two vehicles both attempting to traverse the turn at once. Driving at night only furthered the hazard. I slowed to a snail's pace and sounded the horn as I approached. I only continued after I saw no other headlights were approaching my direction.

After surviving this day, I was not going to be taken out by a traffic accident. Nearing the curve, the headlights shown only forest, as if the road ended abruptly. I was pleased the road seemed rut free, the dirt surface smooth.

It was only my familiarity which got us through unscathed. Once safely traversing the curve, the cabin was only about a mile down the road.

I found the driveway which led to the cabin without any issues. Sam looked horrified when I made the left-hand turn seemingly into a hedgerow and thick bushes. She was relieved once the turn completed and the cabin came into view.

"What the hell! I thought you said we were going to a cabin?"

"We are and we're here."

"Okay, maybe I was expecting something, smaller, something, I don't know shack-like. And I don't mean the guy who plays for the Lakers."

We shared another hardy laugh. I was very impressed by the sports reference. The only exposure she has to sports is when she passes ESPN while on the way to the USA channel or the two seconds it's on in the car prior to her insisting on something different. She may have come across this bit of knowledge through osmosis or hypnosis.

I could understand her awe. Our family always referred to this place as the cabin, yet many would consider this a second house. I spent many a fall day here.

Dad and I would go to ready the place for hunting season. We would travel with friends, leaving on Thursday morning, and returning Sunday night. I made this annual visit from the time I was thirteen until I graduated high school. I learned how to use a chain saw, shoot a rifle, and shotgun. I was given a big-ass knife with a compass and correctly taught to use it. I learned about hunting and hunting safety. I bagged my only buck at the age of seventeen, a ten-pointer weighing in around one hundred and sixty pounds. I learned a lot. Those times were some of my fondest memories.

I also learned to play poker at my dad's hip. Learned how to bluff, when to bluff, and, when to keep your mouth shut. I won my first poker game in the cabin. So this place meant something to me and I was looking forward to seeing this sanctuary once more.

It was no doubt rustic, the exterior composed of wooden

logs capped by a wood-shingled roof. Although I could appreciate Sam's surprise, as the cabin was two full stories and additional crawl space. It was, by and far, the largest cabin on this side of Sand Hill Lake.

A garage was attached to the north side of the cabin, a door connecting the garage with the kitchen. By many, including some of our sparse neighbors, this was considered extravagant. Dad considered it a necessity. He preferred to be comfortable and did not seek personal growth through shitting and pissing in the woods. He also preferred to get out of the car without having to tramp through the snow.

The cabin was surrounded on two sides by large, old-growth trees on the north and south side of the cabin. If this were not considered private land, most of these trees would have been removed in 90', when a large portion of the Adirondacks was deforested.

Any tree larger than eight inches in diameter was taken. There are areas north of the cabin that look like a new forest, as only small trees still stand. A beaver would be unable to find suitable trees in this forest with which to make a home.

Sand Hill Lake was on one side, a neighbor on the other to the east. The lake was not that large - only about a mile wide by a mile and half wide. The lake, like most in the Adirondacks, had been contaminated by acid rain. The water was crystal clear, yet supported no life, other than algae and bacteria. It was a shame - as a younger man I can remember fishing the lake with Dad. We both had pulled rather large bass from its waters.

All told the cabin sat on approximately three acres.

As we approached the locked gate, I put the van in park and got out, telling Sam to take the wheel. Moving to the left gate post, I unlocked the heavy padlock and Sam passed through. After she moved the van forward, I closed the gate, locking it again. I met the van at the garage and unlocked the overhead door, promptly closing it when Sam turned off the engine.

With the gate locked and the van parked securely in a locked garage, I felt fairly safe for the moment. We had been spotted at the grocery store, but the cabin was in my father's name; furthermore, one would have to get inside the garage to find the van.

It was extremely dark outside - there is no light pollution in these areas. At night it's dark, and tonight the moon had not reached apogee. Only the moon on a clear night can offer any guidance. The fact we were in the confines of the garage, which had just one window facing north, made the dark rather complete.

I felt my way by memory to the door, unlocking it with yet another key on my ring. I was eternally grateful the FBI saw fit to return my keys, even though the car key was now rendered useless. Entering the cabin, the flashlight was just where it was supposed to be. I used it to subsequently locate the fuse box and turn on the water heater and lights.

Moments later the lights were ablaze. Sam seemed very anxious as this process was carried out. I think she may have only seen a cabin once, and it was in a movie.

The huge kitchen measured fifteen by twelve. Ample cabinet space had been added one off-season and the area held a table which sat six, with an extension to accommodate twelve. I helped dad replace the sink a few years ago, and the kitchen had been updated, although no one would call it stylish or modern. It, like the rest of the cabin, was built for function. Usability was key.

The additions were completed without the aid of an interior designer. Unless you consider first college apartments a style, then this place is reminiscent of most college abodes.

A wide door led into the living room, which was the same size as the kitchen. Comfortable furniture and a useable fireplace dominated the room. Real wood paneling, real wood ceiling, and real wood floors made the room appear to be a big oversized study.

Sam was slightly disturbed by the various trophies hanging on the wall, their glass eyes following her around the room. There were six mounted trophies, five were deer and one was a bear. Legend has it, the bear was found in the kitchen, rummaging through cupboards. This of course happened prior to the garage construction. The bear, startled by the arrival of people to their own home, panicked and began chasing two of Dad's hunting buddies. The bear, now angry, treed one of the men and decided it best to follow him up. The man climbed as far as the tree would take him. Various shots were fired in the air in an attempt to scare the bear. It failed. The bear's progress up the tree was quick and decisions had to be made. My father shot the bear in the head, dropping him to the ground below. The man in the tree made it to the ground, scared but in one piece. Most assuredly his pants were not dry.

That hide is proudly displayed on the back of the bathroom door.

There is also another story, possibly more plausible, which may have involved a drunken wager. Two men, no longer members of our hunting entourage, were carousing after a fine day of hunting. Drinks were passed around, and a bragging party broke out. Each man insisted his shot was the one which required the greatest degree of marksmanship; shortly thereafter, it was decided there was only one way to judge the better shot. A target was placed on a tree at 100 yards. One shot to hit the center using my father's Winchester. This would offer no man the advantage. Well, each had his shot, and each missed wide, the tree remaining undamaged.

The next day, the men found a dead bear in the small stand of trees, just outside the line of sight for the target challenge. It was impossible to determine which man made the fatal shot. The ranger's station was contacted. Before the ranger arrived, a cover story was created.

The ranger came to investigate and asked to see the felled bear. The two men begrudgingly agreed to show the ranger. Once arriving at the site of the murder, the ranger let out a loud and long laugh. The two men had no idea what was so humorous about the situation. The ranger saw the look of confusion that took up residence upon their faces. He took his hat off, looked in my father's general direction, and stated loud and clear:

"Well now, since you can't kill a bear twice, I believe you fellers have done nothing wrong. Ain't that right, Mr. Prince?"

My father was laughing uncontrollably now, rolling in the snow. He barely managed to get to his feet. When his breath returned, he told the two men about the setup. Uncontrollable laughter again overtook him. Everyone in attendance, lacking the two men involved, thought it to be a hysterical situation.

The ranger was none too pleased that dad had allowed two intoxicated individuals to handle a loaded weapon. Dad very calmly, with his face still red from laughter, explained he had loaded the gun with blanks. He was waiting for an opportunity to present itself, as indeed, he knew about the bear all along. In fact, he had carefully placed the target knowing that the men, would want to determine what caused the shots to be off-target, thus finding the dead bear.

The above story, to my understanding, is factual. It is also a sound example of the lengths a Prince will go to make a joke. To this day, dad cannot share that story without breaking into fits of laughter. Every year we visited the cabin in the fall, it was expected he would tell the tale over a few beers and a roaring fire.

Recalling the story brought a smile to my face as I continued to give Sam the grand tour. Mounted heads aside, the space held an intimate, yet wide-open feel. However; the furnishings did not match, and one could tell this cabin was lacking a "woman's touch". The furniture was oversized and begged you to sit down and let the world's problems melt away. Heaven could not have looked more inviting than this room. I am sure Sam was not quite sure what she was looking at. She was a designer at heart and lived to decorate. Sam was gifted. I could only imagine the list that was being constructed. I figured she was either disgusted or planning the next renovation. First, she would replace the drapes, as they were thick and deep red. They seemed more at home in a monastery than a hunting cabin. Men don't do drapes and I believe these have hung in the windows since dad purchased the cabin.

The TV with satellite was not around when I was in high school; although, the bathroom door looks like it was made from scraps when the rest of the cabin had been finished. The bathroom was much more accommodating than the meager door suggested. It had gate hinges instead of door hinges. We referred to the bathroom as the barn.

The bathroom had been updated sometime last year and included a fully functioning shower and a water conservative toilet. This was pretty much the middle of nowhere but it was livable. No roughing it here.

The kitchen had a propane-powered stove and the heater lie still, as it was too warm to trigger the thermostat.

There were five bedrooms upstairs and one boasted a working fireplace. This was dad's room. Since he owned the cabin his room was half the square footage of the floor below. His room was large enough to accommodate a double bed and a sitting area with another overstuffed chair. There was also a wardrobe. When I was fifteen I found that he hid all of his "gentleman" magazines in this room. I also discovered he was even prone to enjoying a cigar or two.

The rest of the rooms were about equal size, occupying the other half of the second floor. All were connected via a common hallway. The rooms were adequately furnished with a bed, lamp, and a small dresser. There would be little socializing in them; these rooms were meant for sleeping only. If you wanted entertainment you'd better go to the living room.

I also shot my first goose up here at Triangle Point; it was not duck season, but that's a story for later. Suffice to say, it involved a 22 caliber pistol with a hair-trigger. I had a lot of life "firsts" at this cabin. I guess I could add another - running from professional killers.

Sam was strangely quiet throughout the tour. She grasped my hand with an unusual level of pressure. She cleared her throat.

"Are there coyotes and wolves up here?" Her voice was apprehensive.

"Some, but mainly just bear."

"Don't joke," she said firmly.

"I'm not."

A look of total terror passed over her face.

She returned to the kitchen to get the bags that had been left there when we entered the cabin. There was one bag of groceries and another bag holding our clothes. She was not looking pleased, immersed in all of this nature.

With the mere mention that bears do roam this area, she had expected one to jump out of every closet and dark room we passed. I figured the old adage "they're more afraid of us" would not succeed. Sam preferred to see large carnivores behind bars at the zoo, not roaming about the woods.

Sam was a big city kind of gal with big city sensibilities. I am from a small town and am a huge fan of hiking and camping. Those of us that enjoy such hobbies respect nature - we do not fear it. We possibly had three separate groups following our movements. Man is the most dangerous of all animals at the moment. However, I do not believe she saw that point of view.

Holding back the laughter was a difficult but lifesaving fete, as she was about to kill me for my harassment concerning her phobias. I found the radio CD player and inserted a disk into the appropriate slot and started unpacking our meager belongings.

14

August 18 | 10 p.m.

We had returned downstairs, the CD player still spinning the disk. Sam went to the kitchen to organize our bounty.

I was busying myself at the gun closet. Dad keeps a gun in the cabinet year-round, hidden behind a false back. As always the gun was impeccably clean. The rifle was a Winchester .35 caliber. It packed a punch and was very accurate. An extended magazine encased another ten rounds. If the quality of your marksmanship was lacking, there was plenty of quantity to finish the job.

I was loading the weapon, taking the care that my father had shown me so many times before. My quiet world was about to take a turn. Sam was in the kitchen organizing our food and drinks, humming to herself along to the music on the CD player. She let go a scream that could simultaneously boil then freeze one's blood. My heart thumping within my ribs, I felt my flesh wound and twice-broken nose scream with every beat of my heart.

Fairly certain the bear must have made it into the cabin, gun in hand I ran to the kitchen.

I saw Sam defending herself with a broom and backed into

the corner near the stove. A bear had not broken into the house after all, but its diminutive cousin, the field-mouse had.

It was ferocious as it consumed a morsel of food. It was huge and must have been three inches long and two to three inches tall. My laughter could not be contained.

"You never said anything about pests. How can anyone live here? Are there snakes too?"

"Not anymore. I think you scared all the wildlife away in a ten-mile radius."

"This isn't funny you never told me there would be these, these things," she said, motioning with the broom at the mouse, who had the sense to find egress out of the room.

"We are out in the middle of nowhere, that's where these things live."

"You could have warned me."

"Sorry. Good thing this is loaded in case we run into a rabbit. They have vicious, sharp teeth, and could be dangerous."

She said something very unladylike that did not merit repeating and then threw the broom at me. I returned to the living room not attempting to contain my laughter. There was work to be done. I expected the FBI would be arriving soon, closely followed by Fred's friends.

The gun may be the only way out of this situation. I have already seen two men dead today. God willing that would be all.

We must begin our search, reading the newspapers to begin to make that connection. There was a customer somewhere hidden in this database. Somewhere there was an answer, an answer which would end this day, an answer to my problems, so today would not be the day I die for real.

Sam and I started the process of combing through the newspapers while I also accessed the database. The man who contacted me said the secret was in the national papers. I would now turn the tide. My turn to get some idea as to why there were people who wanted me dead.

I decided I would run a query looking for duplicate addresses that had different account numbers. That would, in essence, point to multiple phones being billed to the same address. Thus the mysterious connection which caused today's events.

The query returned two results. One I knew was an apartment complex and the other was my friend Rose. She would take people into her home that needed help.

I quickly created another query to extract customer interaction from the last six weeks. The list was much longer than anticipated.

Back to square one.

The rifle leaned up to the chair next to me. Sam was making sandwiches. I was studying the database. A cross query of the last six weeks of interactions and duplicate addresses yielded zero results.

15

August 18 | 10:30 p.m.

The smell of freshly brewed coffee opened my eyes. I hadn't realized I dozed off. Sam had her hair up and was highlighting articles in the paper. Trying her best to make sense of her findings, trying to figure something out, something that would aid our search for the elusive needle.

She had compiled a list of similar stories each paper carried. People don't get killed for a bus driving off a cliff in Bulgaria. The list was shorter than expected. Sam had put this together while I slept. After her one hour of searching, she found all of the papers carried these similar stories.

One: Various angles on the conflict between Lebanon and Israel, including Turkey and France, countries considering sending troops to aid Israel and the international consequences of said action. Both articles included side notes concerning our involvement.

Two: The British Prime Minister was charged with sexual misconduct over a tryst with a minor. He had been caught with a young female prostitute. He declared his innocence and stated he did not know the girl's age. There was a photo of the girl in the Toronto paper; I thought she looked twelve.

Three: Funeral services for Hussein Abdullah Jafar and his three sons were conducted in Mosul. It was believed Jafar was killed because he aided and abetted Western Forces and Americans in the search for Saddam Hussein.

Four: Various articles debating the ineffectiveness of the Iraq conflict and President Bush's mismanagement. I thought that was assumed - the author did not need to waste ink telling us something we already knew.

Not one of the articles had any clear connection with western New York or myself. We searched and found no names in any article that was from western New York. Back to square one.

Someone wants me dead and I don't know why. I realized the database was sort of a long shot, my recent queries only reinforcing that belief. But I was feeling very disappointed. I considered my options, which at this very moment, seemed extremely limited, like equal to the square roots of negative one. I walked over to the window to gaze upon the mirrored surface of the lake. Maybe the story we are looking for is listed but not reported by all the papers. It may just be listed in one or two. This unfortunately just increased our search. It may be best to look at each international story one at a time, searching for related names in the database.

I again ran through my mind the queries I had run for duplicate addresses. I had spoken to the three men of what I assumed were of Arab-American descent who had different accounts but the same address. I had suggested a rate plan adjustment that would save them some significant money. All three reached out to me stating they resided in separate apartments. The address was wrong on the accounts. Case closed.

Yes, there were various stories concerning Arabs and Muslims. Mistakenly connecting these three men in an attempt to save them money does not lead to people dying.

My hands in my pockets, I think Sam was saying something but at the moment I could not hear her. My thoughts continued further inward. I was calculating how long it would take to compare every story to my list of names. The sky was black and cloudless and the moon was bigger here, seeing it silhouetted against the trees. It's blue-white surface radiating its reflected light on the lake.

My clock read 10:30 p.m. This ordeal had now gone on for fourteen hours straight.

There were no more options. My nose ached. My side hurt. I felt exhaustion try to take me, draping over my body like a blanket. I was through.

I was on the verge of turning myself in at the nearest FBI branch and telling them my story.

Maybe I could help. Maybe they could search my database for whoever was involved. I had assumed it was someone I had met or talked with. It never occurred to me that maybe it was someone connected with Sam. My death a way to ensure her mouth stays closed.

It was time to leave. Sleep here tonight and then Syracuse tomorrow. I was physically and mentally battered. I was not sure where we could rent a room without producing identification.

It was time to bring in the pros. I could do no more to further my own cause. Maybe the Syracuse FBI was on the up and up, and there were none of these mysterious rogue agents in that office.

Standing at the large window, watching the moon wax as it began to dominate the night and appreciating the stars that filled the sky, I was surprised to see a small boat about one hundred and fifty yards offshore. The silver metallic surface of the boat shown brightly in the moonlight.

I had not noticed it before.

I was shocked there were other people out here; I wondered if it was an acquaintance. This was a small community - only about twenty cabins were dispersed around the lake.

The Nodiers were an exception to the rule, as they were only yards away from our cabin. Most others were separated by several hundred feet and thick vegetation. Years before the Nodiers sold a portion of their land to my father and another investor.

The Triangle Point Hunting Lodge described the shape of the land my father was able to hunt. It was a large property and sat between the Nodiers and some protected State land, literally, the property was shaped like a triangle.

The lake was not particularly large, although like most glacial lakes in the region, had some rather deep areas. I was wondering what fish these fine men were going after as there were none remaining in the lake.

I watched the boat floating lazily about the lake; it could not have been larger than a rowboat. As if they knew I was scrutinizing their progress, the boat made a sudden and fast turn toward us. I sipped my coffee and continued to examine their movements, my curiosity increasing with their speed.

Their distance from shore had already been cut in half; as the distance diminished their speed increased. I turned my back on the strangers on the lake.

I was about to share my plan C with Sam when it occurred to me there were no docks on this side of the lake. The neighbors used their places as a hunting camp, sometimes hunting with dad. They also only owned two boats, and on my last visit they consisted of a canoe and a kayak; neither requiring a dock of any kind.

I had last met with the neighbors about two years ago in October. Dad and I were knee-deep in preparations for the upcoming season. Charles Nodier and his wife Jean were doing the same.

Charles was a few years older than dad and often referred to him as kid, which always gave me a chuckle. Consequently, even though I was pushing thirty-six at the time, Charles would call me sport, tussling my hair in the process. I was sure they did not have a dock and were dead set against installing one.

The boat was now nearing the shore. I could plainly see two people occupying the craft. I turned to shout at Sam and tell her to hide.

The first shot came through the window. I heard it squeal past me, burying itself in the wall. I was showered with broken glass, horrified, but unharmed. The FBI usually asks questions before they shoot, mostly. This had to be some of Fred's people.

The second shot missed me by a mile, the bullet now lodged in the ceiling. I stayed low and crawled to the junction between the kitchen and living room, turning off the ceiling light. Sam had the laptop and was hiding under the table looking scared and pissed.

I cleared the table, adrenaline running through my veins. I could have thrown it back to Buffalo. I tucked Sam away in the corner and then moved the sofa in an attempt to slow any more errant bullets.

Sam looked both furious and confused, our moods matched, as being shot at for the second time that day was a personal record I thought I would never break. I could feel the rage building. These men did not have a gun to my back and they were unaware I was able to return fire.

I have never had a poor temper. I have not been prone to outbursts. However, my blood boiled in my veins and I could feel my teeth grinding. The anger I had initially felt with Fred had returned. Time had not lessened my fury. I took a few seconds to slow my breathing before obtaining the rifle.

I had left it leaning against the wall in the kitchen. I retrieved it and gripping it forcefully, crawled past the window to the stairs for a better vantage point. Dad's room had a window which shared a view of the lake.

Panting, running, and feeling the pain echoes surging through my body, I made it upstairs before the men landed the boat. An animal-like yell forced it's way through my throat as I took two stairs at once. I needed to get upstairs before they set foot on dry land. My rage fueled my velocity.

I have never in my life pointed a loaded weapon at a man,

woman, or child. Surprised by my own fortitude, I did not hesitate. I crouched by the window, sliding it open, the gun sighted on the first man in the boat. He now appeared to be carrying an Uzi or a Mack Ten. Definitely not government-issue; the gun was small with an extended magazine. I believe both are illegal weapons. He was no more than fifteen feet from the cabin and closing fast.

I squeezed the trigger twice. Both bullets found their target the first time, putting a nice sized hole in the first man's head. The second bullet ripped into man number two's shoulder, knocking him to the ground, as his partner had fallen. I am not sure if fallen is the correct term; he collapsed without taking a step as if his spine was ripped out of his body, which now lacked the rigidity to remain standing.

The second man while on the ground pulled a handgun out of his jacket and fired in my general direction. Broken glass was the only casualty.

I wondered if they thought that the first bullet had hit me as I was turning away. Neither of the men closed in on the cabin emptying their clips; they may have thought me dead. I am surprised they did not show more care. This struck me as odd, what little experience I had with Fred's comrades lead me to believe they were not only organized but ruthless. They must know this small community was nearly empty, thus should have sent a barrage of bullets toward my position.

I had eight shots remaining in the rifle and I returned downstairs.

Sam clutched the laptop, shaking. Hysteria had control as she crouched behind the couch.

"They are shooting at us why are they shooting at us," she babbled in a shaky voice.

"I think they are shooting at me, but two of those shots were my evening the score. Stay here," I commanded.

"Yeah, I am good right here," she said shaking her head emphatically. She managed to cram her small frame into a ridiculously small space.

I kissed her on the top of her head. I had no idea how badly I had injured the second man. Turning off the remaining lights, I handed Sam a flashlight, and as quietly as possible, slipped out the front door, locking it behind me. The night was silent and still; a bright moon offered ample lighting.

The outcropping of trees was replete with dark, deep shadows. I did not hear any footsteps or the snapping of twigs that infused the forest debris. They may have located the cabin but I doubted that they understood the layout.

I hid behind a cord of firewood, trees to the south side of the cabin easily in view. This copse of trees was dominated by deciduous pines with very short, sharp needles. Dad would know what variety they were; I just required some cover.

From my vantage point, I could cover both the front two corners of the cabin. The moon was the only light in the area as the cabin was dark. I think I managed to turn off all the lights and the thick drapes had not been pulled back to allow any to spill out into the night.

I have shot and killed a lot of animals, both large and small, in my many autumns at the cabin. I don't kill unnecessarily and we only shot what we can use and what we would eat. I can remember my first buck and the excitement and adrenaline that accompanied shooting such a magnificent creature.

Dad and his hunting friends' were very pleased with the kill and all wanted to celebrate my first deer.

As I did all those years ago, I hid, allowing the forest around the woodpile and the night to offer coverage. My adversary did not have an acute sense of smell or hearing as my last prey. I attempted to control my breathing. The anger, forgotten momentarily, was unlike anything I have experienced before. It began building inside again. I wanted to scream out loud, testing the strength of my vocal cords and start firing rounds. I was very fearful that, when required, I would not be able to control this monster growing inside me. The lyrics to "The Animal I Have Become," by Three Days Grace, began playing in my mind. The album was released last month and is on the CD's I kept in the car.

The bile in my stomach grew acidic, and my eyes tightened, as did my grip on the stock of the rifle. The muzzle velocity of the Winchester .35 caliber is 970 feet per second; the round carries twice the powder load than a .35 caliber handgun. The bullet itself was longer and a few grains heavier.

It would pack a punch. Through empirical evidence collected moments ago, the human skull lacked the tensile strength to slow the bullet.

I was so angry and so filled with such hatred I wished the man had survived his wounds so that I could kill him and watch him die again, preferably something slow that involved blood loss and profound agony. The sight of his partner's head exploding after the impact brought an evil smile upon my face. I literally shook it off.

I am worried about my reaction to the shooting. This is not who I am, yet the feelings running through my very tired, very confused, overly caffeinated adrenaline-soaked brain, were pleasant in a way. It made me feel real and alive and that my killing this man with my rifle and eight remaining rounds would somehow be appropriate payback for what had occurred today. A dead man can't speak; and while I wanted him dead, now, I also required information. I decided it best not to kill him immediately.

The fact this man must somehow be connected with Fred and his group made it even better; granted, Fred lay dead somewhere with a nine-millimeter bullet hole in his head. But these men decided I needed to die when they stole my car and burned it to the ground. They chased me. They handcuffed me. They shot me. My actions now were payback. After I obtained the information and answers I needed, I would seek that payback.

These thoughts made no sense. This is not me, forming these thoughts. It was reminiscent of my nicotine-addicted days. The first week after I quit, there would be moments when a second voice lived in my head. Constantly, vehemently, urging me to pick up that pack. To enjoy a smoke. The voice logically urging, "what could it hurt you haven't had a smoke in days, just one will be fine, you can handle just one." The voice eventually lost its war and ceased its cohabitation. Apparently, it has returned, this time and it's not about cigarettes, it's channeling that dark place where no one except movie directors and writers ever dares tread. The anger had created another personality who was directing my actions.

I waited.

And waited some more as the strange thoughts and feelings ran roughshod over my overworked brain. I struggled with those feelings and I doubted I truly had the gumption to carry out my plans.

I doubted my strategy of leaving Sam alone.

I doubted my strategy of staying in one place, wondering if I made myself an easy target.

I wondered if the assailant would try to go in through the busted window. It was about five and a half feet off the ground and the ground sloped to the lake. I doubted he could pull off that feat with a busted shoulder.

Feeling like plan D was not working out, I immediately regretted leaving Sam unarmed. I counted to twenty but with the adrenaline, I'm not sure it took any longer than two seconds. My mind raced back and forth, leave to protect Sam or stay put, and hope that the second man would give up his position first.

These people had training and strategy for these situations; all I had was instinct. Training prevails in these situations. I was also certain he had more than eight rounds of ammo on his person. Out-trained and out-gunned I stayed my position. A cold sweat ran down my back. I really did not know if I was too warm or too cold.

I was shaking, regardless.

The night had gone silent, as the tranquil lake had been intruded by gunfire. The bright moon still hung high in the sky.

Once your eyes adjusted to the bluish light, it could have been confused for street lighting.

My ears straining to hear something in the woods any-thing, all that I heard was the whoosh-whoosh-whoosh of blood flowing through my auditory canal. There was a noise that either was a twig snapping or my jaw breaking from the pressure. I decided to wait, fighting against every urge to run back to the cabin.

I had a clear view of the front door. The kitchen door was not only locked but was inaccessible due to its location in the garage, offering an extra level of security. His only way into the cabin had to be through the front door. I was confident I could stop him before he could enter. Confident, but not one hundred percent sure.

The door was locked. However, the lock was not the stur-diest on the market. I stepped back into the copse of trees, the woodpile in front of me offering some protection. He would have to step into the woods to spot me.

My paranoia was running full tilt. I convinced myself he was already in the woods, waiting for me to make a move and put a bullet in my back. I stopped breathing and concentrated on hearing with all my being.

After a few minutes, I was convinced he had not come this way. Yet the flesh on my back crawled and I now was overcome with nervous sweat. It was not unlike my first hunt; adrena-line fueling my anticipation.

I heard nothing from the house. There was only one win-dow on this side and I could not see through it, as the thick drapes prevented it. I also did not see the telltale sign of a sweeping flashlight. This did little to dispel my fear.

The safety was still off and the rifle was ready to fire at a moment's notice. Eight rounds are all I had. I cursed myself for not bringing extra ammunition; again not thinking ahead had cost me what small advantage I possessed.

I panned from corner to corner of the cabin, using the scope on the rifle, the black crosshairs showing nothing other than trees and cabin.

My palms were oily against the rifle stock and wiping them off on my jeans was not eradicating the problem. Also, I had to pee. I counted the seconds, hoping anything would relieve my zooming mind. The fourth time I reached one hundred I finally saw a thin beam of light poke around the left corner of the cabin.

My ruse worked.

I could have jumped for joy shouting, "Hey Mr. Bad guy you were outsmarted by a customer service manager na na na na na," but I thought it wise to stay in my hiding place although I was dancing the cha-cha on the inside. Again the hate and the loathing building to epic proportions, as the chance to kill one of those involved excited the dark part of me. It seemed this dark place bestowed upon me strength. I could feel a confidence of sort, an instinct that this was the correct path. An urging not to overthink, just react, just do what was required. This strength steadied my hands, slowed my heart, and temporarily removed my conscience.

This new part of my psyche was very worrisome. I was fighting an internal battle, kill the man and dance on his corpse, or question him until he provided information. Earlier the thought of unintentionally causing the death of two men weighed heavy on my conscious. Now, I can hardly fight the anticipation of adding to the body count. If God were out there, somewhere, witnessing these events, I could really use some guidance. I was on that philosophical slippery slope, and my shoes lacked adequate traction.

I stood behind the trees. They offered protection and also completely concealed my position from my adversary. I slowly and noiselessly raised the rifle; the ambient moonlight was sufficient enough to place my target in the black crosshairs.

He was cautiously rounding the corner, his hand cannon leading the way, silver barrel glinting in the moonlight. I had a clear shot at his head, which at the moment was hidden behind a black ski mask, completely concealing his countenance. I hesitated my finger tight on the trigger. All that was required was a few more pounds of force in order to unleash my vengeance.

He looked in my direction and treated it as innocuous. He now completed his turn, stopped, looked in a window, and, satisfied with his viewing, continued to move slowly.

I aimed and pulled the trigger, missing intentionally. The rifle makes a god-awful sound, louder than a twelve gauge when fired.

"Drop your weapon!" I shouted, my voice filled with rage and anger. "Kick it out of the way!" I demanded. The assailant immediately did as he was told.

I moved from behind the trees and pointed the rifle at him.

"I missed on purpose," I informed him, trying to sound

sinister. With the rage that coursed through me, it wasn't hard.

He said nothing.

"What is going on here?" I demanded, menacing him with my rifle.

He said nothing. I shot him in the leg, the bullet penetrating and then exiting the man's thigh, ultimately coming to rest in the cabin wall. It looked like it hurt. It was the first time I shot a defenseless man. Tomorrow would offer me the opportunity to confess my sin.

Tonight I did not care.

It was cold and callous and made me feel a lot better about my general position at the moment. The new me did not take to getting shot at, the new me did not turn the other cheek.

The new me shot back.

"Now are you in a more talkative mood?" My anger was growing by the second. I may have been shouting but I cannot recall for certain. I had the upper hand and I was far from relinquishing it. I stepped closer, aiming the rifle at the man's head, from almost point-blank range.

He flipped me off. He was now on the ground, the blood flowing from two wounds. In the bright moonlight, the dark puddles spread on the ground, absorbed by the dry earth.

"I have seven rounds; do you wish to continue or are you ready to talk?"

He leaned against the cabin, bleeding, and being stubborn. "You can't make me talk," he said between gritted teeth.

Sam had joined us, the report of yet another round of ammunition being fired causing her to exit the cabin to investigate.

"Sam, go inside, grab a chair out of the kitchen, and two towels from the bathroom."

Sam had that "doe in the headlights look." I do not know what surprised her more, the fact I was not dead, or the fact I held a man at gunpoint.

She was looking back and forth, trying to process the information being received via her optical nerves in what might have been the second set of the night in her imaginary tennis match, the first being the ride in the van. "Sam. I am fine. Please, do as I ask. It's important," I said firmly.

She moved from her statue-like pose, slowly backing her way into the cabin.

The man lay on the ground bleeding. His leg wound was seeping blood, the wet stain spreading across his black combat fatigues. It looked like spilled black ink in the moonlight.

I paced back and forth, waiting for Sam to return with the requested items. The anger was building, yet to be honest, what to do next? I have no experience interrogating anyone, let alone a professional killer. I was thinking he would not be swayed with my arguments.

But shooting him made a part of me feel good. Satisfied.

I have been running all day, tossed into the middle of this thing and people want me dead for reasons I cannot start to fathom.

I held the upper hand and it would not be relinquished until some concrete answers were forthcoming.

"Why are you here?" No response from my captive.

"I ask again, why are you here!" I shouted, but more volume was not effective either.

I walked two paces closer, the muzzle of the gun touching the man's forehead.

Sam returned from the depths of the cabin carrying a kitchen chair and two towels. Her face was Casper white, her eyes disbelieving.

"Did you shoot that man in the leg?" Her voice was incredulous.

"Yes."

"God. Why?"

"Do you want me to put the gun back in his hand so he can continue shooting at us, by which, I mean me?" I asked angrily.

"You are above this; this is not you." Her voice was pleading. I didn't care.

"I want to be alive come tomorrow. To do this I need to know what this asshole knows." I took the towel and the chair and headed toward Man #2 bleeding on the ground.

"My girlfriend is correct, I am above this. But I have shot you twice, once from close range. If I were you, I would ask myself, will he shoot me in the head next? The answer may be yes."

No response.

"It must have been quite a surprise to find out I was no longer unarmed."

Wrapping one towel around his thigh and the other around his shoulder, both makeshift bandages appeared tight and the bleeding at least slowed. I grabbed Man #2 up to his feet and shoved him in the chair. His face remained stoic.

In the next few moments, I seriously injured my Karma and conscience. Man #2 would not reply to a single question. There was a part of me that went feral, knowing that whatever he knew was my ticket to freedom. I had been pushed to my personal limits all day, and whatever I needed to do, well, it was going to get done.

That "animal" inside had shucked its shackles and was running full speed at this man gone mute.

I picked up the rifle from its perch against the woodpile.

"I could kill you right now. Show you the same treatment that was meant for me. But I don't think that would do either of us any good."

No response. I placed the rifle on the ground. I looked at Man #2 and with all my might punched him in his already abused shoulder. He grunted and folded himself in half in the chair, sweat on his brow.

He more than likely was in shock or heading there fast. In an ungentlemanly like way he flipped me off again and he held it there as if asking me to record it on my camera phone.

I raised the rifle and taking two steps back, I shot his hand as he held it for my consideration. One's hand does little to slow bullets, and the round passed through his hand in a cloud of blood and bone, then lodged in his shoulder.

Sam screamed and ran back in the cabin.

Man #2 was now busy rolling around on the ground, speaking unintelligently, with a lot of swearing thrown in for good effect. He was on his knees, attempting to get back against the wall. There was only a stub remaining were his hand once perched.

"Are going to shoot me again?" The agony was clear in his voice.

"If I have to."

"Okay. I don't know anything other than you need to be dead, like now."

"Who was in my car?"

"I don't know," he groaned, shock coming quickly. "Someone in some fairly high place found out about our plans. They stole your car, planted a body inside, and drove it into a tree, scorching it in the process."

"What could I possibly know that's worth killing people?" I wanted answers but wasn't getting any.

"I don't know," he said, very sincerely.

"How did you find out that I was not dead?"

"We had a man inside trying to access some database. He saw you at your office." More groans of agony.

I truly didn't care.

"My customer database?"

"Yes, I heard someone say it would blow the thing apart, even if one person outside the agency knew."

I was getting very impatient with the word "knew." But I used it anyway.

"Knew what?"

"Beats me. I am just hired help."

I was pacing. I had been handed another piece to the puzzle. Even though the puzzle had been reduced to ten pieces, none of them could form a coherent picture. It was still jumbled. I did not know if I was holding an ear or a leg, or maybe a foot.

Again, considering a run to the FBI seemed prudent. I hadn't noticed Sam had joined us again. She was looking at Man #2 and at me. I did not like the look in her eyes. It was like she just found out her new fiancé was a murdering sex offender. She was not pleased with the news.

I heard Velcro opening, as it has such a distinct sound. I was going to ask this guy one more question. The knife he removed from some hidden sheath would have hit and inflicted much damage if this man had a hand and working shoulder on one arm. The knife hit the woodpile next to me with barely enough force to stick. Acting out of rage, I knocked him unconscious with the butt of the rifle.

Sam, wild-eyed, looked at me. I saw fear in her eyes. That look will haunt me for the rest of my days. I took a step towards her and she backed away.

"Don't."

Taking a deep breath, I gave her instructions, instead of taking her in my arms as I wanted. "Sam, I need the duct tape from the drawer in the kitchen. Please go get it."

She nodded and darted into the cabin, flipping on the light. It flooded the doorway and in what was only a few seconds she was back, holding out the silver roll.

Sam and I stripped the man of his clothing and I dragged him to the boat. His friend was where I dropped him, still dead. Again, I get the "what kind of savage can do this" look from Sam as we loaded both men in the boat. I used duct tape to handcuff unconscious Man #2.

We launched the boat, sending it back onto the dark lake. We stood in silence as the boat floated off; it will end up on-shore sometime tomorrow. But we were safe for now.

Sam finally spoke. "Are you alright?" she asked, her tone a mixture of fear, confusion, and a touch of concern.

"Yes, Sam, I'm alright. Tired, but alright." We started back to the cabin.

"He told you they were after your database."

"Yes, that's what he said." The weariness crept back into my voice and suddenly I was very, very tired.

"What do you want to do? Continue with the database search, or get the hell out of here?" She was almost pleading.

"Option 2. Let's get our things and head to Syracuse. I'm hitting the shower."

After a short shower a new pair of pants and a tee-shirt, I just may feel human again. Some of the dirt would not wash out with soap and hot water. But the hot water did remove the oily film on my body. There would be time for retrospective later but not now. The events of today have not sunk in. They have yet to be processed and I had no time to digest them now. I shot two men today with a rifle, one at close range after he was already down. Sam can't seem to look at me.

I, myself, have trouble with the man in the mirror. Concerned, I shook my head and took some deep breaths. For a few minutes, my eyes had a wild look, filled with hatred and anger. Sam was right to be concerned. After several more cleansing breaths, my true self shown back to me in the mirror. I had returned.

I don't think Sam is mad, but I am certain I frightened

her. She is not used to seeing her mild-mannered fellow manager gun down two men. The man shot in the head was not a pretty sight - his brains were where they ought not to be, mainly on the grass, the tree, and on the rocks.

I can hear the fear in her voice as she pleaded with me as I tied up the other man. I told her they started it. I finished it. There may have been another knife in Man # 1's pocket that Man #2 could use, and then Man #2 would come back and finish the job. I firmly told her the ride to Syracuse was going to be uneventful.

Returning my gaze to the mirror, I stretched my shoulders and winced when the wound on my side screamed in protest. I was glad I turned the water heater on when we had arrived and was very pleased as my shower was not only refreshing but extremely hot. It relieved some of my maladies.

But not all. There were places the hot water could not reach.

I returned downstairs and we loaded up the van with the remaining food, the laptop, papers, and the rifle with additional ammo, as well as two flashlights from the cabin. Sam drove so I could unlock and relock the gate. I did my best to secure the cabin, but the broken window required repair. Dad had a man that would take care of such jobs; I would call him when we were safe.

I was now totally immersed in this conspiracy, my involvement no longer in doubt. I hadn't the understanding, or the ability, or the training, to get out of this with all my parts still attached. What I wanted was in Syracuse. I was hoping the innocent bystander label would hold. Although our experience at the store told me differently, maybe I would be afforded the opportunity to explain myself.

I opened the door and slipped into the van. There was movement near the cabin next door, at first it seemed my imagination was conspiring against me in my fragile state. When I saw that the figment of my imagination had a gun I told Sam to stomp on it. She complied fully.

16

August 18 | 11 p.m.

The road to the cabin was not designed for speed or comfort. Sam didn't mind bouncing all over the place and neither did I. The van created a cloud of dust in its wake. I couldn't see five feet behind us and I saw no headlights but that really did not matter. We still had about three miles before the road would be paved.

We saw, rather than heard, the bullet fly through the dashboard, killing the radio in an explosion of vinyl and foam rubber.

The barrage of bullets continued. The van was being riddled. I was not sure how long before something more crucial than the radio caught a bullet. The windshield was taking a lot of damage and soon would be worthless. Trying to put my decent size frame into a small area was unsuccessful.

I felt something hit my shoulder like a hammer swung by Thor himself, and the force of the bullet threw me to the dashboard. I wish I killed that man instead of floating him naked out onto the lake. I figured they had to be right behind us; maybe there were two teams at play and his partners managed to bail him out.

Foolishly, I climbed to the back of the van, maneuvering around the seats, trying to keep flat to the right-hand side while bleeding profusely from my newest wound. I was concerned, as I have not stopped to count, by I am certain I was a few quarts low and I could feel the warm, sticky blood running down my arm. Even with the raucous noise, I swear I could hear the drops of blood impacting the floorboards.

The car behind us was about fifteen feet away and closing fast. Bullets continued to fly through the van. For whatever reason, the pain had yet to invade my world, and I was conscious and alert. The bounding, bouncing van made it difficult to maintain my balance. The road conditions must have made it hard to get off a good shot, however, that did little to quell the number of bullets flying through the van's thin sheet metal, discerning from the pattern of bullet holes that were directed toward my side of the car.

I wanted to get the rifle and fire back. But I also did not want to make myself vulnerable and I was thinking all of this while trying not to fall on my face as Sam tried her best to miss the holes, dips, and otherwise uneven surfaces. I have been on smoother roller coaster rides.

Glancing back at the sedan, I saw no headlights. No wonder we hadn't seen them. They were now just following our lead. Looking out the bullet-riddled windshield, I knew what was up ahead. I moved to the front of the van.

Pulling Sam from the driver's seat I took the wheel and managed to put on the belt. We lost some of our speed, but so did the car behind. I could not see it in the rearview mirror.

Sam crouched the best she could to stay out of the line of

fire. She fit under the dash, something my size did not allow me to do. We were traveling well past the "safe" speed for such a road and the seat belt did little to keep my ass in contact with the seat. The van groaned, the sound of metal on metal echoing, grinding. I wasn't sure how much more jarring it could take.

I was gripping the steering wheel to keep control and also hold myself down. I flashed the high beams to get a look ahead and abruptly turned them off. I sped up after extinguishing the high beams and also the taillights, which seemed suicide, but would leave those behind us blind on the road.

This private road did not come complete with streetlights to illuminate the way. I knew this turn. They did not.

I turned sharply to the left, the steering wheel fighting me through the whole turn, the ruts almost wrenching the wheel from my hand. The van pulled left and only at the last moment did I use the lights. A tree branch clipped the driver's side mirror; any further off the road and the van would have been bent around a tree.

Humor visits me at strange times. All I could think about at that moment that I indeed was in a vehicle that had hit not once, but twice today a tree. Combine that with twice having my nose broken, twice being thrown in the trunk, and now twice being shot, I was having a rather banner day.

The car was tailgating us and it remained on a straight path, unable to negotiate the dangerous turn. It was swallowed by the forest with a loud crash. I did not stop to check to make sure they were okay. I had a smile on my face and I wanted to yell for all the hear:

"Don't fuck with me anymore!"

I kept our speed until I hit the pavement on Vaadi Road. The suspension on the van was taxed beyond the normal limits; the wheels and shocks bounded the vehicle down the road. The engine strained, and a noise like metal fatigue was emanating from the block. The barrage of bullets had inflicted much damage; the windshield was a spider web of cracks and gaping holes, and light was filtering through the Swiss cheese back door.

Sam would have some explaining to do when we returned the van. I wondered if the van would make Syracuse. Hell, I wondered if it would make the next mile marker.

Sam extracted herself from under the dash and attempted to mend my wound by standing behind the driver's seat. I was trying to maintain some control over our bullet-ridden ride. At the moment more adrenaline then blood was circulating through my veins. The left side of my shirt was one large, dispersing bloodstain.

I was aware the blood loss was severe. Sam's constant reassurance brought me back to the present when all I wanted to do is pass out. I hadn't realized we were traveling over 80 miles-per-hour while on Route 12, with a vehicle in a current condition that would not pass inspection. She retrieved a shirt from the bags and used one as a pressure bandage.

She retook her seat, continuing to talk me down. I eased off the gas and had a moment to breathe. The oozing wound was not painful; it may have been shock or an adrenaline overdose. I assumed it was the latter. I felt like a strung-out junkie.

The makeshift bandage constructed from the remnants of my new shirt seemed to stop the bleeding.

Her voice was soft and nurturing and almost brought me down to human levels. If this is what it's like to be an adrenaline junkie, count me out. I will settle for a sedentary life.

"Are you sure you're not a spy, Mr. Prince?" She asked, her voice still holding a note of fear.

"No, I am not Mrs. Prince."

"The FBI is right. Your brain works while others' panic."

"I was panicked; I was scared shitless. The only idea was to turn off the lights and wish them off the road." The turn onto Route 81 was just ahead, which meant Syracuse was only an hour away. My heart was back to beating less than 1,000 times a minute, I drew my second breath in what seemed like the last few minutes.

Driving east on Route 12, I knew the Route 81 merger was not far off. I was contemplating my next move. My concern centered on the van. I was anticipating a breakdown. My current condition appeared not to be critical, however, I lacked the strength to walk to Syracuse. The van was my primary concern. I was in a contemplative mood, yet again not knowing what comes next, a theme that had defined this day.

I was not at all prepared for what happened next. The darkness encompassed me too quickly to relinquish the driving back to Sam. As I have been told, I slowed the vehicle before unconsciousness entirely took me. But not soon enough, as the already ravaged van drove off the road, striking a tree trunk with an appreciable force.

17

August 19 | 1 a.m.

My eyelids were heavy. I struggled, but I could not get them to open. There were voices in my vicinity, yet they sounded like they were hundreds of miles off at the end of a very long and deep tunnel. Willing my eyes to open, I was certain death had found me, or the rescuers were working against time to save what remained of my life.

Some inconceivably long time later, my lids no longer were laden, I opened my eyes. The bright lights were harsh, doing little to eradicate the monster headache that was echoing through most of my skull. Focusing, I found myself in a bright room wearing what I figured was a hospital gown. Lines of various lengths and color issuing forth from a variety of vinyl pouches poked my arms, and the rhythmic beep, beep, beep of a nearby monitor was the only sound in the room.

Nurses and doctors came flooding in the room, alerted by the monitors. Sam was the last to join the parade. My shoulder was thick with gauze and my arm was in a sling. I was receiving a blood transfusion and feeling rather thirsty.

Raising the height of the bed, the doctors began their examination, poking, prodding, and recording every conceivable medical test. They ruled me fit to walk among the living one more time. I often wondered if indeed the heart speaks to doctors in some language unbeknownst to the rest of us, or maybe the stethoscope is a recoding device to our souls, as medical professionals seem to be able to determine a lot of information simply by listening to the noises of the body.

I had lost a great amount of blood; some earlier, most within the last few hours. The ER doc was concerned enough to order me both a unit of blood and another of clotting agent. An IV was replacing the fluids that have been leaking out of me at different rates throughout the past 18 hours.

The gunshot wound was a through and through, surprisingly other than the two holes and much blood loss; the damage was relatively minor. The bullet passed through without ricocheting off a variety of bones and such. The doctors were pleased I was awake and informed me of my fortuitous circumstances.

I, of course, was not feeling very lucky at all, but the sentiment was coming from a group of folks who were very fond of saying "this won't hurt a bit." Maybe they did not know that regardless of their diagnosis, my shoulder most certainly had fallen off and had to be reconnected stitch by stitch, the surgery completed most likely with the use of a spoon or some other blunt instrument. Also, the surgery could have been completed with a hot poker, as my shoulder seemed on fire although it had yet to yield smoke. I realize this is the normal treatment of a gunshot wound during the wild west period in the 1800s but for Christ's sake this New York and the 21st century. I was certainly in a hospital and I am cognizant of

JAICO regulations; maybe this facility had failed their last accreditation.

When I am feeling up for some conversation, I might inquire about some pain meds.

They had asked me about my nose, which had been broken twice today, and the "graze" on my right side. It was then I noticed thick gauze had been applied to my nose; consequently it had been reset while the hot poker was mending my shoulder wound.

The big, angry abrasion on the right side of my face was treated with some sort of salve and for a change was not throbbing as it had earlier. Generally speaking, my day was looking up.

As I turned my head to the side as directed so my ear could be examined, I saw a large plastic bag which held my clothes and more noticeably, my torn and bloody used-to-be-white t-shirt and jeans, which I was wearing while being shot. The more surprising fact was the bag had a wide red stripe on the top that read "evidence." I wondered why it had not been logged and taken away by the police. The doctors or maybe Sam had recently relinquished the bloody garments; further, it could be they were awaiting someone to pick it up, chain of custody and all that.

They do not use such bags for innocent bystanders. I would need to lawyer up and convince them I indeed was an innocent bystander. Granted, an innocent bystander that just killed one man and mortally wounded another, but an innocent bystander none-the-less. I remembered, fondly, removing the man's hand with a bullet. Karma and legal wise, I may be in some trouble. The second voice returned, pleading with me to relish the moment.

I slowly moved my head on the pillow which was too thin and not comfortable. My other ear was examined thoroughly and found without defect.

Sam took my hand and explained exactly how it was we found ourselves at this hospital.

I had collapsed at the wheel and driven the car off the road; had my foot not come off the accelerator we would have been dead. Sam's quick thinking saved us both, as she was able to get to the brake pedal reducing our speed as the van hit the tree. Sam got away with a few scrapes and bruises but nothing that would not heal quickly. A gash that had recently been sewn shut crossed her forehead. The crash did not worsen the exit wound, my shoulder was damaged enough. Although, I now know the exact area I had used to stop my head with the steering wheel.

A trooper that was on the verge of pulling us over for speeding was on the scene moments after the collision. The ambulance was not close but arrived within ten minutes of the accident. The trooper was able to slow the bleeding long enough for the paramedics to arrive.

I of course missed all the action being unconscious and all. Sam was allowed to ride in the ambulance on our way to the closest ER, she was not talkative about how I came about my gunshot, but told the paramedics to have the police at the ready.

Once stabilized, I was taken into an OR and my wound was flushed and stitched in the appropriate places, my left subclavian artery, and the subclavian vein had been nicked by a bullet and thus the large amounts of spilled blood, one millimeter higher and I would have bled out prior to the ambulance's arrival at the ER.

Sam did her best to describe the inside of the van, the huge rupture where the radio once occupied, how blood had saturated the passenger's seat, and also the dashboard. Blood soaked the driver's seat penetrating the cloth right down to the cushion underneath. The van was not drivable due to the front axle damage and damage to the U-joint. A bullet had pierced the radiator. The damage report was simple as the van came to rest on a stump, and the few moments it took them to free me of the van, Sam did not require an excuse not to watch.

A nurse arrived in the room, her badge read Renee d'Anjou, and she busied herself, taking vitals and ensuring that my heart was still beating. Following a quick consultation with a nearby doctor, it was determined that I was able to speak with the police for a few minutes. Nurse Renee assured those that I was not to be pushed beyond physical exertion.

What followed was a procession of policemen and officials from a number of agencies. Some took time to display their ID some did not.

Robert Fludd, an agent from the local FBI office in Syracuse, took a moment to indicate that he was in charge. He did so not with words but rather his actions. He, with slow deliberation, removed a notebook from his jacket inside pocket. It was flipped open with a deliberate movement. He was taking notes as he walked around my bed as if the monitor could also determine guilt and innocence.

The others waited for him to start the questions and they did so without rocking back and forth in their stance or clearing of throats. This man was most certainly in charge and he did not tolerate the breaking of the chain of command. He seemed to relish this moment as if I were number one on the FBI's top ten list.

Here assembled in this small hospital, in a small town were twelve officers representing four different branches of law enforcement all gathered to question and interrogate, obliviously the most dangerous man on the East Coast, Ryan Prince.

Had I not been shot twice and reshaped the steering wheel with my cranium, I would have been lost in laughter. I glanced about the room and there were two other men dressed in dark suits and white shirts and ties. I assumed them to be FBI. There were two officers dressed in the purple and grey uniforms of New York State troopers. There in the back of the room stood my good friend and acquaintance, Agent Rocksolid. There were four other officers each wearing the dark blue uniforms, not familiar, maybe locals, and still four others that were dressed in khaki uniforms with insignia that read they were with the Jefferson County Sheriff's office. I had hit for the cycle, a member from every possible branch of law enforcement, local, county, state, and federal.

Fludd was strutting about the room proud to include me as his quarry, and finally, he approached the bed. He quickly informed me Sam had been questioned earlier while surgeons had attended to my shoulder during emergency surgery.

She had answered the questions and had cooperated to the fullest. He did not believe that she told any mistruths, and he was well aware of most of the story of my awful day. He smiled while making entries in his notebook. Agent Robert Fludd did most of the talking while others gathered there were fast taking notes.

"Can you tell us what happened at the cabin?" Agent Fludd asked, a very ominous tone to his voice that sounded like he was prepared to accept my lies.

"We went there to hide out and to discover why I was being targeted."

"Why were you being targeted?" Another disapproving look from Agent Fludd.

"I don't know. I have had two different people try to kill me today, and both had the same answer - because I knew too much and the information I obtained is dangerous and could result in more deaths."

"What is it that you supposedly know?"

"You know, I have no idea. I have been through some contacts in my database and I certainly cannot find anything that seemed relevant."

"Why did you decide to go through the database?"

"Two reasons, one it seemed logical, perhaps a contact I have made through my position at CellNY is the cause of all this mess; and two I have had these people tell me as much. Whoever is behind this thought that I had indeed died last night. Someone was at my office trying to access my database but was unsuccessful. I went to the office this morning to re-activate my phone and this "mystery" person saw me."

"The database is with you then, correct?"

"Yes. We downloaded the database onto Sam's laptop. But honestly, I don't know where that is at the moment."

"It is with her for now. I want to talk with you about the shootings at the cabin."

"I was standing in front of the window looking at the lake. I saw a boat on the water and it seemed odd. What was odder yet, one of them took a shot at me."

"Is that how you injured your shoulder?"

"Is it necessary for you to ask questions when you already know the answer?" I was tired of the pointless questioning.

"What's that supposed to mean?"

"You've spoken to Sam already, yes?"

"Yes, we have. But she could not confirm a few things."

"Why don't you just ask me about that, this is the second time today I have been interrogated and I have done nothing wrong. Why don't you call the Buffalo office they know as much as I do."

"I have. They know nothing about you or this whole affair."

Were the Buffalo FBI office and Agent Boyle part of the rogue group the man had mentioned? I certainly did not imagine or hallucinate my time spent in the interrogation room - Agent Rocksolids' presence here confirms my sanity. Maybe hours spent at the Homeland Security Office was not in the company of the FBI, but rather the NSA. Either way,

I was in trouble. Fludd continued to pace the floor. I decided defense is the best offense.

"Agent Fludd, the man in the back of the room that looks more like a wall than a person, he was present for my questioning. We even shared some special bonding time, didn't we Agent Rocksolid."

Agent Rocksolid stood there mute.

"Ryan," Fludd cut in, "That is Agent Robinson and he's not with the FBI."

"Regardless of which alphabet soup organization he reports to, he was there. He followed Sam and me to the coffee house in downtown Buffalo."

Sam nodded in agreement.

"This was before you two conspired to steal property from ErieOne Mortgage?"

"Yes."

"You admit to grand theft auto. You are in a room full of officers from every branch of service."

"I admit that Sam was granted access to the van, and from my understanding that access was never revoked. We borrowed the van. That doesn't have any bearing on his presence," I pointed to Agent Rocksolid.

"Is shooting a defenseless man considered okay?" he continued.

"He shot first. I was defending myself." Fludd obviously cared not to lose the momentum of the questioning.

"Sam told us you interrogated the man," stopping to refer to some notes "and you shot his hand off when he wouldn't answer your questions."

"He flipped me off and he had it coming. Two men came out of that boat and they both wanted me dead. What would you do? I haven't gotten a straight answer out of anyone today. I was hung out like bait by your office in Buffalo and that guy," I emphasized pointing my finger in his general direction. "I needed answers. I needed them now. I woke up this morning reading an article that stated I died last night. These people obviously wanted to correct their mistake, unlike this morning I had the means to defend myself. I did so to the fullest. The only way I will survive this day is to discover what information I have stumbled upon. I did question the man about what he knew."

"You can drop the story about being held for questioning by the FBI we all know that is strictly fiction."

"He knows the truth, Agent Fludd. Do you think that I may have been signed into the building under a different name, they did not sign me in as Ryan Prince but Joe Smith?"

"Why would they do that?"

"Because they did not want anyone else to know who was in the interrogation room."

"I will check into that, there is no evidence you were at the FBI offices today."

"Why don't you check the camera footage at the Homeland Security Office. Truthfully. I was not told where I being held, I guessed the new Homeland Security Building. I may have been anywhere."

He looked at a man dressed like every other FBI guy and barked out "go check into that now."

The man left without awaiting further instructions.

Fludd continued his questioning. "What did they want from you Ryan?"

"First, they questioned me extensively on my activates that day. And wanted to know what Fred had told me, and my connection to the people that abducted me. I am tired. I heard this line of questioning so many times today, I know nothing."

My voice was weakening by the second and what little strength seeped out of my body. My eyelids started the fight to stay open, dropping against my will. I was curious why he did not ask about Fred and my fun-filled morning hours in Buffalo and Niagara Falls. He hadn't spoken with them if he had would have had some direction to his questions, or maybe truly there was no record of my hours in that building which only furthered my belief that the agents were working their own agenda. I was concerned about Agent Rocksolid's appearance in the room.

The events of today are beyond me; I have become a man I do not recognize. I have crossed a line today. I shot a defenseless man, twice, then rendered him unconscious and exposed him to the elements. I felt a rage that I thought was not possible. I reacted without thought. I have strayed from the path I have followed all my life, follow the rules, make logical decisions, and do no harm, path.

Maybe Fludd did not contact the Buffalo FBI or Homeland Security offices. Maybe he thought the case was open and shut after speaking to Sam. Regardless, I may very well live to see tomorrow, the only problem, would be the next sunrise would be obstructed by prison bars?

Nurse Renee remained in the room during my questioning and now removed the group, stating that I required rest and they could talk with me tomorrow. They grunted but complied. They posted a guard at the door for my "protection." I did not believe I required protection because I was all but in custody at the moment.

Truth is I was exhausted, I could only see this going one way, I was being set up for murder. Agent Fludd's questions and mannerisms indicated that this was going to get pinned on me. He was not here to ascertain the truth. He was fishing for a scapegoat.

He must have read the statewide bulletin that was distributed to all law enforcement agencies. He must know that I was a person of interest in a murder in Niagara Falls. This is common knowledge by now, I wondered if those in attendance also were curious about his tactics. He should have started with the death of Fred. Interesting, I was in full belief that maybe the cops in the grocery store were not tracking me, maybe I had just flipped out, misunderstanding something that came over the police radio.

Regardless, if I was wrong or right about the store, at the moment that was the least of my concerns. Agent Fludd had all he needed. I was certain Sam's portrayal of events only sealed it. I am not blaming her; she witnessed a transformation of sorts from Ryan the runner to Ryan the defender.

I made a promise to myself should the situation was to repeat itself; I would take action. Where could I go? I had no vehicle and at the moment, I was not one hundred percent. I wished the rifle was with me in this room. I now was an especially easy target, limited in mobility.

I was ready to accept my fate as the cards at the moment were highly stacked against me, and the evidence as well. The icing was Sam's testimony stating I twice shot a man after he was down and of no further threat. The line crossed between self-defense and murder.

I don't care, I am not sorry to have to state that so emphatically; but, I got a big chunk of even when I blew that man's head off his shoulders and shot his partner three times. At the moment, I just wanted to bury my face in the pillow and for the next eight hours not think about anything at all, just disconnect and forget.

Nurse Renee took some time to pour some water from a pitcher near the bed, and she fluffed my pillows. She was a very attractive young woman who took pride in her job and aiding people. It was evident through her actions.

Her fiery red hair seemed both out of control and styled simultaneously. Her deep blue eyes reflected her inner person. I liked her immediately. She was upfront.

"How are you feeling?"

"Tired, beat down, broken."

"You're lucky, a few millimeters either way and the bullet would have caused some permanent damage."

"I don't feel lucky. Did you notice that this is my second gunshot wound today?"

"You must have really pissed some people off."

"I guess I did. I got caught up in all this nonsense. It doesn't seem real, it just doesn't seem feasible."

"Who was that pretty little thing at your side?"

"That's Sam. We were going to be engaged today, that was before everything happened."

"Well, congratulations! She was waiting for news while you were in surgery. She was quite concerned."

"We've been together for a while. I wouldn't know what to do without her."

"Ah, such a nice guy. I wish you the best." She squeezed my hand showing her concern.

Nurse Renee spent a few minutes unhooking me from the monitors, unplugging everything except the IV catheter replenishing my depleted blood reserves, an IV that was nothing more than fluids to replace those lost through excessive bleeding, and the IV that was bringing the additional platelets to aid the clotting of my diminished blood. I was relieved to be rid of the beeping monitors.

Sam entered the room. My thoughts now centered on the here and now. She approached the bed extending her arms, she felt good and it felt right I needed her in my arms the same way I would need medication to heal the gunshot wound. Feeling her soft skin brush across my face, I lightly kissed her cheek. I could feel her tears against my face.

"Sam everything is going to be alright. I promise we will make it through this day."

"I am sorry, I'm sorry. It's all my fault." Her few tears had gained numbers and she was sobbing.

"Nothing is your fault these people have been after me all day," I stated as reassuring as I could muster.

"No, no, no. They will arrest you tomorrow. They think

you killed those men. You will be tried for murder. I told them what happened and they asked me if it was justified and I said," her voice trailing off overtaken by tears, "no."

"Well you were speaking your mind and neither of us has had the chance to process today, understanding very little of what has happened. I know that I scared you at the cabin. But I did what I felt was justified. You can only shoot at a man so many times before he starts to shoot back."

"We need to get out of here tonight."

"I agree. Do you still have the clothes we bought?"

"Yes I have those clothes I think two changes for me, a change for you."

"Do you have my cell phone or is it with my other possessions?"

"I have it," she removed it from her pocket "what is that going to do for us?"

"I have a plan."

"Do mind sharing?"

"Step one: don't die."

"You need to revise your plan - that's the same one you been using all day."

"Don't change it if it works. We are still alive are we not?"

"Yes, but you had a close call."

"Yes, I did. We are making a run. See if you can borrow a briefcase from someone or some other bag."

My next thought was rudely interrupted by a hospital employee carrying a very large, very bulky package.

"Mr. Prince, pardon the interruption, my name is JC."

"Well hello, JC, what can I do for you?"

"It's more about what I can do for you."

My mind went wild as he was reaching into his bag. He must have a set of balls to kill a man while the place is overflowing with officers from every branch of law enforcement. Sam instinctively took an enormous step back, awaiting the fight or flight signal from her brain. I was helpless to do much of anything other than await the bullet.

I guess they finally caught me.

In what seemed to be the longest 5 seconds of my life, JC extracted a manila folder from his bulky bag and handed it to Sam. The folder was closely followed by a small pouch.

"Ryan you have friends here. There are discharge papers in the folder under false names. There are keys and alternate IDs in the small satchel."

I watched as Sam examined the bag, discovering the exact items that were listed just moments before.

"We are about to create a diversion. You will be both be able to slip out and be on your way. We will give you both about 10 minutes so that Ryan may don some more appropriate attire."

The bulk of what he carried was actually some lightweight jackets that were not listed among our belongings and a thermos of some hot beverage and a package of food.

JC hesitated at the door, "please make haste. The keys have been acquired from a hospital administrator. You will need to find alternative transportation quickly."

The door shut before either of us asked a question. We both paused briefly as we turned to each other, asking if indeed those last few moments had actually transpired, and I also believe we were both confirming that neither of us was dreaming.

"Okay, let's get out of here."

My money, my shoes, and my socks were all in a bag that our new friend had delivered embossed with the facility's name printed on the side: Watertown Memorial Hospital. My remaining clothes were in the possession of Agent Fludd covered in gun powered residue, the aftereffect of sending four shots into the night.

Sam proudly held tight to the laptop. She told me that she could arrive back in Buffalo with neither the van nor the laptop, and well, the van wouldn't fit in her a bag.

I dressed quickly and with some considerable assistance from Sam. My shoulder felt better but it was more of a liability than an asset. Removing the catheter was far from pleasant, in fact, I won't doubt if some countries may have used it as a form of torture. I felt guilty about the mess it left behind, it was not at all pleasant. The other IVs were removed with a lot less pain, although with a significant amount of discomfort.

I was surprised as Sam very deftly removed all the medical paraphernalia. Sam never ceases to amaze me; I may have discovered that she had some medical training. My brain drew up an image of her wearing a cute nurse's outfit, it was quite satisfying.

The t-shirt would have been impossible to put on unassisted. Further, with only one functioning arm, I did not have the necessary dexterity to button my jeans. I hoped that this sling and bandage could be removed shortly.

I stood up to gaging, doubting my ability to walk about without falling over. I was overtaken by both a great bout of nausea and weakness. I fought back the urge to pass out, my head was spinning and my balance altered via the blood loss.

Thinking that my recovery was farther along than it appeared Sam needed to take my arm, steadying my gait, before my face once more hit the floor. Realizing my condition was a liability: where we decide to run, not only would I require rest, I could not walk ten feet. I wondered if the Red Cross delivered; I might require another blood transfusion.

She helped me to a chair that had occupied the corner nearby niche, there was a tray. The food was cold and made in a hospital cafeteria, despite the fact that it's not gourmet it would help to regain some strength. She was trying to be supportive while simultaneously urging me from the chair.

As I sat, I was trying to summon the last of my resources. I would need to be completely ambulatory in order to see the next sunrise unencumbered by a grave or bars. I was required to walk as if I had not been shot twice today, confidently striding across the parking lot. I was waiting for the go signal from JC. I am certain that the diversion he would create would be subsequently boisterous enough to allow for notice.

I tried not to fall asleep.

18

August 19 | 1:15 a.m.

I turned on my cell phone. The display not only reminding me I was roaming but the time flashed reading 1:15 a.m. Twenty-four hours ago, the police pulled what they believed to be Ryan Prince from the smoldering wreck of a car. A day had passed since that crash: 86,4000 seconds of chaos. I was aware even then that my life had inexplicably changed; these incidents that had rocked the soul of my being.

I have been reborn, I have passed through the crucible of that dark space in us all, a different Ryan Prince would emerge. At this point. I am wondering if the new me would still be welcomed in the world Sam and I had created. Self-lessly, my relationship with Sam could fall apart; my ultimate concern was our safety. If she chooses to move out tomorrow she would still be breathing while removing her possessions. I would accept the trade-off: a Sam that's alive and pissed, over the Sam that took her love to the grave.

I have been shot - twice, pushed beyond my personal limits, and framed for a murder I did commit, and not feeling great about the two men that I had legitimately killed. No one remained that had any concern for my continued existence.

I would emerge from my sarcophagus a fighter with a shoot-first mentality. When I am able to again gain possession of a firearm of any type, if you are a stranger, you had best announce yourself or prepare to dodge bullets.

One of my favorite movies is the "Untouchables." a fictional account of real-life gangster Al Capone and real-life Department of Treasury agent Elliot Ness. There is one key moment in the movie where Ness and a Chicago beat cop, portrayed by none other than Sean Connery, come to the conclusion that they can either die and play by the rules or win and fight back with necessary force. They both agree to the later. I have watched the movie many times over and can now appreciate the decision they made.

There was no set of rules that could be followed. I have tried to the best of my ability to play things straight. If Sam and I were to make it to tomorrow breathing and standing upright; I could no longer feel remorse for those that stood in my way. I would have to shut off that circuit that feeds the guilt portion of my brain, those that had conspired to ruin my day seemed to possess this ability, I will learn by their example.

The infamous Man #2 had angered me beyond my ability to control it. If I could only find a way to tap that reserve anger, the hatred that I felt hiding in the woods, the hostility that was coursing through my veins when I shot the bastard in the leg. If I could only focus that anger and use it to my advantage, I would do what was necessary to persevere. Again, Sam may not be fond of the new me but it is a sacrifice I am willing to make.

The fire alarm began it's noisy alert as a distant voice was announcing that this was not a drill and all patients required evacuation.

I very leisurely walked down the corridor, a few doctors and local cops passed me without notice. I was down the stairs quickly, but with much effort as my legs were not fully functioning. I would not have made it that far without Sam's assistance. Around us flowed the sounds of personnel running through the halls, gathering patients and personal effects, the background dominated by the blaring alarm. Distant sirens growing closer by the moment as turmoil erupted throughout the facility.

Sam was familiar with the layout of the hospital as she had roamed the halls while I lay unconscious in the room. I followed her without asking questions as to our destination. Hand in hand we made our way out into the lobby and without incident slipped out the door. Chaos was a better disguise then the clothes on my back; however, fatigue was swiftly working, wearing on my body, after only a few moments of activity I felt like I could sleep for a week. The laptop and my remaining possessions were in the hospital bag Sam was carrying; and so far this had not attracted much attention.

Outside the parking lot was looking dark and immense. I was in no condition to walk to the other side of the lot let alone go on a search mission for the car that matched the key now in our possession.

The sirens were drawing closer and the patients and hospital personnel were flowing out of every door. It seemed that an evacuation of this magnitude had not occurred before. It was not very organized.

The approaching sirens only added to an already stressful situation. Our passing garnished no attention whatsoever. Raised voices and the uncontrolled scurrying of staff and ambulatory patients dominated the scene. I am certain an elephant may have passed unnoticed. Under cover of this nerve-racking environment, we began examining every car we came across. It sounded like 1,000 vehicles were headed here. There was a tide of vehicles and a sea of red lights pouring into the parking lot wave after wave.

We searched about fifteen cars' breathless, I was resting my hands on knees. The pain medication was losing its effectiveness and the fire and throbbing in my shoulder had increased.

I was out of options. The wind was emptying in and out of my lungs wet; it did not seem to be enough to satisfy my body. I severely doubted my ability to make it back to Buffalo. The pledge to shoot first ask questions later would indeed be difficult to uphold if I am powerless to remain alert for more than ten-minute increments.

I leaned up against a car when I heard someone sound a horn behind me. After setting a new world record for the unassisted high jump, I was able to see Sam behind the wheel, smiling, presently pleased with herself. She leaned across the car to unlock the passenger side door.

"I found the car parked in a space marked the hospital administrator."

Thankful I was not required to complete another step, I made my way to the passenger's seat stating, "well like one bird said to the other - let's get the flock out of here."

My spirits lifted as she shifted into drive and we began to

leave the hospital's massive parking lot. The tide of police vehicles had hit the shore and the entrance of the parking lot was a logjam of too many vehicles and a severely inadequate entrance. It created a bottleneck and emergency vehicles were jostling to enter the lot.

We waited for our turn to exit the parking lot; my heart skipped a beat with every police cruiser passing our position. Patiently we sat moving only inches at a time, drive, brake, drive, brake, drive, park. As of yet, no law enforcement agency had started searching cars, my disappearance at this point must have gone unnoticed. Three cars remained waiting to exit the lot. With any luck, the car would be cruising down the road at any moment.

Two local cruisers embossed with Watertown PD pulled into the intersection blocking traffic as it exited the parking lot. Our current position was now two cars deep at the light.

The officers began searching the cars shining their huge flashlights through driver's side windows, back seats and trunks. The cars before us left the noise and confusion and turned south onto Washington Street.

Sam looked dismayed. I calmly handed her the paper that I obtained from our new friend. Feigning a drug-induced sleep, I was slumped in the passenger seat, my head bobbing with the movement of the car. We pulled up to the two officers. Sam rolled down the window.

"What was your business at the hospital today?"

"My boyfriend broke his collar bone. The stupid asshole was drunk and fell down the stairs."

The bright light illuminated the interior of the car. The

police officer on the driver's side inquired about her stitches. His sole concentration was spent examining Sam's various bumps and bruises. She said nothing, occasionally glancing at me.

"I fell after he grabbed me, caught my head on an end table near the door."

He handed her a business card.

"If you, ah, fall again why don't you call us?"

"It was an accident, but thanks."

The trunk was closed and we were directed to the traffic light. I could hear the two officers discuss what a son of a bitch would beat upon such a pretty woman. There was much talk centered on the next time she would have to call if another accident occurred again.

The traffic light stood as the last obstacle halting our escape, the red light slowly turning to a green arrow pointing to our freedom, it was the second most beautiful sight on which I have laid my eyes. If you need to ask what occupied the number one slot, you have not been paying close attention.

Sam made the right hand turn out of the parking lot onto Washington Street. Traveling south until we reached Route 232, we saw the blue sign announcing the Route 81 merger was ahead. It was as welcoming as grandma's hug. Sam slowed and headed south on Route 81.

Stopping by the local FBI office no longer was feasible. Agent Fludd had determined, with a limited investigation, I was the responsible party. Our options were restricted. Skirting back to Buffalo and Agent Boyle, asking for refuge, was our only option. I was concerned. How many miles could we put between Watertown and ourselves before the car was reported stolen? Should we travel the Thruway using prudent speed, or travel Routes 5 and 20 all the way back? Do we deal with State Troopers or local police? Either plan had its pros and cons. The Thruway would allow us to travel at 75 miles per hour, while the back roads were posted at 55, with many speed zones thrown in along the way. During my contemplation, Sam had managed to put 20 miles between the hospital and our current position with 39 miles remaining to the Thruway. Could we actually make it?

Without asking my opinion she pulled into a truck stop that had a convenience store and attached tourist trap, er.. I mean souvenir shop. The store was called Happy Harry's Hideaway complete with an attached bar-restaurant. I hoped they had some of those 'I was here' t-shirts. I survived being shot at and all I got was this lousy t-shirt, not that I really wanted one but it would make a nice souvenir. Something we could show our guests at our next party.

Sam went inside alone. It was imperative I rest. I was unable to hold my head up, my eyelids lead weights again, would not open on command. I was useless; my condition would not permit me to aid with the driving responsibilities. Sam would have to do this solo. My eyelids were leaden and closed. I did not see or hear Sam approach the car. She had purchased some food and drinks. Pulling the car along the backside of the truck stop she gently woke me up and we enjoyed our dinner and a few moments of quiet. The food consumed in a state of apathy, jaw muscles opening and closing in a robotic fashion. The sustenance was necessary but I did not taste or enjoy the food. It just was.

My shoulder complained - the searing pain may have abided, however; the joint was stiff and grumbled with every movement. Remaining energy reserves depleted; I fell back into the seat losing the war against gravity.

I would never again complain about the rat race or the schedule that we all live our lives by, do A by Monday, B by Tuesday, do C by Wednesday. I could use some boring complacency right about now. The thought of spending an evening with Sam, a movie and, a bowl of popcorn, was like heaven. Some amount of spontaneity in one's life does wonders to dispel boredom. However, a meeting with upper management would be a delight. I am looking forward to garbage day and spring-cleaning, to trimming the hedges and mowing the lawn, to monthly reports and customer retention ratios to gross sales figures, and net profit margin. I am looking forward to a lot of things, those things that have not conspired to ruin my day. Sam often tells me my best quality: I am stable and dependable, i.e. boring. My friends along the way stated many times over that I needed to loosen up enjoy life, live for the moment, and lose my planner. Well if they could only see me now.

Dinner finished Sam pulled the car from the parking lot. She looked tired, the burden of today's activities weighed on her, worry lines played on her face. I was feeling like I had died - my life seemed drained from me. I felt like hell, the stare on Sam's face full of concern told me that I looked even worse. Pain in my shoulder radiated through most of my being, only adding to my malaise, with every beat of my heart the wound felt like fire. Sam's constant prodding, telling me to nap, was met with only minimal resistance. The power to converse was lacking. I refused to give in. Although the day had been long and sleep was a necessity. I avoided the allure. There were things yet to unravel, things yet to come.

While the sun had set upon August 18, I feel it in my bones that my role is not finished. The proverbial target still rested on my back. We were moving, heading south almost to Route 90; however, the car we are driving is not ours. The target still there reminding me that three groups were spending tremendous resources to track me down.

I am now a fugitive from the law.

I am wanted for murder and attempted murder. No one cared that they shot first, no one cared that people have been shooting at me all day, no one cared whether I lived to see another sunrise. I felt like a canoe on a preverbal river without the use of paddles. I was witnessing everything, recording what I saw, yet could not control my destination, I was only along for the ride. Those powerful currents had tossed me about all day. I was defenseless against the never-ending torment of rushing water, the rocks, and vicious white foam forcing me further downriver. I had no control over my destination and was unable to return to my origin. If I did not find that needle, the key point, the one person that ties me to this nonsense, I was a dead man either before long or in forty years drawing my last breath behind bars.

I would have plenty of time to sleep tomorrow. For now, I will remain alert. I will remain vigilant, for the battle had yet to be won or lost, every breath I draw we are one moment closer to Buffalo and possible sanctuary.

The FBI had the tools necessary to complete the search of the database, they would find the connection, and they would put an end to this nonsense. They would allow me once again to return to my mundane albeit wonderful life. Sam and I could resume where we left off as if our lives recorded on a DVR, just simply fast-forwarding past this day, past the pain and the running, past the bullets, past me losing an integral part of myself, past the men I gunned down. With remote in hand, I would fast-forward to Noon, waking up finding Sam by my side and our lives restored to normalcy. If only it were that simple. The time on the car's digital chronometer now flashed 2 a.m. I have now been dead for twenty-five hours, my life ruined along with the mangled carcass of my Subaru.

I wondered if the man they pulled out of the wreck would be willing to switch places if asked. In a very strange way we both were dead, his body in the morgue with my name on it. Would this stranger trade for another day with the real Ryan Prince? The man currently residing at the Erie County Medical examiner's office. Would anyone trade death for a chance. That is all I had, a chance. Granted, I may not be alive come 4 a.m., but I have a chance, a minuscule chance, to remain alive.

The laptop remained at my feet mocking and reminding me that failures outweighed successes. I am an intelligent person; however, I failed to find anything that would connect me with the events since transpired. I am smart enough to realize that this was beyond my abilities, beyond my intangible gifts that have allowed me limited success. Other people trained in the art of intelligence gathering, trained to connect invisible dots. I prayed that they would be counted as allies.

Using the perfect vision of hindsight, I realized that luck and happenstance had more to do with my continued breathing than my own abilities. Other than my mysterious caller and JC, I had no one on my side. To be honest, I was unsure even if that caller truly had my interests at heart. He could be feeding me false intel in an attempt to force my hand, force me out of hiding, and force me to do what he was either unable or unwilling to do.

Maybe JC was part of this mysterious rogue group, aiding our escape so others could follow.

Agent Boyle waited some hours and many miles away, perhaps he could jump out of the bushes and save my skin again. Or could it be he was waiting for my return, the news of my exploits reaching his desk with orders that I was to be taken into custody, either way, Buffalo seemed the best bet.

There is something the FBI understands more about today then they shared. I was convinced they had not allied themselves with Fred and his team. Fred's death was vicious and quick. I saw the gore, I felt the gore, these are not the actions of allies.

I did not have the number for the FBI office, somehow realizing the prudence of calling before arriving on their doorstep. I wondered how I would be received? Do they still want me for questioning, or have my recent actions caused them to change their status?

19

August 19 | 2:30 a.m.

Sitting in the passenger seat watching the blur of the land-scape speed by, watching the light play shadows on the ground as we rushed by, not focusing on any one item, the tightness in my belly returned. I have begun to doubt our return to Buffalo would be met with celebration. The answer to all my problems lies mere feet from my location locked inside my database. It was impossible to sift through 25,000 names in any time we had remaining.

Our agreed-upon plan of running to the FBI in Syracuse had backfired; I certainly lost some popularity. Ryan Prince as an innocent bystander ended when I shot an unarmed man. I don't regret those actions, just Sam's interpretation. That is in the past, there is no time to focus on anything other than what lies ahead. Somewhere on this road, we will meet the future, we will be tested, what occurred five minutes ago will hold no bearing. I am back to living sixty-second increments, cur-rently, we are covering 12 miles every ten minutes. Our first milestone lay just ahead - the New York State Thruway.

The radio brought me out of my mind's wandering; I ac-tually have no recollection as to how long it had been tuned to the 24-hour-a-day news station. One does not hear one's name on the radio often, unless you're a politician or you dropped the winning touchdown pass in last Sunday's game, ordinary folk like us are not usually fodder for the radio heads. I hushed Sam and turned up the volume:

"........there is a multi-agency search currently underway. The FBI has released two photos of the fugitives Ryan Prince and Marie Saint Claire, both residents of Amherst, New York. Prince is wanted as a person of interest in the deaths of two NSA agents killed tonight in the small town of Sand Hill Lake. Prince is to be considered armed and dangerous. If you see either of these fugitives do not approach, call your local 911 operator immediately. The two made their escape from Watertown Memorial Hospital after a false 911 call. They were last seen exiting the hospital. They may be driving a metallic blue 2006 Toyota Avalon, New York State license plate number DPW-1082. This is Ferdinand Gonzague reporting for WWBN radio Syracuse."

Stunned, I was well aware that we had crossed a new line when we "acquired" the car. The news report brought this to reality, it made it real. The two men at the cabin worked for the NSA. I wondered if an NSA agent was in the room while Fludd questioned me.

The flashing red and blue lights in the rearview mirror was a freighting experience; frightening enough to cause many expletives to escape my mouth, Sam, too, adding some colorful language.

The lights were hidden under the grill of the car. The blinding searchlight was unexpected. I wanted Sam to mash the accelerator to the floor and run like hell. However, there had to be more than one police cruiser in the area. I wondered how long they had been tracking us.

If we ran and tried to escape; it may be a shoot first ask, questions later situation. It also occurred to me that perhaps my one phone call could be to Agent Boyle. I would refuse to answer any questions without a lawyer and Agent Boyle at my side. He might listen to what I have to say before passing judgment.

Figuring that a supervisor or captain had pulled our car over, the surprises did not cease as Agent Fludd knocked on the driver's side window. He was carrying a huge Maglite and a handgun.

"Step out of the car now!"

Sam looked at me and I looked at her and there was a brief moment of hesitation but we both raised our arms and exited the vehicle. I grabbed the laptop from the front seat.

"You are both under arrest. Do you understand your rights?"

"Yes," we said in unison.

"At this moment, asshole, you have no rights," he said menacingly, pointing in my general direction.

Agent Fludd suggested we join him; he was very persuasively waving his handgun. It looked like a Smith and Wesson .45 caliber and also appeared that it could possibly shoot through houses.

He looked pleased, as if our short escape had been some sort of personal affront to him, an affront that soon would be avenged. Hands raised Sam and I approached his cruiser. He was very careful about the handcuffs, securing Sam before he moved onto securing my hands.

I removed my arm from the sling, placing both hands in front, he smiled; his grin showing teeth; although it was not a happy smile it was very animalist, a sneer to show dominance. It would not have surprised me if he broke out in a growl. He then handcuffed me, both arms behind my back.

As he turned me around guiding me to the car he emphatically stated, "I hope your fucking arm falls off."

When we were both handcuffed he took turns throwing us into the back seat, twice ramming my injured shoulder into the door frame. I did not grimace after the first "accident." He was especially displeased when I did not grimace after the second attempt; even though he used noticeably more force, and the pain was unbearable, I never showed any signs of discomfort.

When he deemed us safely stowed and no longer a threat, Agent Fludd drove off. He never called anyone on his radio. I was certain that he would need to gloat over this accomplishment. He would be a hero capturing the dangerous fugitives on the lam. It would at least result in a commendation on his personal record.

He looked as if he enjoyed the spotlight - he may even on occasion seek it out. He liked to be in charge as was indicative of his questioning at the hospital. He knew that an FBI badge carries with it more merit than that of the local constables. I thought that nothing would surprise me again, but his cruiser appeared to be the only one in the area. There were no others in sight - his police scanner in his car was on but there was no chatter concerning our escape.

A fleet of such vehicles in the multi-agency task force was nowhere to be seen and did not set upon us.

Sometimes it takes me a minute to catch on: I'll be the first to admit it's amongst my many flaws. As I sat in his back seat wondering why there weren't ninety cars here to help in our capture, what had to be the most famous fugitives ever to run in Jefferson County, the conclusion struck me like a hammer. My conclusion, if correct, could only mean more trouble and an ending that would bring great pleasure to Fred's compatriots.

Agent Fludd removed his cell and made a call. This may be the fifth one-sided conversation I heard within the last 25-plus hours, I was only privy to his side.

"Yes we have them, no one else is aware they have been found." He turned off the scanner as there was talk of a status check.

A short pause -

"He is alive but very uncomfortable."

A longer pause –

"I am looking forward to ending this piece of shit's life."

He ended the phone call.

The radio was on the all-news channel and there was an update from the earlier report. The reporter was interviewing the chief of police, Charles Bourbon, I believe what I found most interesting about the story is how we were still being reported as on the loose. I wish we were on the loose instead of handcuffed and in the back of Fludd's car.

Agent Fludd never called in the tag on the car, he never called in a report. It was to his advantage that others still utilized their energies tracking us down. With all the local police and other agencies concentrating on our capture, he was free to do as he pleased.

He was operating on his own. He had time to carry out whatever plans our capture had set forth. My friend had warned me earlier that there were rogue forces in action today.

I may have just met the master.

20

August 19 | 3:30 a.m.

My shoulder was complaining about being asked to be flexible. I did not want Agent Fludd to be pleased with my discomfort, I said nothing about it. However, I was fearful my body may turn traitor.

Sweat was pouring off my brow and I was light-headed and nauseous. I was unsure how much longer I could maintain consciousness. The grey was closing in; I was losing my peripheral vision. My heart was slowing with every minute we were in the car, and my breathing matched its partner's rhythm.

Sam and I both knew enough to remain silent. It didn't take a rocket scientist to figure out that Agent Fludd was at the moment working off his own agenda. He needed us, or at least me, for some as of yet unknown reason. Once the reason had been determined, I would not be long for this earth. I was certain that a "mystery" person would not be jumping out of the bushes to save my life.

At that moment I wished that he would allow Sam to leave. She really had nothing to do with this nonsense; therefore, she should not have to die. I had come to the end once again; I decided to initiate the conversation.

"Agent Fludd, as contained with my Miranda rights, I wish to have counsel present before any questioning."

"Your rights! Your rights! Let me reiterate your rights: You have the right to shut your damn mouth before you eat a bullet, you have the right to die like those agents you murdered, and you have the right to disappear never to be seen again. Do you understand your rights, Mr. Prince?"

"I must be behind on my law journals. Did they change the Miranda notification?" Sam kicked me in the shin and shot a look at me that could have felled a grizzly.

"Our contacts in Buffalo told me you were a smart ass prick."

"To bring laughter to the world: that's the gift I offer." Sam kicked me again only harder this go around.

"Laugh while you can. You won't be laughing long."

"Why don't you call that multi-agency task force to let them know we are in custody?"

"We are not going to headquarters; we are not going anywhere anyone will find you. You are about to be swallowed by the ground."

"I want to contact my attorney or any other attorney in the area."

"This is the only law you'll find" he cocked his pistol, pointing it indiscriminately about the back seat. "I really don't require your assistance; however, cooperate and you may live another few hours. I will shoot Sam to close your mouth. Are we on the same page now?"

"I suppose so Fludd." I think Sam was grateful that I had no comment at the ready. Agent Fludd released the hammer on his gun and returned it to his holster. He answered his cell phone.

"Agent Fludd, I am not the one to point out such minor offenses, but as a representative of the cellular industry, I would like to mention that it is exceedingly safer to use your phone with its headset while driving. You know, I wouldn't want to get into an accident or anything."

"We are twenty minutes out. They are contained," he flipped it closed and increased the speed of his sedan. His eyes targeted me in the rearview mirror showing his teeth in his canine-like grin and fired a round between Sam and me. The back window exploded in a shower of small sticky glass.

"Fucking shut your mouth or the next round goes in your skull."

"I would rather arrive safely at my murder, is that too much ask, sir?"

Sam was pretending to cry; she was indeed stifling a laugh.

He once again returned his full attention to the road. He would occasionally glance into the backseat like he expected us to bail out of the now absent window. I wasn't sure if he was disappointed or pleased. His large hand cannon was within easy reach on the passenger seat. He received two other phone calls, he said nothing and neither seemed to last longer than a minute.

I was all out of plans. A part of me gave up. It was dark outside and this road was not illuminated by any street lighting. I could not focus on any trees or shrubs or anything as we rushed by at 90 miles per hour.

The green backlit speedometer climbing, the engine readily able to pass the additional gas being thrust into the fuel injectors. He looked determined behind the wheel, he looked like a man with a plan, and he could not reach his destination fast enough.

My body continued to leak fluids, sweat now ran cold down my back, there was a telltale sign that sutures were no longer correctly doing their job as a red stain spread across my shirt. Talk about a day full of milestones - this is the third shirt I have ruined.

Sam followed my concerned gaze, her eyes huge with fear. She knew the bleeding had returned and I was already a few quarts low. I fought the greatest fight of my life and I remained awake and almost alert through the worst of it.

21

August 19 | 4 a.m.

The red stain continued its southward migration and now my shirt was soaked, sweat stains now under my pits and neck, the dizziness worsened, and I was burning hot and then freezing cold. I was in shock and would require some assistance soon.

Agent Fludd was silent as he drove unrelenting. We were not on Route 81 nor any other main route I recognized. And we had traveled 30 miles since he apprehended us. We were on surface streets heading for Syracuse. That was my guess as the digital compass on his rearview read "S."

I do not spend a lot of time in the city so the street names did nothing to aid my bearing. He also had his radio tuned to the all-news channel. The latest update: we had ditched the stolen car and had acquired another one the make and model yet not available. According to the report the Thruway had been closed at Route 81 and cars traveling west on any other major route were subject to searches. The net was tightening and our capture was imminent. If we slipped this noose police in western New York would be on the lookout. Our apartment in Amherst was under constant surveillance and both our offices were covered as well. New evidence had been uncovered that indicated my guilt. Sam was drawn into the whole affair, her innocence as certain as my culpability. A plea was issued on the radio for Sam to contact the police with our position and destination in an attempt to end our flight before someone was injured, or worse.

The "or worse part" had come and gone, we were well past it at this point.

I was pleased to be listed among the living once again, however, the circumstances could not have been less fortuitous.

Fludd continued to drive around, his silence constant. There had been no more contact with whoever was waiting for us. He had gone dark; he was trying to operate under everyone's radar.

We turned on many one-way streets our route taking on a definitely circuitous pattern. Turning right down yet another one-way road except this street lead to a back alley. It was narrow and the surrounding buildings were tall. The fire in my damaged shoulder was now raging.

Without medical attention I was fearful that Fludd would not require a bullet to end what was remaining of my life; twice on the trip I was almost overwhelmed by thirst. I was dehydrated and in need of more fluids than just water.

Approximately halfway down the alley, Fludd braked, placing the car in park, removing the keys. I thought this was rather prudent as this did not appear to be a very good neighborhood. He opened Sam's door first lending her a hand as he helped her out of the back seat. Fludd was none too delicate in removing me from the back seat and the narrow alley did not allow the door to open through its full arch.

I was grabbed by the collar, thrown from the car, the subsequent meeting with the concrete and brick wall re-injuring my broken nose, the blood again filled my mouth with the metallic taste reminding me more precious blood freely flowed and my reserves were already dangerously depleted.

I was thankful Sam did not receive the same treatment. Fludd removed the laptop from the back seat along with our possessions. A quick knock on a heavy industrial metal door caused light to flood the narrow alley. We were led into the building without blindfolds. They cared not if we saw their faces. Thankfully, a man at the door removed our cuffs.

Twelve men awaited our arrival. Some like Fludd wore suits, others donning jeans and sweatshirts, some in t-shirts, and there were two men dressed in full black fatigues, each carrying a nine millimeter. I walked by smiling.

"I think I saw your friends tonight, maybe we should all go out for a drink."

A large well-muscled man stepped in my path thrusting his chest into mine. Fludd caught me before I fell.

"How much paperwork is required when a customer service supervisor takes out two of your fucking goons?' I smiled. Again, with every ounce of my remaining strength, I headbutted the man right in his face, breaking his nose. He stood drawing his gun on me.

"You can't kill me or else I'd be dead already. Fludd, why don't you call off your dog?" I spat blood in his face. I was unarmed but pissed at this point, I no longer cared. I either eat a bullet, or I would bleed to death all over these fine people, either way, I was a dead man.

To be honest, I am not sure these were courageous acts. I had reached what I believed to be my personal limits, I was about to die. I might as well go out in a blaze of glory. I was not about to give these bastards any satisfaction. I know this is not the confessional but I also gained a great amount of satisfaction. I may have been suffering a psychotic break.

My shoulder flared with pain, every step felt like a dull knife was forced into my shoulder, cold sweat was again running down my back. Fludd marched us down a long hallway, doors on each side. My feet had issues maintaining balance on the polished concrete. Fludd was now supporting most of my weight. He was escorting us unattended as the others waited, back near the entrance. I could hear Sam's shoes squeaking on the floor, it was reassuring to know she was behind us.

The very rough appearance of the entranceway quickly transformed to a professional office setting, complete with modular workstations and plush carpet, dividers breaking up the floor into definite units, the grey short walls matching the grey stitching of the carpet, just enough wood accents around the main floor to let one know that some money was spent to make this space appear more upscale than it actually was.

Fludd led us through the work area and down a hallway, it was not at all that different than my own office. There on the right was a conference room dominated by a large darkly stained maple conference table, it was not hard to imagine that just hours ago men in suits surrounded the table discussing topics such as quarterly reports, and customer relations management, or maybe upcoming mergers.

The table was surrounded by overstuffed chairs, the fact that some rogue organization ran this place seemed odd and out of place. Of course, that could be the point to make this place look legit for illicit means. The facade seemed as important as the falsehood, hide in plain sight, conduct business as if this place was run by old men in suits not men in black fatigues. Maybe our tax dollars actually went to furnish this place adding to the air of legitimacy.

I was surprised they had left the carpet uncovered to kill two people in the midst of maple stained tables and fresh carpet. It seemed messy, or were they expecting another carpet to be installed shortly thus hiding their murderous deeds? I could almost imagine our lifeless bodies being carried from this place in the plush carpets to be dumped where they would not be found.

Fludd led us both to the end of the table farthest from the door offering a chair to Sam as if this a job interview and not the end, as courtesies somehow needed to be extended. It was obvious that they needed me for something or else we would have been killed before we reached this place.

I was aware this was the end of the line when Fludd had found us in our newly acquired vehicle. The fact they cared not whether we could identify them led me to believe it was not a necessary precaution on their part. We would be dead as soon as I fulfilled whatever task was ahead. This trip did not terminate in an interrogation room but a conference room not unlike the one at my office. There was no two-way glass or steel table, however, another person not identified nor offered a name joined us in the room.

"Okay smartass time to pay the bills. Fire up that database of yours." Fludd threw the laptop hard to the mahogany glossed table.

"Why don't you do it."

"You know I can't. There's a code to access the information. One you knew we wouldn't crack."

"You could if you had a supercomputer and about two hours' time, it's a 23-digit code containing numbers and letters and some other characters, 256-bit encoding. This, after all, is personal and propriety information, I couldn't allow it to fall into the wrong hands."

"I am about through with you and your bullshit!" he cocked his gun, pointing it at Sam, "do you want to be the reason she dies?"

I itched my forehead with my middle finger, feigning a move I've seen my friends eleven-year child use on his parents.

Fludd was just as oblivious.

I booted the computer. The code was not hard to remember - it seemed to be random digits, my uncle's birthday with month N capitalized, the date my parents met written in European Standard, then the date of my wedding with two digits for the day followed by S, two digits for the month followed by F and two digits for the year followed by another F and then the number sixty-three, just because. It looked like this 12085810056205s21F91f63 The three letters stood for stupid foolish... well, you can figure out the rest. It was to be a constant reminder to never marry again. Bad system it did not work.

Stalling the best I could without drawing undue attention I pretended to have problems remembering the difficult code. I glanced in Sam's direction; her rigid mask wore heavy on her face. She was not going to let these men into her world. They were only going to kill a body - she was hiding her soul from them.

I was trying to formulate a plan, but I drew a blank. I gained strength from her. I would not plead to these killers for my life - I would look them in the eye unblinking. Fludd withdrew a computer printout from his jacket pocket and tossed it in my direction.

I had accessed the database.

"What is it you want from me, Agent Fludd?"

"How far back does your database go? How many customers are there?"

"Six years and over twenty-five thousand."

"These are all customers you have helped in some fashion?"

"Yes, either over the phone or in face-to-face encounters. Whatever it is that you're after, I can find it quickly."

"Can you sort by data fields?"

"Ah, yes that's what the program is for, what they designed it to do. Not exactly Bill Gates, huh, Fludd?"

"Do you need another lesson in how I deal with smartass worthless piles of shit? Access this name and make it fast. There will be no one saving you, do as I say it will be quick."

The computer printout had the words 'Top secret. For

your eyes only. Destroy after viewing' written across the top in a large bold font. There was only one name on the paper - Abu Abdallah Moseb. The name was familiar. It was one of the few names that my earlier query had returned.

I sat at the laptop typing, bringing up the table that allows you to run a query. I set the parameters and waited - the process took seconds.

I stretched, looking at Fludd and said, "Long days like these are killers."

The computer beeped, his eyes diverted to the query, I figured I had thirty seconds left on this lush blue planet. I stretched again, my shoulder was sore and my hands were shaking.

The database allowed a straightforward sorting by data fields and last name was the field I chose. Access was able to efficiently locate the entry. Mr. Moseb was experiencing difficulties with retrieving voicemail messages. I had added some extended notes that indicated there were two other customers with different last names but the same address. One week ago, I sent these gentlemen a letter after completing a rate analysis on all three accounts. It was determined that a rate plan change would end up saving them a small fortune as the majority of the calls were among the three phone numbers. No contract would be required and I would be able to change it; moreover, I was willing to back rate the last three months. These three phone lines had generated well over $2,000 a month in revenue, ranking them in our top five percentile. There were small businesses that did not produce that much revenue. I presumed that they would be thrilled with the savings. Another strange fact was that I had helped all three gentlemen in the last six months. I presented my findings to Fludd. I was dead-on right about one point, an insignificant customer contact had led to the events of today to unfold. How was it possible that a voicemail issue and a potential rate plan change with an explanatory letter could possibly be the factor that caused at least three men's deaths?

I held back a need to laugh as much as a hearty belly laugh would have helped my stress level. This was deadly serious, although still made no sense whatsoever.

"Is this all you know about this one customer?" he questioned, emphasized via his handgun pointing at my head.

I mentioned the letter and the two other customers I found living at the same address, stating in a monotone voice preparing myself like Sam. I was about to die from doing my job too well - a bullet in my skull over a rate plan change.

"Are there only two copies of this database you utilize?"

"Yes, just this one and the one on my hard drive in the office."

"You don't know anything else about these customers?"

"Other than their pant size, I have already told you no."

Fludd extended his hand for me to shake. I refused the offer of his hand and gestured inappropriately. His hand forming a fist found my face, knocking me to the ground and aggravating my various ailments. I grunted unceremoniously when I hit the floor. My injured shoulder broke my fall, blood now flowing from the mended wound again. I could not find my feet and my head was spinning madly out of control. I struggled to regain my feet and my balance.

When I had finally regained my feet, blood was dripping from my nose onto the carpet. Fludd was in my face madly waving his gun about.

"Do you know how much trouble you've caused?" Fludd was so angry spittle came from his mouth. "You worthless piece of shit! You have caused the death of seven of my top field agents - irreplaceable men." He paused to sip from a flask he produced from his suit. "You tell me this Mr. Prince, how can a customer service manager best three of my men? You've had help from somewhere outside my range. I want to know who it is."

"First I have already told you. Someone else killed Fred. I was taken by that person and questioned extensively. They let me go, End of story. Asshole. I have had no help from anybody, no one. I have asked why, why me? It seems you don't know that answer either. Everybody wants me dead, no one can tell me why. It was payback for drilling the one man in his head, he was dead before he hit the ground. How did you find me faster than anyone else, that's the question that needs to be answered"?

"Someone took out a surveillance team of four agents. Four agents doing their job to protect the country from traitors like you."

"They're not missing. I know exactly where they are."

"Tell me now, or your girlfriend gets it."

"Relax. These fine gentlemen you're referring too, have an interesting policy of shooting first. They did not approach badge in hands announcing their intentions. I ran the best I could, they drove off the road about two miles from the cabin, before Route 12."

It was apparent that along the way I did receive help. The guy who did Fred, and the call from my mystery friend, and JC the man with a plan; although I am convinced they did not have my best interest at heart. I was the bait and this joker in front of me is the fish they landed. At the moment, it appeared the fish was about to shuck the hook.

"Well, it seems we have this contained," Fludd said, talking to the other person in the room. "We'll have this all fixed within the next few minutes. Get a team out to that cabin now!"

"Well, before you fix the problem, may I be allowed to ask a few questions?"

"Sure, why not." Another celebratory swig off his flask, a pack of cigarettes appearing from his jacket pocket.

"Who was killed last night, who was in my car?"

"A bum or vagrant - someone no one would miss. They put him in the car, gave him access to good drink. Boom there's an accident. The Brighton Fire department thought that there was something fishy about the explosion. A group, yet identified, was hoping to take you alive and set up a fake accident. The car might have hit the tree going 30 miles per hour - not fast enough to cause an explosion. Once you were dead they closed everything down, turned off your phones, and put a hold on your accounts."

"Was Sam next? She knew I wasn't dead - we were together last night."

"They may have left her alone, unless she made a fuss."

"Fludd, what is it that I know? A few people have been killed because of it. This still makes no sense, no sense whatsoever."

"It makes no difference. You connected dots, dots no one wanted to be connected. That's what caused this whole mess."

At my moment of contemplation, Sam reverted into the chair as far as possible, hiding from another outburst from Fludd. He was sipping at his flask wandering about the room, wondering who needed to be shot first.

I walked around the table, putting myself between Fludd and Sam.

"Why would this information I found result in my death?" I asked, appearing much braver than I actually felt. "Other than these men having a business connection to CellNY, I don't know who they are."

"We weren't sure how much information you knew and how widespread the problem was. Now we know. Two bullets to fix, everything back to normal."

"Who are these men? What do they know and what have I to do with this?"

"You'll have plenty of time to put it all together," He said, laughing and smashing his cigarette out on the conference table.

"Are you sure you want to do that Fludd? That looks like the real deal mahogany. Must have cost a fortune."

The other man who had not uttered a single word during this exchange exited the conference room after answering a call on his cell. Fludd had us both backed into the corner of the conference room. He insisted that we turn and face the wall. Without having to consult one another, we disobeyed his order. Either way, we were both dead. Whether you get a bullet in your brain, through the front of your cranium or the back, the results are generally the same.

The next few moments would rock my life-long belief in God as the supervising executive. Somewhere removed from us in the office complex there was shouting, the exchange of small weapons discharging, and general disarray.

Fludd closed the door, retrieving his cell phone, frantically making calls but no one was answering. He reached for a walkie-talkie he had clipped to his belt. He spoke into the device shouting surnames too numerous to count. The most disbelieving look took residence on his face as sweat began to collect on his brow.

Four men burst into the conference room, the door vehemently removed from its hinges, the force knocking Fludd to the floor, the door striking his head. He was disoriented as he tried to climb to his feet.

The first man through jumped on the door; I could hear the wind quickly evacuating Fludd's lungs. The gash in his forehead bled profusely. In the Armageddon that ensued, Fludd involuntarily relinquished his weapon.

He was disoriented and was trying to catch his breath, gasping for air, using his hand to cleanse the blood from his forehead. I did not hesitate to recover his pistol. With all the strength I had in my body I aimed the weapon at the first man that tried to knock Fludd unconscious.

"Hang on, hang on. Ryan, we are all friends here." The

man put his hands in the air holstering his weapon, "We want the son of a bitch dead as much as you do."

"That's right Mr. Prince," a second man entered the room, glancing at Fludd's limp body bleeding on the floor. He paused a moment, kicking Fludd in his already damaged skull. Much to my surprise, it was JC, the man who had aided our escape from the hospital.

"You two better start to explain what is going on. I have had a bad day, a short temper, and an itchy trigger finger." Aiming the weapon at both men, the promise I made at the hospital now came to fruition, I would without hesitation shoot everyone and let God figure out the rest.

"Mr. Prince, I am your friend - we spoke earlier on your cell and at the hospital. My name is Jean Cocteau. You, my friend, are a very clever man. Congratulations on making it this far."

"Save it for the party. What the hell is going on?"

"We have been tracking you all day. We set the fire to your car with a body we, well borrowed from the morgue." As we walked toward us he kicked Fludd square on his temple again. Needless to say, Fludd did not respond. The carpet became soaked in the blood streaming from the monstrous gash.

"I'm sorry that I could not explain further when we met at the hospital." He took a long drag on his cigarette. "There is too much to explain. I can tell you this is one bad individual. We have been tracking this rogue group for some time. This is my finest hour."

"Were you waiting for me to die? You took long enough to decide to help out."

"I am sorry it was necessary. We needed to see how high the conspiracy went. We have all the information we require. We have a few moments before we take leave of this place." Both men picked up Fludd's lifeless body, dropped him in a chair, reviving him in the process. "Agent Fludd, can you hear me?"

"Yes," he answered groggily.

"I believe you owe this fine citizen an apology."

"Fuck him." Fludd spat out a wad of teeth and blood on the ground, "I hope he rots in hell."

"Mr. Prince, we no longer have a need for this man. Would you like to do the honor?"

"No, I have enough blood on my hands today."

Fludd turned in the chair readying some smart-ass comment. The look of shock in his eyes was worth the price of admission. I held fast as the barrel of the pistol was within inches of his forehead, which at the moment was doing a nice impression of Niagara Falls. The pupils in his eyes were dilated, the adrenaline rush fueling the flight or fight instinctual survival mode. For the first time since we meet he was speechless.

"Welcome to the end of your life." I spat in his general direction.

"We can work something out, we can....." he was not offered the opportunity to finish his last sentence. The gun barrel was spewing smoke as it lay limp in my hand. Regret never settled in my heart or my soul, as a sense of triumph and completion would not allow such thoughts to enter.

The worm slays the fish. I had blood on my hands again and had killed a man at close range. My first thoughts were of Fred waiting to put a bullet in my spine or in my head; he was gunned down before he could complete his task. Fludd had made a similar mistake. Maybe he thought that, after all we had been though, there was no fight lingering, no desire to struggle against the current, like a man on the brink of drowning, we no longer possessed the necessary level of fight.

I know it was wrong, I know that Mr. Cocteau and his associate would have finished what they started. Call it revenge; call it a need to know this bastard was dead so he could no longer haunt my life. So I could continue my life without having to look over my shoulder.

Fludd completed the last few moments of his life. I felt safe: safe for the first time in nineteen and a half hours. His brains had painted the wall behind him, the circular pattern of deep red blood and bone congealing down the wall. His eyes wide open, wondering how his life had taken such a tragic turn, remained unbelieving.

I stumbled back against the wall and tried to control my breathing, trying to steady myself. My shoulder screamed in pain. Sam's eyes held the same unbelieving look as Fludd's.

I did not have a plan for the next sixty seconds. Closing my eyes, head slumped backward, no longer able to fight gravity, sliding ever so slowly down the wall, how easy it would have been to go to sleep, to give in to the need that was pulling my eyelids closed. I could feel my breathing slow to a steady pace; it was only moments away if I give in to it, just succumb to the numb.

22

August 19 | 5 a.m.

I felt a pinprick then all the lights came back on. Passing out again could have been from the stress or the blood loss. Either way, I came back to in the conference room with Fludd dead and our new friends standing in attendance. The entire situation was becoming extremely difficult to follow. Jean Cocteau had been following me all day, along with Fred and the FBI, added to that was a group of individuals from various government intelligence agencies that had gone rogue, or as Mr. Cocteau stated they had gone black.

From what I could ascertain the cause of this mayhem, this destruction, this death, was a letter I sent out to one customer, a letter advising a change in his rate plan to one more cost-effective. How many had died because of that letter, I had a direct hand in killing three, at last count. I had no idea how many had died in the vehicle as it lost its battle with the forest. I am certain that beyond this door lay more bodies than I care to count. These deaths deserved but still tragic, caused by a letter. I do not know if it was ironic or heartbreaking.

Mr. Cocteau was offering me a hand. As I witnessed Fludd's corpse the first pang of guilt echoed through my body.

I had only one explanation, not that it would do much to alleviate the current situation. I think I snapped. The emotional strain today simply was too much. I have subjugated my temper for the last fifteen years, as it is a necessary skill to survive in my occupation. Today was a first, I could no longer contain was what building inside. Although, I relinquished the opportunity, standing there watching Fludd knowing that as he walked this earth, there would be no safe days. I would spend the remainder of my life one eye looking backward to ensure no one followed. I would check every dark alley or ill-lit street waiting for this man. Something broke, something that was the core of what I did and who I was. Broke.

Aiming the pistol was effortless, as he was feet from my position. The trigger was pulled seconds later, wiping that smug grin from his face. Again, I was counting my last thirty seconds. It is an arduous task trying to explain how that rocks you, how it feels in the soles of your feet, in the pits of your arms, and in the abyss of your soul.

You are preparing for the end. It's both the lowest moment and the greatest joy of your life. However, it also seizes your heart and removes the breath from your lungs, when the moment passes the feeling of cool air rushing into the void, its priceless, a moment most people never experience. Certainly, there are those that have counted the last thirty seconds but miss the joy, as their clocks do not reset.

I have no explanation for the two seconds between my denial to pulling the trigger. My finger was not responding to reason, it reacted instinctually, tendons tightening, yanking the trigger, causing the nine-millimeter to fire. It took longer to write that last line than for my finger to decide to end his life. It happened that fast.

"People's life expectancy seems to decline around you, and decline fast," Sam said, disbelief in her voice.

"Would you rather he killed me and then killed you too?"

"Sam, as much as Ryan's actions were not pleasing, you must trust me when I say it was necessary," Mr. Cocteau said coolly, like he was reporting on tomorrow's weather. "Ryan, the time draws near, we need to take our leave of this place the sooner the better. There is a van waiting outside."

We followed Cocteau out of the conference room. Fludd's partner Louis Nevers I was told, lay dead just outside the door. Cocteau explained that all twelve men in the building now lay dead and that they had brought a force of twenty. I gingerly walked over the man in the black fatigues, his brains, like his partners, no longer where they belonged. The other fatigued gentleman fell to the ground in a sitting position, his finger still on the trigger. Smoke hung thick in the air, accompanied by the noticeable odor of burned flesh and cordite. Not pleasant. I tried not to think about it as I tiptoed around the corpses, almost failing to maintain my late-night supper.

Cocteau told me all members of the strike force had but one goal in mind - save my hide. I was grateful but overwhelmed. I was positive that a week's vacation would be justified just to process everything that had occurred within the last nineteen hours.

We hurriedly exited the office complex the van awaiting our arrival. The men had been inside only five minutes and their presence had gone unnoticed.

I followed Sam and Mr. Cocteau outside, activating the safety on the gun as I tucked it into my waistband. It took only moments to evacuate our party.

Mr. Cocteau, Sam, and I were the only three that entered the first van - another pulled up behind us to accommodate the remaining party. There were men left behind, those with computer skills required to hack the systems and extract all available data concerning the operation.

The van we occupied was well-stocked, complete with two physicians at the ready. As soon as they saw me, without asking, I was prepped for a transfusion, my once again broken nose mended. The bed in the van was comfortable. I could feel myself relaxing as my arms were prepared to accept an IV.

I was going to ask if they had my correct type or was it just plasma. I decided they knew my type as they were not willing to risk killing me after the expenditure of manpower spent to wrest me free.

Sam had various bruises still present from the crash but they were clearing now. The back of the van was equipped with a narrow albeit comfortable bed. The transfusion filled my empty veins drop by drop.

However, the doctors lacked the medical training to mend the broken part of my being.

I am changed in a yet to be determined way. I had focused my anger and acted instinctually, hopeful this would not affect my ability to service customers. I was somewhere else, removed. I heard the conversation in the van. A small part of my awareness was able to respond to questioning, but most of me was not in that van. I heard the doctor's quick conversation concerning the sorry state of my shoulder. My pupils responded to light correctly, they ruled out a concussion. The bandages were hurriedly removed from my beaten shoulder and a local anesthetic was administered. My shoulder went numb, which was a relief.

The pain had become intense, and under normal circumstances, I certainly would have been on bed rest, my shoulder immobilized to aid the healing process. Wearing handcuffs and being thrown to the floor had caused more than one suture to rip again, and the bleeding commenced. The doctors wondering aloud to each other how was it possible I remained standing. I was surprised to be among the living after another close call with Fludd. They finished their mending, replacing another bag of blood and an IV.

I could feel Sam's hand in mine. Her face was the last thing I saw before the grayness of unconscious sleep took me once again. I was informed later that I had been given a sedative and there was no fighting it.

23

August 19 | 6:30 a.m.

The return trip to Buffalo was uneventful, being I slept the entire way. I awoke to the van braking to a complete stop in front of a rather nondescript house. The house was not on a main street. I was not a witness to where exactly we had exited the highway.

Mr. Cocteau and his men started to the house, making way for Sam and I. They entered the two-story Victorian, automatic weapons leading the way. I was stunned to discover the nine-millimeter was still tucked away in my waistband. It was as comforting as the bed on which I slept and felt as necessary as the blood transfused into my depleted system.

We were told that the top floor served as the safe house, and a married couple lived in the lower apartment and were in the employ of Mr. Cocteau.

The stairs in the back of the house were narrow. Sam and I quickly climbed the staircase in the middle of the entourage. Sleeping on our return trip and my blood level back to normal, my mood had increased exponentially since being abducted by Fludd and his team.

Nearing the top of the stairs one of our protectors

knocked on the door muttering something nearly unintelligible, but it worked as the door opened outward toward the group.

"You'll be safe here." Mr. Cocteau stated glancing about the apartment, ensuring everything was in place - everything as it should be. "There will be someone stopping by in about an hour, he will want to take your statements."

"Will this mystery guest be part of a recognized agency?"

"Yes, he will be with the FBI. He will be particularly interested in what you have to say about Fludd."

"Doesn't the FBI believe I killed those men at the cabin?"

"Some things have come to light during our trip home. You are no longer considered a person of interest. The media has been contacted and they were given Fludd's name and description along with an explanation that you and Sam were set up."

"So we are safe here?"

"Yes, you're safe. If you need to contact anyone it will be a while. But your respective employers have been called and the situation explained."

"Does someone want to explain this to me? I am at a loss to understand what happened."

"It will all make sense soon. We have not shared the entirety of the events with your employers; however, they were given enough information that you both have been cleared of any wrongdoing. Sam, the company van is being replaced."

We were both relieved. In all actuality, we had stolen two different vehicles: Sam's company van and the Toyota at the hospital. Moreover, twice today, I have shot an unarmed man.

I went too far in trying to extract information from the man at the cabin, Fludd straight out had it coming. We were no longer considered fugitives; as soon as this was finished we could slip back into our quiet lives. I have had my fill of international conspiracies and fleeing from professional killers.

Quiet complacency with a good dose of apathetic withdrawal would be the vacation my soul requires. Mr. Cocteau stated we would be free to leave in about an hour or so; however, it was mandatory we stay for our debriefing with a legit member of the local FBI. I wondered how Mr. Cocteau became involved in all this nonsense.

He defined himself as a civilian consultant to any number of agencies in Washington DC. Mr. Cocteau was a French national that had grown weary with his own country's handling of international affairs. He wanted to be involved to make a difference. He had been recruited after completing his degree in International Business Relations from Georgetown University. Mr. Cocteau was fluent in English, French, German, and Arabic. He was able to go places were American agents, no matter how well trained, were not welcome.

He reported to a variety of agencies, including the FBI, CIA, and the NSA, to name a few. He also was aware of the presence of other less organized forces in Washington. He had utilized his contacts to investigate and infiltrate the members of this conspiracy. Without naming names and pointing fingers, Mr. Cocteau uncovered exactly who was involved: some of the President's inside men were cognizant of what occurred, and my very limited role.

The media loved it when we uncovered terrorist cells

within our borders. I was about to become an integral part of discovering such a cell. The media will be informed of my fictitious endeavors to uncover Arabs for Freedom. A new group that is taking responsibility for bombing various embassies and oversees targets frequented by Americans. This terrorist group had decided to take its fight to foreign soil, in order to defend their own. Mr. Cocteau's ability to move among a variety of intelligence agencies, both domestic and foreign, allowed him to gather this information without arousing suspicion. I was about to be labeled a hero. Through my extensive database, I was able to connect men via their cell phone records and was about to go public with my findings.

This is the reason for the false report on my death and the subsequent events that had transpired. Ironically, my database had located a connection; however, not the connection that was being reported.

Mr. Cocteau gave me a disk and the information downloaded into my database. The numbers on the disk were as fictitious as the cover story, none the less important information to have on hand. Even fabricated evidence had its place.

I surveyed the apartment. It was large, big enough to be in the Elmwood section of town, although its location still eluded me. The streets were too quiet, and there was not enough activity, so this definitely was not Elmwood. We could have been in any number of suburbs. I would not be able to determine our location until we drove to downtown.

The curtains were drawn and little ambient light was present. The room was lit from small lamps scattered about on various tables. The living room was immense and included a dining area. There were three bedrooms and a bathroom each off a small hallway adjacent to the living room. The kitchen was not overly large, yet seemed very accommodating. The high tech equipment and computer monitors numbering at least 10 did seem very much out of place in this less than modern accommodation.

We were advised the apartment was routinely swept for bugs and other listening and surveillance devices. There also were two rather large men in the corner, currently their attention paid to the bank of computer monitors.

Mr. Cocteau spoke briefly to each man in French. They were introduced as Jean and Guillaume de Gisors, men that Mr. Cocteau had personally recruited for missions such as this.

Both men had shoulder holsters, each carrying a Desert Eagle fifty-caliber handgun, making the nine-millimeter weapon I carried seem very inadequate. I supposed they were the first level of defense and my weapon would not be necessary.

"Jean and Guillaume are here to protect you until you are handed over to the FBI. They will give their lives to ensure you see tomorrow." He stated this with such fact that it seemed absurd.

After a brief nod in our general direction, the men went about their surveillance of the monitors. Mr. Cocteau left briefly, returning with a suitcase I would have sworn was out of the bottom of my closet.

"We have taken the opportunity to get some clothing from your apartment. Please excuse our choices as my men were hurried at the time. The shower is through those two doors -

please help yourself. Ryan, the doctors prefer you not to take a full shower to avoid saturating your sutures. Sam, you'll be given all the privacy you need to refresh yourself. You can see we have taken every step to ensure your comfort." You could hear the smile in his voice.

"Mr. Cocteau, how did you gain access to my apartment? It was closed off after the officer was gunned down."

"Ryan, some questions are better left unasked, yes?"

"Yes sir."

"Please, please it is simply Jean, or my friends call me JC, as you know."

"Okay JC. Thank you," I extended my hand and he took it in both of his.

"JC, you have been very accommodating, we can never thank you for everything you've done." There was a sadness in Sam's voice that I could not yet place. She left with her overnight bag, "I need a shower. Ryan, can I use your cell phone? I need to call someone. It's important."

I handed Sam my cell. She might have lost her own in the mayhem. She went about attempting to shower and rid herself of 24 hours of grime. I know exactly how she felt; a single shower would not be a suitable remedy.

"Mr. Ryan, sorry English not so good as Messier Costeau's, we are needing to know how you find these three men." One of the de Gisors bothers asked. "I am sorry, ah my name is Jean."

"Over the last three months I had spoken to each of those men independently, it wasn't until I had spoken to the third man that I made the connection with the addresses."

"Why did these men, ah come to visit you?"

"The first one Abdul, wanted to add international calls to his account, the second, sorry I forget his name, was having trouble with his phone. Our vendor had rushed that model to market and it had many issues. The third, Abdu, was having trouble with his voice mail. There is a large population of Arab Americans in western New York. I cross-referenced their addresses and sent the letter to Abdu."

"Do you know these men?"

"Never met them before they came in."

"Why is it you keep such an extensive database?"

"I manage a one hundred person call center; however, my area of responsibility is customer retention. I keep the database in order to better service our customers, to give them, a special touch. What we refer to as the concierge touch. All carriers offer about the same plan. My hope was my extra level of service would help us keep these customers with CellNY."

"You are very good at your job, no?"

"I like to think so."

"Because you care so much, is that what caused, ah everything to happen?"

"Jean, I have asked myself that question many times today, yes, I guess that's it."

"You are a good man, yes?"

"I hope I am just that."

"Can you please surrender your weapon?"

"No."

"Why not please?"

"If I were armed this mess could have been avoided. I mean

you no ill will but you'll have to pry the gun out of my dead hands."

"Oh, I see. We are friends here; you are surrounded by people that wish you to be safe."

I took the gun out of my waistband. There was one round in the chamber. I relinquished the magazine but kept the gun. I was not in a trusting mood. These people may have saved my life, but I still did not understand their motivation. I may become expendable at any moment. I was not going to be unprepared for the third time today. One bullet may be the difference between escaping with my life and ending up dead for real. Jean had our laptop and he was able to connect to his LAN and began a search, for what I do not know.

"Is there anything to eat? I am starving."

The other brother went to the kitchen and returned shortly with some sandwiches and coffee.

"This is not exactly gourmet cuisine but it will do, no?"

"Thank you."

I was famished and the sandwiches were delicious. The meat and bread were very fresh; I doubted that they were deli. The mayo was seasoned differently than the store-bought variety, it may have been dill, it was hard to place. The brothers watched my gastronomical feat as I consumed eight of the ten on the plate. The coffee was more than passable, a blend that I had not drunk before. It was robust and smooth and no one in attendance gave a damn that I drank it black.

Sam exited the bathroom, her hair still wet from her shower; she sat next to me and began eating the last half of the sandwich on my plate. There is something very alluring about a woman fresh out of the shower. I only wished there was a moment we could enjoy together. But there would be a better time for such things later.

"My boss is pissed."

"Really, did you tell him that the van would be replaced under the circumstances?"

"That's not the point. I was not supposed to have access to the van. I'll be lucky if I am not fired over this."

"Sam, your pending termination should be one of the last things on our minds tonight. I'll work at 7-11 if it means we both are still breathing a week from now."

"You are right. I should apologize for setting you up."

"Sam, it's not every day you see me react this way. I am sorry. I know that I scared you. But I am still the same Ryan you fell in love with."

"I am not sure about that." She quickly jumped from the chair, nearly running from the room, and headed back towards one of the bedrooms.

"I am taking a nap," she said dismissively.

I wanted to walk back and hold her if even for just a moment, in order to ground myself, introducing some normalcy in this rather abnormal day.

"She is a beautiful woman and you are a lucky man."

"Jean, you don't know the half of it my friend."

It was the tension breaker we all required. Too much has happened, too much running, too much being shot, too much bullshit. The group had a good albeit too hearty laugh. Even JC seemed very amused. It had been a difficult day for all involved. I was so self-centered; it took moment to realize these men also had put their lives on the line to ensure that I would see daylight once again.

They must have endured great strain following my activities, intervening at the last moment. I would like to speak with them to understand their motivation. My motivation was simple - don't die and protect Sam to the best of my abilities.

I was reminded of the movie "Signs," where everything was connected and there were no coincidences. My thoughts went back to Boyle and JC and everything seemed connected in a way I have yet to understand. There was a greater power working these last 24-plus hours, a power that had conspired to make certain that I lived to see another day. I stated earlier that I lack the necessary tools to correctly understand what had transpired. It was not unlike a spider web - touching one strand caused the other to reverberate. My belief system which had served me so well throughout my life had been upset. I am not a philosopher, however, we as a human race are connected, connected in ways even I could not explain in my logical world.

I could care less if God was able to make a rock so heavy even he couldn't lift it. Is there betterment in our lives through the discussion of such topics? I am not sure. I am also not alone. I believe in what I see and what I can touch. I believe in the concrete. I don't believe in fate. I am a determinist. Maybe my belief structure was without the necessary tools to completely understand what had transpired. Could it be that my brain is not wired correctly, that it was too logical in its operation?

It is difficult to philosophize or bring spirituality to those events. It is not how I operate. It's not that I don't believe in a higher power, I do. I just don't believe in God the manipulator, forcing man to follow some predetermined path.

I believe in God the observer; feet on the desk, paper in hand, watching the events unfold in the universe he created. Observing, choosing only to scrutinize, not interfere. I also believe in God as an ultimate judge; I may have some problems in that area after today's events.

Maybe God is the ultimate supervisor; God might have interjected these people into my life. Maybe my disbelief in God the chess player was invalid after all. Could it be that through this indirect interference he may be able to shape things to a greater design? That everyone you meet, whether it's for an hour or twenty years, influences your movements and decisions? Could it be through this kaleidoscope of human interactions that His will is carried out? Could it be that God indeed managed the universe, truly supervising certain movements, certain interactions leading to outcomes we could not fathom? Does he play with an adversary on this five billion-piece set? Are there other forces influencing people in a different manner trying to undo every one of God's previous moves? Is this adversary blocking interactions, cutting off connections, breaking the web, stopping the sequence? Is this the battle of good and evil - two adversaries indirectly influencing our future?

Is there truly evil in this game? Could it be that we are offered guidance, yet ignore the call? Is it an intentional act of knowing that we are forcing our way, knowing that we fight the current yet continue anyway? Maybe instincts feel right because we are following some predetermined path? Is what we do when we just react is as important as the decisions we fret over for weeks?

We practice activities like sports and learning to play musical instruments, until repetition breeds instinct. We react without thinking about it, the action is done, just like a quarterback throwing the ball and the receiver that jumps to catch it.

Are our life experiences a type of practice so that we know what to do without conscious thought? Or is this how we are programmed? Is there an invisible hand or a cosmic plan? Is there some being named God who is a manipulator or master chess player?

Questions abound today. So many questions that demanded answers, yet, like my involvement in this mess, are so difficult to answer. I would need to meet with a priest, therapist, and a philosopher for a weekend in order to start to grasp the events of the 20 plus hours. My intellect is not prepared to tackle these questions or provide answers. I may never truly comprehend this day. I lacked the time and the appropriate counsel to settle such things. Either way, the universe was starting to make some sense to a person that believes only in determinism. Even if you don't believe in God, I am under the belief that he knows you. Regardless. I was shaken to my core. My mind accelerating to unheard-of speeds and going places it has never been. I was considering alternatives that two days ago I would laugh off as absurd.

The logical side of my being was determined to break my

thoughts. I was exhausted and making connections where none existed, connecting dots that truly weren't there.

I would not give in. There was a new Ryan, one who found the strength to survive. The new Ryan would expand his horizons, become more accepting of things that one cannot hold, cannot grasp, the intangible and the unexplained. As the day's events unfolded, there was indeed a higher power, someone looking out for me, someone who did not think my time had yet to arrive. For the days following August 18, much contemplation would be required. I am a spiritual person - not necessarily a religious one.

I believe spirituality resides inside, religion is routine and rules. However, it was difficult to ignore what has occurred. My second oldest sister had decided to pursue a religious life and she currently is a novitiate and had taken her temporary vows. We had many discussions – many of which ended in heated arguments.

She might be correct in her instruction. She believed in God the manipulator, as I always believed in God the absent caregiver. The God who did not care about the lives of the human race. It seems that I owe Caryn an apology. She was so steadfast in her beliefs she staunchly argued her side. I had wrongly assumed she was toting the Catholic line.

I was the new member of an emerging Catholic faith, one which did not look to the Vatican for guidance. I believed my fellow American Catholics would break away from the oppression of Rome. We would find our own path where priests could marry and the church would adopt a more open stance concerning gays and abortion. And conservative clergy members who did not heed the separation of church and state would not be allowed to stand atop the pulpit and direct the American voter.

Sam did not often elect to go to Mass with me. I attended a very open and liberal church. One where gay couples could go and participate in weekly mass. I am now in the belief that my liberal views could mesh with those with the more conservative church administration. "God does not play dice," Einstein stated during the birth of quantum physics.

God does not play dice, indeed. He does not play anything. Maybe there are people in this world which He does watch and intervene in their lives. Someone intervened in my life today; someone was ensuring tomorrow would not be my last.

I am steadfast in my belief that God instills upon us certain skills and attributes. There may be those who walk among us which God deems special. Maybe I am that special person. Maybe there are better things to come. That is why I am still breathing, still able to contribute.

It's too much to take in, too much to process. I wish I had a moment to call Caryn and ask her advice. Like my sister Clair, Caryn had corresponded with Sam. She is thrilled with our relationship and would welcome Sam into our tight-knit family. It may be the drugs that have been administered that are making my mind reel into areas that were normally off-limits.

To have the guidance of our family pastor, Father Clemente, would be, excuse the pun, a Godsend. It is not easy to share such thoughts at this moment. I could only hope the days which followed would allow me to investigate these feelings.

My brain is not functioning properly at the moment. Too little sleep, too much adrenaline, too many bullet holes - all conspired to impede its normal operation. There were still gaps to be filled in, connections to be made.

My mind still wandered to how I fit into this puzzle. I had more than three pieces of information now, the corners were starting to form, a picture of sorts building out of this puzzle of chaos. Yet the picture still remained fragmented, puzzle pieces lost, waiting to be found. JC was going to finish placing the last piece and complete the picture. There would be time to contemplate spiritual issues later.

I started to wonder if these people had indeed been in Niagara Falls following me. People who did not know a single thing about Ryan Prince, yet pledged their lives to ensure my safety.

I have only known JC for a brief period; it's obvious his natural charisma added to his leadership skills. His voice was replete with command and authority. I would follow this man into battle if only he gave me the order. He moved me. You wanted to listen to this man; every word he uttered seemed to carry with it certain importance.

I sat in a chair attempting to follow the weird direction my mind was pursuing. This has yet to reach its apex. I am intelligent enough to realize there were things that were yet to unfold. When I am back at home, the ring prominently displayed on Sam's finger, will I allow myself to know God had intervened today?

Did I feel safe? Yes and no. Three men who have pledged to give their lives to guarantee my continued existence surrounded me. After what had occurred it is challenging to trust anyone outside of Sam. My determinist world was still part of my being and I could not shuck off the shroud with which I lived my entire life. I cannot rely on anyone other than the two of us.

There was a feeling today was drawing to a close, yet there were those involved who have yet to surrender their goals. Forces again may be gathering for one last initiative, one last strike. I excused myself and walked down to the bedroom which Sam occupied. I needed a few moments of rest and needed to lie beside her.

Following Sam's lead, I went to the bedroom.

The room was dark, but the new day's sun provided enough ambient light to guide my way. The sun was already warming the room. Today would be much nicer than the 18th. Sam lay above the covers, bathrobe still clinging to her body. I quietly crawled into bed. She stirred, and I slipped my arm around her waist.

It was heaven to have her in my arms.

I could feel the alluring pull of sleep. I succumbed, feeling myself drop deeper and deeper, breathing slower and slower. Without any warning, Sam jumped up and threw me to the floor. My shoulder hit the small nightstand before breaking my fall. It was the second horrible waking I had experienced in the last 24 hours.

"What the hell was that?" Anger and surprise made my

words louder than I had intended. I did quick damage control and was relieved when no sutures had ruptured.

"You are not welcome in this bed! You are not welcome to put your hands on me!" Sam shouted wildly as if I had touched her hand to a hot stove.

"What the hell I ...!" My brain fought to comprehend her words.

"Do you understand?"

24

August 19 | 7 a.m.

A loud knock on the door of the apartment brought me back to the here and now. I instinctively reached for the handgun tucked in my waistband. Exiting the bedroom in a near sprint, handgun leading the way, I was uncertain if I had correctly heard Sam's last sentence. At the moment I had other things to deal with.

Both of the brothers leaped from their seats and ran to the door, waving frantically in my direction, insisting in broken English that I remove myself from the room. I did so, choosing the bathroom. A majority of the living room was still in full view through the crack between the door and frame. Hearing only hushed voices at the door, it was difficult to follow the conversation. Moreover, all of it may not have been in English.

The man who entered the apartment was wearing a dark suit with a white, freshly pressed dress shirt. He was at least 6'2" and looked like his previous occupation may have been a quarterback for an NFL team. His suit was well-tailored and it accentuated his muscle-bound frame. He might have been related to Agent Rocksolid.

If Sam saw this guy the engagement might be off for certain.

The tense situation de-escalated as quickly as it started as the brothers relaxed their posture and greeted this man with a handshake. My heart was still beating in triple-time, but I stowed my weapon as the brothers waved me to join them in the living room.

The mountain of a man extended his hand and I warily took it as he introduced himself as Agent Charles Radclyffe of the FBI. He displayed his badge. He retrieved a laptop stowed in a small satchel he had brought along.

"Let's get started, Ryan. We have a lot to accomplish this morning," he commanded, pointing to the other chair at the small table. I sat as ordered.

"Do you want to talk with Sam as well?"

"If she is resting, leave her be. You're the person I am here to see. Let's get started."

Agent Radclyffe began asking questions and taking notes. I started at the beginning; at the part where I woke up and found out I was dead. I dictated the proceedings in a monotone voice, as if unaffected by the turn of events that would forever change my life.

It was surprising how I could recall them in such an emotionally-devoid manner. I reported Fred's death as morbidly as the weatherman predicts frost.

Agent Radclyffe was most interested in Fred and the men who had momentarily abducted me in Canada. He was unable to find out if they were affiliated with any agency. Even my best description did nothing to help, as I could not provide any names at all, as not once did I hear any of them refer to each other by name.

I admitted the flight to dad's cabin was my idea, also to shooting Man #2 at near point-blank range in an attempt to extract information. However, I was adamant my first shots were retaliatory. Their first shot barely missed me.

My conscious was near clearing, so in the spirit of confession, I also told Agent Radclyffe about the van we borrowed, the car we stole, and about putting a hole in Fludd's skull. I neared the conclusion of my tale, pausing to finish the coffee one of the brothers had placed on the table before me.

I removed my shirt with assistance, so Agent Radclyffe could examine my two gunshot wounds. The first a superficial scratch, the second a blast through my shoulder which occurred during our flight from the cabin.

I told him I was caught up in an international conspiracy and my database of customer contacts caused the whole thing to come unglued. He did not believe me. I gave him the name Abu Abdallah Moseb, who of course Fludd gave me earlier, explaining the connection with the other two Arab Americans all living at the same address. And the subsequent letter that was mailed out.

I informed him Jean Cocteau had aided me along the way, had indeed saved my hide when I had but moments more to live.

Agent Radclyffe tapped away on his laptop, entering data. I was not sure if he was recording my words or searching some database, checking on my story. He would make notes on his pad while sifting through whatever data he had on hand.

Maybe he was collaborating my story. At the very least, I was certain our employer records are being accessed, as well as the name that Agent Fludd had given me and was willing to kill us both for.

Agent Radclyffe took his cell and dialed a number, telling me he needed to call someone in Washington. He stepped out of the room into the hallway. I could hear his muted voice, yet could not discern a single phrase. Mr. Cocteau had assured me I was cleared of any wrongdoing, pinning some of my actions against Fludd's corpse, who would not be surrendering any testimony to the contrary.

The longer Agent Radclyffe talked on his cell, the more I felt my chances of escaping without any jail time dwindling. Every additional minute was an additional year in jail, every second a day off my life.

A year later the phone conversation ended. I could feel the sweat building on my brow, my heart wondering if it could fuel another run.

"Everything checks out Ryan," Agent Radclyffe said, extending his hand. "What you lack in training you made up for in balls."

Relief, a palpable, living thing rushed through my body as I shook his hand. "Thanks, I guess. I did what I had to do."

"If you want we can arrange for a trauma psychologist to talk with you. Some of our agents have used this man before. He's good."

"I may take you up on that offer. There are some things I need to work through."

"Ryan, none of us ever gets used to killing someone in the

line of duty. The first time is the worst, no matter how justi-fied, no matter how unavoidable. It hurts and breaks a part of you."

"Thanks." I knew he was right; the emotional weight of the last day and a half was starting to take its toll. It was press-ing down like ninety atmospheres.

"It has not been easy, I think that would help a lot," I agreed, surprised that the tightness in my gut was replaced by a lump in my throat.

"I'll have a name for you later, okay? How's Sam handling all of this?"

I shook my head, remembering her pushing me off the bed. "Not well. She thinks some of my actions were, ah, over the top."

"Was she there when you shot Fludd?"

"Yes, she was. I shot him after declining an offer from JC. It was at point-blank range. Not pretty. She also was witness to the events at the cabin. I basically interrogated a man and shot him while he was unarmed."

"Did you feel better after shooting Fludd?"

"Did I feel vindicated? No. Did I feel safe for the first time all day? Yes. Either way, he was not leaving that room alive. JC and his men would have finished it."

I wondered if Sam shared this logic or not. I was very con-cerned with her reaction. The urge to talk to her about it was overwhelming. "Excuse me, please. I need to go talk to her." Agent Radclyffe nodded and I turned to leave.

Walking down the hallway, I wondered if I would have to give her a ring after all. Sam had not wanted to touch me;

she distanced herself emotionally and physically. I didn't go see her to be with her. I just wanted to hold her if only for a few minutes. I understand she did not know what to believe, I don't blame her. I did not know what to make out of the day's proceedings myself.

Her live-in boyfriend had killed breathing human beings, killed them with rifles and a handgun. Shooting the last in the head at close range, as if my dying, this time for real, could be justified.

As the madmen had concocted this plan, wasn't my right to defend myself to the very highest level of justifiable homicide the act of a righteous man? I grew angrier. I was tired. I was sore. There was a hole in my shoulder and the gunshot residue was so thick I could see it on my arms and feel it in my hair. I was not certain if I would be clean after one shower, or two for that matter. As for the immediate future, I am banned from full showers.

I walked deliberately and slowly down the hall, unsure what I would find. I wondered what we had left if anything. Consequently, I needed her touch, I needed her to look at me with those blue eyes and see everything would be fine. I needed normalcy returned. I needed to know the one thing in my life on which I could depend, was still present. If all she had for me was contempt, I would be able to read it on her face. It would be evident in her actions.

My bullshit meter was set fairly low after what had occurred. We had been through a hell of a storm, but we had been through it together. I stood in the doorway of the room, watching Sam, who was busying herself with a brush, minding her hair. I could feel her attitude from where I stood, even though her back was to me.

She barely had a scratch on her, while I made it a habit of having a rather intimate relationship with firearms. She was judging my actions. My actions will be judged one day. There would be some soul searching, some retrospective later.

Her ability to sit on that bed was a direct result of my actions; currently better stated, my deplorable actions. I could read her well enough. Well enough to know that an argument of epic proportion loomed on the horizon. It was an inopportune occasion; but, to say nothing would be worse.

We were supposed to be in this together, through thick and thin. I, however, cared not to continue on this way. I wanted to clear the air, even if it caused a schism in our relationship. I saved money for the ring; I had already made the next step. I wanted every morning to start with Sam and every night ending with her by side.

My nerves were raw and my patience as paper-thin as a politician's promises during an election year. I barged into the room without knocking. She turned quickly on the bed, startled by my quick entrance.

"What do you want?" The scorn was thick in her voice.

"Would you rather that guy put a bullet in my head?" I answered. It was hard to remove the sarcastic tone from my voice.

"Which one are you talking about?"

"There are three potential contestants, you pick one," I stated, growing angrier now, pacing the room.

"Your sarcasm is out of place," she said dismissively as if my acts today had no meaning on our well-being.

"So is your judgment! Would you rather that Fludd had been successful, and it was my brains, not his, on the walls? Or yours?"

"That is a ridiculous question."

"Is it? It's not easy to stand here and have you glare at me like there has been some fundamental shift in the person I was."

"You've killed people today. You've shot a man in the head with a rifle. Did you fire a warning shot? No. You shot him in the head, just like Fludd." I could see her eyes were unable to restrain her tears and they began spilling gently down her face.

"You're welcome."

I could feel her reaching for words. She wanted to pick the ones that would hurt and find a target. She crossed her arms. She started and ended at least five sentences. She continued to glare, cold and unmoving.

If she wanted she could have cauterized my wound. But she did not.

"Would you rather I died today? Would you rather I played Mr. Nice guy, negotiating maybe? Those men in the boat, the men you are feeling sorry about. His first shot was a headshot. I moved at the right moment or I would be dead and so would you."

She sat, arms still crossed, but her words now came quickly. "I did not know you had the ability to act quickly, without thought, to blowing a man's brains all over the wall."

My anger over her judgment became harder to contain. "I

acted, but not without thought. I was thinking quite clearly. Thinking if this man got by me you were next. I was not only trying to save my own hide, but looking out for yours as well."

"When you interrogated the man outside the cabin, you tortured him. You shot him as he sat there defenseless. What you did to his hand..." Despite her defiance of my acts, the tears were now flowing freely.

Neither of us was stable emotionally now. The day to end all days had ended. It was time to process. The stress had lifted, the endorphins drained from our bodies. Now, we were crashing hard.

"I have done things today of which I am not proud. I will admit to that. This wasn't a game of hopscotch. Those men at the cabin, Fred and his team, the men who shot up the van, they all shared one goal. Kill me before I could find help. Do it fast and do it quietly." I paused, my hands shaking uncontrollably.

I regained some composure. "I have done what I believed necessary, so the woman I want by my side from now until I die would make it to see the sunrise. If that is not sufficient for you, I will leave." I was pushed to the point of no return.

The sight of the man's hand exploding at bullet impact was playing through my mind, DVD-like, frame by frame. He had only two fingers left on his hand, a bloody stump remaining.

I also saw Fludd's head exploding, brains and blood splattered on the wall three feet away. It did not look real; the DVD in my mind now choosing to stop and freeze, zooming in on the cloud of red debris which preceded the hole in the front of his head. I could smell the cordite; I could feel the gun in my hand.

"I will be judged by many people, and God as well. I was quick in making decisions. I haven't had a minute to myself all day. Not one minute to sit down and plan. When a man points a gun at you, or better yet shoots at you, either run fast and far or shoot back. You shoot to kill. My first response was to run and hide. I am no coward; I did not know what I was up against. That almost got me a bullet in the back."

She sighed as if the wind had gone out of her as well as the fight. "Maybe I just need time to process everything."

"I can understand that. It's been a confusing day, a long day, with too much to process. To be honest, I am not sure if I'll feel any better in a week or even a month. I do not regret what I did today. I feel remorse for some of my actions. But not regret. Whatever you think about me, remember these two things: one, you are here because of those "things" I did today, and two, I acted out of the need to ensure your safety. I would rather have you alive and angry, than dead and content."

Agent Radclyffe was calling from the living room. I walked back, leaving Sam before she could respond. There would be a better time for healing and my anger was about to get me into trouble.

We had things to figure out. JC had the answers and so far he has kept them for himself. Not being big on suspense, I would rather just have my questions answered, questions to puzzle, puzzles that lead to the death of men today. I deserved answers. A few hours ago I was given the third piece to this puzzle, now I had a box full of pieces but no clue as to the completed picture. JC was about to show me the front of the box, and this enigma would be answered.

He was about to give my day some order, some logicality. I was starting to understand the limited role I played. Still, it did not add up. There was something else yet to be brought to light; there remained many unanswered questions.

"Ryan, your boss, Victor Hugo, stated you have unlimited access to your building, correct?"

I nodded slowly, unsure of what was to come next. "Yes, I could get us all in, but why?"

"I need to see your database. It is time for answers. JC will be joining us in a minute."

"Agent Radclyffe, I have my database here. It's in the laptop the brothers have hooked up to their LAN."

"The complete database?"

"A true copy of what sits on my hard drive at work, the only additions that were made were done recently."

"Good. Let's get started then."

I sat down at the laptop and brought up the database. The last query was saved and simple to run again. The name Abu Abdallah Moseb was still in the query field; seconds later, the results of the search was complete.

The hard drive whirred and boom, there he was, immediately under my favorite customer, Rose Lion. I hadn't notice before that their phone numbers were so close. I accessed the notation field and a letter I had sent him and two other people who lived at the same address showed in the comment field in my database.

"What is it that you did for these men?"

"I sent them a letter suggesting an upgrade of services to our family plan to save the trio a lot of money. I had noted the account numbers of the other two mentioned in the letter. They were Mohammad Jafar Emir and Abdo Massai Sahim. I had helped all three customers over a six-month period."

I went on. "Mohammad had been the first point of contact; he had issues with voicemail on his new phone, which turned into a bigger problem, and the original phone was swapped out for a new one at no cost." Agent Radclyffe was busy taking notes on his own laptop as I paused. Without looking up, he waved his hand for me to go on.

"Abdo was looking for a better plan and wondering about international rates. His was a relatively new account. International dialing is not something we normally allow a new customer to have, as those calls can become very expensive. But he waved a handful of bills in my face and I naturally turned that feature on for him. Also handed him a brochure concerning the rates and how to use the service." Since Agent Radclyffe was still busy typing notes I assumed this time he wanted me to proceed so I went on.

"Abu had been the last of my contacts. He wanted me to do a rate analysis on his account. When I entered his house address, I found that these two other men had also resided at the same address."

"What is that address?" Agent Radclyffe asked, finally looking up from his notes. I gave it to him and he typed it in, then took out his phone. He placed a call, and as he related the information, his face went from passive to concerned.

"Did you know this address was non-existent? It's far beyond the street address range of the other houses on the block," he said, looking pointedly at me.

I shook my head. "All of the customers paid their bills online and on time. There were three separate banks, and thus different account numbers." I shook my head again. This still made no sense at all. I had located a connection between three men. I had offered to save them money. This is not information for which men are killed. This is borderline ridiculous.

Agent Radclyffe's cell rang and he gruffly answered it, clearly not happy with my information. After hanging up, he explained Abu had not existed six months ago, and there was no Visa information about his entry in the county. There also was nothing wrong with his INS file, no red flags. Agent Radclyffe had given his contact the other names of the two men in the database and was waiting for information on those as well. We all looked perplexed as to how this puzzle would fit together. Both Sam and I had seen men die to protect this data, and as long as the data existed, there may be further complications.

I remembered the newspaper search. Sam had made notes concerning certain articles she had identified from the papers purchased. All but one carried the story of an Al-Qaida terrorist convicted of killing a wealthy Iraqi man and his three sons. The terrorist had been sentenced to death. During his trial he had professed his innocence; he stated these four men had aided the US in its initial attacks during the early days of the war, and branded them, traitors.

Agent Radclyffe received yet another call. He propped the

phone against his ear and began typing furiously. The call was decidedly one-sided with Agent Radclyffe grunting, his only words an occasional "uh-huh" and "okay." My heart began to beat faster. The nagging thought that this horrifying experience wasn't over yet it put my senses on high alert. For what seemed another hour, but probably was only minutes, he finally got off the phone.

He sighed. "The other two men also fit the same profiles," Agent Radclyffe explained. "They apparently fell out of the sky six months ago, no entry papers at all. Part of the file on these two is Top Secret." His voice held a note of concern.

It was then I remembered the paper Fludd showed me that read TOP SECRET on the top of the page, as if stamped, then copied.

"Agent Radclyffe, Fludd had a piece of paper with one of the men's names on it and it looked like it was copied from a file. It read TOP SECRET across the top. We had access to these records."

Servicing three men of Arab descent in a six-month period may raise flags elsewhere, but for some unknown reason western New York had turned into a popular destination for recent Arab immigrants. The infamous Lackawanna six, the alleged "other group" of 911 hijackers, also took up residence here.

Fortunately, they were never able to carry out any mission, as the cell was discovered quickly, and all involved were apprehended.

Not every Arab immigrant was here to wreak havoc. Some enjoyed the sights and fit right into the community. An Iraqi immigrant recently decided to invest in western New York, using millions of dollars out of his own pocket. He purchased a crumbling hotel, promising to restore it to its previous grandeur, not unlike what Sam's company had done.

He also was bringing investors into the area to build the largest office and retail space in all of western New York. Western New York was much more diverse than the small town where I spent my formative years. We had large populations of Hispanic, Asian, and African-Americans in the area. It added to the ambiance of Western New York. We had some excellent restaurants downtown, most serving delicious regional dishes - much better the usual American fare.

Had I discovered another cell, or something worse? Was Fludd protecting these men or chasing them? If these three men were indeed another splinter cell, they had inside help to get into the country, as there is no proof of entry. Why would someone from the great USA want me dead for connecting these men? All I did was my job, saw an opportunity to further service a customer, and save him money. That's all. Save money.

Agent Radclyffe opened a mapping program I was not aware existed. He recalled the address that was in my database. He turned his laptop towards me, and it clearly showed a satellite photo of a vacant lot at the address the men had given me. Another dead end. When he saw the look of disbelief on my face, he assured me this was accurate.

After looking at the information in my database I could now understand why they had chosen not to receive a paper bill, which we credited their monthly account three dollars. It was not uncommon, as most of our customers preferred our paperless billing system. And because they all paid their bills on time and in full, there weren't any notations concerning delinquency on any account.

Frustrated, we needed to make some headway. JC needed to step in and contribute to the cause. When he entered the room, it was if he had planted a bug in my head, heard the little voice talking, and was making an entrance.

"Agent Radclyffe, please access the name Hussein al-feyd Abdallah," JC said, pointing his finger at the agent's laptop. Agent Radclyffe promptly complied.

Agent Radclyffe entered the information and moments later I thought he was going to jump out of his suit.

"He is listed as a wanted terrorist, operating in northern Iraq. There is some notation indicating he did initially give our troop commanders aid in tracking Osama bid Laden. Although the information was considered compromised."

"Anything else listed about this man?" JC asked, pacing the room.

"He was killed in a car bombing, also taking his three sons. The man involved in the bombing was recently executed."

The newspapers came back to mind. "I saw that article in every paper we bought. All carried the story, word for word, I think it may have been off the AP wire," I added.

JC nodded. "That indeed it was Ryan. You are good at this my friend. Let us get comfortable. Its storytime."

Moving from the table, we all settled into the comfortable furniture. The de Gisor brothers looked like it was movie night. There was a fresh pot of coffee on the coffee table and I filled my mug in anticipation. Finally. Some answers.

JC didn't sit. He started his narrative smoking a cigarette and pacing the floor. He certainly had a flair for the dramatic, allowing everyone's expectations to rise, waiting for the right moment to start his tale.

"In the early days of the war, intelligence gathering was key to locating bin Laden. Generals and others decided to "trust" some of the locals with gathering information. They were surprised when a wealthy, well-established man stepped forward with what seemed some useful intel. This was a high profile Iraqi national, having ties to Shiite clerics. He signed his own death warrant the minute he aided the US. His reasons were actually selfish. The faster the US found bin Laden, the faster stability would be restored to the region and the faster he could again start making money again. He was an exporter by trade and also owned some oil wells," JC took a long drag on his cigarette, finishing it. He fished a pack out of his pocket and lit another.

"His most profitable crop, however, was one not normally listed on the manifests or on futures list. He was responsible for most of the black tar heroin that made its way east to American soil. When he found out that the Sunnis were targeting him and his family, he contacted the CIA through some field agents in his area. He turned over every name he had in the heroin business on both sides of the ocean. He asked for and received refuge in the US, for not only him but his three sons as well. The fake bombing of their death was carried off like a fake mob hit. It was very successful; the US did not investigate the bombing at all, and the local Iraqis followed the planted evidence to the man who ultimately was set up for the bombing. The trial was held two days ago, coinciding with the date exactly eight months ago when these men made their arrival in the great US as detainees heading for Guantanamo Bay," JC paused, taking a drink of his coffee and finishing another cigarette. He did not light another. He must be out, I mused.

"The men never made it to Cuba; this is where Fludd and his men enter the story. Luis Nevers, Fludd's partner, had a connection with the INS, a high reaching one. He was able to give these gentlemen false visas and other IDs and quietly they dissolved into the background. Two of the brothers were believed to be involved with a splinter cell and there were threats made. Fludd threatened to fly them back to Iraq. Since then, they all have been behaving themselves, although Abu was still making a lot of calls back home and our code breakers think they may have discovered a few things."

JC pointed at me. "Ryan, you stumbled across these men accidentally. You ruined what some fifty men and at least two separate government agencies conspired to do. The false address leading nowhere was supposed to be a safety measure if anyone came snooping around. They only received two pieces of mail, a welcome note from the US post office, and your letter. Cell phones are hard to track and companies are unwilling to share customer information unless you have a warrant. Further, the more technology progresses, the harder it is to capture cell signals, correct Ryan?"

I nodded feeling better now that more puzzle pieces were

fitting into place. "That's correct. Our competitors utilize CDMA, or coded division multiple access, with an emphasis on coded. Unless you had an ESN, the ten-digit number, and the code the computer is using, tracking random cell calls is difficult."

"That is why they were given cell phones. However, if they had not used them so much and had issues you would have never found out about these men, and today would not have come to pass. So yes, indeed Ryan, your skills and service ability almost cost you your life. You may want to be a bastard once in a while," JC said, and everyone had a hearty laugh.

It was the relief I needed. "Well, we have a meeting with our parent company in two months. The retention figures had to be improved. If we reached certain benchmarks, we were going to be fully brought under their wing, their logo, their customers, and their financial backing."

"With a substantial bonus to you and Victor?"

"Yes, sir," I nodded. "Substantial."

"Ryan, that letter almost cost you your life, you realize that now, yes?" JC inclined his head towards me.

"Yes, but it still seems absurd. I certainly did not address the letter to "Hey you international terrorists.""

JC became serious, which sent a shiver down my spine. He was already serious. What he was about to say must be very important. And probably required some kind of security clearance I did not possess. "You made a connection the US government was willing to forget about. You compromised some people - some in high positions. Tomorrow, the Under-secretary of Defense is stepping down amid a sex scandal that never happened. And two months from now he will be killed in an accident." He paused his dramatic flair on display once again. My head was spinning from this last piece of the puzzle.

"The men after you may not have felt you to be special, Ryan, but we do," JC said. "We need people like you and Sam. You managed to hold off twenty men with more training and more gun power than you. Men whose sole purpose was to kill you, and they did not even know why. They were told you compromised a high-level project. Did you know this man Boyle that saved your hide in the Falls?"

I shook my head. "No sir, I thought that he was going to shoot me right after Fred missed. Sam did get to meet Agent Rocksolid, and even he makes Agent Radclyffe seem small," I said, inclining my head towards the man filling the small easy chair next to me. "After my release, he followed me at least as far as the Mug Stop. I felt he knew more than he was letting on, and he was trying to determine what I knew first and if I was useful to his task at hand. What that task was, I have no idea."

"How long were you with this man?"

"About two hours. I am not sure, as the interrogation room had no clock, and I spent a good part of the day riding in his trunk."

JC nodded. "Well, we lost you in the Falls, and picked up your track as you left the coffee shop. I have to say, the van idea was brilliant. The local agencies were convinced they had you cornered. They did not realize their mistake until Sam's supervisor showed up to let them in. You were probably in Rochester by the time they even knew about the van." He chuckled and I was not sure if he laughing because he found it humorous, or at the ineptness of the government.

"Ryan, why did you choose your father's cabin?"

"It's isolated, so we set up a trip to Syracuse for all to hear. I figured it gave us some time before anyone guessed our actual hiding place. Plus, I knew there would be a gun ready if needed," I explained.

"Smart indeed, you both have proven your worth." JC paused to light another cigarette. "I run a group of men simply known as the Protectorate. This group is comprised of thirteen men; there are twelve subordinates and one superintendent; I am of course that man. I have personally recruited every man who stands on the council. When the time is right, you will meet these men," he paused, taking a sip of his coffee. "They are from every walk of life, government officials from various countries, members of society that sit on many boards, leaders in commerce, and even some ex-KGB and ex-CIA agents are in the fold. Their connections come in handy once in a while, as they are trusted connections. It is our goal to work in the dark, to keep the world safe from men like Fludd and Neivers. We are not a recognized group, only a handful of people understand what we do. And only twenty men could name the entire group," he explained. "We also recruit a number of citizens such as yourself who have proven their worth. We call these people Allies." JC pointed to the man next to me. "Agent Radclyffe has been associated with us for some time. He has never been asked to compromise his position, he helps when he can."

Pacing again, JC continued. "The world operates in ways

most would not understand; there is a belief that democracy runs the world. This is not the case. Your own government makes choices that seem counterproductive to its cause. The Iran-Contra scandal, the fact Osama bin Laden was once financed by the great USA; these are examples of how the world operates. The old adage your enemy's enemy is your friend has been carried to the extreme. The cold war in the fifties and sixties is the impetus for such endeavors. Much has been done in name of the common good, such as protecting the global oil reserve. So much of what makes the world go around is completed through backroom deals. Publicly denouncing a group when in fact that same group is receiving aid is also a common practice. We have, over the years, "fixed" certain problems the government could not be involved in. They turn a blind eye to our actions for two reasons: one, they have no idea how large we are, and two, we have no central meeting place. We have a training facility, yes, but our organization is not dependent on centralization. We are everywhere, yet we leave no trail. We are ghosts, as the majority of us in the group have no identity, which makes us hard to track."

He paused to take another drag off his smoke. "We discovered Fludd's plot three days ago in the form of an intercepted communication. The men involved in this secret were vast - CIA and even Homeland Security, the very organizations set forth to destroy terrorism supported these men, financed them, and spent many lives to protect them. You must forget what happened, put this behind you. Whatever thoughts you have will be kept private. Twenty men were killed; countless others quieted by force and blackmail. After you leave there will be no record of the men you located. Their names will be erased forever. If these men continue to be good citizens, they will be allowed to live, if they step out of bounds, they will be silenced and no one will be the wiser. There are copies of important files, information being sent to Washington to quiet others; you, Ryan Prince, must play your role. A suitable story will be fabricated to cover up all this mess. Your government owes you an apology, but one will not be forthcoming. Do you understand?"

I let out a deep breath. "Yes sir."

"Can you make Sam understand?" JC asked.

"I understand on my own, thank you. No one speaks for me." Surprised to hear Sam's voice from behind me, I turned to face her.

"Thanks for joining us Sam," JC said, dipping his head at her in greeting. "It was assumed you were resting."

"I was," she said curtly. "We will not forget what you did for us today, will we Ryan?"

I nodded. "Exactly."

"You must never talk of this even in private. There are ears all around, no? You will be followed, your house will be bugged; if not now or not next week, but sometime sooner than later, I guarantee it," he warned. "If you accept my offer, you will receive certain training. Such as how to locate a shadow, or a tail, or how to search your residence for listening devices. You will be given tools and trained on how to use them."

He looked at us point-blank before going on.

"Do you want to help your country further itself despite

the idiots that run it? If you say no that's acceptable as well, but know that today will be the last day you will receive our aid. If you try to expose us, you will be eliminated. I am not trying to scare you, but this warning is necessary. Do you understand your options?"

"Yes, we do," Sam and I said in unison. We looked at each other and without hesitating said "We would like to join."

JC nodded, pleased with our choices. "You'll both request vacation time; you will be booked at an exclusive resort in Virginia. There is a screening process; however, my instincts are right as only about four percent of those that accept training are denied entry. This is a great responsibility. Do not accept this lightly. Don't accept this offer under the premise you owe us anything," he warned. "We intervened for various reasons, but never put those we saved in our debt for the services we performed to save them."

25

August 19 | 8:30 a.m.

After all of the puzzle pieces fell into place, I realized I was such a minor player in this interwoven international conspiracy. I wondered if others would happen upon these men I discovered by accident just for doing my job. I also wondered if past mistakes would be remedied. Most of those involved getting these men into the country illegally, as well as the men involved in the search for my ultimate demise. Had they been silenced?

I hoped the next person to make a connection with these three men would not receive the same treatment as I. The land of the free and the home of the brave made no sense to me anymore. There were brave men putting their lives on the line to save me from a government plot gone awry.

One has to wonder how many resources were expended to silence me. I knew nothing of these men, outside of my business dealings, yet it was determined my level of knowledge was dangerous. I do not remember who first stated, "a little knowledge is a dangerous thing," but I have lived it firsthand.

Sam's mental state was considerably better after her short siesta. JC and Agent Radclyffe left the apartment shortly after we accepted their offer. I was alone with the de Gisor brothers and Sam.

She had returned to the bedroom, taking my cell phone with her. Sam asked me to join her in a few minutes, agreeing we needed to have a conversation. I knew in my heart a breakup might be looming, however, as I had stated before, I prefer her alive and pissed over calm and dead.

Sitting in the living room, I watched the de Gisor brothers at their job monitoring something on the vast network of terminals. They appeared to be arguing some contentious point.

I speak as much French as I do Cantonese; needless to say I could not follow the conversation. Although it was heated, the hand gesturing alone almost made me laugh. JC had opened my eyes and offered an incredible opportunity. He has my allegiance, and I was certain he had Sam's as well.

I would be able to serve my country from behind the scenes, my skills being utilized when needed. It was perfect. There was a certain element I possessed, maybe it's the ability to run on instinct and adrenaline, maybe I have another natural talent that can be grown.

Before joining Sam in the bedroom, Agent Radclyffe took me aside and spent a moment talking with me in private, urging me to join, stating he would consider our inclusion as an asset. After my roller coaster day, his statement instilled me with such a sense of pride and in some ways, I realized a different person emerged.

No one had attempted to extract the weapon now tucked securely in my waistband. While listening to the brother's argue, I walked to the table, taking the magazine I had ejected earlier. I decided to keep the gun until a suitable replacement was purchased. JC indicated that we would be under surveillance at some yet to be determined time; if they were listening to us we may be deemed expendable once again. There were no rifles or weapons of any sort at the apartment. The nine-millimeter seemed necessary. My personal paranoia may have subsided, but it was not all together deactivated.

Agent Radclyffe gave me his cell phone number when he exited the safe house. I was under instructions to call him for anything - anything at all. While we all were hoping everything had settled and there would be no further issues, it's better to be prepared. I agreed.

I walked to the bedroom Sam was using and prepared myself, trying to disable my sarcasm. Sometimes I was not fully in control of it. Right now, I did not want to say anything that I would later regret.

Nearing the room, I heard the last of her conversation on my cell phone. Like the brothers in the living room, her conversation was very heated. I assumed she was speaking with her superiors. I knocked on the door and stepped through the threshold, falling into the bed next to her. She had her back to me and the conversation ended shortly after I entered. Sam lay on the bed, her back still facing me. Although I could not see her face, her entire countenance told me she was sullen.

"Sam, Agent Radclyffe gave me the name and number of a psychologist with the FBI who specializes in cases like ours. I really think it could be helpful if we both went to see this person," I said, in a neutral tone as I could.

"These men are treating you like a hero. I don't see it that way," she said. Her tone was definitely sullen. And accusing. I felt my anger start to rise once again at her judgmental attitude.

"How many times were you shot today?"

"None."

"Then don't judge what you can't possibly understand. That's all I'm asking," I said, weariness over this same argument came onto me suddenly. "I need to lie down for a while. Are you going to push me out again?"

"No," she said, moving closer to the edge of the bed.

I don't know how long my eyes were closed. But I was awakened by the sound of wood splintering and loud voices. At first, thinking that the de Gisor brothers were embroiled in another heated argument, I rolled over.

We were still waiting to hear back from JC when it was deemed safe to leave and be reinserted back into reality. I shot off the bed. The heated conversations were in perfect, profanity-laced English. Ordering Sam to pretend she was sleeping on the bed, I shut the door behind me. Stealthily walking down the corridor, I saw two men dressed in black, currently holding a gun on both of the de Gisor brothers.

"Where is Prince? We want him now!" One of the men in black ordered. The hair on my neck stood up and I retrieved the gun in my waistband.

Both brothers responded simultaneously and in French. This only further incensed the assailants. One of the assailants knocked Jean unconscious with the butt of his gun.

"I know you speak English, you stupid, no good mother fucker. Start talking or he gets it." The man in black cocked his gun to show his determination and pointed it at one of the brothers.

"He left fifteen minutes ago with Agent Radclyffe and Messier Cocteau."

"Who is Messier Cocteau?"

"I met the man tonight, Agent Radclyffe just introduced us."

"Let's search the place."

Using the utmost stealth I made it back to the bedroom before the men rounded the corner to check the bathroom. I shut the door behind me, silently latching the door. I quickly informed Sam of our situation and told her to stay where she was.

I hid in the closet, hiding back into the darkest recesses. I was holding the gun in front of me, ready to fire at a moment's notice. My shoulder could only hold the position required to properly aim the handgun for a few more moments. I had not heard any gunshots issuing from the living room, although I do not think the de Gisor brothers would allow these men unencumbered access to the apartment. I did not have time to process what that meant.

I could hear the assailants leaving the bathroom and then the adjacent bedroom. I could see through the slats on the closet door that Sam remained motionless on the bed, playing her part. I heard the door quietly open and Sam jumped up in surprise and faced the assailant.

"What are you doing here, who are you?" She demanded, almost shouting.

"All we want to know is what happened to Ryan Prince. We need to talk with him now!"

"I don't know where he is. I've been asleep." Fear was in her voice. She was playing her role well.

The man ordered her to sit in the corner, calling in his collaborator. From the slats in the flimsy closet door, I could see one man holding his weapon on Sam, and the other start searching the room.

It was not the largest room I've seen and there were not a lot of areas to search. Basically the bed and the closest held the only places large enough to accommodate a person of my size.

Very carefully the man lifted the bedspread off the floor, shining a flashlight under the bed. He was treating the situation as if I were unarmed. He was cautious, but not that cautious.

He started toward the closest. I wasn't sure if I should exit hands up or shoot him before he reached the door. Someone close to JC must have turned, as this address was not known to anyone outside his reach. Also, these men were not coming in shooting it up. JC at last count considered me to be unarmed. JC himself could have set me up, as well the de Gisor brothers, who could be turning their tails and clearing the house.

Never trust anyone, never trust anyone my mind screamed and I cursed under my breath. The whole thing about the Protectorate and the offer of training and support was all bullshit. It was a nice story he wove. He had held my attention and I had believed every word.

This meant I was not as free as I had been led to believe.

I cursed under my breath again. Maybe the FBI and others were on their way here. I had been debriefed by Agent Radclyffe speaking without concern about my legal rights. Now he had my statement, with collaboration by Sam that I shot an unarmed man. I just signed my own death warrant. Those in charge would ensure I get jail time.

Ensure that I could no longer run.

It would only be a matter of time before I was killed while imprisoned and it would all be chalked up to another case of inmate on inmate violence.

My options were running out. The man had completed his inspection of the bed. Finding it unoccupied, he began walking toward the closet. Although his weapon was in his hands, it was pointed at the floor. Maybe five feet separated him and me.

Two feet.

One foot.

His hand reached for the knob and he nodded to the man behind him. Standing in the shadows, I raised my gun and pulled the trigger quickly, firing off two rounds. Sam screamed, the sound the same as the last time I shot a man.

Each shot had found its target in a rather lethal manner.

Both men were down. Unfortunately, I was getting better at this. Either that or luckier. The men were standing close enough to each other, that aim was not required. The second man had no time to react prior to the bullet finding its target.

Sam was crouched in the corner, trembling and sobbing.

"Wha, where did you get that gun?" Her voice was shaky, almost unclear.

"I've had it since we left Fludd."

"But Jean took the magazine away."

"He did, but as I was on my way to see you, I grabbed the magazine. The de Gisor brothers were arguing so I could take it without causing an alarm."

"Is this going to end sometime? This has to end," she pleaded. "I thought JC said it was all over."

"The bastard set us up. Neither Jean nor Guillaume did anything to intervene. This whole apartment was an attempt to get me to confess. It was a setup."

"Let's get out of here now." Shakily she rose from the corner, grasping the small bedside table to steady herself.

"Good idea." As we exited the bedroom, I put my hand in the small of Sam's back. I was more than relieved when she didn't shy away from it.

The living room was a bloody mess. Both of the de Gisor brothers lay on the floor, blood pooling on the carpet, monitors still ablaze, computers awaiting their input. I could not tell you how they were incapacitated, but both of their throats had been sliced wide open.

I do not believe the scene could have been faked. The blood was congealing and was sticky. The metallic odor of it filled the air. These men did not set us up. They indeed gave their lives in my defense.

I did not have a number for JC, but did for Agent Radclyffe.

I called his cell and explained to him that the safe house had been compromised and both of the de Gisor brothers lay dead. His voice held notes of shock and concern. At this point, it was difficult to determine who in JC's Protectorate was impossible to infiltrate.

He disconnected the call and advised he would be contacting JC. We did not know what to do. We walked downstairs to check on the couple who lived there. We were not introduced; however, we were informed they also were counted among the Allies. The door was busted open and we found the husband in the bedroom, half changed into his business suit. He was wearing dark socks and a light blue pressed Oxford shirt, his stylish tie in place. His pants lay on the bed, as if they were waiting patiently to be included in his ensemble. His wife was still wearing her bathrobe; the pretty white terry cloth showing a huge red stain on her chest.

I called Agent Radclyffe again, notifying him the couple downstairs also had been killed. He stated we had five minutes to gather our belongings; and he would come to pick us up. As quickly as possible we climbed the stairs. Engaging the safety, I replaced the gun in the waistband of my jeans, running behind Sam and urging her to move faster. I would gather what I could as she changed into some clothes. The laptop and money belt were a priority. I gathered both without wasting any more than a minute. I went to the back bedroom. Both men still lie dead on the floor.

Sam looked as if she was deciding what to wear like she was headed to Shea's Theatre. After my constant urging, she finally pulled on her jeans and the first shirt she grabbed.

Agent Radclyffe called within five minutes as promised. He notified me he was at the downstairs front door, examining the carnage and the damage. He instructed me to hurry.

I lead Sam down the stairs where Agent Radclyffe was waiting on the first-floor landing. His car was parked in plain view, the engine still running.

"How many men did you see?" He asked tersely, leading us to his vehicle.

"Two."

"Are they neutralized?"

"Yes, both dead."

"By whose hands?" He looked at me. I think he already knew but wanted confirmation.

I gave him what he wanted. "Mine."

"Did you see any others enter the house?" Agent Radclyffe asked, unlocking the car doors, motioning for us to get in. He jogged around the rear of the vehicle and I slid up front. Sam got in back and buckled herself in, looking small and frightened.

"No. I was napping."

"How were you able to neutralize both men?"

"I still had the weapon from shooting Fludd. The men must have had information that I was unarmed. It had to have come from someone inside, as neither man came in shooting. Their search of the safe house was completed quickly. I concluded they thought I was unarmed."

"When did you retrieve the magazine?" He asked, gunning the car away from the now unsafe house.

"The brothers were having a rather heated argument. They did not even see me take it back."

"Why did you do that?"

"I wanted a gun until I could legitimately receive my pistol permit. I wanted to be able to protect Sam and myself."

"Okay." Agent Radclyffe said. "Fast thinking."

"Where are we going?" Sam's voice came from the back seat, the terror and fear making her normally strong tones shaky and small. I glanced back. She looked terrified. I could feel it. Also, the adrenaline coursing through your veins, just when you thought it was all over. Welcome to my life.

Agent Radclyffe drove us to downtown; I could ascertain the safe house must have been in the Cheektowaga area by the route we took to our destination.

Much to my shock we did not stop at the new Homeland Security building but continued to the Federal Building, located on Elmwood and Huron.

Agent Radclyffe parked the car in the lot and confiscated my weapon. He leaned close and told me I could have it back later, but there is no way I would be permitted to enter the building while in possession of the gun.

Our crazy trio crossed the parking lot. Agent Radclyffe did his best to look unconcerned, yet his hand never moved from its perch on his pistol. The parking lot was only sixty feet wide, yet it felt like we walked a mile. I felt very exposed; again sensing men on every rooftop, scope, and crosshairs targeting our party.

Although we all walked faster than what would be considered normal, we did not run. We were able to cross the parking lot without incident.

We all managed a smile when frisked by the security detail and Agent Radclyffe did his part, talking about things that made no sense. He signed us into the building and we followed him to the elevator. We exited on the sixth floor.

We were given visitor badges and ushered to a conference room. The sixth floor was rather nicely decorated. Real wood walls and doors lined the hallway. Thick, dark blue carpeting ran throughout the floor. Hot coffee and some food awaited our arrival.

The situation was absurd. There we sat as if patiently waiting for our CEO to deliver the great news concerning our third-quarter earnings. As if some screen would drop from the ceiling and a PowerPoint presentation would begin as soon as the doughnuts arrived. However, I was wearing clothes that reeked of sweat and cordite and not my usual professional Oxford shirt, tie, and slacks.

As the door to the conference room remained open, I was able to watch as agents ran through the halls in hurried strides, all looking like they were operating in emergency mode. After yesterday's rollercoaster ride, I secretly wondered when the bar would lift and the ride would be over. But there was there another exciting, steep hill around the corner, where the men were trying to kill me, masquerading as FBI agents, waiting for their moment to stick a bullet in my skull.

I suddenly found tears running down my face at the memory of two more deaths at my hand as Sam sat in her chair. She was even more withdrawn, her gaze examining the intricate wood pattern of the dark table.

The pain returned in my shoulder and it began to throb. My head spun. All that ran through my mind was the men I had killed. At the cabin. Fludd in a conference room much like this one. The two men at the safe house. The manpower expended to keep me quiet over the silliest of all coincidences. It was beyond absurd.

It was beyond all explanation. I shook my head against the events as if shaking it would dislodge the memories from my brain.

I shook it against the fear that filled me.

I shook it, wondering when it all would be over.

Agent Radclyffe had left but now returned with another agent. We were introduced to the local FBI director, Johann Valentin Andrea.

"This is the man that caused all the problems today?" He asked, pointing at me accusingly. I did not like this man and we had just met.

"Yes sir," Agent Radclyffe said. "He is the one who found the terrorists."

"I await your complete report Agent Radclyffe. It should make for some interesting reading." He turned on his heel and exited the room, military-like in his demeanor.

He looked at me as if to say I was unworthy of the praise Agent Radclyffe had already adorned upon me.

"Well, Ryan, it's been a very interesting day, has it not?"

I gave a curt nod. "To say the least. It has."

"I contacted JC when I left the room. He should be calling momentarily. Until then, sit tight."

I laughed grimly as he left the room. Sit tight. I had nowhere to go at the moment. My car still remained burned to a crisp. Sam's car was either impounded somewhere or still in the parking garage at her work. Going home would we feel safe? Could we continue on, or would it be the preverbal look over our shoulders for the rest of our lives?

I looked at Sam, but she was still studying the table, unmoving.

That was the last I saw of Agent Radclyffe. About an hour after we arrived at FBI headquarters, four agents escorted us from the building. We all drove back to our quiet apartment in Amherst in the middle of a caravan of FBI and local police. Two unmarked FBI vehicles would stand watch over us for the next 24 hours.

It was odd to see my apartment surrounded by the yellow crime scene tape. To see our belongings scattered about, holes in the walls, placed there by law enforcement searching for things hidden. Black residue remained on corners and doors and everywhere else fingerprints were present. It would take a few days to clean up the mess. I looked out of the window and there, in the middle of the street, was an unmarked car. Our guardians. Exhausted, neither one of us said anything as we both crashed in our bed.

I was brought to the hospital later in the day to have my shoulder mended and make sure that I was in good shape otherwise. Sam also accompanied me and she was given a thorough once over as well.

The wound on my shoulder did not require further surgery but was bandaged, my arm again in a sling. A prescription for antibiotics was dispensed and instructions to report back as the first sign of fever. It appeared Cocteau's doctors had done a passable patch job on my shoulder after our meeting with Fludd.

JC never determined who leaked the information about the safe house in Cheektowaga. The house was put on the market a few days later after the computer equipment and "other things" were removed from the house. The atrocities which occurred inside the walls were never reported and I was advised the place was cleaned out completely; cleaned of the equipment, cleaned of the bodies. I remembered the de Gisor brothers laying on the floor, more blood surrounding their bodies, more than I thought was possible. I couldn't imagine that floor ever being clean again.

We had lived through the events of August 18 and 19. We saw the sunrise on August 20 as well. We both had a chance to catch our breaths and think about reporting to work on Monday.

Sam's boss had dropped the threat of termination. Victor was not upset at all and my presence back in the office caused much jubilation. I attempted to fill in what had occurred, the cover story still had not been released, so I spoke in generalities. My gunshot wound was the talk of the office, as well as our parent company. My picture was prominently displayed on the company web site and subsequently the employee weekly newsletter.

The quiet, schedule-driven life came back quickly and Sam and I spent most of our free time together trying to mend the wounds in our relationship.

I had not thought much about the philosophical or spiritual aspects of August 18. After a week had passed we were feeling safer and started to relax. My mind was a jumble of those 24-plus hours, a jumble of images coming at me in an incoherent fashion, hard to piece together, hard to understand.

Agent Radclyffe stopped by on two occasions; both times he let us know our apartment was still under surveillance from his office and that we were being protected. He insisted that we start counseling sessions with the FBI shrink. He said talking about these events to a third party may help alleviate the trauma and bring closure. He stated he had made an appointment for two weeks from now and urged us to go.

26

September 27, 2006

I walked out of the nondescript office, just blocks from my own, and headed back to work. I had just finished dropping off my homework assignment to my therapist. Agent Radclyffe fulfilled his promise and I was, indeed, attending counseling sessions with the FBI's best. My shoulder was still quite sore. Physical therapy became as necessary as my mental therapy.

Delayed medical attention was the cause of the stiffness and soreness. My physical therapist, Sandra Botticelli, advised there was extensive damage to my deltoid and trapezius muscles. Both were used in conjunction with the shoulder joint to move it. The sessions were an intense hour, but after two weeks, I was making progress.

Sandra was a Godsend; she was as easy to talk with as my other therapist. She wondered how it was that a customer service supervisor was involved in such an incident. We would talk through the hour-long sessions. We talked about family and careers. We talked about cell phones and plans and muscle abductors and conductors. We talked about a variety of topics; whatever came to mind that day.

My mental wellbeing improved. I did not feel the guilt that Sam demanded. But it's been five weeks since that day I died. Life had returned to normal, whatever that is supposed to be.

My wish came true - the dull patter of our days brought about a healing power. Regularity did not breed boredom; it allowed us to process the events of August 18. We embraced the rat race where others shunned it; we scheduled our lives and our days, sometimes our hours, if needed. We both had our fill of spontaneity. It was in this endless scheduling of the meetings I used to dread and the chores around the house that never cease, that we were able to process that day. Sometimes recalling hours, sometimes living slowly through it, one minute to the next. Unfortunately, we were not able to forget or clear the entire day from our memory. I cannot even say we were able to understand the events, because, more often than not, understanding never arrived.

This Palm Pilot existence allowed us to forget about that day, as our time was planned and calculated, very much like Einstein wore the same suit every day as if wasting creative effort to pick out a suit took away his ability to manage mathematical equations. As I understand, if our brains were not caught up in our activities it could process, we could review, and we could make some sense of it all.

We also planned for other things as well. We both now carried with us a prepaid cellular phone, purchased from an agent of CellNY and under a false name, and using cash to keep the phones active. I now owned a Berretta nine-millimeter - the FBI was integral in getting my pistol permit passed through quickly. Not only was the gun permit forthcoming, but it also came as a permit to carry a concealed weapon, and I did.

We had contingency plans in case this happened again, including a used car we kept in storage. Contingency plans for our contingency plans. But we would not be caught unprepared again. We took self-defense classes and borrowed some books from Agent Radclyffe concerning strategies and planning.

We practiced. We prepared. We were ready. Two weeks from now we would be attending that "exclusive" retreat in Virginia, the invitations arriving yesterday. JC had called to confirm our attendance.

He also called our supervisors, explaining I had uncovered an American terrorist group. ErieOne Mortgage was given a check to replace the van and a warning. Sam was not to be removed from her position, or the media would be informed that this young lady was forced into actions trying to aid her new fiancé, only to be fired by an unfeeling corporate bureaucracy. The van allowed them to flee the area, and thus a certain death.

The Syracuse papers and national media were quick to jump on the story. Victor was pleased, as CellNY was getting free national publicity. I received a personal call from Blanch de'Evreux, thanking me for my efforts.

The Buffalo area FBI director Johann Andrea gave Sam and me a commendation from the Federal Government. Further, the Governor had us spend a weekend at his mansion. We were introduced by our local State Assemblymen, and to the Senate, receiving a round of applause and another plaque for the wall.

For a while, it was fun and enjoyable. But we received so many calls from well-wishers our landline number had to be changed. Often, we were recognized when we went out. Buffalo is, after all, the smallest big town I have lived in.

At the height of the frenzy, a national news magazine TV show requested an interview. We were allowed to participate, however, there was a spokesperson representing the FBI who would intervene once questioning turned to the specifics of my database search. That was listed as confidential and off-limits, as there were still more names to sift through.

Today, I finally was able to purchase the ring and was surprising Sam with it tonight. She was under the impression I was going for a checkup, not to the jeweler. After a few rocky weeks, normalcy returned. After that day, the worst day ever, all I wanted, all I needed, was to complete my task and buy the ring. It was a necessary healing step – one step closer back to the life we would never again understand or know.

After waking up dead, the thought of having to live without Sam was much too much to bear. Life had settled down, the paper printed a correction stating I had not passed in an inferno and that my car was stolen and the body so badly burned it was assumed to be me. I have a new car, complete with a car alarm and Low Jack. If it is stolen in the middle of the night, I'll know.

For my "debriefing," I met with a group of people at the FBI headquarters. I was not told who they were. As I approached the table, I noted we were in a special room. It was soundproof and deplete of electronic apparatus, except a person typing my words on a laptop.

There were eight men and four women at the table, They all wore suits, mostly dark colors, with white shirts and conservative ties. The women present wore business suits. One with pants; the other wore a short skirt and had the legs to pull it off.

They were all very officious, yet not one of them wore any identification or introduced themselves. I was sworn in as if giving testimony, and I asked if I should hire an attorney before proceeding. I was bluntly told no. The questions started. They had access to the written report taken by Agent Radclyffe, its details complete and thorough.

At first, the questioning centered on my written statement. They asked questions about everything, sometimes repeating a question in an all not-too-subtle manner. It seemed as if they were trying to catch me in some fabrication, poke some hole in my story. They were indeed interested in what I knew about the man I called Fred and Agent Boyle. It appeared both Agent Fludd and Agent Boyle did not exist at all, and somehow I was at fault for bringing them to life.

It was believed Fludd was using an alias and his true background had yet to be uncovered.

They asked me about my proficiency with guns. I told them about how my father had taught me to shoot a rifle. And that I knew I would find his thirty-five caliber in the gun cabinet. They seemed not to believe a married man like my father may have had a few things in his man-hunting cabin that his wife was not cognizant of. They admitted that my driving was impressive, and took note of how I shook the guys off my bumper while driving recklessly down a dirt road in the middle of the night.

I told them repeatedly I did not own a handgun. But I received aid from an unknown group of people who never identified themselves. Thus referring to the phone call I received, and the gun I kept after blowing Fludd's brains out. I told them my feelings of being played out as bait, how I killed for those who cared not to have their names attached to such things.

They asked if we ever discovered the connection between the men. I lied, stating we had no other information than a common address. We had theories, but that's all. They told me the database was destroyed and the pertinent data had been wiped from the system. The information that was sought that night would be given to me with a notice I would swear not to repeat it. But I was told it involved the story of the funeral. And that those men did not die. It was a setup and they were then offered refuge in our country in exchange for that lie.

This was a secret that was worth killing for. If those involved with terrorist ties discovered these men had not perished in a bombing, all means would be used to find them and kill them once and for all. We did not need to give any terrorists a reason to come to our soil and in general kill civilians and wreak havoc.

I was the first outsider to make a connection between three of the four men. I was told that I could continue my life without fear, as those inside the NSA who were responsible were reprimanded, as one untrained civilian managed to elude them for so long. I said nothing about JC or the facts he shared. I played dumb, as if this were the first time I was hearing this information.

Even those in the room were not sure who was shot at the cabin. All in attendance would not proceed with any criminal charges, as I was defending Sam and myself. I was offered an unofficial citation for my bravery that day. They concluded that my being able to reactivate the cell phone without raising suspicion, and then my trek to Canada, was indeed perfect moves generated by someone who had received no training.

The unclassified portions of my activities were now being considered as part of a new training initiative. I promised to be a good citizen and stay out of the way of international conspiracies from this point forward.

I left the chamber, the official story of the worst hours of my life was tucked under an arm. Anyone connected to me on that day was to be given the official version, not that a lot of copies were printed. In my coat pocket awaited a surprise for Sam. Some of the new details go something like this.

After finding my car stolen, I reported it to the police department. I have that police report now; never mind the fact it had not existed prior to the meeting I just left. The person who stole my car used it to go bar hopping and was so drunk he caused the horrific accident that ultimately the police discovered.

The date on the police report correctly stated August 18, as I found out my car was stolen and reported it that morning.

Sam stated with so many work items on her mind, she did not notice the car was not in the garage when she left for work.

After reading the article in the paper, I called work to correct the situation and was transferred to the wrong department, and they, misunderstanding my call, deactivated my cell phone.

The official version does not include my reactivating it later, nor my trip to Canada. There was no notice of the database or my activities in Canada.

Since there was no paper trail to trace the phone reactivation, that, too, was omitted from the report.

I had spent the afternoon of August 18 searching my database for contract expirations. After discovering there were thirty-one contracts expiring on the same day, I completed a rate analysis on each account, concluding most of the calls either originated with one of the phones or terminated at one of the phones. I completed a few letters to be mailed out, stating that fact and stating all were eligible for new phones at no cost. After careful contemplation, I approached my boss about my findings. Victor was thrilled we could save thirty-one customers.

My concern grew daily about the international calls and I decided to visit the person who was in charge of CellNY company security. He could understand my concerns and contacted the necessary people to look into the matter. The customers were investigated and it was determined a terrorist cell had been located. This is when the bad guys set up the accident, thinking I was in the car, and then followed Sam and me around until we decided to leave town and head to

Dad's cabin. I emailed my boss (again supporting documentation was produced for this) stating I required a few days off, as I was feeling stressed. Sam also took some time. The aforementioned bad guys followed us there and quite a ruckus occurred.

I was forced to defend myself with a rifle at the cabin. One of the suspected terrorists was shot, the other was arrested (this being easy since he was found dead from hypothermia and still bound with duct tape). Another group of terrorists fled and caused damage to a van we borrowed. This was all legit under the company's (new and never to be used again) regulations.

The terrorist we surprised by our intrusion inflicted the two wounds. Somewhat true. "Insurance" covered the window replacement and filled the bullet holes. Sam and I did not feel comfortable spending the night so we headed back. Being a federal, and not a local matter, we contacted the appropriate parties in Syracuse before heading home.

There was no mention of either Agent Boyle or Agent Fludd. And never would there be.

I exited the building on Elmwood Street, jumped in the car, Elmwood Ave having granted easy access to the 190. I was not going directly home, going instead to the liquor store on the corner of Delaware and Sheridan in Tonawanda. It was a little out of the way, but was the best and biggest in the area, with an entire wall of refrigerated items, including champagne. I also purchased some scotch, as I was in a festive mood and tomorrow was Saturday.

The events of that day now stood more than a month in

the past. They would visit me in the night while I slept. Even killing in the name of honor should not be bragged about. Sam would toss and turn, sometimes her sleep being as invaded with the darkness as mine. It no longer encompassed our entire thoughts - it lessened every day until we were able to joke about it and not have it be such a huge void in our lives.

It was a shared experience we will carry to the grave, an experience of the few. It no longer defines who we are. We have both inhabited this planet for thirty years or more and when taken with the rest of our lives, it was such a small segment, barely a blip on the screen.

I have gained a necessary perspective. Through this perspective, I now understand I was given a gift, a very rare gift indeed. It's like every day is Christmas. I unwrap this gift in the morning, smiling and humming as I go. The present is here in me somewhere, so deep now it's a part of who I am, what I am about. It's Ryan Prince at his most elemental. While showering or watching a movie or even discussing issues with customers, my fingers find that scar on my shoulder. It is not disfiguring, but it is noticeable to the touch; the wound on the back of my shoulder is small, barely larger than the bullet that caused the damage. The wound on the front is a different story, it's quite large due to both the fact it is an exit wound and the wound itself was enlarged in order to repair the damage. The skin is taut; the smooth lines visible, indicating where the skin was sutured to close a huge gap. I have said this present resides in my soul, the festive green and red bow tied across my shoulder.

We are so content to get swept away in that daily routine,

the daily maze. It is the little things that drain the life from us Monday through Friday. Then, with just 48-plus hours to unwind, to get something out of the 40-plus we just worked, seems senseless. Maybe you need to have a loaded gun in the small of your back before you realize how quickly it can all be over, how tomorrow may never come. At its heart, this is the gift that was given to me.

Regardless of how I survived, whether through luck, or divine intervention, or the Grim Reaper taking a sick day, regardless of how I feel or the doubts that often resound in my conscious, I must go on and live my life.

I have no unreal expectations. I will not discover the cure for cancer, or make a car that runs on water; yet I can strive to do my best to live my life in the moment, enjoying every last laugh, or tear, or hug, with Sam. I must remember how it felt, remember the very audible ticking of one's personal clock. For now, that clock has been rewound, another chance to make things right, another chance to make a difference. I could of course spend the next thousand pages arguing for and against how one man could make a difference, so I will digress.

Like those people retelling their tales of survival, to assume that mere chance was all that saved my hide, would be short-sighted. However, to assume that luck and fortune are the reasons I lived to see August 19, could be a slap in the face to the cosmos or the grand scheme of things.

Even after the weeks that have followed, it is an arduous task trying to understand what role we all play in this great place. My personal philosophy has hindered my understanding. My role seemed so minor, so insignificant, yet still, it was my direct actions that brought that day to fruition. It is clear that the actions of others, that did not know me, who had not heard of Ryan Prince, at times laid down their lives to ensure I witnessed the next sunrise.

It could be I am on the next "I survived against all odds" show. Maybe I will be more understanding of the tears and praise. I can now understand the stress, the idea of trying to live from one moment to the next, often not even having time to contemplate the next hour, it is to live your life in one-second intervals. I have been there. It is not a pleasant place to be.

So I will wear this gift of scars for the remainder of my days. I will not mock those that insist that God saved their lives; that sometimes his influence is hidden in the most subtle of ways, that whisper on the wind.

Once Sam was able to come to terms with what I had to do to make it through those hours, we again were close. But understanding what she needed, I gave her space, and last week it felt like we were back to normal. Well, as normal as we will ever be.

My concern, the past few days, is that she is distant once again. Our lives have been on a roller coaster, and not just on those few fateful days. I was under a firm belief we were headed for another downturn.

Ring in pocket, champagne in hand, as well as the official story of our day, I entered the house. It was deadly quiet. Sam must not be home from work. I unloaded my burden on the kitchen table, placing the champagne in the fridge, the folder on the kitchen island. Ice from the freezer and into my scotch glass, I headed into the living room to watch some TV. HBO's weekly show, *Inside the NFL*, was due on and was one of my favorites. My festive mood only increased with the single malt scotch filling my mouth and momentarily numbing my body.

I heard Sam pull into the driveway. Glass in hand, I hurried into the kitchen and placed the ring box in my pocket, readying myself for the moment to come. She took an inferable long time coming into the house. There I stood, goofy grin on my face, waiting for her as patiently as possible.

She finally emerged into the kitchen with that "don't talk to me until I've had a glass of wine" look. I knew she required a few minutes to process her day before the rest of the evening could commence. This the same favor she had done with me numerous times. There was no need to rush. I found myself back in the living room watching *Inside the NFL*, which had not yet finished.

I returned to the kitchen and was fixing another drink. Humming to myself, I practiced the well-rehearsed lines of my romantic proposal. I was looking forward to many years with this beautiful woman.

Her purse was in the chair she always put it, but she had yet to come into the living room. She was standing, looking perplexed and perturbed, searching for the words to start a conversation.

"How bad was your day sweetie?" I asked, a little buzzed by the scotch and what was to come in the next few minutes.

No response. I haven't seen her this bad in a while, but sharing her field of work, I can relate. I walked back to the living room, relaxing in my oversized recliner, sipping on my scotch. I did not hear her approach the living room. I caught her gaze out of the corner of my eye.

"Come sit down," I said, indicating the other chair next to me. She sat down but she did not have her wine glass.

"Are you okay?"

"You're not who you say you are." Her tone was deadly serious, one I had not heard since August 18.

"What is that supposed to mean?"

"They were not trying to kill you over any stupid database. You are one of them, aren't you?"

"One of who? I am not following this conversation at all." I looked at her perplexed.

"Ryan Prince did not exist seven years ago. Like those men in the database who fell out of the sky. You were apparently born of thin air."

"Sam, what has gotten into you today? Honestly, you're not making any sense."

Feeling nervous for no reason, I sipped my scotch.

"I found out two days ago. But I refused to believe it until today. I was approached with more information and I was told to take care of it."

"Sam, what are you talking about?"

She turned faster than I had ever seen her turn before. Gun in hand, a silencer artificially extending its length. There, in her lap sat a badge, not unlike the one Fludd carried, except it read NSA.

"What black ops group do you use, or did you use?"

"Nothing," I implored. "Sam, think about this for a moment. I spent four hours today in front of twelve people who looked into my background and questioned me extensively. Someone is feeding you false information," I pleaded with her, my hands upturned in my lap.

"I found this out for myself. The bank is a front Ryan. We run reconnaissance out of the mortgage office," she said, still pointing the gun at me. "What better front to check credit reports? And other data? I work for a group affiliated with the NSA. You, my friend, do not."

There was a movement in the kitchen. Sam had yet to notice whoever was moving there, as they were using tremendous stealth.

"Who do you work for?" She demanded again. "I should have noticed from your interrogation techniques, there is more to you than meets the eye."

"I guess I can say the same of you my dear." I motioned towards the gun.

"I am not working for them. I am on the right side, I am doing the right thing."

"And I am a customer service manager. That's all, no more. I love you. Put down the gun." I reached for the ring in my pocket and she backed up, ensuring her grip and aim. I slowly opened my hand, a stunning diamond ring now taking up residence there. She did not even look at it.

"I love you, Sam. Remember that. I love you more than anything."

27

Epilogue

I heard the spit of bullets through a silencer, the blood-stains spreading rapidly. I collapsed into the nearest chair, exhaling what seemed to be my last breath. Sam crashed hard onto the table and landed face-up on the floor. I watched her die a quick, albeit quiet death. I was surprised at my reaction; tears were freely flowing down my face. I wish she did not have to die, I truly loved her.

They always tell you not to get involved in relationships - it could only end badly. They are right, I heeded the advice too late. I lay witness to my own stupidity as the life drained from Sam's eyes.

I had not pulled the trigger, but my actions were as responsible as my partners' who lurked in the kitchen. I was caught up in the fantasy of Ryan Prince, the fantasy that I might live like everybody else, that I could love without consequences, and that I could find room in my life for someone special.

Of all of the assignments I have been given, I enjoyed this one the best. I felt like I was Ryan Prince, the best call center manager in the history of CellNY. My strategies were incorporated into other markets, my name tossed about board meetings for promotion. Those in charge knew I held no interest in leaving Western New York. Thus, no serious offers were made.

If my cover had held, I might have been Ryan Prince for years to come. But being brought down by another covert group, using a legitimate business as a conduit for surveillance, is that not the definition of irony?

Boyle would be the first to remind me we are not "normal" folks. We know too much and live too fast. Our lives are not ours to use, we are tools, and as such the decisions are not ours to make. The carpenter does not consult the hammer before starting a project. The hammer gets used to its best ability and then replaced when it's no longer efficiently doing its job. I am the hammer.

When we arrived back at the office, I would be reminded of my place and my indiscretions. I ought to thank God they deemed me too important to kill, or there would have been six shots expended in my apartment instead of the two used.

I would not fault Boyle, as he was only following orders. The hammer pounding the nail, fixing the squeaky board.

Boyle is watching me carefully. We have been involved in more than one project, and he is the closest thing I have to a real friend. I will, however, not try his patience. I look again at the dead body of Sam lying on the floor. Her eyes still open, imploring me to look at the last embers of her dying soul. Even if we could have gone on one more year, 365 more days, this would not hurt so much. I placed the ring on her finger. It sparkled as if illuminated.

I don't have a regular life. We are not regular people. I

know that now, again learning a lesson after the fact, too late to change the outcome. There is nothing here I can change without the use of a time machine.

Maybe if we had not moved in together, maybe if I had never accepted the invitation to that blind date. The perfect vision of hindsight does little to help the here and now. I let myself fall for this special person; she had captured my soul, day one. I should have walked away. I will never put my life ahead of the job again. What we do is too important - it's too necessary.

I watch as Boyle now stands behind the chair, smoking gun in hand. She was indeed everything I ever wanted in another person, she made my day tolerable. She was beautiful, more than likely the most beautiful woman I had ever dated.

"What took you so long?" I was trying to wipe the tears from my face while appearing not to do so.

"Wanted to come in unnoticed," Boyle said nonchalantly.

"Let's get out of here. I don't know how much longer my cover is going to hold." I rose, slammed the rest of the scotch in my glass, and moved to the kitchen.

"Close call. Much too close. We have them, the terrorists, but I don't care what information they gave. They never give you what you want. Never give you what you need."

"Who was at the cabin? I have been unable to find out," I said, my soul was empty, and I was trying not to turn into a slobbering mess.

"They were affiliated with Sam; NSA. We were tipped off to Sam about a week ago."

"I wish it did not have to work out like this. She was beautiful. We could have had a great life together. I was surprised when you found out who she was." Tears threatened to pour out. I breathed in deeply to stifle them.

My cover as the manager of the call center for a cell phone company could not have worked out better. My database held every person I had ever met with, complete with notations the best code-breaker would not have deciphered.

I could pass those numbers I found suspicious to my associates and once they had the number and the ESN, the phone signal could be captured with little issue. Once the third brother arrived at the office complaining about his voice-mail not working, I knew we had them.

Only I knew it wasn't working. I had turned it off in the switch, although still active in his account, it was dead everywhere else. Once I saw the third brother, I was convinced there were factions in the government who wanted these men alive. We thought otherwise.

My superiors had given me a new identity. I have been living as Ryan Prince for almost six and a half years. Now, we'll move onto a new location and start again. My experience at CellNY will come in handy. There are parts of the story that have been fabricated to convince those in my life that I was indeed, an innocent party in this whole affair. Those who wanted me dead knew they could count on Sam. She was part of their plot.

I played dumb, hoping we could go on without any complications. The change in Sam was a direct result of her finding out about my true background; my actions only made it real.

Unlike my co-workers, I did not find out about Sam until two days ago. She played an integral part in the day that I woke up dead. She had disconnected my phone, unaware I would be able to reconnect the cell with little issue. Even though we were careful not to tip our hats to the FBI and Fred's group, she had sent an email to her people informing them of our destination and address.

Boyle informed me just last night that they had flown out to the location to set up the ambush at the cabin. They did not expect me to be armed and able to defend myself. She did not know that I shot first, and the reason the bullets missed me was due to the fact they were the final spasms of a dying man, and not that of a skilled assassin. I killed one of her old partners, splitting his skull in half with a single rifle shot.

She watched while I questioned her other associate. I stayed my role, not knowing she was involved, that she had given them the description of the van, had turned off our home phone. She even called in the ambush at the safe house, giving those involved the address. If I had known, I would not have hesitated to do what was necessary. She had done every-thing except pull the trigger on me. I guess we were even.

I said before we all have a past we keep hidden, even from those we love - those closest to us. I had done the same, hoping I would be able to stay Ryan Prince for the rest of my days, Sam by my side, none the wiser. Two days ago I was informed Sam knew my true identity. My cover was blown. I also was advised to hang in until she tipped her hat; however, caution was advised. Find out what I could. I wished it weren't true.

I also hoped she also truly loved me and I was not just an assignment.

I was told there would be back up when needed. I was also told that she had orders to kill me. I have learned from this experience; I would be better next time. I went to the wall safe and removed the cash from the it, along with a fist full of issued ID's. Time to move on.

Boyle and I quickly left the house. It occurred to me I never thanked him for shooting Fred in the head, thus allowing me to continue my job, continue what was needed.

I followed him. We both had our guns drawn, pointed to the ground, each of us very aware of our surroundings, each aware Sam may have her associates waiting for us. The quick walk to the car was completed without incident. Boyle was behind the wheel exiting the driveway as I slid into the passenger seat and slammed the door.

We pulled away from the curb as the first yellow-orange flames became visible through the windows, the white curtains beginning to combust.

Fire covers up everything. I am not sure who set the fire; it was not me and it was not Boyle. I will heed the advice. I will not become attached, ever again. Boyle put the bullet in Sam, our superiors doubting my ability to complete the task. Maybe they were right. Sam's death, although a necessary evil, did not mend my soul.

The bitter taste of tonight will not sit well on my heart, and it will sour my stomach.

I did not wish for Boyle to notice the tears have returned. I do not want him to see I was hurting. I am the frontman, tough as they come. I am fearful he will judge those tears and assume this job was weakened me. I watched the houses fly by, watched as the city blocks turn to commercial streets as the road merged onto the highway.

I was preparing my report. I was doing anything other than thinking about Sam. My emotions were more difficult to hide. I felt a hand on my shoulder.

"There's a cooler in the back, filled with beer and booze, mixers also," Boyle offered.

"Thanks." I turned in my seat and took two beers out of the cooler.

"Have a smoke."

"No. Beer will do for now."

"Time heals."

"I know." Still staring out the window, I was not satisfied with the answers Boyle was giving. He was trying to help, but for now, no one could help, I would deal with the pain of losing Sam for the remainder of my days; it will be a third scar, and like the rest, just as permanent.

"We are going back to the office for a while. Maximilian Franz wants to talk with you."

"Is he pissed?" Max was our boss at the office. If he was really mad, I would be dead, for real.

"No. He said he was satisfied with the fact your cover held as long as it did. However, you are in for one of his 'people like us speech.'"

"Good. I am in need of such instruction."

I was not in a talkative mood. I was being killed as well. Ryan Prince died tonight. There would be a corpse, or bit of clothing, maybe some teeth or whatever it took. Two bodies would be discovered once the flames were extinguished.

Where Ryan Prince is a pile of ashes, Claude Debussy will rise like the Phoenix. Claude Debussy is my real name. It has been so long since I heard it I almost forgot it. It's been almost seven years since someone spoke that name. The next assignment will be complete with a new personal history and a new identity. Claude will again fade into nothing, as the new me walks this earth.

I am certain our information department will be preparing a complete history from birth as we drove back to the office. My next cover will not be so easy to crack. The lessons learned in Western New York will remain.

Boyle broke the awkward silence which permeated the car. "Not to rub salt in the wound, but your dad gained access to your FBI file. He read your story. He thinks this is hysterical."

"Oh really?" A smile found its way to my mouth, and, fighting the pain, I agreed. "He is really going to let me have it."

"He thinks you should publish. He called it the funniest and most interesting fictitious story he has ever read." Boyle could barely contain himself from laughing so hard he crashed the vehicle.

"It wasn't all fiction. I'm glad Dad got a big laugh from it." Relief did flood through me, enough to forget the look on Sam's face as she died.

"Mostly fiction," Boyle answered.

"Ok, I was shot twice, correct?" I countered.

"Yes twice. Once with a real gun, and once with the hot barrel of my nine millimeter."

"You also broke my nose, remember?"

"Your nose has been broken so many times, I am surprised it's still in the same place on your face," Boyle said. It was his turn for tears. His brought forth from laughing at his own jokes.

"Well, my car was stolen. I also did run to Canada."

"True. Except you knew exactly what caused those events. You were responsible for much of what occurred."

I had to give him the point. "True."

"The whole two hours of your day in the trunk of a car and your subsequent time at the FBI, a total farce."

I huffed. "True, but I couldn't very well tell Sam we met for a planning session."

"You know," Boyle paused, while taking a drink from his beer, "Bradford now insists everyone call him Agent Rock-solid, the baddest FBI agent ever."

"He does work for the FBI," I paused, "Or at least that's what we tell everyone. His credentials are so convincing he was able to be at my interrogation at the hospital. He was making funny faces at me when no one was looking."

I paused. Boyle's plan had worked for but a short time; his distraction brought a smile to my face and a moment of solace. "Do you know what else is true?"

"Sure."

"I loved her with everything I am. I wanted to be with her forever." The confession weighed heavily on me.

"I know. But once we found out she was NSA, you know

that could not happen. You know she was directly involved in trying to get you killed, not once, but twice."

"Yes, I know she sent her men the address of the cabin and planned the ambush. She had the mistaken assumption I was unarmed. She also called in the hit at the safe house. I looked at the call records on my phone."

"And yet you loved her?" Boyle asked, an incredulous tone sneaking into his voice. "That, my friend, sounds crazy."

"She thought she was doing the right thing. I cannot blame her for that." I have told so many lies in the name of patriotism and security; I sometimes forgot what the truth is. Sam was unlike any I have ever met before. I could celebrate my accomplishments publically under my façade as Ryan Prince. Yet there was so much we do that cannot be celebrated. "I really thought I was making a difference," I told Boyle.

I will now accept my fate. I am not in a position to accept another person in my life. To live out my days as a single entity is preferable to the death my actions caused. We are not normal, we are not in control of our lives, and I will remember the hammer analogy. I will remember the office will be all that I know. I will remember there is no room in my life for anyone other than myself. I will not be the cause of death because I placed my personal life above that of our objective.

There will come a time when I am deemed too old to continue my fieldwork. At that time, I may seek the comfort of another. But that day is too far off for it to enter my mind now. There is much work to be done.

My parents played an integral role at the office and would

be informed of the change. They greatly influenced my decision to join them. My Dad told me that it's a quiet war we wage, and this job does not come with accolades.

We operate in the dark, hiding, waiting, concealing our movements. There are those who think the office should have been disbanded after the cold war. However, our impact is even more important now.

It is not a country we fight, not a country we infiltrate. It's an idea: the idea that we are the evil empire the great USA destroys.

We do destroy those who believe fascism is tolerable, that killing in the name of some God acceptable, that training eleven-year-old boys to shoot on sight justifiable, and training men to fly planes into high-rise buildings acceptable.

We frighten those who condone such beliefs. We operate where others can't. Most of our efforts are spent on our own soil, foiling plans before they come to fruition. We find those in hiding, conducting plans, and we are not afraid to infringe on the civil liberties of others. We tap phones and intercept protected communications. I am not the only operative currently in the field. We have at least fifty others throughout the country and in England.

We hide behind titles. We hide in plain sight. Our most productive group works for Internet service providers. There is no longer a counterbalance to our power and will. The scales have tipped.

"Ideas hide where countries can't." That's a Max favorite. He is correct. Our enemy could be your next-door neighbor, the kid who delivers your groceries, or the guy down at the deli.

Our war does not stop at imaginary boundaries drawn in the sand. It is as difficult to contain as it is to identify. Information is our best resource, and my ability to locate sources for that information is my forte.

People still feel the need to be connected - connected to what they deem the greater whole. It's these connections I seek, these connections which lead to sources, these connections which will ultimately lead to one small battle and one victory.

We prefer not to crush our adversaries; but, rather, bother them like a cloud of a thousand gnats. You may be able to slap a few away; however, you'll never get us all. Eventually, we bleed all them dry.

We know who they email and IM, we know about the wire transfers under $5,000 that others ignore, we know that one out every thirty ATM transactions are fraudulent.

What we cannot hear we read, what we cannot read, we deduce. Our victories are small, but not insubstantial. The best thing, these people know not where the attack originated.

My eyes are closed and I pretend to be asleep. Boyle continues to drive, his attention no longer focused on my well-being. In truth, even though I was preparing for yet another assignment, in reality, I was picturing Sam, wearing that summer dress the night we met. She was stunning as she walked across the floor.

I have killed her body, but not her spirit. I do not have so much as a photo of her or us. To do so would be suicide. I could have nothing linking Ryan Prince with my new identity. But she will exist for a while longer in my conscious mind and maybe my dreams. I say farewell to Marie Samantha Saint Clair as I embark on the next adventure.

I will need to call Mom and Dad as soon as I am back. They will be as disappointed about Sam as I am, but they will understand. Dad was the first to remind me of my duties when I told him things were turning serious.

He also had a similar experience and was replete in telling me we all have to learn this lesson. No amount of advice, whether solicited or unsolicited, can take the place of learning this one monumental lesson.

I will also be talking with Dad about setting up another "cabin." This one will be better equipped after this experience. Better equipped for next time, because there will be a next time. There always is a next time. Just remember, I hide, as always, in plain sight.

Read on for an exciting excerpt from David R. Cook's new book, Logical Abstract.

28

Logical Abstract

Introduction

2018 – Google unveils the first natural voice personal assistant. It was nearly perfect, utilizing regional colloquiums and regional dialects. It set the standard for what was to come.

2019 – In a yearlong research project, a marketing team, backed by the tech giants, revealed Millennials had no presumption of privacy. Further, the group stated that if data was collected and analyzed, it should be used to create personalized experiences.

2019 – In a report published by *USA Today*, it was theorized that Artificial Intelligence, or AI, would be a multi-billion-dollar enterprise by 2025.

2020 – The Coronavirus, or COVID-19, changes the world, as countries shut down and locked down. It would change the delivery of home entertainment and the economy for years to come.

2021 – The Bill Gates Foundation, Microsoft, Apple, and Samsung develop injectable chips that would track and compile the general health and wellbeing of the recipient.

January 2022 – A mutated strain of the Coronavirus,

COVID-22, makes a comeback with a vengeance, killing 10 times the number of people that its much less lethal father, COVID-19 did. The country was in lockdown for 9 months.

July 2022 – Google invests millions in an effort to combine streaming services and AI to provide customers the ideal streaming service. The product was nearing completion until the "Second Great Depression" ruined the nation. The economy never fully recovered from the COVID-19 shutdown. The 2022 shutdown witnessed the total collapse of the national economy. All trade ceases.

December 2023 – Google sells its AI/Streaming platform in order to avoid bankruptcy. This company, founded in Arizona, was the brainchild of three software developers who had lost their jobs during the Second Great Depression. The company was named Logical Abstract. It was funded by three men through the proceeds of a winning lottery ticket. It was surmised it would not last a year. After just six months of operation, they perfected what Google could not - wearable tech glasses that worked seamlessly with any mobile device. In four years they would revolutionize streaming services, AI, and the internet itself.

March 2024 – Logical Abstract releases two products; one would revolutionize the cellular phone industry, the other was a platform that allowed users to track their friend's and family's location. This quickly turns into a social media craze. Although not mentioned at the time, it also ended privacy. The company paired the "TechSpecs" with a new cell model that did not have an integrated screen. Many tech periodicals were quick to criticize; however, a few forward-thinking investors not only bought the product, but they also bought the stock.

Chapter One – So it begins

March 5, 2052

Detective David Strahan visually examined the dead body, placing double thick rubber gloves over his hands before opening the small, albeit heavy, metal door. He was doubtful the extremely rusted surface would yield fingerprints; it was not worth contaminating potential evidence. He was calculating the amount of force required to stuff a body into a storage container that was but 12 cubic feet. The metal door frame measured approximately 30 inches on each side.

The metal container was part of an abandoned ranch that had been operational 150 years earlier. Broken fences, standing like skeletons, marked the perimeter of the ranch.

His preliminary visual inspection yielded very few clues. It was apparent, although not yet verified, that the victim suffered either broken bones or compound dislocations of his hips, shoulders, and knees. Even though the container was 12 cubic feet, the deceased only occupied about half of the entire volume.

His TechSpecs measured the size of the opening, providing him with the exact dimension of the fuel container. Using only eye movements, he was able to access the mathematics module through his TechSpecs, confirming 40 to 80 pounds of force was required to dislocate the shoulder joint alone. The range displayed was a comparison between a posterior versus superior dislocation. The module then brought forth the force required to dislocate the knee joint. Detective Strahan was surprised to find it was under the force necessary to dislocate a shoulder.

Perplexed at the scene, he slightly raised his hands. This simple motion brought forth the main menu of his cell. He made an additional gesture that brought up the "call by name" menu.

"Sadie," (this is the name he gave to his personal AI) "Call Sims"

"David," Sadie's gentle voice asked, "Is this a direct call, or a call to his assistant?"

"Direct and tell him he is late." His assistant did not pick up the anger in his voice.

The call was only answered via voicemail.

"Jesus Christ," he muttered aloud to himself. "What kind of sick bastard would do this?"

He immediately dismissed Sadie's request to search all databases for Jesus Christ.

Detective Strahan scanned the scene of the first murder in Pinal County in five years. His partner was late to the scene, again. Detective Paul Sims may be tardy, but the hiking trail, tucked in the Superstition Mountains, was teaming with activity. He had been on-site with the forensics team now for 30 minutes and apparently a gang of six ghosts, wearing size 10 to size 13 generic work boots, had bent his victim into an impossible square and left him for dead.

The man had yet to be identified, as he was without his cell phone and his TechSpecs. Conjecture by the team deduced the man was probably six feet tall before he was turned into a 10-foot cube. Thumbprints were being collected as the team extracted Mr. Cube from the metal container.

Detective Strahan walked the trail, taking care not to disturb what little evidence was left at the scene. Sadie, as always, predicted his next question, confirming via a screen notification that the trailhead was 1.25 miles away with an average elevation of 500 feet.

Detective Strahan slowly made a wide circle, allowing Sadie to record the elevation of the surrounding foothills. He waited patiently for the team to extract the body while waiting impatiently for the arrival of his partner. His anger rose. He knew why his partner was late. This only further fueled his growing temper.

Ten minutes later, the forensics team had fully extracted the body.

Detective Strahan sent a text to all team members, letting them know he was going to survey the surrounding area. He had hiked this trail many times. It was not well marked - only an occasional cairn lead the way. These small, pyramid-like structures had saved him many times. A bone dry river bed comprised the majority of this part of the trail. During the wet season, it would meander around uprisings of vegetation, creating mini islands. It was easy to get turned around and GPS was not always accurate. The men who brutally murdered the victim must have possessed knowledge of the area that most do not. The trial was also riddled with rattlesnakes. There were no signs a vehicle had accompanied the caravan of suspects. A ridge surrounded this part of the trail and averaged a height of 500 feet. The growth on the ridge was stained a dark green after being feed by winter rains. In another two months, the dark green would be replaced with the light golden color of desiccated grass.

Something was flawed with the whole scene. There was many more easily accessible places to dump a body. This location required planning, manpower, and hacking a system that is reported as being unhackable.

Detective Strahan returned to the location where the victim had been viciously stuffed into a metal tin can. His mind was trying to make sense of this crime. Does this place hold some sort of importance to those that committed the crime?

Paul Sims appeared at the summit of the ridge. Strahan met Sims halfway down the steep hill. Paul was disheveled and smelled of booze. Typical for most days that ended in Y.

"I am not going to ask where you have been and why you're late," Strahan said, his tone laced with disgust and a touch of contempt.

Sims shrugged his shoulders while poking his boot into the granite which littered the trail. "It was a rough night. It won't happen again." At least he had the sense to apologize. But it wasn't the first time Strahan heard those words.

"I won't bring this to the Captain," Strahan bit out. "But straighten up now or you're out!" The "out" was emphasized with a stiff poke to Sims' chest.

"Go get yourself cleaned up and meet me at the station. When you get to the office and review the forensic findings, schedule a trip to the Logical Abstract corporate offices," Strahan commanded through clenched teeth. The anger roiling off of Strahan caused Sims to avert his gaze to the ground. "We need to figure out how this guy was offline for over eight hours."

Sims gained his composure. "I have someone tracking all offline reports for the last 10 hours. I called tech on my way here."

"How many offline alerts were there?" Strahan managed to keep his tone level despite still being angry.

"None so far."

All citizens were required to have their cell phones attached to their hips 24/7/365. The lone exception: Charging the unit. However, that information would have been included in the alerts. Once a citizen reached the age of 14, they were provided with a cell phone. Today these devices did not resemble their ancestors in the least.

Strahan instinctively placed his hand on his cell, which rested on his belt. Simple in design, yet extremely technologically advanced, this device managed every aspect of a person's life. They were in constant communication with a connected watch, which required no charging and was worn constantly. All this tech was developed and maintained by Logical Abstract, the largest company on the planet.

"Good. Go get cleaned up and meet me at the house in an hour."

Strahan turned his back on Sims before the man could respond.

He began traversing the scrub brush which outlined the

path. Sadie mistook his angry mutterings as a request. He declined the request from his assistant before she could proceed.

The forensic team had removed the body from its metal prison. The distinct and distant sound of a helicopter heading toward the scene washed over them. A member of the forensic team used his TechSpecs to focus on the victim's thumbprint and seconds later the team had a name. Strahan hastened his pace to join the others.

"Timmie Robbins. Director of Software Development at Logical Abstract." The forensic tech delivered the news in the same manner as if he was talking about the nightly stock index.

"Interesting," Strahan said. "Sadie, is there a missing person report filed for Timmie Robbins?"

"No David, he has not been listed as missing," Sadie replied in her very sultry voice.

"Marital status?"

"Single," she replied.

"Sadie, please access the Logical Abstract employee files. Was he scheduled to work today?"

"The files indicate he was finishing a vacation."

"That is very curious." He did not need a response, but one was offered.

"He was scheduled to report to work in two days," she reported.

"Thank you, what was his last known location?" Strahan waited for a response; the nature of the request required time for Sadie to access several location databases.

Strahan's access level to such information was much more

advanced than even his partners. As a Detective Third Grade, he had the second-highest level of access issued to local law enforcement.

"Mesa, Arizona. Hybrid Bar located at 112530 Main Street...."

"I know where it is, thank you." He cut off what certainly would have been a very lengthy explanation from his assistant. "Please reach out to Tamara Burris' AI and inform her she is down one employee."

"Will do David." It took less than a second for Sadie to further respond. "That has been completed."

The Hybrid Bar was one of many which specialized in top-shelf liquor, oxygen therapy, and alkaline water. He had frequented the place before.

Strahan knelt by the body of Timmie Robbins, knowing the last few moments of his life were spent in excruciating pain. The men around him seemed perplexed. Some have never been called to a murder scene and they wore their disgust like masks. He didn't judge, not many people have witnessed a murder victim.

Strahan asked Sadie for a statewide search matching today's incident parameters and return the report when completed. He stood to leave, thanking the men and women for their efforts.

While making the 1.25-mile trek back to his police cruiser, he received a notification the forensic team's report was available for viewing. He would review that with Sims when he reached the precinct office. His thoughts were his only companion. This murder not only seemed extreme but also personal. He could not understand why someone would murder a software developer. Sadie, always anticipating his needs, was downloading Timmie's social history and his circle of friends. There would be much to review upon his return to the office.

The remaining 100 yards to the car were difficult. Dressed in black tactical pants, a light blue shirt, and carrying forty pounds of equipment, the sun's constant abuse on this body was noticeable. The temperature had reached 95 degrees.

"Gotta love the desert," he muttered to himself.

David Strahan was a native Arizonan, Growing up in the baking desert heat, he hated the sun the way East Coasters hated the snow.

David R Crook
Photo by Christine Wolfe

David R Crook is a native New Yorker who transplanted to sunny Arizona after shoveling snow for 40 years. He is an Information System Manager by day and author by night. Visit him online at davidrcrook.com.

www.ingramcontent.com/pod-product-compliance
Lightning Source LLC
Chambersburg PA
CBHW030827110726
47900CB00006B/1780